BLISS

BLISS

Fiona Zedde

KENSINGTON BOOKS
http://www.kensingtonbooks.com

KENSINGTON BOOKS are published by

Kensington Publishing Corp.
850 Third Avenue
New York, NY 10022

All Kensington titles, imprints and distributed lines are available at special quantity discounts for bulk purchases for sales promotion, premiums, fund-raising, educational or institutional use.

Special book excerpts or customized printings can also be created to fit specific needs. For details, write or phone the office of the Kensington Special Sales Manager: Kensington Publishing Corp., 850 Third Avenue, New York, NY 10022. Attn. Special Sales Department. Phone: 1-800-221-2647.

Kensington and the K logo Reg. U.S. Pat. & TM Off.

ISBN 0-7582-0919-3

First Kensington Trade Paperback Printing: August 2005
10   9   8   7   6   5   4   3   2   1

Printed in the United States of America

BLISS

Chapter 1

Bliss Sinclair walked in from the rain, brushing sparkling raindrops from the sleeve of her gray suit. She stopped and shook herself like a cat. More droplets scattered, flying from her large haloing Afro to the carpet that lined the main lobby of the Volk Publishing building. People walked around her, some watching her display with something like amusement. Others were too focused on the clock, already beginning to chime nine A.M., to pay her any attention. She shrugged again, to better settle the jacket on her back and shoulders, and headed for the bank of elevators at the rear of the lobby. The gray carpet muffled the sound of her footsteps as she stepped into the chrome elevator and pressed the button for the twenty-third floor.

Just as the door began to close, a woman slid quickly between them. She brought with her the light, mossy scent of Chanel No. 19 and nodded briefly at Sinclair before staring ahead at the mirrored wall of the elevator.

Despite her coolness, the woman immediately drew Sinclair's attention. She was a clever mixture of elements. Her hair was tamed Africa, thick and permed to tumble to her shoulders in shiny waves that framed her square-jawed, Anglo-Saxon face. Freckles sprinkled like brown sugar over her nose and cheeks. As Sinclair watched, a hint of a smile pulled at the woman's full mouth. She was beautiful, Sinclair decided. And her creamy milk and coffee skin looked delicious in silk.

"Hello." The woman's voice was a velvety southern drawl.

Sinclair slid her gaze to the elevator doors, embarrassed to be caught staring. "Hi."

The woman took Sinclair's reply as an invitation and looked fully at her travel companion, her mouth still curled in that almost-smile. "Do you work here?" she asked.

Realizing that the woman wasn't offended by her blatant ogling, Sinclair relaxed. "Yes, on the twenty-third floor."

"You must do some pretty expensive work for Volk to be that high up in the building."

"Not really, just a little accounting." Sinclair turned to look at the woman. "What are you doing here?"

A real smile captured her mouth. "I don't look like I work here?"

Sinclair figured that honesty was best in this case. "Not really."

"Then I must be a writer. Coming to meet with my editor."

"Ah. What have you written for us?"

"A couple of books. Essays."

"Hmm." Sinclair sized the woman up again. She didn't seem at all like the intellectual type. Rather like one of those hard-edged businesswomen, in her tailored silk pantsuit. "I don't read much nonfiction, although I've been meaning to start."

"That's funny that you say that. I could never really get into fiction." The woman's mouth twitched. "I'm Regina, by the way."

"Sinclair."

Regina nodded just as the elevator door slid open. "I guess I'll see you around."

"Sure." Sinclair watched the woman walk toward an unfamiliar cloister of offices. She blinked when the gunmetal gray doors closed, cutting off her view of the silk-clad backside gliding down the hallway.

"Baby got back." Sinclair coughed when she realized she'd

said that out loud. Still, she chuckled to herself as she stepped out of the elevator and down the carpeted hall to her office. Shelly Romero, her secretary, was already at her desk when Sinclair walked in. Shelly looked like a child who'd come in for "bring your daughter to work" day and just stayed. Dark hair in two ponytails, glitter eye shadow from the kids' section and barely business attire. She was a liberal arts college graduate still safely ensconced in her twenties and with ambitions of being a published poet. That ambition was what drew her to Volk Publishing three years ago and the belief that as long as she had some link with the publishing house she had a chance of having her first book published by them. As far as Sinclair knew, Shelly was still unpublished.

"Good morning, Shelly."

"Don't you look cheerful this morning?" Shelly grinned and handed over a large stack of mail. "Did you get lucky?"

"Wouldn't you like to know?" A smile shadowed Sinclair's mouth.

"Only if it involved at least one other woman. Otherwise save it for the boys in the break room."

Sinclair rolled her eyes then stepped away as Shelly's phone rang and the secretary turned to answer it. Ever since she had "accidentally" walked into a lesbian bar uptown and ran into the younger woman over a year ago, they'd become more than open with each other. Shelly was the closest thing she had to a friend in this city. In her office she put her briefcase and purse away, humming a light tune under her breath. When she found herself tapping her feet to the same song as she opened the mail, Sinclair laughed softly, wondering at her sudden good mood. An image of the woman in the elevator immediately came to her. So what? Regina was an attractive woman. It wasn't like anything was likely to happen between them. Though a girl could dream . . .

That night, Sinclair's boyfriend, Yuen, coaxed her out for a book release party, an event that she had offhandedly mentioned to him weeks ago and where his favorite author was launching her latest book. When they walked into the hotel ballroom it was chaos of flashbulbs, megawatt smiles, towering displays of food, and free-flowing alcohol.

"This is great," he whispered, tilting his head to kiss her cheek. "If I'd known you were this well connected I'd have asked you out years ago." His thick black hair fell over his eyes. He seemed nothing like the thirty-five-year-old lawyer he was. His full lips were more prone to smile than not, and his slim youthful body could have easily belonged to a teenaged underwear model. There were days when Sinclair wondered what he was doing with her.

She lightly pinched his wrist. "It wasn't that big a deal. Everybody in the office gets an invitation."

When they walked through a mirrored archway, Sinclair gave her hair a discreet fluff and threaded her arm through Yuen's. Today, like most days, she wore her hair in a large Afro to rival Angela Davis's. The makeup she'd brushed on thankfully didn't look out of place. It was just enough to emphasize her full mouth and wide, slightly tilted eyes. Yuen once said that she looked like a hungry fox, beautiful but inclined to bite a hand off and swallow it whole if someone was stupid enough to try and get too close. It didn't help that there was a reddish cast to her skin. Sinclair acknowledged that she looked a bit too thin, but could think of no immediate remedy for the situation. Sometimes she just didn't feel like eating.

"Linnet's over there." Yuen drew Sinclair's attention to the author and her entourage who had set up a display on a large dais at the front of the room. The walls of the ballroom were lit with artfully done track lighting that brought the eye straight to the life-sized mock-up of Linnet Costa's book jacket. Naughty nubile angels were her latest obsession. Apparently they photographed well.

"And the best part is that the food and drinks are on the house," Sinclair teased.

"Nice." He sounded like a college kid let out for his first spring break.

The guest of honor worked the room well, looking wicked in head to toe fire-engine red. The latex and metal dress sparked as much conversation as her book. Sinclair hoped that she looked half as good when she turned fifty.

"Go on and introduce yourself, Yuen. I'll be back here getting a bite to eat." He looked at Sinclair as if he thought she was joking. "Go ahead," she said. "I won't leave without you."

"Funny. Since I drove."

Her smile faded as he walked away. She glanced at her watch. *Two hours should be a reasonable amount of time to stay*, she thought.

"Hello, Sinclair."

It was the woman from the elevator. Tonight she wore black slacks that sat low on her hips, emphasizing their soft curve and her flat belly. The blouse was a sheer white and showed off the lift of her slight breasts under a white camisole. Her upswept hair made her seem taller than before. Still, she had to be at least three inches shorter than Sinclair's five feet ten. Her scent, Chanel Coco if Sinclair's nose was correct, invited her a closer inspection.

"Good to see you again," Sinclair said.

"Believe me, the feeling is mutual." Regina's glance traveled quickly down Sinclair's body, taking in the loosely draped burgundy dress and high heels. "I never figured you for a Costa fan."

"I'm sure there are lots of things you figured about me that were wrong," Sinclair smiled to lessen the sting of her words. From the corner of her eye she saw Yuen pause and clear his throat, preparing to approach his idol.

"Touché." The corner of Regina's mouth lifted. "Would you like a drink?"

"Sure."

They walked to the bar together where Regina ordered a

tequila sunrise for herself and a gin and tonic for Sinclair. With their drinks in hand, they left the bar for the cozy comfort of the attached lounge with its overstuffed love seats and thick rugs, all in shades of red and copper. They found an empty sofa in the midst of the shifting crowd and sat down.

"So what other things would I have figured wrong about you?"

"I don't know." Sinclair eyed the smaller woman over the rim of her glass. "You haven't told me what other conclusions you've jumped to."

Regina laughed. "I'll keep those to myself for now." She sipped her drink and nodded toward the guest of honor. "So, do you know Linnet?"

"No, not really. I've seen her in the building a few times, but that's about it."

"You must run into a lot of women in that elevator." A smile settled on Regina's coral mouth.

"Not many interesting ones."

Regina smiled at the implied compliment. She leaned closer, draping her arm along the back of the sofa, tickling the other woman's nose with her lightly floral perfume. Sinclair's breath caught. She could've counted the freckles on Regina's nose if she'd wanted to.

"This is her, right here." Yuen's voice made Sinclair look away. He stood a few feet away with a smiling Linnet Costa next to him.

Regina leaned back from Sinclair as they drew closer.

"Linnet Costa, this is my girlfriend, Bliss Sinclair. She was the one who invited me here tonight."

"Ms. Costa." Sinclair stood up and extended her hand to the handsome woman. Still seated on the couch, Regina watched the introductions with a curious smile.

"Please call me Lin." Then the writer turned to Regina. "Nice to see you, Regina. I thought you were on tour."

"Not until the end of next month." Regina stood up, too,

and gathered Linnet in a surprisingly intimate embrace. "Your book is terrific, by the way. When is the next one coming out?"

"Spoken like a true fan." She turned to the man at her side. "Yuen here was just telling me about his pro bono work with the Delancy witches three years ago. That case gave me a great idea for a book."

Regina shuddered theatrically. "You're right. Madness, group sex, witchcraft, and murder. Sounds right up your alley, Lin."

The others laughed, but Sinclair wrinkled her nose. Of course, Yuen noticed.

"What?" he asked.

"Should you even be talking about that case? Client confidentiality and all that?"

"It's been—"

"Oh, I'm sorry," Lin said with a smile that wasn't the least bit apologetic. "You're very right, Sinclair. I was just so fascinated with the whole story. I was the one who brought it up."

Yuen's smile held a trace of embarrassment. "I was just helpless to Lin's charms." They shared a guilty laugh.

"You wouldn't be the first," Regina said. She and Linnet smiled at each other.

"Linnet! Linnet!" A man loaded down with camera equipment waved frantically to get her attention. He was having issues pushing both his bulk and his equipment through the crowd.

"Pardon me, everyone." Lin excused herself and started to make her way to his side.

They watched her graceful back disappear into the crowd.

Sinclair was the first to speak. "She's a very nice woman."

"And gorgeous too." Yuen tilted his head close to his girl-friend's. "Though nowhere near as beautiful as you, of course."

"No need to be diplomatic, my lovely boy toy. She's definitely gorgeous and any man would be a fool to kick her out of bed."

"Or woman."

Sinclair turned to Regina. "Why would you say that?"

"She's bi. It's pretty common knowledge." Her eyes flicked over Sinclair.

"Yup." Yuen gave his best leer. "Maybe you and Lin could hook up while I—"

Sinclair poked him in the belly before he could finish. "Don't be a pig."

He oinked. Regina laughed. "By the way, we were never really introduced earlier, but I'm Regina Velasquez. Lin and I are old friends."

"A pleasure." They shook hands then started laughing again. Sinclair rolled her eyes.

"I had a good time tonight. Thanks." Yuen held Sinclair's hand as they walked through the gilt-edged revolving doors and emerged onto the street.

"I'm glad you liked it."

A scent of rot rose up from the gutters, mingling with the smells of old fruit and spilled alcohol that poured from the doorway of the market they quickly walked past. On the wind, the acidic tang of piss floated from the alley near where Yuen's car was parked. They hurried to the black Lexus convertible and drove off.

"Want to come back to my place for a drink and a little sex?" Yuen asked as they drove uptown. He wasn't joking.

Sinclair shook her head and manufactured a smile of regret. "No. Not really. I'm tired. That party wore me out."

"I forgot that it's only Wednesday and you have work tomorrow."

"Yes." Sinclair didn't need reminding. She already had her suit pressed and laid out for the next day.

At her apartment, Yuen kissed her good-bye, touching her

with a possession that seemed odd for him. "I'll call you later." His hardness pressed against her belly.

"OK."

As soon as Sinclair crossed the threshold of the apartment, she shrugged off her coat along with any lingering traces of tiredness. It wasn't deliberate. She wanted to be tired. But even with a long soak in the bathtub and a luxurious cuddle in her grandmother's old cotton robe, she still had too much energy to sleep.

After almost five years the insomnia still caught her off guard, as if there was something she could do on one particular night that would put her right to sleep. Instead of sleeping, she read. Thousands of books filled her neatly arranged shelves, every genre, every author she'd found even mildly interesting from all her years of working at Volk. She turned on the bedside light and curled up under the covers to read.

Morning. Sinclair stepped out of the shower, toweled herself dry, and put on her robe. The apartment was quiet. No music. No noise of someone else stirring in the bed. And up this high on the fifteenth floor, not even the noise of traffic intruded. Sometimes she thought that could be part of the problem. She was so separate from everyone, no real friends, no family. Now, as the days passed, an unfamiliar sense of loneliness was beginning to invade her life.

Her only real pleasure came from being in her apartment, sheltered by its sand-colored walls, comfortable earth-toned furnishings, and memories of her grandmother. Photographs that she had taken a long time ago hung in their expensive, oversized frames all over the apartment. Bare-limbed trees weighed down by snow, boulders framed by magnificent blue skies and tinted gold by the sun. An old photo of her and her grandmother on a faraway beach, laughing. All images from the happier and well-traveled life she had before her grandmother died.

Her Gram had had a fascination with America and its landscape. She took endless pictures of it, mostly crooked, underexposed, or unrecognizable shots that keenly disappointed her and eventually drove Sinclair to take photography classes in high school. She and Gram saved for months to buy the camera that ended up documenting their last few years together. Sinclair put that camera away years ago, stuck it in the back of a storage closet along with a few other things that she didn't want to see anymore.

Even though Gram had been long past her youth, her death still took Sinclair by surprise. The elderly woman had left the apartment to indulge in one of her favorite things— nocturnal shopping—but hadn't gotten very far. A stroke laid her out in the middle of the sidewalk while Sinclair slept. Less than an hour later she was dead. There was so much more that Sinclair had to share with her, so much that they still had to do together. Mavis's granddaughter hadn't been able to sleep through the night since.

Her robe whispered against her legs in the dim morning quiet as she moved by habit from room to room. A morning ritual. With all the lights still off and the glow of approaching dawn stretching equal parts light and shadow across her apartment, she could feel the night's change to day, and welcomed it. If she closed her eyes long enough, she could imagine being home again, standing in the kitchen of her father's old house in Jamaica, the one where she'd spent her first thirteen years, waiting for her mother to come down the hall and begin making breakfast. She opened her eyes and resumed her walk through the apartment.

Sinclair took pride in the order of her space, in the certainty that she knew where everything was and why. It was the way her Gram raised her. Even her habits now were still influenced by the fifteen years she'd lived with her grandmother. Gram loved tea. She used to drink it all the time. They'd shared countless mornings with their heads bent over the first cup of Darjeeling—lots of milk, lots of sugar—just talking.

"What are you going to study?" Gram had asked a fifteen-year-old Sinclair, smiling but perfectly serious.

"Accounting," Sinclair had answered. Not because that was what she wanted for herself, but because that was what she overheard her grandmother say was best.

With a sigh that no one else heard, Sinclair slipped into the kitchen to make herself a cup of tea before getting ready for work.

At five o' clock that afternoon she closed her office door behind her and prepared to leave. "Miss Sinclair," Shelly stopped her. "A woman came by and dropped these off for you earlier. She was a cutie."

Shelly handed her two neatly bound hardcover books. Between the crisp white pages of the top one lay a card. *Regina Velasquez. Writer.* Her phone number and uptown address were neatly written below that. Sinclair's eyebrow rose.

"Thanks, Shelly." She ignored her secretary's curious look and slid the books into her briefcase. "See you tomorrow."

At home, Sinclair propped the card up on the edge of the tub while she took her bath. Earlier, she'd sniffed the card, brushed it under her nose, and found the light scent of mint that clung to it. She stretched out under the bubbles and leaned back against the inflatable pillow propped up against the back of the tub. Irresistibly, her eyes wandered to the card again. Regina Velasquez. At the book release party, Regina had been polite yet mischievous, especially after Yuen came back with Linnet. She flirted shamelessly with Sinclair as if putting on a show for Yuen, touching the small of his girl-friend's back, refilling her drinks, even kissing her lingeringly on the cheek when they said their good-byes. At first Yuen seemed titillated, then annoyed. By the end of the evening he and Regina both seemed to be in competition over who could be the most solicitous to Sinclair's needs. Sinclair had been content to sit back and enjoy their attentions. She hoped that neither of them had known just how much Regina had intrigued her.

Fresh from her bath, her body still steaming from its heat, Sinclair slid naked into bed to read Regina's first book. It was a collection of essays on sex and love. *Making Sex, Having Love*. Nice title.

> *The first time someone else touched me with the intent to pleasure, I fell in love. Not with that person, but with the act itself. Such intimacy and accord. Even with the awkwardness of first time lovers there was a grace and purity, carnal and beautiful, that I knew from that moment on I could never live without.*

Sinclair slid down into the covers and continued reading. This was a woman who unabashedly loved sex. The more she read, the more descriptive and less academic Regina's prose became. Sinclair squeezed her thighs together and crossed a hand over her stiffening nipples. Regina was very good. She imagined the slight woman reading the words aloud, her soft red mouth shaping the seduction, an invitation to fall into her silken trap. And Sinclair *was* seduced. In the cool seclusion of her bedroom, she felt Regina's hands on her, touching her skin, teasing, satisfying. All these things that she wrote about aroused Sinclair's curiosity—the good-natured teasing among friends that eventually became a thoroughly gratifying group orgy, going down on a lover in a crowded subway station, the scorching wave of a shared orgasm in a cozy bed for three. All these were alien experiences to Sinclair. Regina's words made her long for them. Her fingers slid down between her thighs. She didn't fall asleep until almost five in the morning.

The office intercom buzzed and Shelly's voice filled the air. "Regina Velasquez calling for you, Miss Sinclair."

Sinclair's fingers twitched against the computer keys and typed three extra *t*'s.

"Put her through."

She took a deep breath and picked up the phone.

"You didn't call me last night." Regina's southern drawl wrapped around the words like hot molasses.

"I didn't know that I was supposed to."

"You were, but I forgive you. Did you read any of my essays?"

"Yes. A few." Sinclair wiped her damp palms on her slacks.

"What did you think?"

"They're good. Very . . . vivid."

Regina laughed again while Sinclair's stomach rearranged itself. "That's something, I suppose."

"Is that how you pick up people?"

"What makes you think I was trying to pick you up?" Regina asked.

Sinclair had walked right into that one. In all of Regina's essays, she never once mentioned the gender of the person she was with. There had been body parts sprinkled throughout, a liberal mentioning of penises and vaginas, breasts and buttocks that left Sinclair absolutely bewildered and painfully aroused.

"Are you?" Sinclair felt bold enough to ask.

"Yes." The other woman's laughter was full bodied and captivating. Sinclair imagined Regina throwing her head back, white teeth flashing, her long neck arched.

"Well, you know that I'm seeing someone," Sinclair said. Her hand tightened on the phone. Yuen had never made her feel like this. Hot in her belly and dry-mouthed. Sinclair knew that she should have been more nervous, hesitant, but Regina's seduction was so shameless and genuine that her own responses were too.

"So am I," Regina said. "Do you want to come to dinner with me tonight?"

She couldn't say no. Her body remembered the promise in Regina's book, in her low laughter. But she hesitated. What about Yuen? He would be expecting to see her soon, maybe even tonight. What would be her excuse? *Sorry darling, this stranger propositioned me and I was a little curious about my attraction to women so I'm going to try her out and see what happens.* That obviously wouldn't work.

In the end Sinclair called to invite him to breakfast on Sunday, apologizing that she couldn't see him before then. Still, she knew he would call to wrangle an invitation to Saturday dinner as well. She'd deal with that when the time came. In the meantime she tried to convince herself that there was nothing for her to feel guilty about. At least not yet.

Dinner was at a Mediterranean restaurant near Regina's house. The décor was stark. Sky blue walls and white columns, the scent of olives in the air despite whatever else was going on in the kitchen. Regina pulled Sinclair's chair out for her, then waited until she sat down.

"I have a few suggestions, if you don't mind," she murmured near Sinclair's ear.

Sinclair didn't mind. She'd never been to a place like this before and welcomed guidance. When the dark-haired waitress appeared, Regina took charge.

"We'll have the moussaka, dolmas, the stuffed shrimp with spinach and feta, tirópita, and a bottle of your house red."

That was her idea of making a few suggestions? She saw Sinclair's expression and laughed again. "I know. I'm overbearing, but you'll love it. I promise." Her eyes gleamed. "You have to try everything."

When the food came, Sinclair picked over it cautiously, prodding the dolmas—grape leaves stuffed with rice and herbs, apparently—and barely tasted the moussaka with its unpalatable blend of eggplant, ground beef, and zucchini swimming in a god-awful white sauce. The spanakopita was good though. Sinclair sipped her wine and watched Regina. The writer ate her meal in big, voluptuous bites that left her mouth white with béchamel sauce. Her pink tongue swept the paleness away in preparation for another bite.

"Come, taste this." Regina held a dolma perched between her thumb and index finger. When Sinclair lifted her hand to take it, she pulled it away and shook her head. "With your mouth."

Regina fed her the dolma, waiting patiently while her teeth bit through the thick concoction of grape leaves and seasoned rice, the soft pads of her fingers resting against Sinclair's lips all the while. Sinclair couldn't meet her eyes. She wondered briefly if she shouldn't be more uncomfortable with this. It didn't matter. She ate the other half of the dolma in one neat bite.

"So the person that I met the other night, was that a man or a woman?"

Sinclair almost choked on her wine. "Very funny. Yuen is very much a man."

"A very beautiful one."

"Yes. We've been together for about two years."

"It's a serious relationship, then?"

"It's exclusive, if that's what you mean."

"Up until now." Regina's eyes danced in the candlelight. She was so sure of herself.

"Until now." Sinclair released the admission, finally voicing her desire for much more than a friendship with this woman.

"Does he please you in bed?" Regina bit into a flaky spinach pastry, then licked the crumbs from her mouth.

"Yes. Yes, he does."

"You don't sound so sure."

"I think you're the one who doesn't want me to be sure. He does satisfy me in bed. Can we move beyond that, please?"

"Of course." Regina sipped her wine. A bit of red lingered on her mouth. She caught Sinclair's gaze and smiled. "Curious?"

Sinclair knew that she would be lying if she said no. Instead of replying she bit into her dolma and chewed as if that would save her from answering. Regina stood up over the low candles and leaned in to kiss her. Sinclair stopped chewing. Regina's lips pressed harder into hers, then softened. She licked Sinclair's mouth, bit the plump softness of her lips until the other woman sighed and opened her mouth for more. Sinclair's body began a slow melt, heating until every bit of moisture in her body was pooled between her thighs. Her fingers slid into Regina's hair to pull the woman closer. When Regina drew back, Sinclair's dolma was in her mouth. She finished chewing what Sinclair had started and swallowed.

"Does that satisfy any of your curiosity?"

When the check came, Regina took it before Sinclair could. As the waitress leaned over to pick up the bill and its generous tip, Regina smiled over the flickering candles, her eyes lazy with seduction.

"Come home with me."

Those simple words ignited a fire between Sinclair's legs. She couldn't say no. In the elevator to the penthouse apartment, Regina watched her from the other side of the copper-and-bronze fitted cage, smiling.

"I'm not going to touch you now. If I do I won't be able to stop. Don't want to frighten my neighbors."

Sinclair tried for levity. "They spook easily, like horses?"

"Something like that."

The elevator bell sounded. Regina ushered her through a well-lit hallway into an apartment that was all darkness and warmth. The scent of pine filled Sinclair's nose. The apartment was ornate but impersonally furnished. Anyone could have lived there. Sinclair trembled with an unknown fear. They moved through the darkness to the bedroom.

"Relax."

In a rustle of sound, Regina was on her. She kissed Sinclair, softly, as if trying not to frighten her. It was just like kissing a man, Sinclair decided, except for the press of two soft breasts against her.

"Touch them if you want," Regina murmured, nibbling on her lips then the slope of her neck.

Sinclair took a deep shuddering breath. With no table between them, no restaurant, no ambiguous flirtation, it was on. Regina took Sinclair's hand and pressed it against her breast.

"I'm going to fuck you." She bit Sinclair's lip. "If there's anything that you don't want, just tell me. Otherwise I'm going to take this." Regina cupped her through her trousers.

There was only one word left for Sinclair to say. "Yes."

Regina pushed her into the mint-smelling sheets and pressed her fingers into Sinclair, devoured her mouth, her breasts and pussy until she was incoherent with want.

"This isn't a man touching you, is it?"

"No." Sinclair gasped when the other woman's fingers slid deep inside her, quickly finding the spot that made her breathless, made her sweat and beg. She didn't even know that it existed. "God!"

"Just call me Regina." Still in her silk suit, she turned Sinclair over and slid up behind her, biting and caressing, inviting her to stain the silk with her sweat and cum.

"Come. It's all right. That doesn't mean the night's over."

Sinclair did, panting like a freight train as she collapsed beneath the other woman. Her own loudness made her blink at the ceiling in surprise. She half expected to see a mirror up there.

Regina shrugged off her skirt and blouse. She was completely naked underneath, ready with her small hard breasts and curvaceous hips. Sinclair reached for her, cupping her hips with wonder. They were soft and laced with fine lines that were almost invisible until the flesh was close enough to kiss. Sinclair's fingernails traced the rounded ass, the thick thighs.

"Time for that later, baby." Regina touched Sinclair's mouth with damp fingers. "Open your legs for me." She slid down Sinclair's body and tasted her, licked her, slid her tongue in and over her until Sinclair's throat was raw from gasping.

With the last of Sinclair's noises echoing in their ears, Regina lifted up her head, then her whole body. "That was your first lesson. I'm about to give you a pop quiz." Regina straddled Sinclair's face, opening up her shaved cunt to her inspection. "Do your best. I'll guide you through it."

Sinclair wanted to stare. The writer was pale and pink, and glistening, her clit hard and distended. Above her, Regina caressed her own nipples, squeezing and pinching until they were the color of raspberries.

"It's just like eating a peach, only you don't use your teeth." She undulated her hips above Sinclair, signaling her readiness.

It wasn't like eating a peach at all, Sinclair decided. It was better. The soft, wet flesh slid under her tongue like a salted oyster. She smelled gingery here, too, her musk addictive and, right now, very necessary.

"A little lower, sweetheart. Slip your tongue—hmm. Exactly . . ." Regina's voice trailed off on a deep moan.

Sinclair was a fast learner. She remembered how she liked to touch herself. With her tongue lavishing Regina's clit with focused attention, she slid two fingers deep inside her new lover and was rewarded with a sharp gasp and the trembling of the soft thighs bracketing her face. Regina pressed harder against her mouth. Her thighs quaked and started to give out. Sinclair sped up the hummingbird-like flutter to her tongue and thrust her fingers deeper. Regina gasped again, bucked on Sinclair's face as she growled long and deep and came hard around the long fingers.

Regina laughed softly. "I knew you'd be a keeper."

Rain started to fall, and Regina opened the windows to let the sound in. It was not a romantic gesture, she assured Sinclair as she stood bathed in the soft light from the bedroom lamps. She just liked the quiet noise, and so far above the streets she didn't have to smell the filth of the city. When Regina sank back into the bed, Sinclair propped herself on her elbow. "Doesn't this seem at all odd to you?" she asked.

"What? Sex with a near-stranger?"

"Yes, for one thing. I don't know anything about you. For all I know you could be a mass murderer or something."

Regina showed off her gorgeous teeth. "What do you want to know? I like dogs, I'm not into adventure sports or bingo. I'm HIV-negative and otherwise disease-free, unless you count manic depression as a disease."

"Interesting." And so very uninformative. Perhaps that was the point. Could she be satisfied with this? After Yuen's compulsive soul baring, Regina's reticence was a kind of relief. It made her more compelling and much, much sexier than the boy Sinclair had left at home.

"Does that mean you're satisfied?"

Sinclair traced Regina's collarbone. Desire hummed through her veins again, steady and loud. "I wouldn't say that."

Red-blushed nipples puckered and rose under Sinclair's gaze. With a soft laugh, Regina slid her fingers around the back of the other woman's neck and pulled her head down.

"Good."

At work the next day, Sinclair was useless. She pressed her legs together and stared at the computer screen until all she could see was Regina's face, wet with cum and sweat, her lip tight between her teeth. Sinclair left as early as she could and called Regina on her way to the train.

"Come to my house tonight. I want to show you some-thing."

The writer's throaty chuckle stirred up the moisture al-ready on Sinclair's panties. "I can't tonight. How about Sunday?"

What else could she do but agree? Sinclair called Yuen when she got home.

"I can't see you anymore," she said.

"What? Where did this come from?"

"Nowhere. I—"

"I'm coming over." He hung up the phone.

The doorbell rang twenty minutes later.

"Is it someone else?" he asked as soon as she opened the door.

Lying wasn't Sinclair's forte. "Something like that."

"What does that mean? Is there or isn't there?"

"I—I met a woman."

Silence.

He walked farther into the apartment. "You did what?"

"Three days ago." Had it only been three days?

"This is crazy." He turned to her, his face softening from its initial anger. "Is it that woman I met at Lin's party?"

Sinclair flushed hot and looked away. Had she been that obvious?

"It is, isn't it? I knew that bitch wasn't joking around." He looked at her across the pale expanse of the living room. "Three days. You're throwing away two years because of three days?"

Her tongue felt too heavy to speak. Yes, it was sudden. But she felt more in these past three days than she ever had with Yuen. Sinclair didn't want to say any of that out loud. It was too cruel.

"Sinclair. You have to know how insane this sounds. A week ago everything was fine. We were making plans for a weekend upstate."

"*You* were making plans for a weekend upstate. I wanted to stay home."

"But you always want to stay home. That's why I always make plans for us."

"Maybe that's the problem."

"You know what, Sinclair? This is bullshit. You'll come to your senses in a little while." He slid her a look. "Have you slept with her yet?"

"That's none of your business, Yuen."

He looked intrigued by the possibility of it, then shrugged. "Call me in a few days. Take time to sort this out. I'll be here for you." He moved to kiss her, but seemed to think better of it. "Call me." Then he left.

Sinclair collapsed against the closed door with a tremulous sigh. She felt limp and exhausted. Still, her mouth curved in a bittersweet smile. In two days, she would see Regina.

Regina called Sinclair on Sunday morning. "Where do you live?"

She came over with strawberries, whipped cream, sliced peaches, mangoes, and lychees. Her body looked delectable in a black jumpsuit that showed off her lean length and high, round ass. "I hope you haven't eaten yet."

"I have, but my Gram said that there's always room for dessert."

"Don't bring your grandmother into this. She probably wouldn't approve of what I have in mind for you."

Regina glanced briefly around the apartment, at its high ceilings, tasteful furniture, and spectacular view, before focusing fully on Sinclair. "Let's get you in the shower."

She was soft all over, despite her leanness, and eager as a puppy to play with Sinclair, to slide the soft fruit inside her and suck it out in loud, juicy slurps. Regina approved of Sinclair's bed. Its size and softness were apparently perfect for what she had in mind, although it had never been this sticky before. When all the gasping was done, she lay beside Sinclair, staring at her while trailing still-wet fingers over Sinclair's skin in long, lazy sweeps. Sinclair could almost see the tape recorder in her mind, making note of this scene. Fodder for her next book.

"Is the book you're working on essays or fiction?" Sinclair asked.

"Essays, of course. I could never get the hang of fiction. Too many lies." Regina leaned down and licked Sinclair's nipple. Her breath caught. "You're very responsive. I like that." Regina bent to show her just how much she liked it.

Chapter 2

At lunchtime Sinclair looked with distaste at the apple she'd brought for lunch. She wasn't looking forward to takeout either.

The phone buzzed. "Miss Sinclair?"

"Yes, Shelly?"

"You have a visitor. Ms. Velasquez."

A smile replaced her grimace. "Send her in. And go ahead and take your lunch now."

Regina walked in, delectable in a salmon-colored Yves Saint Laurent suit that came barely halfway down her thighs, and closed the door. She held a picnic basket in a manicured hand.

"I knew you did something expensive for the company," Regina drawled as she took in the plush carpeting, the dizzying view of the street, and smog-dimmed sunlight arcing through the large windows. "Hope you haven't eaten yet." She didn't wait for a response. Instead she set up a blanket on the floor, laid out wineglasses, a plate piled high with sliced fruit and tiny sandwiches with the crusts meticulously cut off. "Come."

Sinclair kicked off her shoes and obediently sat down on the blanket. Getting used to their intimacy now, she slid her hands in Regina's heavy hair and inhaled her scent. Today it was Lalique laced with a hint of sweetness—peach-scented soap—and underneath that her own spicy ginger scent.

"It's good to see you," Sinclair said. All day her senses had been alive with expectation. Waiting for this moment, even though its coming had never been a certainty.

Regina poured from a bottle of pinot noir. "I have a meeting later on this afternoon with my editor. I figured, why not steal some fun out of this business trip downtown?"

Sinclair smiled. "Do you come downtown often?" She felt like a fifteen-year-old on her first date, giddy and obscenely happy.

"If you'll let me, I'll come at least two times today." She sipped her wine and met Sinclair's gaze. The accountant's nipples pebbled noticeably under her blouse.

"Have a sandwich," said Regina. "I bought them myself. The ones on white bread are chicken salad, the wheat are tuna."

Sinclair nibbled on a chicken salad sandwich though she could have easily put the tiny square in her mouth whole. Regina dropped a slice of strawberry in her wineglass and bit into another.

"Your secretary is a sexy little thing. Have you fucked her yet?" Her eyes teased Sinclair. She knew very well that she was the only woman Sinclair had slept with. But maybe she didn't. Maybe she assumed that just because she fucked indiscriminately that everyone else did too.

"No," Sinclair said. "Not yet."

Regina's eyebrows peaked. "So does that mean you've thought about it?"

"Of course. Shelly has a beautiful body. Her breasts are the perfect size. Who wouldn't think about being with her?" Sinclair was playing a dangerous game. If there was one thing she knew about Regina already it was that she liked a challenge. Sinclair didn't put it past her to invite Shelly in to join them. She hoped that her secretary had already left for lunch.

"Really. What about *my* breasts?" She unbuttoned her blouse and left it open to frame her smooth caramel skin in foam green silk. She didn't wear a bra. She didn't have to. Her breasts were like two alert sentries, brown tipped and hard. Done with her posing, Regina slid off her blouse and crawled to where Sinclair sat.

"Are these the perfect size?" She straddled Sinclair, moving closer until her small breasts were a mere breath away from her lover's mouth. Her skirt rode up until it barely covered her ass.

"They're perfect." Sinclair leaned in to kiss a nipple, but Regina pulled away. "Let me see yours first."

Hadn't she seen them enough yesterday? Still, Sinclair quickly pulled off her blouse and bra.

"Eager, aren't you? Lie down." She grinned down at Sinclair. "Now, these are perfect. They only need one thing to make them to my taste." She slowly emptied her glass of wine over Sinclair's chest, dribbling the pale cool liquid down her collarbone and the hard brown nipples. Sinclair gasped at the sensation of cold then moaned at the first touch of Regina's mouth. The smaller woman's tongue, like wet velvet, slid over her sensitized breasts. Regina licked her until all the wine was gone from her skin, then she crushed a strawberry in her fist and dripped the juice over Sinclair's lips. Sinclair opened her mouth to lick at the red drops, thirsty for anything that Regina had to give.

Regina kissed her once, a hungry sweep of her mouth that took away most of the red liquid and whetted Sinclair's appetite. Then she pulled Sinclair's skirt up to her waist and pulled her panties completely off.

"One day I'm going to train you not to wear these things." She mashed the pulpy remains of the strawberry against Sinclair's cunt and started to eat.

A surprised breath left Sinclair's throat. Her skin goose-pimpled in a hot flush and she blinked uncontrollably at the ceiling as her body went up in flames under Regina's ruthless mouth. Deep inside, she trembled. The muscles in her thighs groaned as she whimpered, burned, and pushed herself more firmly against her lover. No one had ever. . . . Breath hissed past her teeth as all thought left her. She became animal and seeking, a needy thing caught in the twisting vines of Regina's desire. Against her flesh, Regina laughed.

She walked out of Sinclair's office nearly forty minutes later, her blanket folded neatly on top of the picnic basket, her clothes and hair in perfect order. Sinclair, however, was a trembling mess. Even after a quick shower in her tiny attached washroom, and a cup of herbal tea, her fingers still refused to hit the right keys on the computer. Eventually she gave up and spent the next hour staring out the window and trying unsuccessfully to keep the smile from her face.

Chapter 3

Early Sunday morning the phone woke Sinclair. "Yes?" she croaked.

"Meet me at Francesco's for breakfast in an hour." The dial tone punctuated the unexpected command.

She sat up, rubbing her face. Then she realized what this meant. Regina could play with her this weekend. Within less than an hour Sinclair was showered, shaved, and waiting at a corner table in the neighborhood restaurant when Regina walked in.

"'Morning, sexy." Regina's eyes wandered with approval over Sinclair's blue floral sundress with its cleavage-enhancing neckline.

When she sat down, Sinclair pulled Regina's head briefly to hers for a kiss. She tasted like strawberry lip gloss.

"I hope that wasn't too presumptuous of me." Regina tucked her purse under the table. "But I woke up thinking about you this morning, so . . ." Her eyes twinkled.

The restaurant was small and well lit. Even though they sat in a corner, sun poured liberally over their table. It was like being on the sidewalk without the constant intrusion of people or traffic. Shelly had once recommended the place to Sinclair.

"I think I can handle that." Sinclair's belly danced, fluttering at Regina's attentions. The other woman's powerful and commanding personality was charming, something Sinclair could never stand in a man but now she found it inexplicably arousing.

"The Bloody Marys here are amazing," Regina murmured, pulling her chair closer to Sinclair's. "What are you having?" she asked.

"Eggs and toast." Sinclair couldn't eat anything else with her around. She was too stimulated. Her hands trembled against the tablecloth.

"Have at least one drink with that. It'll spice up your morning." She draped her arm over Sinclair's chair.

Awash in sunlight, Sinclair's skin tingled, begging to be touched. As if Regina had read her mind, Sinclair felt a hand on her knee.

The restaurant was crowded. Jaded urban animals, still hung over from last night's debauches, drooped over their drinks. Their faces were gray from having been forced to face the light of day so early. There were some people who'd traveled in just to go to the fairly popular restaurant. Excited chatter rolled side by side with low growls of reluctant conversation. Regina's fingers traced the skin on the inside of Sinclair's thigh.

"How was your night?" Regina asked.

"Good. I had a long bath, watched *Buffy* reruns, and even read a little."

"Anything of mine?"

"No." She was such an egomaniac.

"Too bad. I was hoping you'd fall asleep thinking about me."

"That was the night before that." Sinclair met her eyes across the table.

Satisfied, Regina sat back. Her fingers traveled higher, brushing the lace edge of the panties Sinclair had worn just for her.

"I don't do too much on Friday nights either. After a little red wine, all I ever want to do is write."

"What? No research? I thought your search for more knowledge on your subject matter was limitless."

"You're right. My curiosity has no bounds." Her eyes flickered to Sinclair's mouth. "But one has to take some time to write down the results of all one's tireless research."

"Of course, silly me."

A waitress in low-rider jeans and a rainbow belly ring came over to take their order. Sinclair was vaguely surprised that Regina let the young girl go without trying to chat her up.

"Silly, never." Her long fingers lightly touched Sinclair through her panties then, after a teasing stroke, disappeared. "Other things, absolutely."

Sinclair took a deep drink of water.

"What kind of women do you like, Sinclair?"

"I'm not sure. I haven't given it much thought."

"Yeah, you have. Don't bullshit me." It was strange to see her elegant mouth shape that curse word. In the sweat of the bedroom, it was OK. Here in the restaurant it was raw, surprising.

She thought of the woman she'd most imagined touching. At Volk, while meetings dragged on, she'd imagined Margo Phelps fucking her until she screamed out the year-end financial goals to the whole building. Margo, Sinclair was convinced, was a closet lesbian, too, with her broad shoulders and short fingernails.

"Powerful women." She grinned, feeling bold. "Women with apple-sized breasts and high, round asses."

"Crab apple or Gala?"

Sinclair glanced at the other woman's breasts. "Granny Smith." They shared a naughty smile.

The waitress came back with a plate of artfully arranged toast and eggs and a pitcher of Bloody Marys. Regina poured a tall glass for each of them.

"A toast." She lifted her glass. "To apples."

Sinclair giggled. "To apples."

* * *

They went through two pitchers of Bloody Marys together, lifting their glasses to toast various parts of the female anatomy until all they had to work with were toes and hair follicles. Sinclair barely touched her food.

"You're very beautiful," Sinclair said over the fifth glass of her morning cocktail. "The first time I saw you I was totally thrown for a loop."

Regina laughed. "Was it the ass or witty repartee?"

"Neither. It was your mouth. It's so . . . damn sexy," Sinclair's thoughts swam in her brain, mostly remaining out of reach. The words that came out of her mouth didn't seem to have any forethought attached to them. "The ass came later. When you were walking out of the elevator."

"My ass has been known to drop many a woman to her knees."

"Mm, can we practice that one again later?"

"We can practice it right now. They have nice big bathroom stalls here."

"OK, let's go." Sinclair stood up.

"I'm just kidding, honey." Regina pulled her back down with a soft tug and a laugh. "There's time enough for that later." She looked at her watch. "There's something else I want to show you today."

Sinclair leaned forward with childlike enthusiasm. "Is it a surprise?"

"Yes. Are you ready?"

Sinclair drained her glass in long, luxurious gulps. "Now I am."

Regina drove them in her Mercedes to a warehouse near the wharf. The sun slid over the wooden boxes and pallets in haphazard piles, making them almost beautiful. Quiet hung in the air. As they walked toward the single electronic door, it began to rise with a series of clangs and squeaks. As soon as they walked through it, the door started to lower. It hit the concrete floor with a loud bang, then a sound came out of the darkness, a fumbling of keys as if someone were locking it, locking them in.

"What is this?" Sinclair asked.

"You'll see."

Regina took Sinclair's hand in reassurance, then let go. An arrow of light from a high window led them to another room, or maybe it was a corner of the larger room. Sinclair couldn't tell. She couldn't see. But she could smell things. Oil from a car or large equipment. The scent of women and sex and baby powder. Regina led her up a flight of steep stairs.

Sinclair's head swam, but was getting clearer by the minute. Soft light flooded the room.

"We're here," Regina called out in a light teasing voice. Laughter greeted her announcement as women—tall, short, white, Asian, black, Latina—suddenly began emerging from the corners, all wearing some bit of lingerie or other.

"And we're ready," a tall woman chuckled, walking up to kiss Regina softly on her mouth. Her ebony skin gleamed in the faint light.

Sinclair counted five women. They looked at her and Regina with various degrees of amusement and anticipation.

"Is that all, Reggie?" the ebony queen asked.

"Is that all? Ha! You don't know what I've got." To Sinclair, Regina said, "Don't worry. You'll enjoy this."

A tall Asian woman with short hair clipped close to her head walked toward the trio. "You haven't told her what's going on?"

"And ruin the surprise? Of course not."

A few of the women laughed, low and predatory sounds that made Sinclair shudder in the warm warehouse.

Regina squeezed her hand again. "It'll be fine," she whispered.

Then at a signal from her, the women converged on Sinclair, pulling her deeper into the warehouse, where there was more light and what looked like a large sitting room with a mishmash of chairs and tables. A high platform bed with white sheets sat in the middle of the room.

"Come, make yourself comfortable," someone said.

As if Sinclair was being given a choice. They tugged her over to a leather Queen Anne chair the color of fresh blood and started pulling at her clothes, sweetly, if one could describe forced stripping as such, while looking at her with their heavy-lidded eyes. Regina stood a few feet away, watching, smiling.

"This is going to be fine," she mouthed. At least *she* would enjoy it.

"You've got pretty skin," a voluptuous woman said with a slight Spanish accent. Her long black hair tumbled over Sinclair as she leaned close. It smelled like cloves.

"Look at those fingers." The Asian woman smiled at Sinclair. "They're so long."

"She's skinny but still cute."

The woman with skin the color of night stroked Sinclair's face. "You could have been a model, baby."

"Or a stripper. Look at those hips. I bet you could bump and grind real good." The tall butchy woman with pale caramel skin wearing tight white boxers and a hacked-off tank top pulled Sinclair's dress over her head. She winked when she saw Sinclair looking. Her muscled belly pressed briefly against the accountant's cheek. Sinclair could smell her cologne and the spicy scent coming from inside her shorts.

"Gorgeous tits." Cool fingers brushed Sinclair's nipples. They let her keep on her panties.

"Can we tie her up?" This from a woman with brown hair and a soft, touchable body.

"No. Not yet." Regina still watched, still smiled.

Sinclair shivered in anticipation and fear. What had she gotten herself into? She didn't even know this woman. Did

Regina even work for Volk? That was probably a fake name anyway. Why—?

The Asian woman pulled her clothes off, revealing a pleasing blend of soft breasts, lean belly, and narrow hips that were barely hidden by a low-cut bikini. She blew Sinclair a kiss and took off the bikini. Sinclair felt herself blush and she looked down, away from the woman's body.

"She's sweet," someone said.

"We'll fix that before the day is through."

Regina chuckled. "Open up your eyes, honey, the real show hasn't even started yet."

Sinclair had watched Regina perform in bed before, touched herself to some inner music only she heard. But this was nothing like that. These women were strangers. Sinclair was terrified, yet intrigued in a way that Regina must have known she would be.

"I'd never introduce you to anything that I thought you wouldn't be ready for," she'd said to Sinclair once. She should have paid attention to whatever else Regina had said that day.

The Asian woman was the only one naked. Everyone stayed in their provocative clothes—ripped denim shorts that sagged over boxers or bare skin, this season's Victoria's Secret panties and matching bra, lace negligee and bare feet. All on bodies that ran the gamut from full and fleshy to hard and toned, then back again.

"Watch."

They started to perform for Sinclair. Or rather, for Regina. Sinclair was just an incidental observer. The brown-haired woman touched the hard-bodied angel in the boxer shorts and ripped tank. She brushed her lace-covered breasts against Hard Body's back and was rewarded with a hand on her ass and a kiss. Breasts touched breasts through cloth, then fingers brushed the lace negligee aside for lips to kiss the revealed nipple. Hard Body quickly rid the other woman of her clothes. A tattoo of entwined, lushly green ivy wound all the way around the voluptuous woman's waist. Sinclair's panties suddenly felt too tight, too wet.

"You like?" Regina stood at Sinclair's chair, her mouth curved in that smile, clothes on, like the director of the show. Sinclair didn't know what to say. But her body was interested.

Regina looked down at Sinclair's hardened nipples and smirked. "I'll let you get back to it." Then she stepped back.

The women converged on the bed and on each other. Naked now, Hard Body sat down on the bed, and spread her legs for Ivy. She was shaved, with small and delicate lips that Ivy breathed over then began to lick. Even from where Sinclair sat she could see that Hard Body was already wet. Venus with the long black hair and heavy breasts sat higher up on the bed, watching as she stroked herself, caressed her thick brown nipples while her mouth opened in a delighted O. She knelt just above Hard Body's head, close enough for her to smell and see, but not touch. Hard Body groaned and arched her pussy up toward the tattooed woman's mouth.

At the sound of that deep, delicious sound, Ivy gave up her cat licks and dove into her pussy as if she was starving, licking and eating her with hungry wet sounds that made Sinclair squirm against her chair. The Asian woman came up behind Ivy and interrupted her view. Sinclair blinked at the unexpected addition to her lean dancer's body—a dash-toned dildo attached with leather straps to her hips. It was already covered with a condom.

"Get on your knees for me." She guided Ivy to her knees, without interrupting the other woman's hungry, pussy-eating rhythm.

Her long hands spread the full curves of Ivy's ass, then with a graceful, practiced move, slid deeply inside the tattooed woman. Ivy grunted but continued to dine on her well-muscled lover, stroking the dark nipples above her head as she ate. Hard Body laughed softly. "This ain't no pettin' zoo, baby. Squeeze my tits like you mean it."

Venus took pity on her and interrupted her self-pleasure to push Ivy's hands away. She leaned over the muscled woman, brushing her thick hair aside to fasten her greedy mouth on Hard Body's breasts. Her tongue moved with sure, hard strokes while her finger pinched and rolled a dark nipple until the muscled woman gasped and groaned her encouragement. Venus's eyes swept up to meet Sinclair's, whose panties were now soaking wet; her breasts tingled beneath a thin layer of sweat. She wanted to be touched. Badly.

"Sit here." Someone guided Sinclair to a chair with a better view. "This is much better. Don't you think?"

Now she could see the long arch of the muscled woman's body draped across the bed, her neck stretched back against the sheets and vibrating to her heavy breaths as Venus with the long hair suckled her breasts from above, biting and squeezing the hard nipples. The long-haired woman had a hand buried between her own spread legs. Ivy's wet mouth rode Hard Body's undulating pussy while her hands anchored themselves on the dark thighs. As if Sinclair's eyes touching her was the signal, the Asian woman reared up behind Ivy, burying her brown dick deeper in the tattooed woman's drenched pussy. Ivy gasped, then groaned deep in her throat. A chorus of moans and gasps overtook the room.

"You like that?" The chocolate goddess sitting on the arm of Sinclair's chair finally pulled her attention from the scene in front of her. Sinclair licked her dry lips.

"They're very uninhibited."

"You could say that."

"Jesus—!"

Sinclair looked up in time to see Hard Body's hands wrap themselves in Ivy's hair, pulling her deeper against her pussy. Her gasps became louder in the lofted space. Suddenly Sinclair couldn't see. Soft cloth brushed her cheekbones and tightened behind her head. She stiffened.

"Relax." Regina's voice dripped, melting sugar sweet, near her ear.

"Did you bring us an innocent to corrupt, Reggie?" some-one murmured from nearby.

"Me? Never." Regina chuckled, then brushed her lips against Sinclair's. "Listen," she commanded.

Noises slipped out at her from the darkness—the slap of flesh against flesh, ragged moaning, hisses, gasps, the slide of sweat-drenched bodies.

"Faster," someone urged breathlessly. Beside her, Sinclair heard hands against cloth, the sound of someone undressing, lips meeting in a wet kiss, a giggle. A hand brushed Sinclair's throat.

"If you ever want to stop, to go home, just say the word." Regina's breath hovered near her ear, waiting.

"I will."

She rewarded Sinclair with a deep kiss. "Good girl."

When the sounds shifted back, she felt a hovering at her mouth, then the soft brush of something. "Open your mouth."

It was a finger, fragrant with the scent of a woman's body. She took the whole finger into her mouth, licking until it was completely clean.

"She's a natural at this," someone, not Regina, said.

Soft laughter teased her. She bit into the finger in her mouth.

"And she's got teeth, too." The finger withdrew.

Gentle hands brushed her neck and jaw. "So pretty." Lips grazed her throat. Waves of sensation rolled from the contact point and pooled between her legs. Something brushed against her lips. Sinclair licked it and was rewarded with a soft hum of delight. A nipple. She started to lift her hands, to keep the breast close, but other hands held down her own. Sinclair nuzzled the breast, teasing it with her mouth and adding her own sounds of pleasure to the ones raining down on her.

A weight pushed her legs apart. The chair slowly reclined. Warm breath brushed her toes, her knees, her thighs. The sounds in the warehouse burned through her, the gasping breaths, soft frantic sucking, the grunting of someone wielding a dildo, a loud cry for Jesus. Hands tugged her panties off. The chair reclined all the way back, and a body straddled hers. The breasts returned to her face. This time she didn't even try to touch them, her mouth arched up and devoured soft flesh, tasting and testing the firmness of the underside of one heavy breast. The nipples were like blackberries. She bit them gently.

When a mouth touched her pussy, she gasped, then arched into it. The skin under her mouth became even more interesting. She wanted to take more of it inside. Two hot mouths enfolded each of her nipples at the same time and sent her body into sensual overload. A deep moan vibrated against the soft flesh under her lips. She widened her legs for the mouth eating her and arched against the twin mouths that were driving her out of her mind.

"What are you feeling, Sinclair?"

It took a moment for her to hear Regina's voice. Then another moment for her to respond. The full mound of flesh eased back to allow her voice room.

Sinclair nodded then gasped as the mouth between her legs reached her clit, its tongue doing a miraculous dance against the bundle of nerves. "Good," she murmured. "It feels good."

"I asked how you feel. Be specific." Regina's voice was so damn cool. It sent sparks shooting across Sinclair's skin as if she'd touched her.

"Li—like . . . like a piece of volcanic rock." She gasped as the mouths worked her breasts, making soft liquid sounds that distracted her from Regina's voice almost as much as the tongue between her legs. "Like I'm in a mountain . . . churning in hot lava . . . waiting for the explosion."

"Ladies," Regina's voice lowered. "Why are you keeping her waiting?"

A soft mouth brushed hers. A hard tongue slid deep inside her. Teeth and mouths tightened around her breasts, milked them until the connection between her cunt, tits, and mouth was liquid but unbreakable. Her mountain exploded in a haze of fire. And that was just the first time.

"I think we wore her out, poor thing."

"She looks so cute."

"Can we take her home next time?"

Soft laughter followed them back into the lowering sun. Sinclair snuggled into the scented leather of Regina's car, curled into the backseat, her mind and body completely exhausted.

"Home, Jeeves." Sinclair weakly tapped on the back of the driver's seat.

Regina's soft laughter gently nudged her into sleep.

Sinclair woke up in Regina's bed. Sunset had come and gone and now night was beginning its slow descent upon the city. The curve of soft gray light pouring through the window reminded her of a woman's back, shadowed, hollow, curved. She turned away from the light and closed her eyes. The hours that had led to her exhaustion and her eventual nap came pouring into her brain like acid. She rolled away from its awareness, but the images came at her in clear Technicolor. She couldn't even blame the alcohol for it. If anything she had been drunk on Regina, on the power the writer had wielded over her. Still, that was no excuse. Toward the end she'd wanted it, wanted the spectacle almost as much as Regina, wanted to see what heights these women could take their bodies, and hers, to.

And now she was here. From far off in the apartment she could hear Regina puttering about. Top forty R & B floated into the bedroom and just below it was the sound of Regina's voice. The woman was adventurous, uninhibited. Sinclair had known that when she read her books, had even looked forward to fulfilling some fantasies with her. But was this too much? And what about this other mysterious person that

Regina was seeing? Were they getting as much of a workout as Sinclair?

Outside the window, city lights flashed, winking on in a domino of brightness that quickly spread out farther than Sinclair's eyes could see. She heard Regina approaching the bedroom with sure footsteps and still carrying the melody of a song on her lips. Sinclair slid back under the covers and pretended to sleep.

Chapter 4

A soft knock sounded on Sinclair's office door. She paused in the act of putting away paperwork in the filing cabinet and glanced at her watch. Five thirty-five. Sinclair felt a moment's regret for allowing Shelly to leave at the dot of five. This better not be business.

"Come in."

"Hey, there," Regina purred as she walked into the office. She could have done nothing else in the outfit she was wearing—black skintight leather pants, boots, and a corset laced so tight that she almost had cleavage. Catwoman come to life. "Come play with me," she said.

Sinclair stared at her lover, at the sleek skin that shone with body glitter, the ornate makeup and cornrowed hair. Her belly tightened with sudden desire to do anything and everything that Regina wanted. But Sinclair shook her head. "Can't. I have some things I need to do at home tonight."

"But it's a Friday."

"Sorry." Sinclair slid the file drawer closed and walked back to her desk. She'd been out with Regina almost every day this week. Tonight was her time to regroup, cuddle into her easy chair with a good book and a cup of rosemary tea.

Regina hummed deeply in her throat as she stalked Sinclair across the room then sat on the edge of the desk. "Come on, sugar." She brushed a thumb across Sinclair's nipple through the thin black blouse. "I'll make it worth your while."

Dinner and dancing. That's all she said it was going to be. But when they ended up at the Burning Rose, Sinclair knew that she'd been had.

"Welcome, ladies." The slim woman dressed in a rubber French maid's outfit took their coats and guided them to a table. A corner one, at Regina's request. The table was intimate, set far enough away from the main dining room that it was private, yet still had a good view of the round, stagelike area that was now empty except for a single chair. People stared as the two women walked past, sliding their eyes along Regina's leather-covered flesh with undisguised delight. Sinclair was glad that Regina had taken her back to the uptown penthouse for a change of clothes—simple leather pants, high heels, and a halter top that covered her breasts and almost nothing else.

"A gift," Regina had said with a seductive smile.

At least she fit in with the leather- and rubber-wearing crowd. The lights in the restaurant, provided by glittering crystal chandeliers, were golden and dim, giving the Burning Rose an air of romance and mystery. A pale-skinned waitress brought two menus and tall glasses of water.

"Would you like something else to drink, ladies?" Her Western European accent sounded fake.

"A bottle of your house red, please," Regina said with a dismissive wave. The girl nodded and left them alone.

"Are you going to tell me what kind of place this is?" Sinclair's curiosity was piqued. But not in a good way.

"Why spoil the fun, when I can just show you?" An impish smile teased her burgundy lips. "What would you like to eat?"

"I'm suddenly not hungry."

"No? At least look at the menu. You might find something that intrigues you." Regina opened the velvet-bound menu in front of Sinclair, smiling expectantly.

Sinclair sighed, but skimmed through the elegantly scripted menu anyway. Duck à l'orange, escargots, lobster bisque, truffles, spanking, public humiliation, foot worship . . . Sinclair stopped reading.

"Are you kidding me?"

"You can order anything on the menu, either for yourself or your dinner companion." Regina arched an eyebrow. "Do you want to punish me for bringing you here?"

"Oh, for God's sake!"

"Look, someone ordered something special." Regina pointed to the stage where a woman, a gorgeous Anjelica Huston look-alike, wearing impossibly high-heeled boots and a very short leather skirt with slits up both sides, stood with her whip at the ready. Her breasts looked ready to spill from its black leather corset. A man was being led up to the stage by the rubber-wearing French maid.

"On your knees, bitch!" Anjelica ordered as she snapped her whip in the air. The man flinched and immediately dropped to his knees.

"Now clean my boot with your tongue. I want every inch of it wet." The boots laced all the way up to her thighs.

Sinclair looked away from the stage with mild disgust.

"I never figured you for a prude, darling," Regina murmured, looking at her companion with slightly narrowed eyes.

Sinclair closed the menu with a quick snap. "I'm not a prude. I just don't find this scenario the least bit arousing or interesting."

Regina lifted a hand to summon the waitress. "I'll have the filet mignon with shallots and cognac. Darling?" She looked at Sinclair.

"Lobster thermidor, please."

"And," Regina pointed to something on her menu. "I'll have one of these, as well. Heavy."

The girl nodded. "Would you like to keep the menu in case something else appeals to you later on?"

Regina smiled up at the girl. "You know, I think I will."

The waitress left with the soft sound of rubber against flesh and the smell of talc in her wake.

"Are you angry at me, darling?"

"Don't call me that. It's meaningless." On stage, the man had finished his task to hearty applause.

Leather creaked as Regina bent close to Sinclair. "What do you mean it's empty? You are a darling." Her voice was light, teasing. But Sinclair wasn't buying it.

"Are you ever serious?" She'd been seeing this woman for almost a month and she could honestly say that she knew next to nothing about her. Except that she liked sex.

"For you, darling? Never. That would be boring."

Next on stage was a leatherman. His body was completely hidden except for his maggot-white penis that flopped through a silver-toothed opening in the black leather. A woman wearing a schoolgirl's uniform approached the stage, led again by the French maid.

Sinclair looked away before she could see any more. "Do you enjoy this?"

Regina's eyes flickered to the stage, then back to Sinclair with obvious reluctance. "It's entertaining."

"I'd hate to see what disgusts you."

"Me, too." Regina twisted her red mouth.

Sinclair shook her head again. What had she gotten herself into? Yuen's explorations into sex—whether it had been light bondage or talking dirty—had amused rather than surprised her. Now with Regina she found herself being shocked at the things the woman was teaching her about herself, about just how far she could be pushed and manipulated sexually.

"What are you thinking about?" Regina asked.

"You."

"I'm flattered."

"It's the truth. Don't bother pretending to be surprised. What else can I think about when you're around?" Sinclair knew she sounded resentful. But she was getting tired of this one-dimensional affair. "Do I mean anything to you?"

"Of course. You're an incredible fuck. Yet you're so naive. You're like my lost childhood. My virginity."

Now that said it all, didn't it? Sinclair thought with a wry smile.

The maid interrupted whatever else Regina might have said. She brought the wine and poured them each a glass before looking finally at Regina. "Madame?"

The writer stood. "Ready."

Sinclair watched her go, admiring the motion of her ass under the leather and the gold-dusted bare arms that looked both sensual and strong under the restaurant's soft lights. She may be fucked up, but she was still gorgeous. Sinclair sipped her water to moisten her dry throat.

For purely masochistic reasons, her mind dipped back into the past, to one of the many nights she had been trying to find satisfaction but could not. It was not that long ago when Yuen had invited himself over with a gourmet dinner, aromatic teas, and sex. Their dinner was long gone and the tea cooling on the kitchen counter when he got her into bed, undressed her, and slid down between her thighs. Despite his enthusiasm, Sinclair hadn't quite been able to get into it. Yuen toyed fruitlessly with her sore clitoris, working to get a sigh, a sound, something, out of her. She had sighed eventually, but it was a sound of impatience. The sound was lost in the pulse pounding rhythm of the M'shell CD playing in her bedroom and in the loud, eager noises that her boyfriend made whenever his mouth encountered her skin. Her body tingled, generating heat between her thighs, but as usual, fulfillment eluded her. She felt disconnected from herself, as if the things Yuen was doing were being performed on someone else. A possibility of pleasure existed somewhere out there, but she knew that it wouldn't be realized that night. Still, Yuen liked to touch her, so she let him.

He loved to look at her and, even after two years of being together, marvel at their different-shaded skin. In the beginning she had been entranced, too. They were beautiful together—his gold-touched porcelain flesh and hers the shade of freshly shaved nutmeg. If only all he wanted to do was lay in the sun together and talk. Then he could be the best friend that she never had. Instead he was someone she held back from. Someone with whom she reluctantly shared her body.

"Yuen, sweetheart. Can you just hold me?" She had made her voice soft, childlike. He looked up and his dark hair fell over his eyes, making him look no more than a child, certainly not like a thirty-two-year-old lawyer with an overactive libido.

"You sure?"

"Yeah."

They adjusted themselves until she lay in his arms with her ear over his chest, listening to his pounding, unfulfilled heart. She touched his belly.

"But let me do this for you first," her guilt said.

Work the next morning was her excuse for him not to spend the night. Once he finally left her apartment, she scoured her mouth with Listerine, showered, and changed the sheets.

That was just one of many nights Sinclair had labored under a man, searching without success for her pleasure. And now, Regina could easily slide it out of her, with a single word or one skillful application of a finger. Unexpectedly, Sinclair's panties shifted over her agitated flesh.

She watched Regina walk up to the small stage as if the maid had shown her into a wealthy aristocrat's parlor and she was waiting to be received. The maid bowed to Regina and stepped away. Sinclair could feel the crowd respond to her lover's presence, drinking in her tight, beautiful body, her confidence. This woman was coiled, patient energy and, obviously, she was used to being the one wielding the whip. The entire restaurant perked up and any residual conversation died.

A tall, dark skinned woman joined Regina on the dais. She walked around Sinclair's lover as if sizing up a prized new toy. Her dark eyes lingered on Regina's ass and hips. The woman wore what could only be described as a Gibson Girl outfit—a long black skirt that brushed the floor and a simple, bell sleeved white blouse with a cameo fastened at the throat. The entire outfit was made of rubber and moved over the woman's skin like freshly poured oil. Her straightened hair, pinned up in an elegant topknot, haloed the severe face. Like a schoolteacher from the old days, she carried a wooden paddle in one hand.

A chair already stood on the platform, a simple thing with a metal frame and a round, red velvet seat. The schoolteacher whispered something to Regina and the other woman immediately bent over the chair, gloved fingers curling into its dark metal back.

"This woman," the schoolteacher said loudly, "needs to be punished. She tricked her lover into coming here. Her lover is very angry with her. How many strokes of the paddle should she get?"

Various responses erupted from the suddenly whispering audience.

"Fifty," came a soft southern voice.

"One hundred," came another. "She looks like she could take it."

The teacher raised her hand for silence. "How about the woman in the halter top with the beautiful Afro?" Her eyes found Sinclair. "How many do you suggest?"

Sinclair looked at Regina. From so far back, she couldn't see her freckles, only the impression of her loveliness and the sweeping curve of her sensuous, smug mouth.

"Twenty." They had been together for twenty days.

"Twenty it is then." Her voice was like warm honey. "Twenty," she said again and turned to Regina and stroked the writer's spine with a long, graceful hand.

The audience could see the two women in profile were in the perfect position to appreciate the graceful bow of Regina's back and the outline of her breasts, hips, and thighs in the leather.

The first slap was loud. More sound than pain it seemed, since Regina barely moved. Her face was a calm sea. The second was louder still, as the paddle hit the fleshiest part of her ass. The teacher was just warming up.

She heated the soft leather with each slap, testing the endurance of the skin underneath the butter-soft pants. On number five, she got serious. The entire restaurant heard Regina's soft hiss of breath. She wriggled her hips and tightened her grip on the chair. Was Sinclair the only one who noticed her tightening legs? The schoolteacher's hand was a precise metronome, swinging in a slow, solid rhythm, making sure that the thick wooden paddle touched every part of that delectable ass.

Regina jerked forward with the force of each slap, like she was being taken from behind. She bared her teeth in a feral smile. Fifteen. Her face and shoulders flushed pink. Sixteen. She turned to look at Sinclair and licked her mouth. Seventeen. The chair slid abruptly across the floor. Eighteen. Sinclair held her breath as the teacher began to put all of her weight behind the remaining blows. Nineteen. Regina clenched her teeth and closed her eyes. Twenty was the loudest. As the echoes of it died away, Sinclair could hear the teacher's labored breathing. Her skin glowed under the light as if she'd drawn energy from the flushed and twitching student.

Regina straightened. "Thank you."

The restaurant erupted in applause. Nearly every head turned to watch her walk back to her table.

"What was that supposed to prove?" Sinclair asked.

"Not a thing." Regina stood near her chair and picked up her glass to take a sip of wine. "It was supposed to be fun."

"And you had fun?"

"Oh yes." Her eyes blazed under the lights. "Would you like to come to the ladies' room with me?"

Sinclair looked at her, amazed. "No."

"Then, if you'll excuse me, I'll be right back." She left without another word.

By the time she came back, their meal had arrived. She was quick.

"Did I miss anything?" Regina asked.

"No."

Regina's hands trembled as they manipulated the knife and fork. Her cheeks and throat were flushed a postorgasmic coral. Had she gotten off by herself or did someone who was already in the bathroom help her? Sinclair swallowed a forkful of lobster and wondered if she even cared.

"Dancing next?" Regina slid two hundred-dollar bills in the leather binder with their check.

"I have a bit of a headache, actually. I don't think I can take any more excitement tonight."

"You'll like this kind of fun, I promise." Regina tugged her into the night, then into a taxi heading downtown.

The yellow cab let them out in front of the Pleasure Kitten, a place that Sinclair had never heard of, but everyone else apparently had. The line to get into the club stretched all the way down the block and beyond. Women waited patiently, some hugging their scantily clad bodies in protection from the brisk spring breeze. Regina pulled Sinclair to the head of the line and, after a brief word with the flat-topped butch bouncer, dove into the club. The large building was full of women, all vibrant and humming with the excitement of the night, their skin shooting sparks of electricity and heat as Sinclair squeezed past them.

"Excuse me," she said when her hand accidentally brushed another woman's full hip.

The woman turned and smiled with her dark red mouth. Her hair fell into sloe eyes as she scanned Sinclair's body. "No problem, baby."

Regina gave the woman a dismissive look, then tugged Sinclair after her to the bar.

"Want a drink?" Regina had to shout above the music.

"Sure. Gin and tonic."

While Regina leaned over the crowded bar to order, Sinclair turned around to get a good look at the club. Women were packed side by side, breast to back, hip to ass in the glittering room. Colored lights flashed from the complex equipment hanging from the ceiling periodically illuminating the large speakers perched from black shelves in each corner of the club. On the dance floor, women danced frenetically to the hard-driving salsa music, whirling and spinning by themselves, in couples, even in trios that somehow managed not to slam into each other. There wasn't a single man in sight. The flashing lights changed to silver, capturing the women in mid-movement again and again like a series of still photographs.

Regina slid a cold glass into her hand. "Here you go, baby." She'd stopped calling Sinclair "darling" three hours ago.

"Thanks."

Torn between wanting to see what else women did together in a space like this and being angry at Regina for being so damn domineering, Sinclair eventually ignored her in favor of the invigorating crowd. Her feet tapped in time to the music as her chest vibrated from the heavy bass line.

Regina knocked back a glass of merlot. "Come dance with me."

"No. You go ahead." She was enjoying telling her no far too much. Sinclair smiled, then watched Regina walk off to the dance floor without a second look at her. She leaned against the bar, watching and sipping her drink. It was enough. Sinclair turned to the bartender.

"Tell Regina I went home, will you?" She had a feeling that they all knew Regina here.

The Billy Idol look-alike with breasts flung a white rag over her shoulder and nodded. "Sure thing."

Sinclair left the club and took a taxi home.

In the cab she leaned back against the creaking leather upholstery and slid her fingers through her hair. The control that Regina had exhibited in the beginning had been erotic, sensual in its sureness. Now it seemed like she had the whims of a spoiled child, pushing Sinclair into experiences that she had little or no desire to dabble in. The outings seemed simply for experience's sake, not because she thought that Sinclair would enjoy them.

The taxi pulled up at her apartment a few minutes before one. Once inside, Sinclair turned off her phone, then showered and washed her hair, scrubbing to make sure she got out all the club smoke. The lingering filth from Regina's attitude she'd have to deal with later.

Sinclair had settled down under the covers to the quiet purr of the bedside radio when the downstairs door buzzed. She let it ring twice to make sure she wasn't hearing things. It was 3:28 A.M.

She pressed the intercom button. "Who is it?"

"It's me. Who else would be coming to see you this time of night?"

"What do you want?"

"To talk."

"We can talk tomorrow. I'm tired." An obvious lie. By now Regina knew Sinclair didn't sleep more than a couple of hours a night.

"Please. It won't take long."

Sinclair always put her hair up before going to bed, twisting it into six big plaits that made her look closer to fifteen than her almost thirty-three years. She touched her hair in a moment of discomfort. She didn't let anyone, not even Yuen, see her like this. Then she twitched with annoyance. This was only Regina, after all. Sinclair buzzed her in.

Regina was dressed in softer clothes than before, blue jeans and a simple long-sleeved shirt. Her hair hung loose around her face and she smelled clean, like she'd just arrived fresh from the shower.

"I'm sorry, Sinclair." She presented a bouquet of bright yellow daffodils as if she was performing a magician's trick. "I was being a pushy bitch. Forgive me."

"Come in." Sinclair stepped aside.

"You look nice," Regina murmured, looking at Sinclair's long T-shirt and bare legs. She smiled.

"I was in bed."

"You're not in a forgiving mood, are you?"

"Not especially." Sinclair took the flowers and walked to the kitchen to put them in a tall glass. Regina followed. The loud splash of water rushing from the spigot filled the silence.

"Even if I grovel?" Regina dropped gracefully to her knees onto the tiled floor. "Even if I beg?" She smoothed her cheek against Sinclair's leg, brushing her soft skin against the beginnings of stubble.

Sinclair looked down at her, exasperated. "If this is all you came for you might as well go home. Like you said earlier, I'm not in the mood."

But she was getting in the mood. Slowly. She knew that Regina could see up her shirt from her position on the floor, could see that she wasn't wearing anything underneath the thin cotton.

Regina kissed the back of Sinclair's knee. "I know I fucked up. Let me make it up to you." She slowly began to stand, nuzzling Sinclair's thigh, then the soft hairs she found under the shirt. Her breath swept over the other woman's belly, breasts, and soft neck. She met Sinclair's eyes. "Please."

Regina tasted like wine and clove cigarettes. Her slick mouth moved over Sinclair's while her hands roamed the taller woman's back before settling on her hips, gently pressing their bodies together. "Come."

Regina took some of the flowers, dripping, from the vase

and pulled her quarry along behind her. Sinclair raised an eyebrow but didn't ask. The liquid fullness between her thighs demanded more immediate attention. The bed took her languid weight and she watched as Regina plucked the yellow daffodil petals from their moorings and released them all over her body.

"All I want to do tonight is make you happy."

She didn't remind her penitent lover that it was already morning. Regina kissed her through the petals, mixing the sweat of their bodies with the heady scent of the flowers. The sight of her lover stroking her breasts, licking them with her avid tongue, filled her senses. Desire churned hot and full under her skin, her legs widened and she arched her back, pushing her nipples into the other woman's hands. Regina slid down her body with naked intention.

She could tell that Regina was trying to take her time, trying to be gentle, but couldn't. Soon she was slurping at Sinclair's pussy as if it had all the nourishment she needed, licking and sucking her, making deep sounds of pleasure that became guttural moans. Sinclair reared up, gasping, as Regina slid two fingers inside, then three. She grabbed the headboard and held on. Her hips kept time with the quick rhythm Regina set and her pussy opened hungrily, fucking as it was being fucked, taking it all and demanding more, more, more. The scent of daffodils swam sweet and thick around them, feeding their desire. She gasped sounds of encouragement, urging her lover on. In response, Regina pinned her to the bed with the powerful thrust of her fingers and her lightning-quick tongue on Sinclair's clit. Pinwheels of light spun behind her eyes as she came, bucking hard against the relentless mouth and hand.

"God!"

She sagged into the sheets, shuddering still, and barely moved when Regina moved up her body to lavish wet, openmouthed kisses on her face. Her damp thighs fell in a sprawl across the bed. Regina clambered on top of her and straddled one thigh. Watching Sinclair's face, she worked her clit against the lean flesh until her body stiffened then trembled extravagantly. She sighed, chuckling.

"Even when you don't do anything you're a great fuck." She sighed again and snuggled up to Sinclair's slick, petal-dotted skin. "Am I forgiven?"

Sinclair stretched around the invasion of Regina's body into her personal space, before relaxing against her pillows. "We'll see."

Dawn found them asleep. Regina curled like an inverted question mark perpendicular to Sinclair, her cheek resting in the curve of her lover's lower back, a hand spread posses-sively over the full curve of Sinclair's ass. As the light pene-trated deeper into the room, turning it a uniform shade of gray, Sinclair blinked and turned her head to face it. She'd only slept for two hours.

Two mornings later, Sinclair woke up to a message from Regina to call her at an unfamiliar number. She stumbled to the kitchen, belting her bathrobe and dialing the phone at the same time.

"Hey," she said when she heard Regina's voice.

"'Morning, sexy." Regina chuckled at Sinclair's sleep-roughened voice.

"Very funny. Where are you anyway?"

"I'm up in the country for the weekend. Why don't you come up?"

Sinclair opened the cupboard and peered in. "I don't have a way to get up there."

"My car's at Volk. Just drive it up here and we'll ride back together."

"I don't drive." With the phone propped between her cheek and shoulder, Sinclair took out a container of loose tea leaves and a bottle of honey before taking them to the stove.

"It's OK out there. Traffic won't be that bad this—"

"I *can't* drive." She put water in the kettle and put it to boil.

"Oh, sweetie," an edge crept into Regina's voice. "Get a car with a driver, for heaven's sake. What do you do with your money if you don't use it?"

Sinclair looked at the phone in her hands as if it'd grown a coat of slime. "Why don't I just see you when you get back into town, Regina?" Her voice was hard, final.

"Oh. OK." The other woman prattled on about something else for a few more minutes before Sinclair stopped their conversation on the pretense of having to eat breakfast.

"Have fun," she said, then broke their connection. *Pushy broad.*

Chapter 5

Sinclair knew that she was walking around like a clown with her face always cracked in a brighter than bright smile, but she didn't care. Despite the minor disagreements and power struggles that she'd had with Regina, this was the first time she'd ever felt totally free with someone that she was seeing. Even in college, the period when she should have been experimenting, she'd kept to boys, suffering through one disappointing encounter after another and trying to convince herself that it was the newness of the activity that made it so disappointing. Now she knew better. Sinclair occasionally thought of the other person who Regina was seeing, but she figured that as long as they didn't mind sharing, neither did she.

Her smile surfaced again as she looked away from her computer screen when Shelly buzzed to let her know that Regina was outside her office waiting to see her.

"Hey, baby." As Regina walked into the office Sinclair was instantly suffused by memories of last night, her writhing on the hardwood floor of her apartment in a sea of her own juices, begging Regina to fuck her harder.

"Hey." Sinclair stood up to claim her hug. "This is a nice surprise."

Regina was wearing her Bohemian drag, faded jeans that hugged her hips low and showed off her amazing ass, and a tie-dyed tank top with a picture of Jimi Hendrix on the front. Sinclair knew that if she slid her hands under Jimi's Afro she would find Regina's breasts bare, nipples hard from the arctic air-conditioning.

"Maybe not so nice. I actually came by with a bit of bad news."

"What's wrong? Are you all right?"

"I'm fine." Regina paused. "We can't see each other anymore."

"Excuse me?" Sinclair's hands dropped away from the other woman's waist.

"Yeah. This has been great and everything, but . . . you know. It's time for me to move on."

"Are you joking? Things are still great. What about last night?"

"Yeah." Her mouth curved in the familiar smile. Then she looked away. "Remember, I told you that I was seeing somebody. Well, it's more than that. So I can't get too attached or stay with the same person for long. That's the deal. One month." She shrugged. "Sorry."

Sinclair didn't try to stop her when she turned to leave. The door clicked softly behind Regina as Sinclair sank into her chair. Tears burned behind her eyes, but she refused to let them fall. There was still work to do. Shaking her head quickly, Sinclair turned back to her computer and brought the month's-end reports back up on the screen.

Twelve hours later, she felt betrayed. Regina had rubbed her hard edges soft, alchemized her from steel to warm toffee in those thirty-one days. And now Sinclair was softened, melted, and alone. She glared at her computer screen, trying to work past the pain. By noon she had succeeded and pushed Regina from her mind to slog through the reports and financial statements that had been piling up on her desk all week. Hours later, she barely looked up when Shelly knocked on her door to wish her a good night.

Sinclair's office darkened when the sun fled the sky, but she turned the lights on, tilted the chair to make herself more comfortable in front of the computer monitor, and continued to work. Only when Sinclair heard the vacuum cleaner just outside her door did she realize what time it was. Even then she wasn't anxious to go home. Nothing waited for her there except more solitude, more time to think about Regina. But, reluctantly, she shut her office down for the night, turning off the computer and pulling the office shades closed.

Sinclair was tired, arms heavy with the weight of sadness, face tight and pinched from thinking about Regina, then not thinking about Regina. Her stomach chewed on itself to make up for its lack of breakfast or lunch. At this rate, dinner looked like it was going to be a miss, too. She took one last look around the office before walking into the hallway. The door whispered shut behind her.

On the underground platform, the stink of trapped air and the olfactory memory of a thousand sweating bodies pushed itself into Sinclair's nose. People stared listlessly up and down the empty train tracks, waiting for that bright white light in the tunnel to tell their feet to move. Eventually, the train came in a rush of sound and wind to dump off its load of passengers and pick up some more. Sinclair sat far away from the small crowd on the train, tucking herself in a seat under the railroad map and an ad for pheromone-laced perfume.

She didn't notice the man until the train jerked to an abrupt stop, forcing her to grab the beam in front of her and look up. He was dirty and bearded and had a red bandanna tied around his neck. His eyes were fastened on her. Sinclair looked away, but not before noticing his gaping fly and the hand he had shoved into the hole, massaging himself as he stared. She glanced quickly around the train. Heads bobbed over open newspapers and paperback novels, all intentionally angled away from her and her new admirer.

Sinclair looked away, but just below the steady rhythm of

the train, she could hear the slap of the closed fist against flesh. Her face burned. She turned away, trying to tune in to the conversations of other passengers, to her pain, anything. When that didn't work, she took out her book and tried to read. The words lay flat on the page, making little sense to her twitching eyes. She still heard him. A smell rose from him, like rotten oranges and bay rum. Vomit darted up in her throat and she gagged. As the train lurched to its next stop she rushed through the doors, pushing past the crowd on the platform and up the stairs. Sinclair barely made it to the warm air and warmer-still piss smell of the surface street before she vomited into the gutter in a bitter, pale arc. People backed away from her, careful not to come too close as her stomach heaved until there was nothing left. When she could finally take a breath without gagging, Sinclair stumbled to the corner to hail a taxi for home.

At home she didn't know what to do with herself. She tried to make something to eat, but by the time the microwave beeped to get her attention, Sinclair's interest in the bowl of nuked ravioli had already cooled. The processed tomato paste with its thin layer of grease made the meal a chore even her iron stomach couldn't complete. Losing Regina had locked up her throat, allowing in only the barest amount of oxygen. Her dinner ended up in the trash.

Sinclair stood staring in the garbage then choked on the lone sob that rose up in her throat. She shouldn't be taking it this hard. After all, she was used to people leaving her to wallow in the pain of their absence. Sinclair closed the garbage can and went to pick a new book from the shelf.

A taxi picked Sinclair up from her apartment at seven o'clock the next morning. By eight, she was in her office working on spreadsheets that weren't due for another three months. Shelly buzzed her at ten minutes to nine to let her know that she was in.

"'Morning, boss lady."

"Good morning, Shelly." Her voice sounded tired, even to her own ears.

"Are you all right?"

"I'm fine. Just didn't get enough sleep last night."

"OK." Sinclair heard the shuffling of papers. "You have a meeting at nine thirty. The reports you need for that are at the top of your in-box in the green folder."

"Thanks. Just give me a ten-minute warning for that, please."

"Sure thing."

Sinclair scratched and clawed her way through the rest of the day, trying to make it all the way to five o'clock without walking out. At five on the nose, Shelly walked into her office.

"You look like shit," her secretary said. She sat on the edge of Sinclair's desk and dropped a bottle of scotch in her boss's direct line of sight. Glenfiddich. The deep green bottle was only three-quarters full.

"What's going on with you?" Shelly asked.

"Nothing. Absolutely nothing." Sinclair turned to her secretary, annoyed. "Aren't you still on the clock?"

"Nope. My slave duties for Volk ended"—she glanced down at her neon pink watch—"two minutes ago."

Sinclair blew out a harsh breath and gave in. "I have glasses and ice over there." She waved to her mini fridge.

"I know. I was just waiting for you to offer." Shelly retrieved the glasses and poured her scotch neat, but dropped three ice cubes in Sinclair's glass before filling it nearly to the brim. "Here you go."

Sinclair drank it in two quick gulps. Ice tinkled against the crystal as she put the tumbler back on the desk. "Don't you have a boyfriend or something to go home to?" Shelly seemed like the kind of girl to do the domesticity thing.

"If you don't want me here, all you have to do is say so and I'm gone." Shelly refilled Sinclair's glass.

Sinclair lingered over the comment, watching Shelly through the sweating tumbler. Finally she sighed again. "Women are really fucked up, Shelly."

"Especially the one who just screwed you over?"

"Are you talking about that Velasquez woman?"

"Yeah, that one."

Sinclair didn't bother pretending surprise. Regina had visited her often in the past month, leaving too many smiles on her face for her to be "just a friend."

"The screwing wasn't a problem. Apparently that was all she wanted me for."

"You're that good?"

"If I had been any good then maybe she would have stayed. But she got all the material she could use already." She finished off her scotch. "On to the next gullible bitch."

"I heard through the grapevine that she was a good lay. Is that true?"

"I thought you were trying to make me feel better?"

"Yeah, but I might as well get some juicy info, too."

Sinclair laughed bitterly and held out her glass for more. "If you're in the market for a month of the best sex you've ever had, then give her a call. But don't expect to get any more than that. She's got a misses or mister at home."

"A girl could get off a lot in thirty days." Shelly looked like she was thinking about it.

Sinclair leaned back in her chair, already taking on the lazy slouch of the pleasantly inebriated. "She was amazing. She made me feel like I had a golden pussy and she couldn't get enough. This is going to be hard as hell to get through."

"But you'll make it, boss lady. You better. That bitch is not worth the breakdown."

"You're right." Sinclair sounded utterly unconvinced.

"Maybe you should use another woman to bury your troubles in." Shelly raised her thin eyebrows and did a fair imitation of an old man's lecherous leer.

Find someone else? This was the worst thing that had happened to Sinclair in a long time. She couldn't compare this to her grandmother's death five years ago. That was the only thing that had shaken her harder, made her question living. Today made her wonder why, after all these years of successfully protecting her feelings, had Regina slipped inside her so easily? Because she was a woman, stupid. Your first. It had never been like this with men. Never.

"You definitely need a break," Shelly said. She dangled her feet over the edge of Sinclair's desk.

"This little pep talk and drinking session are doing wonders for me, thanks." There wasn't an ounce of sarcasm in Sinclair's voice.

"But what about tomorrow or the next day? You can't drink your unhappiness away. Don't become another dyke statistic. That's *so* not sexy."

The woman was right again. This was going to have to be her last glass. It wouldn't be smart to get on the subway stumbling down drunk, no matter how appealing the relief would be. At least she would be able to fall asleep quickly tonight with no more than an hour or two of tossing and turning.

"Tell me about yourself, Shelly. Tell me anything that will make this shit disappear for a little while."

"What do you want to know?" Shelly's voice was soft.

"Anything. Tell me anything."

I'm screwed, Sinclair thought with a bitter smile as she sat in a taxi crawling toward home in rush-hour traffic. But worse than that, Regina had changed her. Now she knew what fulfilling sex was like. She knew what happened when her body was satisfied and her mind at rest, not wondering if she was normal for not wanting to be close to the person who she was supposed to be with. Sinclair finally understood that she loved women—even this woman—more than she'd ever loved any of her boyfriends. And Regina made her pay for that knowledge.

If she had told her in the beginning that all it was and could ever be between them was a fling, a monthlong diversion, then there would have been less letting go on Sinclair's part, less trust. She felt duped. After the night that Regina took her to the Burning Rose, after she'd apologized and touched Sinclair like she meant something, Sinclair had started to believe that they were going somewhere together. That was the worst betrayal, making her believe that she had a chance to be with her. Maybe Sinclair was being punished for leading Yuen on. Yuen. She hadn't thought of him in a long time. He swore that she would come back to him, back to men. But Sinclair would rather hunt down Regina and beg on bloodied hands and knees to be taken back.

When she walked into her apartment, she picked up the phone and dialed Yuen's number.

"Sinclair." There was no smugness when he answered the phone, just the familiar upward lilt to his voice when she surprised him with a call or visit. Sinclair was grateful for that.

"How have you been?"

"Good." He cleared his throat. "How about you?"

"I've been great up until recently."

"Which is why you called, right?"

Her mouth twisted into a crooked smile. He always knew how to cut to the heart of things. She took a breath. "I called to apologize. I didn't do well by you a month ago. You didn't deserve to be treated like that."

"Is that all?" He hesitated. "Are you all right?"

She imagined him leaning against his kitchen counter like she'd seen him do a hundred times, his bare ankles crossed as he watched the river ripple and flash beyond the window.

"Yes. I'm fine. I just wanted to call now that my head isn't so far up her ass anymore."

"What did she do to you, besides the usual, that is?"

Very funny. "Nothing that I shouldn't have seen coming." As Sinclair spoke she realized that she was reaching out to him in friendship, reaching out for the type of relationship that she'd always imagined with him, one not based on sex but on all the things they had in common. But as she silently asked for that very thing, she knew that she could never have it. Not with him.

"She left you for a man?" Yuen asked.

"No. She just left."

There was a hard, pointed silence, an "I told you so" without words.

"Anyway, that was the main reason that I called, so I'm going to go now."

"You can come over if you want. I'm not doing anything tonight."

"That's all right, I have some work that I need to catch up on. I'll talk to you later."

"Sure. Just call me if you need anything."

Sinclair made some more good-bye noises before hanging up the phone. Well, that was a disappointment. Not that she knew exactly why she had called him in the first place. Absolution from her stupidity? She made a rude noise.

With nothing better to do she began to look through the pile of mail she'd just picked up from the mailbox. Under the usual pile of junk mail and bills, she unearthed a square envelope with a Jamaica return address. She smiled. It was from her father. Was it her birthday already? She checked the date on her watch. April 8. No, he was just early this year. By three weeks. Sinclair tossed the bills and junk mail in their basket in the kitchen to be sorted out later and sat down to read her birthday card.

Happy 33rd, it said. *Come down and celebrate your birthday with us. There's always a place for you here.* She put away the letter he'd enclosed in the card to read later and leafed through the photographs. Her father looked thin but happy with his very young wife and their four-year-old boy, Xavier.

They posed on an oversized beach blanket. Around them, coconut trees pregnant with fruit waved in the island breeze.

Xavier stared into the camera with wide, gorgeous eyes. His smile was blinding.

Sinclair looked out at the gray fog beyond her window. Although they hadn't seen each other for some twenty years, her father had always been there for her, sending birthday cards, short letters, the occasional package with current photographs of him and his new family. In turn, Sinclair remembered his birthday and wedding anniversary, sending appropriate cards, money, and gifts when her electronic calendar reminded her to. She'd never sent any pictures of her own.

Every birthday he invited her down to Jamaica to stay with him and his family. Every year she refused. Work was always her handy excuse. Sinclair looked around her. The apartment, a product of her tireless work, was beautiful but cold, especially without her grandmother to share it with. Once a week a cleaning woman came by and did something to it. There was never enough of a life being lived in the apartment to get it dirty. With Regina's betrayal so fresh, she couldn't help but feel that there was nothing here for her. Not really. If now wasn't the perfect time to escape. . . .

At the bottom of the card, as always, was her father's phone number. Before she could change her mind, she called it. The phone rang four times before the machine picked up. A child's voice told any brave caller to leave a message.

"Hi, Papa and Nikki. This is Sinclair. Thank you both for the card. It's beautiful. I'm thinking of taking you up on that offer to come down and visit." Her voice faltered. "Give me a call at home or at work when you get this message."

She left her numbers and wished them both a polite good evening. For the rest of the night she worried that all the invitations—all twenty years of them—had been for politeness' sake alone and no one would return her call. She fell asleep earlier than usual thinking about coconut trees and smiling children.

*   *   *

The next day Shelly was in the office before her. Sinclair stopped at her secretary's desk.

"You're in early."

"I didn't want to give you the chance to avoid me again." She grinned, looking not at all like someone who'd knocked back half a bottle of whiskey the night before.

Today she was in head-to-toe pink, like an extra from that Audrey Hepburn movie, *Funny Face*. Knee-hugging pink skirt, matching jacket, pale pink blouse and high-heeled pink shoes. A pale pink pillbox hat sat on top of her French-twisted hair.

"You're not funny," Sinclair muttered to her earlier comment. "But you do look lovely today."

"Thank you, boss lady," she said to Sinclair's retreating back.

Sinclair was just putting her briefcase and purse away when Shelly buzzed her.

"Your father is calling for you," Shelly said.

"Thanks." Sinclair took a deep breath. "Hello?"

"Sinclair!" His voice came hearty and loud over the phone line. "What a surprise to get your call last night."

"I hope it wasn't an *unpleasant* surprise."

"No, no. Don't be crazy." He laughed. "So, after all these years you're coming to visit your old man?"

"If I'm still invited, yes."

"If you're still invited . . . daughter, please. When are you coming?"

"When's best for you?"

"Any time you want to come is fine. I'm not going anywhere off this island anytime soon."

"How about next month? How long can you stand to have me?"

"Next month is fine. If the burden of your company gets too much I can always ship you off to a family friend." He laughed long and hard at his own joke.

"How about four weeks?"

"That's fine. Just try to get a flight coming in after three in the afternoon and let me know when to come get you from the airport."

"All right. Um . . ." Sinclair glanced at her desk calendar. "Let's say four weeks starting the eighteenth of next month." She scribbled down a note to herself to buy the plane tickets. "I'll call you when I know exactly when my plane lands."

"Sounds good. Nikki and Xavier are glad they will finally get the chance to meet you. Especially since you didn't send any pictures." He tut-tutted, then laughed again. "Seeing you in person will be better than a hundred photographs."

"Don't talk too soon. You may not like what you see." She wasn't entirely joking.

"There you go talking crazy again." He didn't laugh this time. "I know that you're at work and everything so I won't take up too much more of your time."

"That's all right."

"Sure it is. Just call me later on."

"I will. Talk to you soon." She disconnected the line, then rang Shelly.

"Shelly, could you put in four weeks of vacation down on the company calendar for me, please? Beginning May eighteenth."

"A month?"

"Yes." A trace of impatience touched her voice.

"Are the big bosses going to allow that? You're not exactly dispensable here, you know."

"Use your sweet talk to make it happen, Shell." Sinclair's mouth twitched with amusement. "Bryony and Steven can handle my workload until I get back. And don't worry, I'll leave plenty of work for you to do while I'm gone."

Chapter 6

On Sinclair's last day of work before her vacation, she invited Shelly to share a drink with her. The dark-haired woman seemed pleasantly surprised and said so when she walked into the office.

"Don't worry, I'm not turning senile or anything. I just wanted to thank you for going above and beyond when I was having a rough time."

"It was for my own sanity as well as yours, trust me." Shelly threw her an arch look. "But you're welcome. I'm sure you would have kicked my ass, too, if I'd walked in here for days looking like someone had just stolen my lunch money."

Sinclair poured her a glass of whiskey and winced at the reminder of Regina. Shelly touched her hand gently in apology before taking her drink to the leather-covered window seat. She sighed as she looked down at the street below. "I'm sure going to miss your sour puss every morning."

Sinclair sat beside her with her gin and tonic in hand. "Can't say I feel the same, Shell. I'm really looking forward to being gone from here for a while."

Shelly pouted in mock pique. "And here I thought I was the new love of your life."

"No, ma'am." Sinclair gave an exaggerated shake of her head. "I'm through with love. You'll have to settle for my everlasting friendship."

Shelly smiled and a dimple appeared in the soft oval of her cheek. "I can do that."

"Would you like anything, miss?" A blue-clad flight attendant appeared at Sinclair's elbow.

"Gin and tonic, please. No ice."

After a slight nod, the woman disappeared. Before Sinclair could wonder what kind of gin they used, the woman was back, drink and napkin in hand.

"Thank you." Sinclair watched the twitch of the flight attendant's hips under the navy blue cloth as she walked away. Something in her stride reminded her of Regina. The liquor burned its way down her throat before settling with a comforting warmth in her belly. For the rest of the flight, she buried herself in a novel, ignoring the bitter taste that Regina's brief memory left on her tongue.

Sinclair stepped off the plane to a dizzying sense of home. A confusion of voices and accents bombarded her in the busy airport. She limped through them with her heavy shoulder bag and two suitcases propped up on a rolling cart with a mind of its own.

"Can I help you with your bags, miss?" a young man in jeans and T-shirt asked.

"No, thank you." Sinclair had gotten the offer at least five times since she got off the plane, but her city-bred paranoia kept her from accepting any of them. Eventually she made it to the busy curbside where her father said he would meet her.

Sinclair didn't even know that she would recognize him when the time came. Sure he had sent pictures, but photos often stole the animation from your face and turned you into someone else entirely different.

She glanced at every middle-aged man she saw, searching his face for some similarity to her own or at least to the photo in her bag.

"Sinclair?"

She turned around. Her rehearsed greeting fell back down her throat.

A face from her childhood looked back at her. He wore the same thin mustache. His face, framed by long, neatly trimmed sideburns, was still narrow and handsome, even with the balding head and sleepy eyes. There wasn't a trace of gray on him anywhere. Victor Daniels greeted her with Xavier's wide guileless smile.

"Hi, Papa," she stammered when his faltering smile made her realize she was staring.

He hugged her, gathered her up through the straps of her luggage and embraced her with his warmth. He smelled like shaved wood and of the outdoors. "Sinclair. You look so much like your mother."

She smiled, not knowing what to say.

"The car is over there," he said, gesturing to a bright yellow Honda Accord, circa 1970, with fuzzy purple dice dangling from the rearview mirror. "I borrowed it from a friend," he said with a laughing mock-whisper.

Nikki and Xavier waited near the car for them. The boy stared at her with naked curiosity, while Nikki said a nervous hello and hopped into the front seat of the car. She was a bright-skinned girl with pale gray eyes and short reddish hair that stood up around her head like a tamed flame.

"The drive is short, only twenty minutes or so. After that, I'm going to have to leave you at the house for a bit while I take the car back to my friend in town and pick up my bike."

"Sorry to cause all this trouble."

"What trouble? We're glad to have you. The season's been boring anyway." He started the car. "Nikki is always saying that I don't take her anywhere. Well, I'm doing the next best thing, I brought my sophisticated daughter from America for her to talk to."

Sinclair laughed. "I'm hardly sophisticated. Sorry, Nikki. I'm a bit of a disappointment in that regard. All I can do is show you all the scars I got from living in the city, including the slash above my eye where I got mugged a couple of years ago."

That got a response out of Nikki; she turned around to look at Sinclair, trying, the accountant supposed, to reconcile her elegant appearance with the bruised, battered, and defeated victims of city crime she saw on American television shows.

"What's 'mugged,' Papa?" Xavier chimed from beside Sinclair, naked curiosity lighting his features.

"That's when bad men beat you up in the street and take what you have without asking."

"That's stupid," the boy said. "Why don't they just ask for it?"

"Some people won't give up their stuff."

"Did you give up your stuff, Clair?"

"Oh, yes. I didn't have much with me but they got all I had."

"That's wrong, isn't it, Papa?" He leaned against the back of the driver's seat, straining against his seat belt so he could have a good look at his father.

"Yes, it's wrong, Xavie. But remember when I told you that there were people doing wrong all over the place and that it was up to you to do right things so you can balance them out?"

That was a big job for such a little guy, Sinclair thought with a smile. Her father caught her look and grinned.

They drove slowly from the airport, navigating through the surprisingly thick traffic that led them out of town to the more rural area where her father lived. The streets were alive with color, food vendors with their carts painted with the black, green, and gold Jamaican flag; coconut trees rustling in the light breeze; muscular and handsome boys dashing about the streets on bare feet, on bicycles, on ratty shoes, their faces predatory and sweet. On people's faces was a curious mixture of resignation and hope, their eyes darting periodically to the large jumbo jets taking off from the airport and heading for places unknown. High in the hills Sinclair could see large, looming houses painted island yellows and hibiscus reds, ocean blues—vacation colors. They looked, curiously, like sentinels, as if they were guarding, or imprisoning, the people down below.

As the car eased out of the city, the landscape changed. It became more green, twisted jungles of scenery; its sounds broken occasionally by the honking horns of other vehicles as they turned particularly narrow corners. Soon they pulled up to the front gate of the house.

Sinclair's father helped her with her bags while Nikki looked on, holding Xavier's hand. The girl seemed quiet and intense. It was only now that she got out of the car that Sinclair could get a good look at her. Her body was . . . eye catching. Even in a loose T-shirt and knee-length gray shorts, Sinclair could tell that she had a body that was porn-star lush—high C-cup breasts, tiny waist, and round, full hips. It was no great mystery why Sinclair's father was with her.

The gate creaked as Sinclair opened it to allow her father to pass through with the bags. He glanced at the shoulder-high wire-and-steel contraption with surprise.

"I need to oil that," he said, sounding like he'd noticed that creak at least a dozen times before.

The small house looked the same as it did in a long-ago photo—cozy, but beautiful, with a well-tended front garden dominated by fat hibiscus bushes sprouting red, pink, and white blooms. Two tall crape myrtle trees flanked the front gate, their pods of blossoms curling out like lavender-colored lace. From everywhere else in the yard, miniature clay women peeked out at them. They seemed mischievous but friendly. Nikki walked up to the verandah to open the door, then closed it behind them, not once letting go of Xavier's hand.

The inside of the house smelled like fresh furniture polish, a hint of lemon and Murphy's oil. Sinclair left her shoes at the front door as she'd seen the others do. The tiled floor was cool under her bare feet, a welcome change from the enfolding heat outside. Curious about the man she hadn't seen in over twenty years, Sinclair's eyes darted around the house, searching for clues to his current identity.

From his letter, she knew he was a builder and that he was now working on a mansion not far from here. His passion for woodworking was reflected throughout the house, from the handmade checker set to the wood trimmings around the windows and door, and even a low unstained table sitting at one end of the couch that seemed to have become a receptacle for drinks and the occasional reading material, if the multiple coasters and bookmarks were any indication. Then there were the beautiful handmade mahogany bookshelves. They lined the largest wall of the living room and were filled with neatly stacked books and magazines. In a single glance Sinclair saw books on astronomy, bookkeeping, cooking, stamp collecting, and Jamaican history. The bottom shelf had a few fiction titles that she reminded herself to check out later. On the walls hung framed likenesses of Marcus Garvey, Nanny of the Maroons, Paul Bogle, and some other Jamaican heroes she couldn't name. Light spilled in through two large windows above the couch. The overall effect was harmonious and comfortable. Sinclair told her father as much.

"Thank you, daughter," he said, aiming a smile her way.

"I'm going to put on some hot chocolate," Nikki said. "Anybody want some?"

"Me, me, me!" Xavier squeaked from the other end of her hand.

"Fix some for me and Sinclair too, please, sweetheart." Sinclair's father looked at Nikki with something more than fondness in his eye. Sinclair glanced from husband to wife, thinking suddenly that he was treating Nikki like a skittish colt, one who could bolt at any moment.

The young woman nodded and disappeared into the kitchen.

"This is your room for the next month," he said, showing her to a bedroom that was nearly identical to the one she had as a child. "The bathroom is down the hall and to the right, just before you get to the kitchen. Tea is going to be in the living room, so come through when you're done." He squeezed Sinclair's hand once before leaving her alone.

The bedroom door closed her in the quiet time capsule of a room. A north-facing window, the small dresser with neatly laid-out comb, toiletries, and a few porcelain figurines. All of it looked so much like her old room. Even the bed. Sinclair felt a moment of disorientation. She remembered her own bed, the one she'd bled on, not knowing what was happening to her body, not having anyone to tell, when day after day, month after month, she laid on the mattress, bleeding, imagining the death that would surely come from such massive loss of blood. Her mother was gone a week by then when, at thirteen, her stubborn child's body finally decided to change into a woman's. Her father finally had to throw the old bed away, although it had been an heirloom, her parents' first bed together. But it was bloodstained and ripe with the smell of confused womanhood and sweat. Even the wood had taken in the scent and color of blood.

Before that, the bed had been the stage for many happy memories. Her mother used to nudge her awake from it each morning to get ready for school. At barely seven o'clock, Beverly Sinclair's skin would still be softly scented with sleep. Sinclair remembered one morning when her mother had come, mock-whispering her name before crawling into bed with her. Sinclair had made a game of trying to wake her and mother and daughter ended up fighting over the covers, overcome by an attack of the giggles. At least until Victor came in with his warnings about being late for school and swung her up in his arms leaving Beverly sprawled in the covers to stare after them with her fading smile.

Sinclair unpacked her camera and put it on the dresser before digging in her luggage for her bag of toiletries. She didn't know why, at the last minute, she'd dug out the old thing. It was still heavy, still in good working order just like the day she and Gram took it home from the pawnshop.

After a quick wash in the bathroom, Sinclair slipped into the kitchen to see if Nikki needed some help. The younger woman stood at the stove grating a ball of pure chocolate into a pan of boiling water.

"Hey."

Nikki turned around, startled.

"Sorry. I didn't mean to frighten you."

"You didn't . . . It's OK." Nikki's pale skin flushed. She darted a quick look at Sinclair before looking back down into the pan of water.

Sinclair apologized again. "Need any help?"

"No, it's almost ready. I can just bring it to you in the living room."

"Oh. OK." Sinclair backed away, feeling like an intruder. As she was leaving the kitchen, Nikki looked up at her and their eyes met. A smile touched the younger woman's mouth and she shook her head, a light motion that could have meant anything. "See you in a minute," she said.

Sinclair returned the smile and went to find her father and Xavier in the living room. Victor waved her over to sit beside him.

"So, how was your flight?"

"Not bad. It was quick." Sinclair tucked her bare feet under her on the couch. "I didn't have the time to worry about getting airsick or hijacked."

"Hijacked I can understand, especially living in America. You get travel sickness?"

"Just on planes, though lately I've been getting twinges of nausea in cars if I'm in one for more than an hour." When she and Gram had gone on a road trip together in their second-hand Ford Escort, loaded down with all their camping supplies and food, Sinclair had been fine. No sickness; just stomach-fluttering excitement at being on the road and with her grandmother for a whole month.

Gram had been as excited as Sinclair about the trip. She'd made sandwiches; bought a tent, sleeping bags, and special camping pots. On the road, she had become talkative, willing to share stories of her past in Jamaica, about how she fell in love with a man—not Grandpa—who'd told her about the fiery mountain sunsets and white sands of New Mexico. Gifting Sinclair then, as she always had, with beautiful unforgettable moments meant to replace the emptiness that her mother's death had left behind. She had fun on that trip. They both did.

"You used to get carsick all the time when you were growing up," her father said, bringing Sinclair back to the present. "We couldn't take you on any long-distance drives. One time we were on a bus heading for Kingston and you threw up all over the back windows. Some woman didn't have her window closed."

Sinclair winced.

He laughed. "You forced your mama and me to toughen up."

Nikki walked into the room. "Where should I put this?" She held up a tray heavy with steaming mugs and hot buttered toast. A soft laugh bubbled out of her when both Xavier and Victor rushed up to lend a hand with the tray. With their help, she put the heavy tray on the low coffee table, then sat back on the couch with a sigh. Sinclair shifted to make room for Nikki and Victor took her feet and put them in his lap.

"How are you doing in America, Sinclair?" her father asked around a mouthful of bread.

"I'm doing all right. Volk hasn't fired me yet. In a few years I can afford to take off for a year and travel. Maybe even start my own business with the money I have saved up." Sinclair tasted her cup of hot chocolate, surprised at its thick and creamy taste. The flavor, hinting of spices that she couldn't name, wasn't like any she remembered having in America. It was good.

Nikki looked up. "So you're rich."

"No. Not really."

"You're skinny though," Xavier said, pointing at Sinclair's bare knees, his cheeks bulging with toast.

"It's called being 'fashionably thin.'" She stuck her tongue out at her brother but pulled her skirt down anyway.

"Fata—fash?" His long-lashed brown eyes questioned her.

"It means that it's OK for me to be skinny." Sinclair bit into her toast with gusto as if to prove that she really did eat and eat a lot. "Really."

"Xavie." Nikki touched his head, her voice softly chiding. Victor laughed and shook his head at his young son. "Anyway, as long as you didn't suffer because of the money you sent down here to us." Victor lifted his mug to her. "It really came in handy, especially when I lost my job at the factory a few years ago. Now that foreigners are moving to the island and want their houses built in grand style, I'm not so bad off as I used to be."

"I was relieved to hear that things worked out." Sinclair picked up another slice of the thick toasted bread. "All the money did was sit in the bank anyway. I figured that I might as well send it to someone who could put it to good use."

Victor laughed and raised his mug again. "Here's to practical daughters."

That night Sinclair lay in bed staring out at the stars and remembering. Seeing Nikki's closeness to Xavier reminded her of her childhood; of Beverly Sinclair's soft voice and the way she used to tuck in Sinclair with whispered stories of far-off lands. If Sinclair closed her eyes and took a careful breath she could almost smell the Soft Sheen spray that had clung to her mother's hair. Sinclair and her mother had been as close as Nikki and Xavier were now. Only her mother died in a freak bus accident and left Sinclair to her grandmother. It could have been worse.

From down the hall, she heard faint sounds of lovemaking.

A talkative bedspring, sumptuous sighs. Xavier, whose room she'd taken over, had long ago fallen asleep on the pullout sofa in the living room, lulled by the flickering gray light from the television. Outside her window, crickets trilled, frogs croaked, the moon burned. All in a clear Caribbean sky. No police sirens, no smog, no Regina.

Hours later, the sun's flame began to replace the moon's softer glow, creeping into the window like a clumsy thief. Only then did she sleep.

Sinclair woke to a knock on the door. She tried her voice several times before it actually worked. "Come in."

Her father poked his head in. "Want to come eat with us?"

Sinclair rubbed her eyes and sat up. "Sure. Give me two minutes."

For a moment, she watched the spot from where Victor just disappeared. Then shook her head. As she fumbled in her suitcase for clothes, barely paying attention to her actions, delicate tendrils of memory began to unfurl in her mind. Twenty years ago, she had loved this man, worshipped him, and thought him the sun that revolved around her mother's earth.

She remembered now that he had been more crippled by Beverly's death than even she was, often staring down at his daughter as if he had no idea who she was, at times leaving her in the middle of a conversation about a torn button or a hemmed skirt. His eyes were so sad. Her grandmother's arrival four months later was a welcome distraction for them both. Mavis—a woman who before that had always sent cards on birthdays and holidays, who visited every Christmas and seemed so exotic with her foreign accent, flowing dresses, and sandalwood-scented hugs—fell into their lives like healing rain.

When Gram suggested taking Sinclair to America with her, her father only nodded as if he had been expecting it. He asked her how she would feel about living with her grandmother in America. Sinclair, mesmerized by Mavis's smell and distracted from her own pain by the woman's complete devotion to her, said yes, she would like that very much. At the airport Victor took her hand and squeezed it, warning her to dress well for the cold weather in her new city.

Sinclair reluctantly pulled herself from the past and shuffled to the bathroom where she washed her face and teeth. Light from the sun-filled kitchen assaulted her eyes as she walked in. Saturday morning reggae oldies played from a tiny radio on the windowsill, competing with the frantic singing of the birds outside the window. Everyone was already seated at the small kitchen table with full plates and cups in front of them. An empty chair waited for her next to Xavier.

"Good morning," Sinclair said, her voice still low from sleep.

"Callaloo, saltfish, and dumpling," her father said, gesturing to her plate. "I hope you still eat Jamaican food."

"Why would I stop?" She smiled as she sat down. "Gram raised me on it."

"Your hair looks nice like that," Nikki said shyly. Sinclair realized that she'd left her hair in its usual nighttime plaits the same moment that she noticed that her father's young wife wore her hair in a similar style.

"Thank you. Yours looks nice, too."

With her hair in fat, sectioned plaits and the tiny gold hoops in her ears, Nikki looked even younger than she had the day before. She blushed at Sinclair's compliment and broke open her dumpling.

Sinclair eyed her plate with its two fat, round breakfast dumplings and the respectably sized heap of callaloo with bits of salt-cured codfish. She hadn't tried to eat this much in a long time. But she would now. The smell of her breakfast— freshly risen fried dough and the earthy spiced scent of greens—reminded Sinclair sharply of her grandmother.

"Did you cook?" she asked Nikki, breaking open the crisp, tongue-melting dough with its soft and steaming insides.

"No, Victor did." She smiled over at her husband.

Xavier smacked happily at his meal, his cheeks bulging like a chipmunk's. Under the table, his bare feet swung blissfully back and forth to the music from the radio.

"It's very good," Sinclair said after she swallowed her own mouthful. Almost as good as her grandmother's.

"Good. You'll get the chance to practice your cooking, too, while you're here." He winked.

"Hmm. I'm not sure if you want that." Her mouth quirked up around her food. "But I'll give it a try."

"You can't cook?" Nikki asked, eyes wide with surprise.

Victor chuckled. "She left us and became a modern American woman."

"What do you know about modern American women aside from the stuff they show on foreign television?" she said, pointing her food-heavy fork at her father. "All that stuff is made up, you know."

Nikki paused her chewing. "Even *Cops*?"

"Especially *Cops*."

"But you still can't cook?"

Sinclair chuckled ruefully at her father's question. "I don't cook. My boyfriend used to do all the cooking when we were together."

"And when he didn't cook, what did you do?"

"I'd get some takeout, frozen food, or just eat out."

"What did I tell you?" her father laughed, touching Nikki's arm. "A modern woman. Just as efficient as one of her frozen foods."

"I think I resent that."

"Don't take offense, daughter. We're people from different times, different cultures, and I'm just having a bit of fun." He pushed his chair away from the table. "I enjoy reading about Americans on the Web and in the papers, but unlike many of my countrymen, I don't envy you the lifestyle."

"Can you make American popcorn?" Xavier looked up from his nearly empty plate.

Sinclair nodded. "If I have the right corn, I can."

"Tomorrow?"

"OK. Tomorrow."

Despite protests from both Nikki and her father, Sinclair washed the breakfast dishes and pots, before disappearing into the bathroom to shower and wash her hair. Later, with her wet hair fluffed out to dry, she wandered out into the backyard and found her father watering the plants. The house was conspicuously empty.

"Where is everybody?"

"Nikki and Xavier went up the street for some groceries. They'll be back in an hour or two." He swept the spray of water along the length of a tall banana tree. "You lonely already?"

"Not while I have you here to keep me company."

"She's a sweet talker, just like her mother," he said to the air above his head, laughing.

Sinclair grinned and thought for the second time in as many days that this man was nothing like she'd expected. Her childhood memories of him were few, limited only to the ones that had resurfaced earlier that day and mental snapshots of him smiling down at her from a great height, his voice telling her not to forget him as she waited for a plane to take her off to America with her grandmother.

After her mother died, it was hard to see him and not think of her, and of her absence that was a constant flinching pain. Sinclair cried when Gram took her away. She didn't remember if it was with relief or sadness. The distance between her and her father made things better, so did Gram's unwavering love. Before she knew it, a year went by in America, then two, then twenty. When the reason for not seeing him faded it just seemed natural to stay away.

"Give me a hand tying back this sorrel tree," her father said, "then we can go on the verandah for a beer."

"All right."

The backyard was easily as large as the house, lined with thick green grass, banana trees loaded down with fruit, gungu pea trees with their delicate branches and leaves dotted by small purple flowers, plus at least a half a dozen other types of trees that Sinclair knew nothing about. The sorrel tree was short, the tallest branch barely reached her father's six-foot height, but its branches spread wide, spilling over and beyond the waist-high fence that separated the jungle of fruit and bean trees from the rest of the grassy backyard. Heart-shaped burgundy fruit dusted with fuzz hung from its drooping branches.

"What do I do?"

"It's easy. Just hold the branches back while I tie them up with string."

Easy. Right. Forty-five minutes later Sinclair was covered in the tiny white bugs that she didn't realize lived in the sorrel tree and her skirt was dirty from where she had crouched on its hem in the mud. Her bare arms itched.

"You're a cruel man," she said to her father as she disappeared into the house to take another shower.

"Do you still want that beer?" he asked.

"You better still be offering it."

She closed the door on his laughter.

Chapter 7

Victor walked out to the verandah with two beers in his hand. He closed the door behind him and approached Sinclair.

"Is Guinness all right?"

"Yes, thank you."

He offered his daughter a sweating bottle of the dark beer and sat down in the rocker next to hers. With a low sigh of contentment he arranged his long legs in front of him, cradling the beer in his cupped hands.

"Do you have a good life in America?" he asked, staring out into the sun-baked front yard,

"It's all right. Things have been a little hard since Gram died five years ago." She took a long sip of her beer, wincing at its bitterness. This was the first time she'd admitted to anyone that she'd been more than a little affected by her grandmother's death. "How about you? How is married life treating you the second time around?"

"Things are good. Nikki is a good woman. I feel like I'm finally doing things right this time."

Sinclair looked at him with a question in her eyes. As she opened her mouth to ask it, a pale blue Jeep Wrangler pulled up to the gate. Its doors and roof had been taken off, leaving the driver and passenger unprotected from the midmorning sun.

"Hey, Mr. Daniels!" the woman behind the wheel called out. Her hair was in long, loose dreadlocks that tumbled around her face and shoulders like black lace. Another woman, older with her hair plaited around her head and strung with cowry shells, hefted two well-wrapped packages from the back of the Jeep and walked toward the house. When the driver noticed Sinclair sitting on the other side of her father, she waved.

"Why doesn't that girl come into the yard instead of shouting out my name to the whole neighborhood?" Victor asked no one in particular.

The woman with the packages shrugged. "Young people." Her smile teased Sinclair's father but he wasn't biting.

"Nikki's not home. She's on Market Street." He took the heavier package from the older woman, then gave her an envelope. "But she told me to give you this with her thanks."

"Tell her I'll stop by on the weekend to see her and the baby."

Sinclair watched their byplay with curiosity. This woman was beautiful, with short but well-shaped legs and a tight backside covered in mid-length khaki shorts. Sinclair looked away wincing with sudden guilt. This woman was the same age her mother would have been.

"That baby is four years old now, Della," Victor said.

"So what? He's her only one. Until you give her another one, Xavier will stay the baby."

Victor opened the front door for Della and waved her ahead of him. They disappeared into the house. In the meantime, the woman in the Jeep made herself comfortable behind the wheel. She dangled one bare foot outside the vehicle's door as she lay back in the seat that was reclined as far back as it could go. Sunlight poured over the subtle hills and valleys of her body like honey. The slim-fitting white tank top and cutoff shorts gave Sinclair an excellent view of all that beautiful dark skin. She gawked shamelessly, even tilted her head to get a better view.

If she'd been someone else, maybe like Regina, she would have walked up to the stranger in the Jeep and struck up a conversation, found out if she was into women. Her sleek, athletic look screamed "dyke" but Sinclair wasn't one to risk embarrassment on an assumption. Sinclair looked away from the woman as her father came back out of the house.

"Della, this is my daughter, Sinclair. She's visiting me from America for a few weeks."

"Hello," Sinclair said.

"Mercy! I thought that was Lydia sitting right there." So she was rude enough to never speak to Lydia? Whoever that was.

"Good to meet you, child." She looked at Sinclair again as she shook her hand. "Sinclair? Does that mean you're Bev Sinclair's daughter?"

"Yes, ma'am."

"Don't ma'am me, young lady." She squeezed Sinclair's fingers gently. "Well, I'll be . . . . I knew your mother a long time ago. Used to even babysit for her. I can see that the resemblance to Lydia is only superficial. You have your mother's mouth and eyes." She made as if to touch Sinclair's hair but the younger woman moved back.

"Sorry."

Sinclair's smile put even more distance between them. "That's OK."

Della dropped her hand. "Well, I'll just head out. Hunter and I have a few more things to do before it gets dark. Good to see you again, Victor. Take care, Sinclair."

Sinclair nodded in response and watched the older woman walk away and climb back into the Jeep. The woman behind the wheel waved at Sinclair again before driving off.

She turned to her father. "Who was that?"

"One of your mother's old friends." He made an impatient gesture. "A potmaker."

Sinclair smiled. "A potmaker?"

"That's what she does. Make pots. And other things, too. Nikki spends at least half her paychecks on her clay." He waved at the neat arrangement of potted plants ringing the verandah then to the yard where all manner of sculpture sat among the shrubbery and flowers. Nikki certainly had an eye for arranging.

"Nikki must like her work, or her, a lot."

"They get along." Her father made a noise that could have been anything. But Sinclair could see the emotion for what it was. Jealousy. He was jealous of his wife's friendship with Della. She looked at her father in surprise but didn't press the issue.

They spent the rest of the afternoon talking, discussing the books they'd both read and other things they had in common despite the twenty years they'd spent apart. When Nikki and Xavier came back the discussion continued over homemade popcorn and checkers, lasting until dinnertime and beyond. After Nikki and the boy went to bed, Sinclair and her father went back to the verandah and beers. Their laughter rang out in the warm air until the sun blushed the Blue Mountains a soft pink. Only then did their drooping eyes force them indoors for sleep.

In the morning, Nikki and Xavier lured Sinclair out with the promise of showing her the sea. They took Victor's motorcycle. Nikki crushed her fire hair underneath a black motorcycle helmet, then put a smaller one on Xavier's head. Earlier she had urged Sinclair to leave her hair plaited so now the thick mass had no trouble fitting under the helmet Nikki offered.

"Hold on tight to me, Xavie." Nikki's soft voice fluted gently into the late morning air.

"I remember, Mama." He hopped up and down with excitement at the thought of riding the noisy bike.

Nikki and Sinclair got on the bike first, then they squeezed

Xavier between them. He giggled when Sinclair's fingers floated over his ribs before settling firmly around Nikki's waist. And off they went.

Nikki was a competent and cautious driver, honking the horn as they rounded narrow curves in the road to let other, larger vehicles know they were coming. The wind stung Sinclair's eyes, making them squint and water. At first, the speed and vulnerability of it frightened her, but she remembered her childhood when she'd been where Xavier was now, safe between two people who loved her. Then she relaxed, enjoying the push and pull against her body as the bike slowed down for traffic then sped up again.

Their journey ended on the beach, a quiet area of white sand and lulling waves with only a few other people wandering its length. Nikki parked in a grove of tall coconut trees and took off her shoes before unstrapping a small bag from the back of the bike. Sinclair and Xavier hopped off the motorcycle and waited for her.

"This is my quiet place. Not many people know about it." She slung the bag over her shoulder and took Xavier's hand. When the boy offered his other hand to Sinclair, she smiled down at him.

"It's beautiful here," she said.

"Yes, it is."

The women walked toward the water with Xavier strung between them like a twinkling Christmas light.

"Ah! Bird!" Xavier broke away from them to chase a flock of tiny seabirds.

"Careful," Nikki called after him, but did not follow. Sinclair watched her young stepmother, smiling at Nikki's ridiculously young age.

"How old are you, Nikki?"

"Twenty-two."

She was too busy watching her son to see Sinclair's expression. When she turned back to her stepdaughter, Sinclair cleared her throat. "Do we have to be back at a particular time?"

"Not really." Nikki looked at the little Timex on her wrist. "We have almost the whole day to play."

"Great."

They pulled bathing suits from the bag that Nikki carried and quickly changed in one of the tiny huts that lined the beach before all three of them ran into the warm lapping water. Sinclair sank into the wet embrace with a laugh while Nikki and Xavier circled her, splashing each other and laughing at their own childish antics. The sun was hot on their faces.

It wasn't long before Sinclair, who wasn't at all used to exercise, stumbled out of the water with her limbs heavy with exhaustion. She collapsed on the blanket, breathing in the light scent of sunscreen from her own body and the intoxicating salt of the sea. A sigh and an unwelcome thought disturbed her contentment. Sinclair rolled over onto her belly and cradled her face in sun-warmed arms. She wished the sun could burn it all away—the pain, the humiliation, that clawing part of her that still wanted Regina back. Sinclair dozed in the sun, only stirring when Xavier poked her with his toe.

"Mama says come back to the water."

She squinted up at him. "Why?"

"Because—" he looked behind him. "Mama! Why?"

"Because she doesn't want to spend her time on this beautiful place spread out on the sand like a beached whale," Nikki called back.

A whale? That's one thing Sinclair had never been compared to before. Had Nikki ever seen a whale? Then she realized that this was the longest sentence her stepmother had ever spoken to her.

She sat up. "If I were a more physically substantial person, I'd take offence at that."

"I'm sure they have skinny whales out in the sea somewhere," Nikki laughed back.

It served her right when Sinclair took a flying leap into the water and doused her in a gigantic tidal wave that left her choking on water and her own laughter. Sinclair's young stepmother was as much of a child as Xavier, with her high infectious laughter and sweet playfulness. Sinclair could see how she could make a lover feel young again, or very old.

Hours later, they rode back to the house in silence with the grit of sand on their tongues and in the intimate crevices of their skin. Nikki hummed as she drove and Xavier leaned into her, his ear pressed against her back. Sinclair could admit to being happy and being, at least for a little while, free of any thoughts or feelings related to the recent past of the city. Nikki and Xavier's unexpected friendship, like the sun, had burned them away.

Sinclair suddenly blinked her wind-stung eyes to look around her. This road seemed unfamiliar. The route from her father's house had been filled with high forests of trees wrapped in dark dripping vines dotted by the brilliant plumage of exotic birds. By comparison, these streets were tame, paved avenues leading to bigger houses, to ruthlessly pruned and controlled gardens, and to money. They stopped at an intersection.

"Are we taking a different road home?" Sinclair asked.

"No. Just a little stop on the way."

Sinclair nodded as Xavier snuggled deeper into his mother's back and giggled. They stopped at a house with a high steel gate, where at least a dozen cars were parked out front. It was tall and stately with a New Orleans feel, ringed by an ironwork balcony upstairs and an identical one above that. A hammock swung suspended from the lower verandah and was stacked with colorful, inviting pillows.

"Let's go in." Nikki parked the bike and fluffed out her hair. Sinclair was startled when Nikki touched her, brushing sand from her face and collarbone, before straightening Xavier's shorts and T-shirt, then her own red sundress and the flowing black pants underneath.

"Come on."

Sinclair didn't bother pretending that she knew what was

going on. She just followed. From the door, she heard a hush of voices, then when Nikki rang the doorbell, all noise stopped. After a moment's hesitation, Nikki opened the door. She and Xavier took Sinclair's hand, leading her through a sitting room that smelled vaguely of leather and lemon furniture polish. The house was beautiful, decorated in a soft feminine style that reminded Sinclair of something out of a decorator magazine.

"This is a little strange, you know. They don't have laws against breaking and entering here?"

They rounded a darkened corner.

"Surprise!" a chorus of voices sang out.

"Shit!" Sinclair jumped back, truly surprised.

"No, it's a birthday party."

Her father stepped out of a crowd of over a dozen people, most of them unfamiliar. "Happy late birthday, daughter."

Sinclair's belly felt warm as if she'd drunk a glass of gin, no tonic. She laughed nervously, feeling overwhelmed. "Thank you." *Who were all these people?*

Her father turned to the room at large. "Everyone, you know my daughter. Either you met her recently or knew her when she was little before she left for America. Everyone, this is my daughter, Bliss Sinclair. She likes to be called Sinclair now, after her mother's family."

"Welcome home, Sinclair!" the group chorused, reaching out to surround her. Embarrassed heat raced under Sinclair's skin.

"Thank you."

"Come meet everybody," her father said.

Her father introduced her to people she had only the vaguest memories of. Yet they all claimed to know her or her mother in some way.

"America must be treating you well, you look good."

"A little on the bony side, though."

"I hear American men like that in their women."

"Well, you're in Jamaica, girl. Remember that Jamaican men like a girl with meat on her bones."

Nikki's friend, Della, suddenly appeared at Sinclair's side, laughing. "Don't let them get to you, girl. They're just jealous."

Of what? Sinclair wanted to ask. Della took her arm and led her to the main dining area where a buffet had been laid out. Sinclair stared at the extravagant arrangement of Caribbean food—okra in a clear, herb-scented broth, roasted breadfruit, both ripe and green, cut and displayed around a bowl of ackee and saltfish, slices of starfruit, guavas, mangoes, hog plums, pineapples, rice and peas, and jerk pork. Sinclair gawked. A colorful platter of thinly sliced raw vegetables was the most ordinary thing on the table. She hadn't seen a spread like this—all the foods that reminded her so strongly of her childhood—in almost twelve years, not since her grandmother had cooked for her college graduation party. Her mouth pricked with sudden hunger.

"It all looks good, doesn't it?" Della said, gesturing to the table with a flourish. "Your father sure can cook." She scooped a spoonful of perfectly steamed white rice onto a plate before turning to Sinclair. "I hope you brought your appetite."

Sinclair thought that was something she'd packed up years ago and left buried in a closet somewhere, but from the urgent noises coming from her tummy, that was obviously not the case. Still it was satisfying just to watch Della make her way down the long table, sampling from everything that looked good to her. Sinclair's gaze fell to her trim backside again. *Where did all that food go?*

A tall woman with her hair hidden by a brilliant orange head wrap approached Della, who looked at her with recognition and put her plate aside to hug her. Sinclair hung back. The tall stranger said something that made Della laugh, then she plucked a slice of pineapple from the older woman's plate and ate it. She leaned her mouth, still wet with pineapple juice, closer to Della's ear then whispered something that made her friend almost drop her plate. Della used her free hand to tap the woman lightly on the arm in reprimand then turned away to pay more attention to her food. But she was smiling.

Sinclair looked away from them to gaze around the rest of the room. Most of the furniture had obviously been cleared away to make room for the party. The peach-colored walls were hung with paintings of local scenes, women with baskets of fruit perched on their heads, long stretches of beach with nary a soul to spoil the view, vivid watercolors of jungle scenes, complete with waterfalls and exotic birds. Sinclair hoped that she'd get to see some of these things for herself while she was here, with or without the aid of her father's motorcycle. She smiled at the thought of Xavier and Nikki being her guides around the island. That wouldn't be a bad way to spend the month at all.

She looked away from the painting of dense mangroves and wilting hothouse orchids to see what looked like a familiar back and spill of hair.

It was the woman from the Jeep. Up close she was even more impressive. White chinos and a sleeveless blouse, also white, showed off her perfect ebony skin and sleek body. Her dreadlocked hair was loose around a face that looked almost Ethiopian with its narrow cheekbones, nose, and full flower of a mouth.

Sinclair waited until the person that the woman was talking to wandered off before approaching. "Hello," she said before she could lose her nerve.

The woman turned around. "Hullo and happy birthday." She made a noise as if something suddenly occurred to her. "By the way, I hope you don't mind me being here since I am a stranger and all."

Her English was very precise, each word perfectly enunciated, yet made more interesting by a faint Jamaican accent.

As if that wasn't enough, her voice was low and deep, re-minding Sinclair of a tropical rain forest, or the version of one that she'd seen at an I-Max theater when she was younger. The woman's every word was infused with a low-grade heat that seemed to brush over Sinclair's skin, unexpected but pleasant.

"Not a problem. If Papa had only invited the people I knew it would have just been him, Nikki, and my little brother, Xavier." Sinclair unconsciously rocked back on her heels and linked her hands behind her back.

"You've got a point there. By the way, I'm Hunter. Hunter Willoughby."

"A pleasure. And now we're not strangers anymore."

"True." Hunter nodded, then looked behind her, briefly, into the crowd. "How long are you going to be down here for?"

"About a month. Or until Papa and Nikki get tired of me, whichever comes first."

The other woman's eyes settled on her with more than ca-sual interest, moving over her braided hair, slight body, and the loose terra-cotta-colored sundress. They were the same height, Sinclair noted as she met Hunter's eyes again.

"Della was right," Hunter said. "You do look a lot like Lydia, more so a few features than the whole package." Her eyes flickered down Sinclair's body again, as if responding automatically to some stimuli. She ate from her saucer of car-rot sticks as she spoke, dipping the stalks of vegetable into the herb-flecked ranch dressing. Sinclair felt her face heat up, as if Hunter's mouth was nibbling at every feature, tasting her, comparing her flavor to the mysterious Lydia's.

She cleared her throat. "I haven't met this Lydia person yet so I don't know."

"Really?" Hunter looked surprised. "She should be around here somewhere. It seems a little strange that you haven't met your own sister yet."

Sister?

"Hey, there you are." A low voice came from behind Sinclair. She turned around.

"Hey." Hunter greeted the woman with a soft kiss on the cheek, but the woman pulled slightly away. Still, Hunter's hand rested lightly on the woman's waist. "I heard that you haven't met your sister yet."

"No, I haven't." The woman smiled and extended her hand. "I'm Lydia."

She really does look like me, Sinclair thought, staring at the narrow face and full, heart shaped mouth with amazement. Her hair, though, was very different. She wore it straightened and parted down the middle to frame her vulpine face and brush her shoulders in a perfect silken fall. Lydia was shorter and her body was fuller, more voluptuously rounded than Sinclair's. Her skin, too, was lighter, a light-through-amber color compared to Sinclair's red oak. An impressive wealth of cleavage lay in the scooped neckline of her yellow dress.

"Sinclair." Her sister's hand was soft. Up close she smelled like rosewater and couldn't have been any younger than twenty-five.

She felt an acute sense of disappointment. Not only that Hunter was obviously involved with her, but even worse, that their father had cheated on Sinclair's mother.

"Do you live around here?" Sinclair asked.

"This is my house."

"Ah." Sinclair's eyebrow twitched in surprise. "You have wonderful taste. I especially love the paintings in this room."

"Hunter did some of them, actually. The ones you saw when you first came into the house. She's a computer scientist with a soul." She turned to the woman at her side. "Unfortunately the only way you can see it is through her paintings."

Hunter chuckled. "Thanks, Lydia. Good to know how you feel about me."

"Are you two dating?"

They looked at her as if surprised that she could see the level of their intimacy.

"Not at all." Lydia said. "We're good friends who sometimes get together for nocturnal activities." Her grin was devilish.

"Stop it." Hunter shook her head, though her own lips twitched as if fighting a smile. "Don't let her tease you. We are seeing each other."

"I'm sorry, I didn't mean to be nosy. I just thought that—" she gestured to Hunter's hand still draped across Lydia's hip. "This meant you were together. Sorry."

Hunter moved her hand away with a guilty start. "No need for you to apologize, though," her voice lowered to a mocking whisper, "perhaps I should because Lydia's not really out to her family."

"I don't hide it either." She grabbed Hunter's hand and forced it back on her hip.

The dark woman sighed and took her hand back. "Did I mention that your sister was temperamental?"

Sinclair glanced from one woman to the other, curious to see how their little game was going to play out.

"Hey, Sinclair." Her father appeared suddenly at her side. "Having a good time?"

"Yes, thank you. I just met Lydia."

He spared his other daughter an affectionate glance. "Good. She was nice enough to lend her house for this party. I hope you two get to know each other well. She's a good person." No explanation about why she had a twenty-five-year-old sister when he and her own mother were still together that exact amount of years ago. *Maybe it just didn't matter. Maybe that was the way men and women dealt with each other here. What's a lover or two in a marriage?*

"Thanks, Papa. All that because I lent you my house for the afternoon?" Her teasing smile gave Sinclair a hint to the sort of relationship they had.

He shared an affectionate look with his middle child before turning to the woman beside her. "Hunter."

"Mr. Daniels." They shook hands, but that was the extent of their interaction. Sinclair made a mental note to ask him about that later on.

"Come dance with your old man, Sinclair. All this good music is playing for you and I haven't seen you dance one step yet."

"I was taking my time. You know, warming up." Truth was, she wasn't much of a dancer. Being out there in front of all those people made her self-conscious. She'd never even danced for herself in the privacy of her own apartment.

"You've had enough time. Let's go." He dragged her out to the middle of the room where two couples and three children danced to an old Beres Hammond song.

Over her father's shoulder, she watched Lydia and Hunter talking. The ebony-skinned woman caught her eye and toasted her with a glass of clear liquid. Sinclair smiled, then turned her attention back to her father.

"Thank you again for doing this for me. This whole thing was very unexpected."

"That was the idea." He chuckled. "I'm glad you like it. Now maybe you can go out with some of these people while you're here. They can show you some real island sights.

"What are you going to be doing in the meantime?"

"Working mostly. But not all the time. In the middle of all your new socializing just remember that I'm going to want some of your attention, too."

"No problem. I'll always have a space on my dance card for you."

They twirled around the floor, surprising each other with their fancy footwork.

"Can I ask you something?" Sinclair asked.

"Yes, yes. Anything."

"Who is Lydia's mother?"

He didn't seem surprised by the question. "A bush woman I knew for a while."

"Did she know Mama?"

"Yes. But not very well. She used to come down from the hills to sell her fruit and things. I think that was how they met."

"Should I be upset that you had an affair with her?"

"Why? Your mother knew about her. I'm sure that she had herself an outside man too."

"You're sure about that?" *Or does the thought of it just make you feel better?*

"I'm sure. She was happy at times when I didn't give her any reason to be. She had somebody else. I'm very sure of it."

Just like she had been Regina's somebody else, Sinclair thought suddenly and tripped over her feet.

"You all right?"

"Fine. Just a stray thought."

He swept her into an intricate turn and shimmy that didn't quite work. They both laughed and threw themselves back into the dance. Two songs later, they walked away from the dance floor and headed for the bar.

"Have some rum punch," he said. "It's the best on the island."

"What's in it besides rum?"

"There's something in it besides rum?" he asked innocently. At the look on her face, he laughed. "Just try it. The thing won't bite."

A tall pitcher of punch landed on the bar in front of them. Her father poured two tall glasses. He hoisted his glass.

"To my daughter. Happy birthday and welcome home."

Their glasses touched with a sound like music.

Four hours and four glasses of rum punch later, most of the party had already gone home. Lydia and their father sat in the sunroom laughing about familiar things and, drunk from one Heineken and a shot of white rum, Nikki had already curled up for a nap in the guest bedroom with her son. Sinclair walked out to the back patio with her fourth glass of rum punch in hand and sat down at a small table to feel the night breeze on her face.

"Having fun?"

Sinclair would have known Hunter's voice anywhere. She peered into the dark to see the other woman rocking in a hammock a few feet away. "Yes, I am. Thanks for asking."

Sinclair drank the last of her rum punch and put the glass very carefully in the middle of the table.

"Is everything here what you thought it would be?" Hunter asked.

"Not quite." She still wondered if her mother really had taken lovers like Victor obviously had. "I certainly never expected to find Lydia."

Hunter chuckled. "I can imagine. Jamaican men think nothing of having more than one woman at a time; the more pussy around the better." Her teeth flashed in the dark.

Sinclair realized then that Hunter was more than a little drunk. The British precision in her voice had mostly disappeared, leaving it softer and more mellow.

"What about you? Do you believe the same thing applies to you?"

"The more pussy the better?"

Sinclair nodded. Then, realizing that Hunter probably couldn't see her in the dark, voiced her answer.

"Nah. I've always been the one-woman kind. My father and I had that in common. It was my mother who fucked around and got caught." Her voice was matter-of-fact. "I guess that just proves that some people want more while others just want the best."

"Hmm." *That sounded nice. The best.* "Is that what you have with Lydia? The best?" Sinclair looked over at the other woman in the dark, more imagining her shape than seeing it. *Did Hunter mind her asking these intimate questions?*

"Don't have us engaged already. She and I just recently got together. We're trying this dating thing to see how far it takes us. So far she's a nice woman. A very nice woman." Hunter sounded faintly amused. "What's your story, then? You looking for the perfect vacation fuck or what?"

"I'm not looking for anything here." *Except maybe a temporary rest from my life.* "I had a bad experience a few weeks ago and I'm just trying to take my mind off it."

"Somebody in the States broke your heart?"

"She broke it in a million pieces."

A scented night breeze drifted over them, ruffling the tiny hairs at Sinclair's temples and the cloth over her breasts. She closed her eyes as a voluptuous sigh eased from her throat. Her head felt pleasantly weightless, like it was a balloon floating into the night sky.

"So was she any good?"

"What?"

"I hoped you got some nights of good loving out of her before she turned her back on you. Sometimes that's the only consolation a girl can have."

Sinclair flashed Hunter a look in the dark, at her bare leg rising like a dark mountain in the hammock, the color of her skin disappearing and appearing again in the inky darkness of night.

"We were good together." Images of her and Regina entwined bombarded her brain. "But in the end it wasn't enough."

"Did you want more than that?"

"I don't know. I think I just *expected* more. Before her I was with a boy, and he and I met, we went out for drinks, then dinner, then we slept together. After that we just kept seeing each other, building toward something for the future. I suppose that I expected the same thing to happen with her."

"Not every love affair ends up like that, you know."

"Obviously. Some people just want to fuck and dump you." She looked across at Hunter. "Sorry."

"It's all right. If you can't say these things to a stranger, then who else can you tell them to?"

Sinclair laughed wryly. "Thanks for listening to me go on about this. I know it's boring."

Hunter chuckled. "It's life. It's not always squeals and giggles."

"That's an interesting way of putting it." Sinclair reached for her cup then, remembering too late that it was empty, drained it dry of its last few drops of punch anyway. "What about you? Is there something troubling your soul that you need to vent about?"

"No, not really. I tend to meditate for that sort of release."

"What about your other kind of release." *Shit!* Sinclair almost bit her tongue off. "I didn't mean to ask you that, sorry."

Hunter laughed softly in the dark. "It's OK. I didn't take offense. You'll find out soon enough that it takes a lot to offend me." She moved in the hammock, popping the vertebrae in her back before settling once again into the cushions. "These days it's me and my own right hand. Lydia and I aren't quite there yet. It takes a lot for her to become intimate with somebody."

Really? Sinclair would have thought the opposite. She eyed the other woman again. "Your patience is admirable."

"Hey, you asked."

"Yes, I did, didn't I?" Sinclair murmured, amused.

"I'll be sure to hold back next time."

"Don't be too hasty now." They both laughed.

The night fell in gracious silence around them, bathing their stillness with meaning and possibility. *She's your sister's woman, be careful.*

Sinclair shook her head. Hunter was like a cliché. Dark, stormy, and wicked. She'd be the one in those old black-and-white movies to twirl her mustache and smile viciously. Sinclair took strange comfort in that. She wasn't the type to fall for a cliché. She needed depth in a woman. Something that would make her interest last beyond the frantic fuckfest of the first few weeks. Her eyes slid to where she imagined Hunter's mouth to be. *Hmm, but what a fuckfest that would be. . . .*

"So what do you do in the big city?" Hunter asked.

Sinclair swallowed past a suddenly dry throat. "Accounting."

She laughed. "Seriously?"

"Why is that so funny?"

"Maybe I watch too much American TV like a lot of my neighbors." She laughed again. "I thought model or actress or escort would be the default job for people who looked like you."

"Are you saying I look like a whore? I'm insulted." But she couldn't get the energy to appear truly so. The best she could do was a narrowed gaze, which Hunter couldn't see anyway.

"You'll be fine," Hunter said, chuckling.

Sinclair closed her eyes and leaned back in her chair. "I should go back in," she said, not moving a muscle. The rum punch spun her head faster than any number of gin and tonics she'd ever had. Sitting at this table seemed the best cure for her spinning head and lack of judgment.

Fabric rustled as Hunter turned to her. "I thought you were leaving?" Laughter rubbed against her voice like a mischievous cat.

"I was, but my legs weren't ready to go yet."

"I've been there a time or two myself. Let me guess, rum punch?"

"Yep. Right on the money."

In the darkness, Hunter laughed again. The sound dragged like silk over Sinclair's sensitized pleasure centers. "What is it with you Americans and money metaphors and clichés?"

"You Americans," Sinclair mocked. "Don't try that condescending tripe with me. Like you are above needing or wanting money."

"I didn't say that, but I don't incorporate it into my everyday speech."

"A girl makes one comment and she's indicted along with the rest of a capitalist society for being too fiscally focused." She rolled her eyes. "You're no fun. This time I *am* going inside." She stood. "Good-bye."

But it was deadly boring inside. People were talking, though not about anything interesting. The truth was that Hunter's company was far *too* interesting. Even if she was drunk and had a dirty mouth. Instead of going back out to the back verandah, she crawled into the queen sized bed with Nikki and Xavier, hoping that neither of them snored.

"Wake up, sleepyheads."

Sinclair rolled over when she heard Lydia's voice but didn't immediately get up. She opened an eye. "What time is it?"

"Not that early. Come on, we made breakfast."

Hunter poked her head through the open door. "Actually, *I* made breakfast. She just made the tea."

Sinclair blinked at the unexpected treat of seeing her first thing in the morning. Of course, she looked divine. Their eyes met briefly and Hunter winked. Did she spend the night on the couch or in Lydia's bed? Had last night been the night to wear down her girlfriend's chastity?

"Come into the dining room, ladies. Breakfast has been served." Hunter's head disappeared from the doorway.

Lydia poked Nikki's shoulder. Sinclair's stepmother had slept like the dead. Even after she'd joined her in the bed last night, she hadn't moved from her position in the center of the bed. By morning they had ended up in the spoon position with Sinclair, being the taller one, behind her. Nikki groaned and slowly woke under Lydia's unkind ministrations.

"Hey," she said, blinking up at Sinclair. "Where is Xavier?"

"At the breakfast table with the rest of the family like you should be."

"I guess that's a strong hint then, huh?" Sinclair slid off the bed. "Do you have a spare toothbrush or something that I could use on this breath?"

"Everything you need is in the bathroom cabinet." She motioned toward a door to the right of the bed. "Use whatever you want."

"Thanks."

By the time she made it out to the dining room with clean teeth and face, everyone was sitting at the table eating, including Nikki who looked much more alert than she had earlier.

"There's water for tea on the stove," Lydia said as she reached for the platter of scrambled eggs. "Coffee is in the machine on the counter, you can get cold water from the dispenser on the fridge. Everything else is on the table."

"Thanks."

Sinclair sat beside Nikki with her glass of water. "Pass me a plate, please. Thanks."

"Did you have a good time last night, Sinclair?"

"It was great. I haven't had a birthday party in years."

"Good. It was Papa's idea." Lydia smiled over at their father.

"Thank you for having it at your house. I know how hard it must be cleaning up after a party."

"Well, that's what family and friends are for." She looked pointedly around the table. "Hint, hint."

"We can definitely stay to help you," Nikki said.

"So can I."

Sinclair didn't miss the look that her father threw Hunter as the woman volunteered her time.

"You don't have to stay, Hunter," he said. "We can manage."

"I'll take all the help I can get, Papa," Lydia said. "The sooner we finish then the sooner we can enjoy the rest of this gorgeous day. Maybe we can have a cookout on the beach or something."

Hunter and Victor exchanged a glance of cool understanding. Sinclair watched the two of them, wondering what that was all about.

Chapter 8

Sinclair dreamed about her sister's girlfriend. She woke up swimming in rapidly disintegrating visions of Hunter smiling and stretched out on a forest floor on a bed of thick green leaves, her dark skin glistening with moisture from Sinclair's tongue.

"I think she's dreaming."

A weight pressed down on the bed beside her. From the light scent of honeysuckle, she could tell that it wasn't her father or Nikki. Sinclair opened her eyes.

"Papa told me to take you out for the day." Lydia watched her with a smile playing at the corners of her mouth. She looked like she'd been up for hours in her white cotton dress that showcased her gorgeous cleavage and narrow waist.

"'Morning," Sinclair croaked from beneath the parting layers of sleep.

"'Morning." Hunter's voice greeted her from the doorway. Even in a white A-shirt tucked into belted slim-fitting jeans she managed to look like a dyke's wet dream.

Sinclair resisted the urge to grab the sheets up to her chest like a shy virgin, and instead sat up, baring her oversized Sesame Street T-shirt. She just knew that her braids were flat against her head. Not sexy. "Hey. I get the pleasure of both your company today, huh?"

"Two for one," Lydia chimed in. "Today only."

"Unless you'd rather have Lydia to yourself. I can disappear if you want."

"No, it's fine. You can even come sit on the bed if you want," Sinclair, even with her bad breath, dared to tease.

The woman called her bluff and came in to sit down on the other side of her.

Sinclair's body temperature started to rise. "I don't suppose either of you made breakfast?"

"Not yet. But Hunter could."

Hunter cleared her throat to get their attention. "Actually Hunter had just planned on buying you ladies something to eat after we leave here. So the sooner you," she looked at Sinclair, "shower and dress, the sooner you can eat."

Sinclair turned to her sister. "She's harsh, huh?"

"Yes, usually."

Sinclair left the women in her room and went to shower and dress. Twenty minutes later, with her camera bag and purse slung over her shoulder, she was ready. "Where are we going?"

"To find food."

They climbed in Lydia's car, an old Cadillac convertible with a blood-red paint job and black-and-white leather seats that looked like they'd just been peeled off a cow.

"Nice car," Sinclair murmured appreciatively, sinking into the spacious backseat. Lydia pressed a button and the roof slid back. The cool morning air snuggled into the car with them. This was the indefinable quality to mornings that Sinclair had always loved—the brightening light, the slow-moving shadows that spoke of the beginning of things, and especially the crispness that lay in the air before the filth of the day could get a chance to set in. Sinclair inhaled a deep lungful of that air and sank deeper into the suede seats. She could have fit at least two other people back there with her. "Very nice."

"Don't get any ideas about my backseat, young woman."

"Don't worry. I'm sure it's nothing that you haven't

thought of or done before." Sinclair met Lydia's smiling gaze in the rearview mirror.

After a sinfully good breakfast at one of Hunter's favorite restaurants, they drove through town, pointing out sights of interest, and keeping up a running commentary meant to amuse Sinclair. At times the two women were like a married couple, bickering back and forth with a spontaneous ribaldry that made Sinclair laugh, despite her minor crush on Hunter. After almost two hours driving around the island, Hunter got bored.

She turned to Lydia. "Let's go find someplace for a snack, then head over to the market in Winslow."

"You hungry already?" Sinclair turned to her in surprise.

"I'm a growing girl. This body needs its vitamins and protein."

Even though she knew better, Sinclair took a close look at the body Hunter indicated. It was perfect. Just like the last time she checked.

They stopped for food at a patty stand near the beach then leaned against the hood of the Cadillac to drink their sodas and eat the thick pastries filled with spiced ground beef. The sea lapped up on the sand a dozen feet or so away from where they stood. Only a hillock of pearl gray sand, bits of dried seaweed, and a few coconut trees separated them from the water.

"So how long do you plan on being here?" Lydia asked.

"Just four weeks, although I wish I could stay longer." Her family's warm acceptance and the resurfacing of childhood memories were making this trip even more fun than she thought it would be.

"Anybody special waiting for you back in your big city?"

"No, not really." The memory of Regina burned briefly. "I'm footloose and fancy free, as they say."

Hunter swallowed a bite of her pastry. "Who's 'they' and what the devil does 'footloose' really mean?"

"Ignore her, she's being difficult today," Lydia said to Sinclair.

"I am not being difficult." Hunter took a sip of her ginger beer. "This is just me all the time."

"Does it ever get tiring?" Sinclair asked, all innocence. "Being you, that is."

"Funny." Hunter stuck her tongue out at her.

Caught off guard, Sinclair giggled.

Lydia ignored their byplay. "So back to my question, why don't you have someone waiting for you over there?"

"Would it stop you if I said that I didn't want to talk about it?"

"Of course."

"Right." Hunter made a noise of disbelief. "And you have two brass ones hanging underneath that dress." She moved as if to lift Lydia's dress, then stopped herself. "Wait, that might actually be true."

"Very funny." Lydia slapped at Hunter's straying hand.

"I'm hanging out with a bunch of comedians today," Sinclair muttered.

"That's one thing that I've never been called before." Hunter said as she backed away from Lydia, laughing.

"If not comedy, then what do you do to make your living?"

"Scientist. I'm one of the computer nerds at the University of the West Indies."

"Sounds interesting."

"It is and it isn't." She flashed Sinclair a smile. "I'm glad for days like this when I can be out doing what I like. But some days it gets frustrating because of the university's substandard equipment." She shook her head. "But enough of that. The last thing I want to do is bring my work into any conversation that I have on my day off."

"Everyday can be a day off if Hunter wanted," Lydia said. "She practically works as a freelance scientist with freelance hours."

"That doesn't translate into me not working at all, Ms. Nine to Five."

Sinclair knew that Lydia was the manager of a hotel on the beach, one of the Sandals hotels, and that she sometimes worked an ungodly amount of hours during the week. This she'd gotten from low-voiced conversations with Nikki on the verandah while Xavier slept on her lap.

"I don't work nine to five any more than you do, Willoughby."

"Ohh, she called me by my last name. That means she's really upset with me." Hunter turned to Sinclair. "Have you ever seen another person who's as touchy about her job?" She laughed, then jumped away from Lydia's pinching fingers. "Neuroses aplenty, this one."

"Let's lock the car up and go down to the water," Lydia said suddenly.

Still chuckling, Hunter finished off her soda and dropped the empty bottle in a nearby trash can. "Sure. Why not?"

They went to the beach together with Lydia walking between Sinclair and Hunter. The afternoon was a pleasant amalgamation of sounds, of squalling birds, schoolgirls in their dark blue uniforms running on the sand, laughing and splashing seawater at each other. On the boardwalk beyond the sandbank, the sky juice man hawked his wares, advertising his flavors in a deep singsong voice. On the wind, Sinclair could detect a teasing hint of sage, a scent she realized that Hunter wore.

The women eventually left the beach for the market. They parked the car and headed for the tall, colorful booths that sold incense, oils, crocheted hats, and anything else a local bohemian would want to buy.

"This is nice. We have a few places like this back in America, but I never bothered to visit them for one reason or another."

"Are you a snob?" Hunter peeked around Lydia to look at Sinclair.

"Not that I know of."

"She's a snob," Lydia confirmed.

"Hey! It's not 'pick on Sinclair' hour, OK? Leave me out of your little bitefests."

Hunter laughed. "Take it easy. I was only joking."

"No, you weren't, Brit."

"Oooh, she called you a name." Lydia skipped ahead of them to look at some handmade sandals.

"I hope you don't think I was being offensive."

"Not yet, but you're close." Sinclair glanced at her sister's woman. "Do you really think I'm a snob?"

"I don't know." She touched Sinclair's nose. "That turned-up nose of yours gives me the idea that you might be."

She batted the finger away. "I'll remember you said that."

"Hey, what do you think of these?" Lydia called their attention to the brown sandal on her foot. A little on the plain side, it looked odd next to her own strappy, high-heeled shoe.

Hunter appeared to consider the matter. "I think it looks better here," she knelt at Lydia's feet, took off the shoe, and put it next to its mate in the booth's display.

Sinclair nodded. "I agree."

"What do you two know about fashion anyway?"

"Did she just insult us?" Hunter looked at Sinclair.

"I think she did. I don't know why. You look pretty fashionable to me."

"So do you." Hunter's voice took on a high, singing quality. "I think what you're wearing is the absolute pinnacle of rugged expatriate fashion." Her eyes swept over Sinclair's pale slacks and tube-top blouse. "Stunning."

"Why, thank you, Robin Leach. I don't even think this fashion has even reached the colonies yet, my mode is just that far ahead of the current one."

"You two are not funny."

Hunter snickered. "*We* think so."

Sinclair's lips twitched with amusement as she glanced at her partner in crime.

"Come on, don't be mad at us." They rushed up to Lydia from behind, fawning over her in an excess of passion, kissing her cheeks and the backs of her hands.

"A lesbian them, man." Sinclair flinched at the harsh voice. "'Specially the one in the pants."

The women kept on walking, but Hunter had stiffened next to Sinclair.

"You a lesbian?"

The other people walking near them looked around, looked at the boy who had spoken, then at the women. They did nothing.

"You want some dick in your life?"

The voices followed the women. From the corner of her eye, Sinclair saw that they belonged to four men, still boys really, with the hard muscles of laborers but none of the honest intentions.

"Pussy don't belong with pussy, you know. You need this—" he grabbed his crotch, "every time."

Lydia turned around. "Fuck off."

"Keep that as an inside thought, my dear," Hunter murmured near her girlfriend's ear. "We don't want any trouble from these assholes."

"Unfortunately, I think we already have it." Sinclair laughed nervously.

"You dykes think this is funny?"

"Not at all." Hunter stepped back. "So since nobody is amused let's just call it a day and go our separate ways. OK?"

A ring of spectators was beginning to form around them.

"No. No damn way some man-woman is going to disrespect me and walk off."

"Disrespect?" Hunter made a rude noise. "Didn't you start this?"

This was going to get ugly. Sinclair's fists tightened convulsively.

"No, man. You bitches started this. And we're going to finish it."

"Can these punks be any more clichéed?" Hunter turned to Sinclair with a sneer.

"Don't piss off the nice man, Hunter."

"What nice man would that be, sweetheart?" Not the one who was advancing closer and closer toward them.

"Any of you fucks touch me and you're dead!" Lydia hissed, anchoring her purse across her body.

The one in orange took her up on her dare. Her punch was solid, loud in the enclosed space. It set off the other three like firecrackers. They came at the women, fists flying, teeth bared. Sinclair had never felt such fear in her life, not even when she was mugged in the city. She kicked and punched, grateful that her body remembered the lessons from the self-defense course she'd taken two years ago. Her elbow connected with something solid and someone howled.

"Hold her down!" Sinclair felt hands pull at her limbs, then at her blouse. Pain exploded in her side and against her face. She kicked at the body closest to her legs and felt a jolt of relief when he screamed and fell against the concrete. Hands grappled roughly at her arms and breasts. Somewhere glass shattered.

"Back the fuck up!"

Sinclair looked up to see Lydia with a broken bottle in one hand. "Get off my fucking sister or I'm going to shove this glass up your ass, then come back for your balls."

A cold fever swept over Sinclair's skin, then suddenly she was free. The boy backed away from her with his hands up. Lydia feinted closer to him, stabbing at him with the broken bottle. A hand tugged at Sinclair's and she recoiled, bringing her elbow sharply up. The body next to her staggered and cursed.

"Fuck!" Hunter's voice was loud next to her ear. "It's me, dammit! Come on. Let's go."

The mist cleared. She could see one of the boys on the ground, holding his crotch, his body gripping itself in the fetal position. His arm and back were bloody. Another held his nose, making harsh gagging noises as blood gushed between his fingers. The other was nowhere to be seen. Hunter stood next to her, gripping a rock in her bloodied fist, chest heaving. The crowd stared but did nothing. It backed away as the women emerged from their human boxing ring, thrusting their way through the suffocating heat of hostile bodies to find Lydia's car.

They didn't talk on the ride back to Lydia's house. The wind filled the silence in the car, brushing like a soothing salve over naked bruises. Lydia's face was the worst. An ugly purpling bruise smudged the right side of her mouth. In a few minutes it would start to swell. Aside from a slightly bruised mouth, Hunter's face was still intact. Little gashes decorated her knuckles and the palm of one hand where she had gripped the rock. She held that hand outside the car to let the cool breeze ease its burning. Sinclair's arms were a mottled purple where the men had held her down and her cheek had a small cut, probably from someone's ring. Right now she was just tired, her mind still shied away from the fact that grown men had done this thing to them, and no one from the market had tried to help.

When they parked in the garage, Sinclair stumbled from the car, then followed the two women into the house.

"Can I go lie down in your guest room?" she asked. "I'm a little tired."

"Sure, go ahead. I'll call Papa and let him know you'll be spending the night here."

"Thanks."

Sinclair went into the bedroom and took off her clothes. The bed was soft, but she felt suffocated, and instead of being comforted by the paintings on the walls—images of banana trees and coconut groves, of young men walking through otherwise empty city streets—she felt threatened by them. Sinclair turned away but her mind replayed scenes of the attack, the terror and violence of it. She finally got up, wrapped an over-sized towel around her like a sarong, and walked through the empty sitting room and made her way to the back patio. She pulled off the towel and sank into the silken hammock with a sigh. The breeze immediately comforted her. Within moments, she fell asleep.

Moments later, voices from beyond the opened double doors interrupted her rest.

"I can't believe you're asking me that. Was I the only one getting beaten on in that market earlier?" Lydia's voice floated out on the faint breeze.

She heard the whisper of leather against flesh as someone sank into the sofa near the door.

"I'm asking you that *because* of what happened today. This makes being out to your family and friends even more important. When you come home with bruises from so-called god-fearing Jamaicans who beat you up for being who you are, don't you think that you could get your family to see the abnormality in that, that a person who tries to destroy or hate someone because of who and how they love isn't much of a person?"

"I don't see the perfect harmonious vision that you see. In my eyes there are no benefits to being out. For what? So that I can get my ass beat again by some boys on the corner?"

"What about your life? Don't you think that you're living it just a tad bit dishonestly?"

"This is not America, Hunter. This isn't even your precious England. I can't walk around here holding my girlfriend's hand like it's nothing. Women get raped and beaten for that kind of stuff around here."

"I'm talking about your family, your friends."

"You are so damn naive."

From her swaying hammock, Sinclair could feel the heat of her sister's frustration and hear her harsh, angry breath.

"Do you think us being more out would have saved us from

almost being gang-raped in the market? Do you? Nobody tried to help us. They didn't give a damn what happens to three lesbians. They probably thought that a little forced entry was going to save our souls and pussies for Jamaica. Because surely we can't be real Jamaican women and be dykes." Lydia made a low sound of frustration. "It kills me that you women who leave here and come back understand the country so little that you bring your foreign ways here and expect us to adapt."

"Don't you ever get tired of hiding? Of lying about who you're going to see and why?"

"This is what I get tired of." Sinclair imagined Lydia gesturing to her bruised arm and the swelling at her mouth. "I get tired of being called names when I go out to get my shopping done. I wished that I lived in San Francisco or Manchester but I don't. I don't believe in Jamaicans the way that you do. I don't think they can change, or at least not soon enough for me not to be a casualty in this useless war."

Hunter sighed. So did Sinclair. This fear that Lydia was talking about, the threat of violence, could happen everywhere. She could have just as easily gotten gay-bashed walking to her apartment after a date with Regina as she could have walking down her father's stretch of country road.

"Unless you plan to date a different kind of woman from what you prefer now, I say that you out yourself almost every day. Don't you think it would be better for your family to know because you told them rather than for them to speculate and get all the facts wrong?"

"No, I don't. You need to stop thinking about what's best for me, because obviously you have no idea what I need to do or be."

"Just because I've been gone from this country for most of my life doesn't mean I understand it any less. When I was fifteen I left Jamaica. I knew that I was a lesbian then and, because of what I looked like, I was an *out* lesbian. It was hard for me. It was hard for the thirteen years I was in England, for various reasons, and it's going to be difficult here as well. I don't anticipate anything being easy. But I'd rather suffer the chance of someone accosting me for being a dyke than suffer the emotional violence I'd do to myself if I wasn't honest about who I am."

"I don't see it as hiding, like I said. I see it as saving my skin. And I have absolutely no problem with that." Lydia's voice was final.

The leather creaked as someone stood up. "This is a difficult conversation. We should finish it some other time. It's too soon after what happened today."

"Yeah. I guess you're right." The sofa creaked again. "I'm going to bed."

"OK. I'll just stay out here awhile and clear my head."

"All right, I'll see you in the morning." Soft footsteps gradually faded away.

Sinclair heard Hunter's low sigh. "What the blazes did I get myself into with this woman?"

In the morning it was just Lydia and Sinclair.

"She left to do some work," the younger woman said. Her voice was strained. Although it was seven in the morning, she was already made up and ready for work. With her skillfully applied makeup, it was nearly impossible to see her bruise from the fight.

"You can stay here while I go to work if you like, or I can drop you at Papa's on my way to town."

"I'll stay here. You have a good collection of books to keep me occupied all day. We can go over to Papa's for dinner after you get back."

"In that case I'll try to come home at a decent hour for a change."

After Lydia went off to work, Sinclair changed into a pair of borrowed shorts and a shirt and went to explore the large subdivision and its adjoining woods. Despite its manicured façade, the neighborhood still managed to keep many of the natural elements that made it beautiful. Sinclair took out her camera and quickly lost herself in the landscape.

By the time Lydia came home it was too late for dinner, so she just took Sinclair back to their father's, promising that they would do something less dangerous sometime soon.

Chapter 9

Sinclair couldn't sleep. When for the second time that morning she heard someone stirring in the house, she decided to get up. It was Nikki, already showered and preparing to leave for work. It was barely six.

"Hey." Sinclair stood in the doorway of her room, yawning.

Nikki smiled a greeting.

"Going to work already?"

"Yes. I have to be there by seven thirty after I take Xavier to school."

In the kitchen, the boy sat quietly eating his breakfast of hominy corn porridge and fruit juice. Apparently, he wasn't much of a morning person.

Sinclair glanced at the clock on the refrigerator. "Mind if I tag along?"

"Uh . . . sure you can come. But it's going to be boring."

"That's OK. Just take me up there with you and I'll find some way to occupy myself."

"All right. Hurry up, though. We have to leave in about twenty minutes."

In less than fifteen minutes Sinclair was showered and dressed in a long denim skirt and a thin white blouse that covered the bruises on her arms. Sturdy sandals and a bag with some personal essentials, including her camera, completed the outfit. Xavier waited by the front door for his mother, propped in the doorway with his full backpack nearly dragging him backward to the floor. He looked like a pint-sized zombie.

Nikki came up behind Sinclair. "Ready?"

During the walk to Xavier's school, the boy slowly livened up. By the time they arrived at the school's gate he was blinking happily into the sun and waving at his classmates playing a few yards away. They left him to play while they caught the bus heading into the hills to the house where Nikki worked.

"I work for the Breckenridges," Nikki explained as they rode the small minivan up into the Blue Mountains. "They're nice white people who came here from England about five years ago to settle down with their retirement money."

"How often do you work?"

"Only four days out of the week. They pay me good enough that I don't have to get a second job."

They passed miles of luxuriant greenery, hanging vines, an occasional splash of color from blossoming fruit trees. The road was rough. Unpaved dirt and gravel kicked up as the bus passed, leaving it and any passenger unwise to leave the window open, brushed with red dust. They got off on the third stop, walking past a half dozen expensively built houses with their electronic gates and satellite dishes, before they found the Breckenridges' bright yellow, two-story Tudor mansion with its high white fence.

"It's beautiful up here." Sinclair said, breathing in the crisp mountain air.

"Yes. One time I wanted to live up here with the rich people. Then I realized I was afraid of heights and mountain goats."

Sinclair laughed. "What time do you finish up here?"

"Around five thirty. Why? Are you bored already?" she teased Sinclair with a tiny smile.

"No, not yet. But I know that you have to work so I

planned on going for a walk to take in the sights up here. I can come back when you're on your lunch break."

"OK. That sounds good. I'll let them get used to the idea of me bringing somebody up here before they actually see you." Nikki surprised her with a quick hug. "Come back at one o'clock. And be careful."

The roads here weren't quite as rough as the ones they had encountered on the bus. At least it was easier to walk in her sandals without worrying that she'd turn up at the end of the journey looking like she'd walked through a bauxite mine. These roads were paved with asphalt that was spread out like a beautiful black rug then abruptly stopped three feet from the growth of vegetation on both sides. A slight breeze came up, bringing with it the unexpected smell of the sea. Sinclair took a small dirt road that led from the main one, being careful to note where she came from so she wouldn't get lost trying to get back.

The houses along the dirt road were smaller and less pretentious than the ones she just left, lined up like giggling schoolchildren in their small yards. Their façades were painted in wild gorgeous colors, scarlet splashed with blues, carmine, and yellows, teal ribboned with pink. One house was straight out of a fairy tale with ceramic goblins crouched in the flower-ringed yard. The fairies perched on the walls with their nimbus-cloud hair and soft brown faces looked ready to separate from the wood and fly into the air. Sinclair took out her camera.

Hours later, the front of her skirt was dusty from her kneeling in the dirt to take photos and her stomach complained mildly of being empty. Sinclair ignored it and walked back into the forest.

The shifting canopy of plants welcomed her with their sheltering coolness. Sinclair put her camera away, anxious instead to explore the beauty around her with her own eyes. She sat at the base of an old mahogany tree and leaned back into the smooth bark. Its familiar scent brought back the childhood memory of playing with neighborhood children, digging in the dirt for whatever it was that children looked for back then. The smell of the earth was the same and the breeze on her face felt intimate and familiar. If she narrowed her eyes just so, with the sun playing in her lashes, Sinclair could almost see her mother rushing out to usher the children inside before the rain came.

"You look comfortable."

Sinclair let her illusion go and opened her eyes. "I am." She hugged her knees and glanced up at her sister's gorgeous girlfriend. "What are you doing here?"

"Talking to you of course." Hunter stepped closer. "You know, you shouldn't be walking up here alone like this. It's not safe."

"What about you? I don't see your escort."

"I'm different."

Darkness slid suddenly across the sky and thunder rumbled overhead. The air became ripe with the smell of impending rain.

"The sky is going to fall down on our heads any minute."

"Yeah, I should be getting back." Sinclair definitely didn't want her camera to get wet.

"You'll never make it back to the Breckenridges' in time. Come with me."

Without turning to see if Sinclair followed, Hunter walked out of the forest, unerringly finding the dirt road and the few houses that lined it. Moments later they arrived at an unassuming stone house, mostly hidden by dense layers of flowering plants and shade trees. A profusion of hibiscus in lavish shades of red and lavender nearly hid the gate from view. Hunter lifted the vine-covered latch and held the gate wide for the other woman to pass through. The rain began to fall in slow sparkling drops. By the time they were inside the house, it was pouring in violent bucketfuls, slapping against the plants that surrounded the house with a fierce roar.

"Come in. Make yourself comfortable."

But Sinclair was too busy gawking to do that. The walls of the entranceway shimmered a vivid cobalt blue. Two bookshelves on either side of the hallway held pale, silver-shimmered blue vases of varying sizes and shapes. Their glazed surfaces were smooth and warm under Sinclair's touch. They reminded her of Della and her clay garden figures.

Paintings of blueness hung from the walls, a dark blue woman with pale blue eyes and red lips, a day sky bleeding away its vivid colors under the slow retreat of the sun. The entryway's vivid, eye-catching blue faded as they walked deeper into the house to a softer shade, the blue of the sky in the afternoon, lazy and welcoming. Every bit of furniture, the long velvet couch, the draperies, the ottoman in its solitary corner by the window, the rug thrown down on the red tiled floor, was all in shades of blue. The harmony of the room was absolute. The calm it evoked, complete.

"This place is gorgeous," Sinclair murmured, sinking into the velvet sofa.

"Thank you." Hunter brushed a hand through her hair to rid herself of a few errant raindrops. "I'm going to put on some lunch. Do you want to share?"

Sinclair's stomach growled the answer, but she said yes anyway.

Hunter laughed. "Feel free to look around. The food will be ready in about half an hour." She disappeared into the kitchen. A few minutes later she came back with a phone.

"You might want to call Nikki and let her know that the rain didn't wash you away."

Sinclair thought that was a good idea, but she had no idea what the Breckenridges' phone number was. She said as much to Hunter.

"I have the number here somewhere. Hold on." She turned before she could see Sinclair's expression of surprise.

"How did you know that I came up here with her and where she was?"

"I know where she works, Sinclair. It doesn't take a detective to figure any of that out."

Sinclair couldn't argue against that. While she called Nikki, Hunter hurried back to the kitchen to check on the food. She was back from the kitchen within a half hour with a tray of food and drinks for them both.

"Let's eat outside. The rain doesn't come in on the verandah."

They sat down at a rattan table with four well-padded chairs. The verandah was large enough that even with a brisk wind, the rain kept itself far away from the table and their food, splashing instead on the fragrant pink and white frangipani that leaned their small, golden-throated blossoms and green leaves over the railing toward them.

"This looks good," Sinclair said, salivating at the rosemary-flecked baked chicken wings and mashed sweet white potatoes on her plate. She was starting to think that everyone on the island knew how to cook except for her.

"Of course it's good. I made it."

The potatoes melted like butter over her tongue. Their light, starchy sweetness loosened an involuntary groan that Hunter heard over the deluge of rain.

"I haven't been the cause of a noise like that in quite a few months," Hunter grinned at her from across the table. "Thank you."

"That long?" Sinclair murmured between bites. "You don't seem like the kind of woman to endure celibacy."

"I'm not. But for Lydia I made an exception."

"She seems very special."

"Lydia is all that and more. I'm just wondering if it's more than I can handle." Hunter's mouth twisted in a parody of a smile.

"I'm sorry."

"It's fine. It's not your fault that neither our politics nor our bodies are compatible." She saw the look on Sinclair's face. "Sorry. Spoke out of turn."

Sinclair blushed at the mental image that Hunter's words conjured, two bodies moving together, frantically trying to fit.

"No need to apologize. I like to think that I'm not so naive that honesty will shock and insult me."

"And you certainly don't seem like the naive type. But I was actually apologizing for talking like that about your sister in front of you. I usually say those kinds of things to her face so I don't have to repeat myself."

Sinclair nodded, thought of pursuing the matter, then decided to let it drop. She focused instead on the meal in front of her. The chicken was tender, with just a hint of pepper to complement the aromatic seduction of the rosemary. Sinclair finished off her meal and sat back in the chair with a satisfied sigh. The rain still fell heavily outside, but she didn't care. With her belly full and her camera safe, life was good. She stretched out her legs, wriggling her toes when runaway drops of rain bounced off the railing and splashed on her bare feet.

Across from her, Hunter devoured her meal even more completely than she had. Sinclair watched her sink sharp teeth into the chicken bone, heard it snap, then her soft grunt of satisfaction. She made soft sucking sounds then emptied her mouth of the tiny ground-up remains on a corner of her dish. Hunter ate with rabbitlike intensity, biting and sucking and spitting in an even rhythm until all that was left on the plate was a small brown and beige pile of ground bones. She finally looked up and caught Sinclair staring.

"Want to try it?"

Sinclair shook her head, but Hunter scooted her chair closer and urged Sinclair to pick up her barely nibbled chicken bone with its thin curls of meat still attached.

Goaded by the look of disgust that had flared in Sinclair's eyes, Hunter guided the still moist bone to the other woman's mouth. "You have to clean off all the meat first. Come on."

Quelled by her unwanted attraction to this woman, Sinclair was helpless to stop her mouth from obeying.

"Now, bite into it."

Sinclair blinked when the marrow squirted inside her mouth, released from the remarkably soft prison of bone. It slid over her tongue and she swallowed. The marrow was smooth, like pâté, and infused with a taste of iron that made it rich and unexpectedly good.

"Well?" Hunter's smile said she knew exactly what Sinclair was thinking.

"It's not bad. Is there a way to eat this without the messiness of biting into the bone?"

"I could suck it out of the bone and spit it into your mouth."

Disgust wasn't quite the emotion that twisted her stomach and made her take in a quick breath.

"I'm joking, American girl. I swear." She laughed softly and moved back to her side of the table.

"I'm starting to understand that you're a truly wicked woman."

"You're a little slow then, aren't you?"

"I'm fast when it counts though."

"Ah." The exhalation left Hunter as a sigh.

Smiles lingered, deliberately playing with each other.

Sinclair's eyes fell to Hunter's mouth, noticed its softness, the wet gleam of lips a shade or two lighter than her skin. She imagined another place on Hunter's body that would also be two different shades of dark. Her cheeks burned.

"Can I paint you?" Hunter asked.

Sinclair helped Hunter clean up after their lunch, wiping down the table and the rest of the kitchen while the other woman washed the dishes and pots. When they were finished, Hunter took two Popsicles from her freezer.

"Want one?"

Sinclair nodded. "Red, please."

"That's not very adventurous of you, is it?"

"What?"

"Red is such a safe color. Why don't you take this white one? Live a little."

Sinclair looked at Hunter as if she'd lost her mind. "I don't think so."

"Fine. Your loss."

"OK. Why don't we just share? You have the top half of the white and I'll have the bottom half. Same for the red."

"Very diplomatic. I commend you."

They moved back out to the verandah and put their feet out for some of the cooling drops of rain to hit them.

Hunter licked the side of her white Popsicle. "So, may I paint you?"

"If you really want to." Sinclair made a face.

"I do, so when can I start?"

"Whenever you want. I'm not on a schedule. How long is it going to take?"

"Not long. If it's all right, I'd like for you to pose for me for a few hours one day, then I'll take photos of you and use those for the rest of the painting."

"I don't have to be naked, do I?"

"Only if you want to be." Hunter wiggled her eyebrows, startling a laugh out of Sinclair.

"Are you ever serious?"

"Yes. But only when I'm alone."

Sinclair watched her for a moment, idly wondering what else Hunter did when she was alone.

Hunter drove her back to the Breckenridges' house and let her out at the gate. "Come back to my house in two days and we can get started."

"OK. See you Friday."

"I was starting to get worried," Nikki said when she came out to get Sinclair.

They walked up the long drive together, with Sinclair stopping occasionally to admire some part of the large yard's landscaping.

"Hunter took pretty good care of me," she said as they walked into the house. "I ran into her before the rain got started."

The smell of cooking food floated in the air, oddly out of place with the sterile décor. Everything that Sinclair saw was expensive and tastefully placed, but the house didn't feel lived in. The bone-colored furniture and white walls weren't the least bit welcoming. White drapery fluttered at the windows.

"Good. She's nice," Nikki said.

Was she? "Well, she's at least interesting."

She didn't see the look of speculation that Nikki threw her way.

"This is a beautiful house." As beautiful as a Tudor squatting on a jungle hilltop could look.

Nikki hummed an agreement. "Nigel and Barbara are going to be in town for another couple of hours. After I finish making their dinner we can go."

"Since I'm the one sitting up at your job, please take your time. I'll just go have a look around the house and the gardens."

"Go ahead, but be careful. The Breckenridges are very particular about their things."

Sinclair threw her a wicked grin. "I'll try to break only the cheap stuff."

She didn't get much sightseeing done. A little corner in their solarium seduced her into stretching out in the windowed alcove with her head propped up on a white pillow. The sun burned tiny kisses all over her skin as she looked out the window on the abundant green of the land below and the miles of blue sky above. Tall trees danced in the breeze. Her eyes fell closed.

Victor was waiting on the verandah with Xavier when Sinclair and Nikki walked through the gate later that evening. The two boys sat in serious deliberation around a game of checkers while Xavier's cup of milk and Victor's bottle of Guinness sweated nearby.

Nikki sat in the rocking chair after briefly touching her child's head then her husband's. "I'm tired. Who's going to cook tonight?"

Victor laughed. "Sinclair?"

"Don't look at me," she said, glancing over Xavier's shoulder at the close game. "If you don't want to wake up with ugly stomachaches in the morning, one of you will cook."

"Daddy made dinner already."

Both women looking at Xavier in surprise. "Really? You were both good boys while I was away, then?"

Xavier nodded in response to his mother's question. "I helped clean the fish and everything."

Nikki perked up. "What kind of fish?"

"Stew parrot fish." Victor looked up from his game with an indulgent smile.

It was apparently one of Nikki's favorites. Her pose in the chair became one of contentment instead of exhaustion. "I could eat that," she said.

Sinclair knocked on Hunter's door later in the week with a bottle of wine and a loaf of still-warm bread.

"Hello." Hunter's eyes immediately fell to her guest's impromptu gifts. "I should invite you over more often. Come in. Let me take those." She immediately put her nose to the damp plastic that covered the bread. "Lovely."

Sinclair closed the door behind her and walked into the softly scented house. An oil burner on the living room table was the source of the fragrance. Sage, she identified, following Hunter's almost naked back deeper into the house. The woman wore loose denim cutoffs, paint splattered and ripped, and a white halter top that left her back bare except for a bit of string that dipped across the solid expanse of flesh. Her hair was wrapped in a bright blue cloth and coiled on top of her head like a giant sleeping snake.

"Would you like some of the wine and bread to help you relax?" Hunter waved her toward the sofa. "I'm sure I could find a bit of cheese around here somewhere."

"If you have to scrounge for the cheese, don't worry about it. I don't like my dairy European."

Hunter smirked, then disappeared into the kitchen. She came back with two wineglasses and a plate with cheese already sliced into neat, appetizing rectangles.

"You are a domestic goddess," Sinclair murmured appreciatively, watching her wrestle the cork from the bottle and pour the merlot.

"Only a few of my talents are in the kitchen, my dear," Hunter said, stroking an imaginary mustache.

"That's good to know."

Hunter sank her long fingers deeply into the soft white dough of the bread and ripped it apart. "Et voilà!"

She sat down beside Sinclair and sipped her wine. "Umm. And she has good taste in wine too. I love it."

Is she flirting with me? Sinclair hid her warm cheeks by tearing off her own hunk of bread. "So what are we doing today?"

Hunter finished her mouthful of bread and cheese before she spoke. "Come, I'll show you." She picked up their meal and stood up.

The house was even larger than Sinclair thought. They passed by the familiar kitchen to a small anteroom with walls hidden by empty and half finished canvasses and hanging white cloths splashed with paint. The scent of oil paints and turpentine laced the air. A long cloth-covered couch lay a few feet from the easel, waiting for a body to fill it. Just behind the couch was a large window facing the backyard, allowing a view of at least a quarter acre of land wild with fruit trees and flowers. A hammock lay empty underneath a fiercely blossoming royal poinciana tree. Bright red blossoms from this tree lay scattered on the low, small bladed grass that provided at least twenty feet of good rolling around room.

"How do you ever get any work done here? This place is gorgeous." Sinclair had to take some photographs of the house before she left the island.

"Discipline. The need for a paycheck." Hunter grinned. "Sit. Eat. Think about what position would be most comfortable for you on the couch."

Hunter set up the platter of bread and cheese along with the wine on a small table within reach of the couch. She put her own wine near the palette and sat down on the stool to watch Sinclair, who squirmed under the close scrutiny but tried to sip her wine and pretend nonchalance. It wasn't quite working.

"Should I take my shirt off? What do you want me to do?"

Hunter smiled as she put the wineglass to her lips. "Hm. Those words are music to my ears. Too bad I'm not a pervy sort to take advantage of your willingness to sacrifice your virtue for art."

"Is that how you get women to put out? Ask to paint their portraits, then . . . ?"

"That's only one of my wicked, yet effective ways. You'll have to stick around to find out the rest."

Sinclair shivered in response. Tempting. *She's your sister's girlfriend, dammit!*

Under Hunter's eyes and the influence of the wine, Sinclair relaxed. She leaned back on the couch, stretching her arm above her head. Her sandals hit the floor with the sound of two light slaps and the cotton shirt she wore sighed over her breasts, baring the tiniest hint of cleavage. She closed her eyes, enjoying the early morning heat that slid in through the large window.

"That's perfect." A camera shutter snapped. Once, twice, then again.

"What kind of camera do you have there?"

"A digital Olympus Stylus that I picked up a little while ago." The shutter clicked again. "It works great. Haven't had a single problem with it."

"I'd love to see it later, if you don't mind. I take photographs, too. Of landscapes mostly, no nude girls yet." Sinclair peered at the other woman. "Though from seeing you at work, it's suddenly something worth thinking about."

The corners of Hunter's eyes crinkled in amusement. "Yeah, you can come by and see my camera anytime. And while you're at it, take a closer look at my all-booty-all-the-time lifestyle."

"I hardly think that about the way you live. But I like it. It's peaceful. You're happy. What's not to be envious of?"

"Sinclair, honey, you're only on vacation. This is my *life*." She rested the camera against her thigh. "I'm sure that city-bred girls like you would get bored in this place in no time at all."

"Maybe." She looked up as Hunter adjusted the camera and took another shot of her. The dark woman gave her a stern look and indicated with one finger that Sinclair should turn back around. With a sigh, she turned her face into the back of the couch. The camera clicked again.

"I'm going to start painting now. You can sleep if you want to, just don't move."

"Not a problem." She breathed in the scent of paint and, underneath it, the smoky scent of sage that clung to Hunter. Her mind easily followed the path of the sage, wondering where it clung. Was it all over her skin, laying just on the surface of that bitter chocolate flesh, sinking into her pores and becoming part of the woman that was Hunter? Or was it in her hair, caught in the dark, snaking strands, trapped and unwilling to escape? Sinclair thought about the feel of all that heavy hair against her belly. Or would it be light, resting against her shoulders like a hundred black feathers while Hunter whispered hotly in her ear? Would this same sage-scented hair fly like a wild banner around Hunter's head and back as she moved, teeth bared in passion, above Sinclair? Sinclair's eyes snapped open. But she didn't move. Her body was damp under the cotton dress, ripe as an August mango. Had Hunter noticed?

"If you don't mind me asking," Sinclair murmured over the sound of the brush moving across the canvas. "How do you know that your body wasn't compatible with Lydia's?"

"I don't mind you asking, as long as you don't mind me not telling you."

"Fair enough."

Sinclair closed her eyes again and Hunter's brush continued to stroke the canvas.

"I tried to touch her and she wouldn't let me." Hunter's voice woke her from a light doze. Sinclair opened her eyes but didn't turn. "Whenever that happens with someone you've been dating for almost six months, that's usually a bad sign."

Sinclair blinked through the fog of sleep and adjusted her breathing; made a small noise to let Hunter know that she was listening.

"I've never had a woman back away from me before and mean it. For the past few weeks I've been thinking about that." Sinclair heard her swallow more wine. "Do you think that means anything?"

It was simple curiosity that Sinclair heard in the other woman's voice. No pain, just a desire to know. "I don't have that much experience with women to give you any insight," Sinclair said. "I'm not the best one to ask relationship-related questions."

"You're wrong about that. I think you're the perfect one to ask. If someone reached out to touch you with the intention of making love with you and you backed away from her, what possible emotions or motives could be moving you those few feet backward away from that potential lover?"

Sinclair thought of Yuen and all those times he'd wanted to have sex and she'd found something else to do, something else to occupy his mind. She'd never felt repulsed by the thought of Regina's lovemaking. Even now her skin tingled at the memory of it. There had never been a time when she had shied away from the woman's touch. Well, except for that night at the Burning Rose when Regina was being an asshole.

"Repulsion, right?" Hunter answered her own question. "But why?"

Sinclair breathed softly into the fabric of the couch. "I can't say because I don't know how the two of you fit together."

"We don't seem to." The brush continued to move across the canvas in smooth, languid strokes. "And that's the problem."

They finished the sitting by late evening. Hunter took Sinclair back to her father's house, dropping her off at the gate with a mocking salute. "Thanks for the therapy session, Ms. Sinclair. I hope it was as good for you as it was for me." Then she drove back up to her mountain.

Sinclair watched the Jeep until it disappeared completely out of sight, leaving only a trail of dust and unasked questions. During the sitting with Hunter, her curiosity had been piqued along with her libido. What in all the seven hells could drive Lydia out of that woman's arms? If Hunter had been *her* girlfriend . . . she cut that thought off before it could go any further. Thoughts like that would just lead to another masturbation coma and Sinclair didn't think her fingers were up to the challenge tonight. She sat on a rocking chair on the verandah and dropped her bag tiredly at her feet.

"Rough day?"

She slowly turned her head to watch her father close the front door behind him and claim the other chair. "No. Not really. It was actually pretty good. I went back up with Nikki to the Breckenridges', then I spent most of the day with Hunter Willoughby. She's painting me."

He looked sharply at her. "Be careful."

"Of what?"

"That woman. She's not someone you want to hang around with."

"What does that mean?" Sinclair looked at her father in surprise. "Why don't you like her?"

"It's not that I don't like her. I just don't like her with Lydia or with you. She's a bad influence."

"What do you mean?" Sinclair hoped he didn't say what she thought he was going to say.

"Well, look at her." He made an abrupt gesture into the evening as if Hunter were somewhere out there. "She looks like a half-man, trying to corrupt Lydia. It's not right. *She's* not right."

Sinclair sat up in the rocker and looked sharply at her father. "What if she's not trying to corrupt Lydia?"

"I just don't like her hanging around my daughters. She went off abroad and turned into a dyke. Now she wants to spread that disease to Lydia, maybe even to you, too. I don't want that. The Bible says that's not right and I believe it."

"Are you joking?" Sinclair's sandaled feet slapped against the tiled floor as she abruptly stopped the rocker's motion. "Since when do you believe in anybody's bible? You committed adultery. How come you pick and choose what you believe out of this book? Since when is it OK to hate someone because of what she and another consenting adult do in the privacy of her own home?"

Her father looked at her with dawning suspicion. "Are you one of those . . . lesbians too?"

"What if I said yes, would you kick me out and tell me never to call or write you again?"

He stared at her. "Why didn't you tell me this before?"

"Before what? Before you started making ignorant comments about people you don't even know? Before you started talking crazy that Lydia was being corrupted by Hunter when my sister has probably had more pussy than Magic Johnson?" That was when she knew she'd crossed the line.

Sinclair took a deep breath and slowly released it. *Apologize, dammit!* she chided herself, but the words wouldn't leave her mouth.

"What did you say to me?" Her father stood up. "Don't you even come in here with your American ways trying to tell me about my Jamaican-born and -bred daughter. Don't mess with her good name. I don't appreciate it and I'm damn sure that she doesn't either." He didn't raise his voice once. With a look of sharp disappointment, he turned and walked back into the house.

"Fuck."

Sinclair sank back into the chair. She was suddenly very aware of the darkening sky and the empty noise of crickets just beginning to chirp their evening song. Her grandmother used to caution her all the time about trying to change somebody's mind when it came to such touchy issues as religion, sexuality, politics, or food. Be prepared for a fight, Gram said, and be prepared for failing in the attempt to convert someone to your way of thinking. But she hadn't been trying to convert anyone. There was just no way that she was going to sit there and let him call her diseased or let him talk with impunity about sin when he had fucked around on his first wife. The hypocrite.

But with deepening night came a new attitude. Sinclair left the comfort of her rocking chair to look for her father. She found him in the living room, watching television and drinking carrot juice.

"Hey." She sat beside him on the sofa. He looked at her once then turned back to the television to watch an old *MacGyver* rerun. Sinclair sighed and bit her lip.

"I was out of line earlier. Lydia's business is her own, I had no right to speculate about what or who she does in her spare time."

"You're right about that."

She rolled her eyes. On the screen MacGyver was building

yet another explosive device with chewing gum and duct tape. Her finger itched to turn the damn TV off.

"Papa, look at me."

He turned off the television. After a moment of tense silence he faced her, turning his whole body to give her all his attention. "What?"

This wasn't going well at all. "I'm not going to stay here if you feel that you can't be in the same house with a lesbian. That would only hurt us both and that's the last thing that I want." He opened his mouth to speak, but she held up her hand. "Nikki doesn't have to know why I left. I won't tell her. I can fly back to the city and we don't ever have to speak again."

He made a low noise of dismissal. "None of that is going to happen." With a sigh, he leaned back into the arm of the sofa and rubbed the bridge of his nose. "I know about Lydia. I have since she was in basic school, but it doesn't mean that I like it. Having that girl Hunter here just puts it in my face all the time. It puts it in the neighborhood's face. I'm just afraid that people are going to talk and worse, that they're going to hurt her." He paused and took a breath. "Before I knew about Lydia I used to think that . . . homosexuals were masochists. I mean, why choose a life of hardship and pain? Isn't it enough that black people are treated like slaves still, that this island is poor and in need and is like a sinking ship where the rats are scrambling over each other trying to escape? But I know her and she would never choose something like this. Sometimes I look in her face and I see how unhappy she is. I just want to do whatever I can to make things easier for her."

"Can't you see that hating Hunter and acting like she's the cause of all Lydia's problems is not going to do that?"

"I didn't say the way that I was dealing with this made any sense." He rubbed his nose again. "You want some carrot juice?"

"Uh . . . sure."

When he got up and went to the kitchen Sinclair collapsed against the sofa with a barely audible sigh. The last thing she wanted to do was leave, but if he had insisted, she would have. He came back with a tall glass clinking with ice cubes and juice.

"I made it this afternoon. It's nice and sweet."

"Thank you."

The juice had a crispness that was reminiscent of the outdoors, with its combined flavors of fresh carrots, vanilla, nutmeg, and a creamy sweetness that Sinclair could not name.

"I could teach you to make that if you want."

Sinclair wrinkled her nose and laughed. "You could try, but we'll see if I learn anything."

He turned the television back on and they watched the rest of the show in companionable silence.

Chapter 10

It was late. Even Sinclair's body knew that. She'd been able to get more and more sleep since coming to the island, but that still only meant five hours of sleep each night if she was lucky. Four when she wasn't. Tonight the silence of the room wasn't nearly as comforting as it had been on other nights. Her earlier conversation with Victor still weighed on her mind. Disturbing thoughts of Lydia, Hunter, and of herself plagued her, precluding any possibility of rest. Finally she just couldn't lay in bed anymore. She crept through the house, picked a book from the shelf, and made it to the verandah without waking anybody up. It was nearly three o'clock in the morning.

Sinclair was just getting into the first chapter when she heard the distinctive rumble of Lydia's Cadillac pulling up to the gate. The half moon lit Lydia's way up the gravel path to the textured gray tile of the small square verandah with its ring of lush, flowering plants. Lydia sat in the chair beside Sinclair and took something out of the paper bag she carried. It was grapenut ice cream. With two plastic spoons.

"I knew you'd be awake. Hunter told me you have trouble sleeping at night."

Did she? Sinclair wondered what else she had told Lydia about her.

"It's not really trouble," Sinclair said. "My body doesn't

need that much sleep so I end up staying awake most of the night." She took the spoon that her sister offered and waited while Lydia peeled the protective plastic from the top of the pint of ice cream. "So why are *you* up so late? Or so early?"

Lydia put the plastic wrap on the ground near the container's cover. "Well, I haven't been to bed yet. I spent the last few hours at Hunter's but didn't feel like going home to sleep."

Sinclair couldn't imagine spending an evening with Hunter and having the strength to do anything but sleep afterward.

"We just talked. She and I talk a lot." She dug her spoon into the ice cream, sounding disappointed. "I think that this relationship is going to drive me crazy."

Sinclair nodded although most of her attentions were focused on the dessert melting slowly in her mouth. The ice cream was sinful; a creamy French vanilla with grains of softened grapenuts spread throughout. Sinclair swirled the soft granules over her tongue and thought, reluctantly, of Lydia and Hunter together. She asked the question that Lydia seemed to be waiting for.

"Why?"

"We're just not compatible." Her mouth smiled around the ice cream. "Although I usually like older women, from the beginning there was something about Hunter that really revved my engine." She licked her spoon clean and sat back with a tiny grin. "Her eyes are gorgeous. Have you ever really looked into them? God! There's a whole universe in there." Lydia shook her head. "But we're just not going to work out as a couple."

"Why?" Sinclair asked again, not really caring. She breathed out into the night air again pushing aside her irritation at having lost her night's peace to Lydia's romantic troubles. *Then again,* she said to herself, *the woman did bring ice cream.*

"Because she slept with Della. They used to be girlfriends."
Ah.

"I mean I understand that we live in a very small community. There's bound to be incestuous contact. But that's too much."

"Just who is Della anyway?"

Lydia looked at Sinclair as if she'd forgotten that she was there, or that she had another function besides being the silent witness to her confessions. "She's a big flirt, that's what. And she doesn't mean a damn thing that she says."

What?

"She's also Papa's friend and Nikki's." She tucked a smooth sweep of hair behind her ear and considered the empty spoon in her hand. "She and your mother were lovers for a little while, too."

Sinclair stiffened and stared at her sibling. "How do you know that?"

"Like I said, the lesbian community here is very small." Lydia shrugged and looked at her through a lush forest of eyelashes. Sinclair had the sudden urge to pluck them out one by one. *How do you just drop a thing like that on a person?. . . Later. I'll ask someone else about this later.* She took a calming breath and forced herself to refocus on Lydia's problem.

"I still don't understand this compatibility thing with Hunter. So what if she slept with Della. That just means that she likes all kinds of women."

Lydia made a harsh noise. "I can't touch Hunter. I can't have sex with her, not even close." She stuck her spoon in one corner of the ice cream carton. "Every time we start to do something I tense up. I just can't do it."

Sinclair tapped the spoon against her mouth. "I still don't get it. It's not like she's your mother or even that she slept with your mother."

"It's just Della—she's disgusting. I can't stand to be in the same room with her."

"Did you feel this way after or before you found out that Hunter slept with her?"

"I'm not even sure," Lydia said. "I feel like she preyed on

Hunter's feelings, that she's a viper or some sort of . . . succubus."

That's the stupidest thing I've ever heard. Sinclair said nothing, merely spooned more ice cream into her mouth. It melted over and around her tongue, sweet, rich, and impossibly delicious. "What are you going to do?"

"I don't know." Lydia's voice sounded far away, as if she'd lost her favorite toy and didn't know where to look for it.

Sinclair gently patted her sister's hand and reached for the ice cream.

Chapter 11

Lydia knocked on Sinclair's open door and poked her head into the room. "Hey, Sinclair. Want to go out?" It was after eleven on a Friday night.

"Sure." Nikki and Xavier laid on the cot already half asleep, hypnotized by the dancing blue lights from the TV. Deeper in the house, Victor sat reading an old copy of the British *Financial Times*. Sinclair put her book aside. "Let me change and go tell Papa that we're leaving."

Lydia went into the kitchen to greet her father. "Hey, Papa. What are you reading?"

"An old paper." He put it down. "You girls heading off somewhere?"

"A little party up the hill."

He glanced at Lydia's see-through blouse and slim-fitting black slacks. "Take care of yourself, now. People run crazy this time of night."

Sinclair changed into tight low-rider jeans and a thin white blouse.

"Nice," Lydia said once they were in the car. "The girls are going to be nuts over you."

"I'll settle for them just buying me a drink and leaving the nuts at home."

* * *

The house was hidden in the wilds of the mountain. As Sinclair got out of the car she could hear the quiet rush of a nearby waterfall.

"The place belongs to Phyllis Chambliss and Sabrina something or other," Lydia explained. "They are some rich, rich women who made a lot of money in real estate in America, then came back to Jamaica to settle down and spend it."

At least two dozen cars lined the long, paved driveway, everything from Jaguars to Honda Civics. Sinclair noticed Hunter's blue Jeep parked close to the high, marble archway that served as the entrance to the house. Even out here they could hear the sound of women's laughter entwined with music. High double doors parted under Lydia's hands.

"Lydia." A woman in beige slacks and a matching blouse that gaped over her full breasts greeted them as they walked in. "I'm so glad you could come." She kissed Lydia's cheek. "You look marvelous as usual."

"Thank you, Phyl." Lydia reached a hand back for her sister. "This is Sinclair," she said, "my American sister."

"Pleased to meet you." An expensive, powdery perfume lingered on the woman. She left traces of it on Sinclair's skin when she pulled back from the unexpected hug. "Come in. The party is just getting started."

Despite the obvious wealth of the two women who lived there, the house was relatively modest. The walls were done in soft beiges and browns, not unlike Sinclair's own apartment, but while hers lacked sensuality, this house certainly did not. The velvet tapestries in luscious shades of chocolate and cream begged for a naked back to rub against them. The same could be said for the low suede couches and chairs. The rugs were thick and full, inviting bare toes to curl into them. Arabic music played in the main room, bass-heavy and mellow.

Beautifully designed trays of finger food sat on small tables in every corner. The women lounged about in their soft clothes, lightly touching each other, whispering, laughing, and sharing sips from the same cup. It was like a scene from a seraglio, very stylish and decadent. Sinclair immediately noticed a dark couple sitting under a soft golden light with their fingers linked, their mouths moving to shape words meant only for each other. One woman had long black hair that trailed down to her hips like a silken scarf. In her glittering silk pants and cropped top, she perfectly complemented her partner's plain black dress and closely clipped hair. They were exquisite together.

"Come, let me show you the rest of the place."

Sinclair's gaze left the stunning couple as Lydia gently tugged at her hand, pulling her away. They walked through a long hallway decorated with unusual paintings and pottery and books. Lydia obviously wasn't intent on showing Sinclair any of these things. Her sister pulled her through a door at the end of the hallway and into chaos. Loud, hard-driving dance-hall reggae poured over them. This was where most of the women were. They surged en masse to the music, swaying hips and tossing hair, flailing arms and shaking breasts. Sinclair could feel the music in her chest, feel it reach into her heart and vibrate the organ to its insistent beat. Her hips twitched to the rhythm.

"This is fabulous," Sinclair said over the music.

"What?"

She raised her voice, "I said, this is great."

Lydia shrugged her shoulders. She still didn't hear. Sinclair shook her head. "Never mind."

Although it was mostly dark in the room, the faces of the women were visible in the flashes of color from the strobe lights and the disco ball that shot tiny darts of light all around the room in time with the music. There was every variety of woman here—jet-skinned, gold, red, long-haired, short-, and everything else in between. Sinclair thought she saw Hunter but wasn't sure. The lights shifted again and what she thought was dark, snaking hair solidified into a long fall of midnight weave. Lydia tapped her hand and signaled toward the door. The quiet of the hallway was deafening in its abruptness.

"I bet you have a lot of places like this in America."

"We do, but I've only been to one. And it wasn't quite like this."

"What do you mean? Better?"

"No, just different. There were white women there, for one thing. And it was a public club so there were more people, more chaos, and it smelled like liquor and sweat." She remembered Regina rushing onto the dance floor to join the other gyrating bodies, ignoring her for the anonymity of a group grope.

"I'd love to see that one day," Lydia said, leading Sinclair down the hallway and up a spiral staircase.

Sinclair trailed her fingers along the cool iron banister as she walked up after her sister. Her nose twitched at the scent of fresh lemons. At the top of the stairs they stepped through a half open door then closed it behind them. The lemon scent disappeared. Inside, women lounged about on the floor on soft pillows, talking softly amongst themselves while low jazz music drifted through the room's smoky haze. Some of the women looked up as Lydia and Sinclair walked in.

"Lydia," a woman greeted in a quiet, dreamy voice.

Her sister knelt in the nest of pillows to hug the woman who spoke. "How's it going, Jean?"

"Not bad." The woman ran her thick fingers through Lydia's hair. "Want some ganja?"

"No, thanks. Maybe later on after I finish showing my sister the rest of the house."

Several pairs of eyes touched Sinclair at once. She smiled in greeting.

"You two could be twins," a tiny woman in green said from her bed in another woman's lap. "And what a good time having the two of you would be."

Laughter eddied around the room.

"Don't scare her off," Lydia said. "She's only here for a few more weeks as it is."

"You should come by and see us again."

A chorus of agreement rose up.

"Don't just stand there all stiff, girl," Jean said to Sinclair. "Have a seat." She indicated an empty pillow on the floor nearby.

Sinclair eased down in the silk and suede pillows, willing herself not to shrink back at the predatory looks some of the women gave her, their eyes squinting through the sweet, blue-tinged smoke. Lydia looked comfortable, like she could stay cuddled against Jean's large breasts forever, or at least for the rest of the night.

"You seen Hunter tonight?"

Sinclair looked up at Lydia's question. Most of the women had quietly gone back to smoking their blunts, leaning back to discuss some finer details of esoterica or simply to cuddle against each other and laugh at nothing.

"She's downstairs somewhere."

"With Della."

"Of course."

"They're inseparable," Lydia said to Sinclair, rolling her eyes. In the swirling smoke, her face looked ghostly and unfamiliar.

Did that mean that they were still seeing each other? No. Hunter would never deceive Lydia like that.

"I'm sure they're just hanging out as friends," Sinclair said.

"So what if they are just friends? The whole idea of them—"

Jean touched Lydia's shoulder. "Calm down before you say something mean."

Sinclair was getting bored. She at least needed a drink if she was expected to sit around these listless women and pretend interest in what they were doing. She glanced around the room again. Maybe two drinks. Lydia stirred in her cocoon.

"I better get down there and find her." She kissed Jean on the cheek. "Call me later on in the week. Come, Sinclair. Let's go find the rest of the party."

"Is there a particular crowd you like?" Sinclair asked, noticing the sudden lines of seriousness that settled in her sister's face.

"Not really. I just drift from room to room until I get bored and go home."

Sinclair wondered idly when that time would come. "This space is nice. It's better than a crowded club. At least you know everybody and feel safe here."

"You'd think so, wouldn't you?"

Hunter sat cross-legged on a chair, laughing. Her white teeth flashed in the faint light, leading the eyes to fall naturally on the white T-shirt that hugged the curves of her breasts. A girl couldn't help but look. Sinclair forced herself to notice the other women in the room.

"There's Hunter," Lydia said.

And not far away was Della. The older woman looked ethereal in a pale dress that skimmed her body from throat to ankle. It wasn't until she got closer that Sinclair noticed that the dress was made from several layers of sheer material that gave teasing glimpses of the body underneath. Della stood among a group of animated women, soaking up their energy and throwing hers back into the mix.

"I'm going to talk to her. I'll be right back." Lydia slipped easily through the crowd of women. From halfway across the room, Hunter noticed her. The laughter faded from the dark woman's eyes and the woman who had been entertaining her—a slim little thing with wavy hair cut close to her head—touched Hunter's hand briefly before turning away to talk with someone else. When Lydia reached Hunter's side, the taller woman stood up and led her out of the room. Della waved Sinclair over.

"Hello again," Sinclair greeted.

"Hey, Ms. America. Where did those two go?"

"Off somewhere talking, I suppose."

"Trouble in paradise?" Della chuckled.

"Who knows? They could be getting married for all I know." She didn't feel right talking to Della about her sister's business.

"Really? That would be different." She turned to her friends. "I'm being rude. Sinclair, this is everyone. Everyone, this is Lydia's sister, Sinclair." No one looked impressed. "She's Beverly's daughter."

The women looked at her with sudden interest, peering closely at the features Sinclair shared with the Beverly Sinclair they had known.

"The cheekbones are the same," the woman standing next to Della said.

"And her mouth too," another chimed.

"How would you remember what her mouth looked like?"

"Believe me," the woman laughed. "I would know."

They all cackled like witches around a particularly steamy cauldron, leaving Sinclair just a little disconcerted. She hadn't thought about her looks one way or another. In pictures that her grandmother left behind in the apartment, three faces—Gram's, Mama's, and hers—beamed from behind an old-fashioned glass frame. They were each versions of the other, matron, mother, and baby. That had given her some measure of comfort. Her mother had been beautiful, so was she. Her grandmother was graceful in her winter years, still lovely with her thick white hair and most of her own teeth. And later on, so would Sinclair. Now here were these women suggesting that she had more in common with her mother than just looks.

"Stop it," Della softly chided her friends. "Come on, Sinclair. Let's go find you something to drink around here."

Della showed her where they kept the rum punch. This time Sinclair was determined to have no more than one glass. She wanted to be able to walk out of this house under her own power.

"It looks like you're adjusting just fine to island life," Della said with a smile. "It's not too boring for you, I hope."

"Far from it, actually. Between my family and Hunter and the gorgeous landscape I'm plenty entertained."

"So you've discovered Hunter's charm too."

"It's hard not to. She's a very nice woman."

"That's all she is, huh?"

"You should know better than I would."

"Touché." Della raised her glass of rum to Sinclair.

Sinclair realized then that the older woman still loved Hunter. Or at least still wanted her as more than a friend.

"I hope those two aren't going to be gone long. I don't want to spend all night here."

"There would be worse places to spend the night, I'll tell you that much." Della swept her gaze around the house, at the pleasantly inebriated women and the abundance of liquor and music.

"I agree. Still, I'd like to sleep in my family's house tonight." Sinclair sipped her punch and looked over the crowd of women for the sight of either Hunter or her sister.

"While they're talking, let's go dance," Della said. "Come on."

Sinclair finished the rest of her rum punch before putting her glass down and following Della out the door. They spent a good portion of the night on the dance floor, finally emerging sweaty and laughing close to four thirty in the morning. They collapsed on an oversized scented sofa in the midst of three other equally sweaty women.

"Although I usually don't dance, that was great," Sinclair said breathlessly. "Thank you."

"You're welcome. Anytime I could do something for Beverly's little girl, it would be my pleasure."

Sinclair fanned herself with a bundle of napkins. "Why?"

"Why would it be a pleasure?" The sweat of the dance seemed to have relaxed Della's inhibitions, made her tongue and body loose. "Because she was a good woman. I respected her. She was my friend."

"Someone said that you might have been lovers."

"We were."

Sinclair stared at her.

"Why are you surprised? You were confident enough to ask me." Della leaned back into the sofa, watching Sinclair with her dark eyes.

"I—I guess I just never thought that my mother—"

"They say that this sort of thing is in the blood. At least my son is in England where he can be himself." At the look on Sinclair's face she laughed. "Of course I have a son. Just like your mother had a daughter."

"But you're nothing like my mother."

"You never knew your mother, little girl. I knew her inside and out." Della's mouth twitched. "Better than anyone she'd been with before or after me."

OK, that was a little too much information. Still, Sinclair wanted more.

"When were you two together?" she asked.

"The right question is when were we *not* together." Della leaned back in the sofa. "She was my next door neighbor grow-ing up. I was her first lover and her last. Despite the others, she always came back to me. And I to her." Her eyes fell closed as she sighed then became still.

Della didn't speak again. She dropped into a light dose, de-spite the shifting women on the sofa and the hurricane of conversation coming from every corner of the room. Sinclair watched her, at once frustrated and sympathetic. Did Della hate Victor for being the last person Beverly shared her life with? Sinclair knew that if she had been in Della's place she would have hated both Victor and Beverly for denying her the comfort and happiness of setting up house with the woman she loved.

"There you are." Sinclair turned to see Lydia walking toward her. "I've been looking all over the place for you." Her sister glanced down at the snoozing Della then suddenly seemed wounded, as if she'd gone into battle and lost. "Are you ready?"

"Sure," Sinclair said. "Whenever you are."

Sinclair leaned close to Della and whispered a quick goodbye, then she and Lydia left the party without another word to anyone, cutting through the throng of dancing and meandering women as if they had somewhere to go, urgently. Sinclair didn't bother to ask her sister about Hunter.

Chapter 12

"Wake up, sleepy," Nikki's voice trilled from just beyond the bedroom door. Sinclair rolled over and opened her eyes very slowly. Though she hadn't had nearly as much rum punch as she'd wanted to, the little she'd had made her sluggish. And her body ached. The muscles of her belly, thighs, and legs hurt. Even the bottoms of her feet were sore.

"I'm up," she croaked.

"We're all heading to the beach today. Come in for breakfast, then get ready to go."

"Now?"

"In a couple of hours."

"Umm . . . I'll skip breakfast. Just wake me right before it's time to go."

"All right." Nikki's laughing voice drifted away from the door.

No more rum punch, Sinclair vowed as she burrowed back into the sheets and promptly fell back asleep.

High noon found Sinclair still half-conscious but spread out on a beach towel next to her father's coconut-branch lean-to. After a soak in the warm seawater and a surprisingly skillful massage from Nikki, her body wasn't nearly as sore as it had been in the morning. From under her beach umbrella, she watched Xavier and Nikki running and playing on the long stretch of sand. Her stepmother looked barely older than a child herself in the cutoff overalls and baggy T-shirt that hid the curves of her body. Nikki's hair, pulled up into two Afro puffs above her ears, fluttered in the breeze as she ran after her son.

"Hey, everybody!" Sinclair looked up to see her sister walking toward the lean-to where Victor sat.

"We were worried that you wouldn't come," their father said. "After I saw the condition that you left Sinclair in last night we were sure that you looked just as bad."

"What are you talking about?" She dropped to her knees in the sand and kissed Victor on the cheek. "Sinclair looks great and I feel even better."

Lydia was lying about how she felt. Did that mean Sinclair looked liked hell, too? "Don't do me any favors, Lydia," Sinclair muttered from her blanket.

"Hey, Xavie and Nik." Lydia waved at the two shapes dashing over the sand like seagulls, flapping their arms and carrying on like theirs was the only family on the beach. Others were far enough away that, hopefully, they could only hear faint echoes of the two's birdlike shrieks.

Lydia kicked off her shoes and spread out her own blanket near Victor's. With a quick, graceful movement, she slid off her white shorts, leaving her dark amber body covered in a tiny bikini. Lydia stuck her tongue out at Sinclair then lay back on the blanket.

"Are you doing all right over there?" Sinclair asked.

"I'm OK. When I got home last night I fell straight to sleep. I barely had time to take my clothes off and brush my teeth."

"Lucky you."

Sinclair wished that she'd had that easy a time of it. After getting back home a little after five, she'd been too keyed up to rest. Between her aching body and her hyperactive brain, she hadn't been able to fall asleep until the sun was full in the sky, and that was barely an hour before Nikki knocked at the door telling her it was time to get up. After packing up her beach gear, struggling to the bright yellow Honda that her father had once again borrowed for their outing, then struggling back out of the car to set up the lean-to and supplies once they got to the beach, Sinclair was exhausted.

"Do you need any help, Papa?" Lydia asked.

"No, not yet. If you want, you can help Nikki and Xavier get the wood for the fire." He looked down the beach. It was obvious his wife and son were doing more playing than gathering, but he settled back in his chair with a laugh. "By dinnertime we should have a fire going." His eyes settled on Sinclair for a moment, on her bleary eyes and sluggish movements.

"What can I do to help?" she asked, hoping he'd say "nothing."

"Can you gut and clean fish?"

Later on Sinclair found out that her father was joking, but she *did* have to wrap several cold, fishy bodies in foil to get them ready for the fire. Xavier laughed at her as he carried his unwrapped fish, held close to his chest like a baby, toward the large blaze that their father had started.

"Don't do that, Xavier," Nikki cautioned. "You're getting your fish dirty." He pouted but brought the fish back so that his mother could season it with lime juice, salt, butter, and pepper, then wrap it in foil. She put it on the fire for him.

Sinclair stood up. As she walked to the water's edge to wash the stink of raw fish from her hands, the sound of her family's conversation and laughter faded into the background. Her eyes narrowed on the horizon to see the sun falling slowly behind a sprinkling of clouds. Brilliant shades of burnt orange, red, and gold colored the beach and the water tumbling up to the sand in a joyous symphony of gurgles and whispers. She crouched and washed her hands in the playful waves.

"Wipe your hands with this." Nikki came up from behind to offer her a towel, damp with lime juice and water.

"Thanks." Sinclair wiped her hands then gave the folded towel back to her. They walked back to join the rest of the family.

"How are things going with the picture Hunter is doing of you?" Nikki asked.

"It's going well. At least, I think so." They shared the over-sized blanket near the lean-to, sinking into the soft cotton with twin sighs. Nearby Victor hovered closer to the fire, checking on the food and talking with Lydia. Xavier stood beside them, poking the flames with a long stick. "I haven't seen it yet, but she says that she'll have it done long before I leave."

"That's good because I want to see it." Nikki stretched out on the blanket, pillowing her head on folded arms. "Nobody ever did a picture of me."

"If you want her to paint you I'm sure she wouldn't have a problem. Just ask."

"You didn't have to ask."

Sinclair smiled thinking of the day Hunter had asked to paint her. "True."

"She must like you a lot."

Does she? "Sometimes I wonder if it's just for my resemblance to Lydia that makes her interested in me." Sinclair's mouth twisted at the thought.

"No, no." Nikki rolled over and touched her arm. "I'm sure that's not it."

"It's OK if that's the reason. After all, she and I are just friends. We get along fine and she's a nice woman. I traded some good wine for her painting my boring picture."

"Boring?" She released a snort of laughter. "I don't think so."

"We'll see."

They sat in silence listening to the soft voices of Lydia and Victor a few feet away. The evening was quieter now, with only the call of seabirds, the whisper of seawater spilling on the sand, and the occasional shout of laughter, to disturb its peace.

"Do you live alone in America?" Nikki asked suddenly.

Sinclair sighed at the remembered sense of peace that being in the apartment alone gave her. "Yes."

"You weren't scared about being alone like that?"

Sinclair shook her head. "I like being alone. The quiet is nice."

"Victor says that, too, about the way it was before I came to live with him, but it's hard to believe that people actually like to be alone." She glanced quickly at her husband, then away. "When you're alone it's too easy to be lonely."

"Not really. It's easier than being alone in a group of people. I enjoy my alone time, especially now that I'm here."

"But what about America?" She propped her chin up on a fist and fixed her rapt gaze on Sinclair.

"It's OK. I have a lot of advantages being there, but I wouldn't say that it's better than being on the island." Sinclair didn't want to tell her how it had *really* been, especially after Gram died—the sense of isolation, of not belonging, and always feeling like she'd been missing something. "It's beautiful here. The sort of place where I could be happy living."

"I thought you'd be bored here. No theaters, no sushi."

"I don't eat sushi."

Nikki laughed. "The television was wrong about that, too. I thought every modern American woman loves sushi."

"Some do, but not this one. I prefer my fish well cooked." Sinclair grinned. "But I do like sake though."

"What's that?"

As Sinclair explained the pleasures of Japanese rice wine to her stepmother, Victor, Xavier, and Lydia finished cooking their dinner and took it off the fire.

"Food's ready!"

The family sat under the large lean-to sharing the fragrant

meal of roasted corn, fish, and ripe breadfruit, their fingers scooping up the hot, roasted food to appreciative mouths. The sun's glow slowly disappeared, allowing a blanket of stars to spread out above them. Lydia, Nikki, and Sinclair sat together, eating and talking about American men and what they found acceptable in their women. Victor sat with Xavier on his knee and watched the women, his eyes straying occasionally to the stars.

"Where's Hunter tonight, Lydia?"

Sinclair glanced quickly at their father, wondering what he knew about Hunter and Lydia's current situation.

"Probably at home. I thought this was a family thing so I didn't invite her."

Even Xavier could tell that she was lying. "She been to other things before," he said.

Lydia shot him a look of annoyance, but said nothing.

"Is everything all right with her?" Nikki asked with concern.

"Everything is fine. Really. She just has a lot of work to do and I needed some time with my family."

Victor and Nikki exchanged a look. Sinclair bit into her corn and focused her attentions on her sand-flecked toe. Lydia's pain was so raw and obvious that she couldn't bring herself to look at it.

Chapter 13

Sinclair stood on Hunter's steps with an umbrella protecting her hair from the rain. The wind whipped fiercely around her, tugging at her clothes and flinging raindrops all over her. After the cookout on the beach she'd found herself thinking of Hunter more and more, wondering if she and Lydia were still together, and if not then.... Sinclair had managed to wait as long as Wednesday, three days after the cookout, to go find Hunter. Her belly trembled with nervousness as she knocked on the door.

"I came by to see how the painting was going," she said when Hunter answered her knock.

She smiled tiredly. "It's almost done, but you can't see it. I'm working on other not-so-fun stuff right now."

"Spoilsport." Sinclair made a face. "Can I at least come in?"

"Absolutely." The other woman's eyes slid over her. "You're always welcome here." She leaned against the doorjamb and her smile widened. The exhaustion slowly bled from her face. "It really is good to see you."

"Really? Then why won't you let me in?"

Hunter laughed. "Because I like to see you getting wet?"

"Very funny." Sinclair tucked her umbrella into a corner of the verandah, then sidled closer to the doorway. Hunter didn't move. If possible, the rain started coming down harder.

Lightning split the darkened sky and a roar of thunder quickly followed. Hunter stepped out of the doorway toward Sinclair. "Come on. Let's try something."

"What?" Sinclair looked at her with suspicion and took a step back. "Are you talking about getting me killed?"

"Come, fraidy cat." She tugged at her fingers. Like a fool, Sinclair went with her.

Without her umbrella the rain was cold and wet, sliding into her hair and under her shirt with chilled fingers. "Oh! This is *not* fun."

"Yes, it is." Hunter grabbed her hand and pulled her to the backyard. The stone bench looked like a fountain with sheets of water pouring from it, flooding the grass and covering Sinclair's toes. She kicked off her waterlogged sandals.

Hunter released her hand. "Isn't this nice?" She twirled in the downpour, flinging her arms wide and laughing. Her hair flared out around her and rain fell into her open mouth and down her neck. A reluctant smile touched Sinclair's mouth. The other woman's excitement was contagious, bubbling up a fever of appreciation inside of her. The rain no longer felt cold, it was clean, with the heaviness of a friendly touch or a lover's worshipful kiss. The leaves whispered under the rain's caresses, talking to each other, celebrating. She felt a pull at her shirt and refocused on the other woman.

"Let's get naked in it," Hunter said. She might as well have been naked already in the white T-shirt and pale blue pajama bottoms that clung to her wet skin.

"What?!"

"It'll be great. One with nature and all that."

"It's storming, you crazy woman!"

"I know! So let's get naked." Her fingers pulled at Sinclair's shirt again, loosening a button.

"No." She backed away a step, then another as the other woman came after her.

"Don't run," Hunter growled.

Of course Sinclair ran. She ran screaming around the yard,

dodging the stone bench to run deeper into the wooded area, jumping over high, twisting roots and tall shrubbery. The rain stung her eyes, but still she ran. Hunter was a blur of white and dark behind her, then right at her heel. She squeaked, an embarrassingly girlish sound, when the other woman's hand latched onto hers, and brought her up short. Still she tried to pull away, darting around a tree and using the wide trunk to force Hunter into releasing her. The rough bark abraded Hunter's arm and she let go with a loud curse. Sinclair ran back to the grassy area of the yard, past the bench, her toes squishing in the wet grass, when Hunter grabbed her. They both heard the shirt rip. Sinclair swung around. Damn! The back door had been so close. . . .

Hunter's face became hard under the rain, focused. Sinclair looked down at herself, then blushed. She gathered the torn ends of her shirt together and backed away.

"Shit. I'm sorry." Hunter shook the hair out of her face. "I tend to get a little carried away."

"It's—" Sinclair cleared her froggy throat. "It's fine." The rain and wind continued to howl around them as they stared at each other.

Hunter arched her head back, apparently still feeling the wildness of the storm rush through her.

"Go ahead," Sinclair said. "I'll be in the house." She slid into the back door, then dashed to the bathroom, trailing wetness behind her. Her nipples were hard, shamelessly begging through the wet material to be touched. And Hunter had seen. Sinclair toweled herself dry after dropping the shirt and jeans in the tub. Her hair she squeezed dry and quickly combed into two short French braids. A knock came at the door.

"I brought you some dry clothes." Hunter's hand appeared through a crack in the door. As soon as Sinclair took the oversized shirt and cutoff shorts, the hand disappeared.

Only after she was dressed and composed, did Sinclair leave the bathroom. Hunter must have thought she fell in or something. But the other woman was patiently waiting in the sitting room, dry in a sky blue head wrap that completely covered her hair and yet another pair of cutoff jeans and a T-shirt. She had tea waiting, two cups of hot peppermint along with biscuits on a shared plate.

"Sorry again about your shirt. I didn't mean to get quite so out of hand." Her speech hardened into precise British syllables. `

"There's no need to apologize. I got taken in by the storm, too." The drum of rain on the roof and the shudder of the trees just outside reminded them that the storm was still there. "You'll just have to buy me a new shirt and we'll call it even."

Hunter smiled, then opened her mouth. She closed it again.

"What?" Sinclair asked.

"Nothing. I was about to speak out of turn then I caught myself. Don't worry about it." She waved a dismissive hand.

Sinclair wanted to know. Somehow she felt that it was important. "What were you going to say?" she asked softly.

"That you look good in my clothes." Hunter sprawled back in the chair. That wasn't all she had to say. "And I'd like to have been the direct cause of you getting wet, the reason for you to take off your underwear."

Sinclair felt herself swell against the seam of Hunter's shorts.

"Are you wearing panties now?"

"You're right." Sinclair took a deep breath. "You *were* about to speak out of turn."

Hunter laughed. "Chicken."

"No, just cautious. You are my sister's girlfriend, after all." Sinclair took a sip of her tea.

"I was." Hunter dipped a digestive biscuit into the cup of steaming brew. "Now I'm just me."

Sinclair almost choked on her tea. Abruptly, her world shifted and resettled itself into a different arrangement. Hunter was available. Sinclair no longer had an excuse not to pursue her. Sinclair swallowed twice then carefully put the cup down. "I see."

"Do you?"

The china made a soft noise as cup met saucer. Hunter pursed her lips and watched Sinclair. Her eyes were warm with humor and something else.

Sinclair held out her hands like she was warding the other woman off. "I'm not up to playing with the big girls."

Hunter continued to watch her. "Is this cautious attitude because of the girl who fucked you in the big city? The one you're running away from?"

"Fucked me, huh?" Sinclair's mouth curved into an unexpected smile. "You have no idea." Then she sobered again as Hunter's look became predatory, sharpening and focusing intently on her.

"Does that mean she was good in bed?"

"Very. She introduced me to multiple orgasms."

Hunter's legs widened in the chair. She leaned forward and braced her elbows on her thighs. "Big shoes to fill, indeed."

Sinclair laughed out loud. "You are so full of yourself."

"No. I just want you."

And there it was. Out in the open at last. A trembling breath left Sinclair's mouth.

"When you and this girl first got together, did you make the first move or did she?" Hunter asked.

Sinclair wondered where Hunter was going with this. "She did."

"Is that typical of you, or—" she smiled, "if you want something badly enough do you just take it?"

Against her will, Sinclair glanced down at the wide V of Hunter's thighs and imagined the scent and taste that lay there.

"So, do you?" Hunter's eyes dared her.

But, like Hunter said, Sinclair was a fraidy cat. She looked away to the rain-swept verandah and the plants that whipped like dervishes in the mad wind.

"I guess not." Hunter stood. "Do you want some more tea?"

"Uh, sure," Sinclair stammered and watched confused as the other woman disappeared into the kitchen, then came back with a porcelain kettle. She poured herself another cup and topped off Sinclair's before sitting once again in her chair.

"Listen." But Sinclair stopped, sighed, and could not go on.

"I am listening."

Sinclair sighed again. "Regina really hurt me. I'm not up to playing any more games."

"Games are for children. I'd like to think that we've both passed that stage. You have a few weeks left here." Hunter's voice deepened. "I know that you're attracted to me and I certainly, absolutely, am attracted to you. I also know that my previous involvement with Lydia makes things . . . problematic." She chuckled ruefully. "But let's not dwell on the past, instead we should spend some time together. I could be your perfect vacation fuck."

A blush warmed Sinclair's face. But that was nothing compared to the heat that flared between her thighs at Hunter's words. "Let me think about it," she said.

"Fair enough." The seducer abruptly retreated as Hunter stood up. "Would you like a formal tour of the house?"

Chapter 14

Would sleeping with Hunter really be that bad? Sinclair walked down the road from the Breckenridges' house, plucking at the wild reeds growing from the roadside as she went. Her footsteps took her on the path to Hunter's house. Whether her mind was ready, her body was fully prepared to answer the question she'd just asked herself.

"Hey, there."

Sinclair jumped at the unexpected voice, then turned to see Della walking toward her. The woman looked fit in loose capri jeans and a salmon colored T-shirt tucked into its belted waistband. She carried a bunch of wildflowers in her hand. "Where are you heading?"

"Nowhere. I'm just killing time while Nikki is at work."

"Good. Then you can come with me."

"Where?"

"To see your mother." Della held up the flowers. "I'm going to take her some garden-grown sunshine." The older woman took Sinclair's hand. "Come on."

A controlled wilderness reigned in the cemetery. Beyond the tall, iron gates of Hilltop View Rest Home, vines tumbled from thick overhanging trees to trail the ground like green lace. Each tombstone lay distinct and well tended in the marble and granite jungle, protected by the trees except for where sunlight slid between the gaps in the natural canopy to light the names on the tombstones. Samuels. Belvedere. Chin. Sinclair.

The ground was soft near Beverly Sinclair, the grass, green and prickly against Sinclair's palms as she sat down next to Della. The older woman tucked her flowers into a vase built into the base of the headstone and arranged them neatly against the gray marble.

"The people here take real good care of the grounds. When they first put her here I was worried. But I'm glad all that was for nothing."

The grave was a narrow marble bed raised a half a foot off the ground, dark gray and new looking. Patches of tiny, crimson tea roses grew around her grave, as if someone had taken the trouble to plant them just so, then tend them year after year. Their bright heads lay in beautiful disarray against the marble.

"Hey, Bev. I brought your baby to see you." Della touched the grave as if it could feel. She turned to look at Sinclair. "I know that she's not really here, but I like having someplace where I can come and feel her presence."

Sinclair nodded. The lines marking her mother's name on the marble slab were still deep. Her fingers traced them. BEVERLY SINCLAIR. BELOVED. 1948-1985.

"Why did you bring me here?"

"Because, if memory serves, they never allowed you to go to her funeral. You've never been up here."

No, Sinclair had never been to see her mother's grave. Too many of her nights had been spent wondering why she hadn't been with Beverly Sinclair that afternoon twenty years ago when she'd gone out to buy groceries on the town bus and ended up at the bottom of the gorge under two tons of twisted metal and steel. Her thirteen-year-old mind had been unable to grasp her mother's death for what it was. Sinclair remembered being told of her mother's absence, then asking who would iron her clothes for school the next morning.

When her grandmother came to take her back to America less than a month later, she was still wondering where her mama was.

In the twenty years of living in America she'd healed from the violence of her mother's death, taken Beverly Sinclair's last name as her own—with her grandmother's blessing—and even fit reasonably well into society. The memories of her mother, of her comforting Soft Sheen and baby powder scent, the warmth of her hand in Sinclair's, even the remembered taste of the hot chocolate she made in the mornings, were all Sinclair had needed. And now here was Della and the whispered hints of what Beverly Sinclair had really been like. She traced her mother's name again then silently turned away from the headstone. After all these years, did any of it really matter? Sinclair got up and walked a few feet away to lay in the grass, watching the powdery clouds shift above her. Nearby, Della whispered something to her dead lover, leaning closer to the deaf tombstone as the first trickles of raindrops began to fall.

Chapter 15

Sinclair heard Hunter's voice in her father's house. It wasn't whispering the usual litany of sweet nothings, so she figured it must not be a dream. With her robe belted tightly around her waist, she walked into the living room.

"Hey," Hunter greeted her with a cheeky grin. "Just woke up?"

"Something like that." She wasn't about to confess that she'd spent a restless night thinking about her and all that she'd offered a few days ago.

"Either you were asleep or you weren't, so which was it?" She tugged on Sinclair's robe. "Oops." The bit of espresso brown silk had never revealed that much before.

"I guess you sleep naked, huh?"

Sinclair smacked the other woman's hand and stepped away. "Stop behaving like a twelve-year-old boy."

"I can't help it. You bring out the hormones in me." Her crooked grin made Sinclair laugh.

"Fine." She sat on the far end of the sofa away from Hunter. "What are you doing here, anyway?"

"Just dropping some pottery off from Della." She pointed to a pile of brown wrapping and Styrofoam. For the first time, Sinclair heard the noises in the back room. Evidence of Nikki being up and already catering to Hunter's needs.

"She couldn't come herself?"

"She could, but I offered." Her white teeth flashed. "So what are your plans for the day?"

"Why do you want to know?"

"Why don't you want to answer?"

"You're incorrigible."

"So I've been told. What are your plans?"

Sinclair shook her head and gave in. "Nothing much. It's Nikki's day off so I was just going to hang out with her for the day and then walk with her to pick up Xavier from school."

"Sounds fun."

Nikki walked into the room. She looked much more presentable than Sinclair did in her oversized shorts and T-shirt.

"Can I steal Sinclair for a bit, Nikki? Her day with you sounds deadly dull and you know how city girls like to have nonstop fun on their vacations." Hunter winked at the young woman.

Nikki giggled. "Take her. She's been in the house too much as it is." She stooped to pick up the discarded paper and Styrofoam.

"What if I don't want to go?" Sinclair looked from one to the other with disbelief.

"Sure you do." Hunter leaned back in the couch and propped her foot up on one knee. "Go ahead and shower if you want to. I'll wait."

Nikki left with an armload of packing material, still giggling.

"You'll be waiting a hell of a long time. I told you that I'm not going anywhere with you."

"Come on. It'll be fun. You can even bring your camera. And your bathing suit."

A bathing suit? The thought of spending time with Hunter dressed in only her bikini sent shivers of apprehension through her body. Still, her body *wanted* to shiver for Hunter, wanted to shudder and call her name and twine its legs around the dark woman.

"Fine. Give me fifteen minutes."

It was half an hour before they left. Sinclair couldn't decide what to wear or how to fix her hair. In the end it was a loose cotton dress with her one-piece bathing suit under it. Her hair she first combed loose, then ended up tying back up with a light blue scarf.

"You look nice."

"Thank you," she said graciously. "Nikki, we're leaving."

Faint noises of good-bye floated to them from the kitchen.

"I guess we're off, then."

The Jeep was noisier than it looked even though Hunter had put the doors back on, in deference, she said, to Sinclair's city sensibilities. Sinclair wanted to push her out of the truck. Though as they sped over the winding paved roads into the hills, she was grateful for the doors. She clutched onto the Jeep's sturdy frame, praying not to be lurched out the window during one of Hunter's quick turns.

"I don't suppose you could slow down?" Sinclair shouted over the wind.

"Sure." Hunter shouted back. "But only under penalty of being considered an irredeemable fraidy cat."

"Meow."

The Jeep slowed down a little.

"Are you going to tell me where we're going now?"

"Sure. Why not?" Hunter looked over at her, eyes sparkling with mischief and fun. "We're heading to the falls. It's quiet and private. I heard you haven't been out much since you've been here, so I'm making it my duty to make sure that you reacquaint yourself with the real Jamaica before you go."

"Are you part of this experience?"

"Of course. Although to hear Lydia tell it, I'm not authentically Jamaican enough. Hopefully you're not that picky."

"I *am* very picky, thank you very much. But—" Sinclair's gaze flickered over the other woman's body. "You'll do."

*　　*　　*

The Jeep stopped under a canopy of trees. Sunlight filtered through the wide maze of banyans, but only in jewel-like flickers that enhanced the beauty of the trees without compromising any of their shade. Nearby a waterfall roared, full throated and loud. "Here we are."

Hunter pulled a picnic basket and blanket from the back of the Jeep. "Come on. We're going just down here."

Sinclair followed carrying her own light bag. The place was indeed deserted, clean with the smell of highly oxygenated water and freshly turned earth. At the falls, white water spilled down moss-covered rocks in an explosion of sound before diving through masses of hanging vines and plants to plunge into the deep pool below. Lily pads floated on the water's surface.

Sinclair looked at her guide in surprise. "Thank you. This is . . ." Her voice faded away.

"Just enjoy it. That would be thanks enough." Hunter set up the picnic basket and blankets on one of the high, smooth boulders that surrounded the water.

Sinclair put her bag behind her on the driest rocks and took out her camera. Through the lens she noticed new things, the subtle splash of color around them, shy hibiscus that lurked behind large fronds of deep green plants, orange and yellow lantanas with their tiny bouquets offered up as gifts to anyone who cared to pluck them, and Hunter stripping out of her cutoffs and T-shirt. The shutter clicked.

"Are you going to come here and enjoy me, or just take pictures all day?" Hunter was already stripped down to her bone white bikini that showed off her muscled body and the black diamond shade of her skin. Her loosened hair rode the curves of her shoulders and back. Sinclair couldn't help but notice that her breasts filled out the bathing suit rather nicely.

"Is that a rhetorical question?" Sinclair put her camera away and walked over to where the other woman had laid out the food and wine. "This is quite a spread."

"I'm trying to impress you, remember?" Hunter reached

up and tugged on Sinclair's hand. "Let's talk later. Come into the water with me."

"Wait! Let me take off my dress." She pulled the white cotton quickly over her head and dropped it on the blanket before jumping into the water. Her skin goose pimpled from the sudden coolness. She allowed herself to fall deeper into the pool, past the wavering weeds, and small orange fish that scattered at her sudden presence. The pool's depth was only about fifteen feet. Sinclair pushed herself off the ground back up to the surface, past Hunter's paddling legs and to the other side of the pool that was frothy with the fall of water from the rocks above. A fine spray misted the air around them.

"You have a beautiful body, Sinclair." Hunter swam close, her hair loose and floating behind her like trails of black ink in the water. "I hope you aren't trying to hide it from me."

"You found me out." Sinclair ducked away from the other woman, dipping back beneath the water's surface to swim to the other side. She knew that she was thin. Much thinner than the lush body Lydia showed off in her delectable frocks and culottes. Even though Hunter had never seen those riches of Lydia's bared, how could she not compare even that hinted abundance to Sinclair's too-thin body?

Hunter's arms circled her under the water. Without even trying she hauled Sinclair up with her. Water sluiced from their faces and shoulders. Below the surface, their legs briefly entwined and their thighs slid closer. Sinclair resisted the urge to swim backward and surge away from her like a frightened fish.

"We're here to have fun, to relax." Her hands spanned Sinclair's waist. "Nothing's going to happen here that you'll regret later. I promise."

Sinclair relaxed for the first time all day. She felt like a fool, like a child unable to govern her body's own responses. But she also felt relief and a heady sense of freedom. At her smile, Hunter groaned. "I think I'm going to regret saying that."

Sinclair swam off toward their blanket, laughing.

After they ate and finished half the bottle of wine, Hunter drowsed in the sun like a big sleepy cat, spread out on the blanket in the white bikini that barely covered any of her skin. The sun and sunscreen made her glisten, irresistible to Sinclair's eyes. Her palms itched to touch that wonderful skin, to know if it was as soft in reality as in her suddenly out-of-control imagination. Hunter shifted next to her and rolled over to her stomach, cradling her cheek on crossed arms. Sinclair could feel her stare under the protection of the mirrored sunglasses. The muscles in Hunter's back rearranged themselves as she watched, curling under her skin like lazy eels. The dark woman took off her shades and dropped them on the blanket. Sinclair resisted the urge to pluck the edge of Hunter's hide-and-seek bikini out of her backside. Instead she leaned over to briefly kiss her mouth before she could lose her courage.

"Thank you for bringing me out here. I know you didn't have to."

"Of course I had to. It's part of my diabolical plan to get you into bed."

Sinclair's eyebrow rose. "You're very direct, aren't you?"

"That's the only way to get what you want most times." Her eyes dropped to the slight swell of Sinclair's breasts under her bathing suit. "Don't you agree?"

Instead of answering, Sinclair took up her camera and stood to go looking for more beautiful things to capture on film. Hunter tugged her back down. "OK, I'm sorry. I don't mean to be a pain in the ass, really." At Sinclair's look of disbelief she laughed. "Show me your camera. What does this thing do?"

After a suspicious look at Hunter, Sinclair cradled the

camera in her lap and gently turned it over. "That's the manual film advance and rewind crank."

"Are you joking?" When Sinclair rolled her eyes and shook her head all in one go, Hunter picked up the camera and pointed to a dial at the front of it. "How about this?"

"That allows you to control the shutter speed. It works with the lens aperture to control the brightness of the picture."

"This all seems needlessly complicated. Why go through all this when you can just get a digital camera, take the photo, hook it up to your computer, then print it out?" She looked so genuinely confused that Sinclair had to laugh.

"For me it's about the process. I like taking photos. I also like going in the darkroom and developing them by hand. It's therapeutic."

"I knew you were a weirdo the second I laid eyes on you."

"Very funny. Give me my camera back."

"I was just joking, touchy girl." Hunter handed over the camera with exaggerated care.

"This camera has gotten me through some rough times. I didn't pick it up again until recently."

Hunter's eyes were soft on her. "Are you still having rough times?"

"No." Sinclair murmured, watching the face before her transform with a smile. "Not so much now."

After her food settled in her belly Sinclair went for a swim. She floated beneath the surface of the fertile pond, watching the cascades of water from the fall but not being able to hear them. The water rippled like silk above her. Through it she could see Hunter, her long, graceful body spread out on the rock, steaming in the sun. She was so beautiful. Sinclair watched her until her oxygen-starved lungs forced her up for air. As she broke the surface, her insecurities came rushing back. She pushed a hand through her dripping hair, sure that it was sitting on her forehead in unattractive clumps.

"One day I'm just going to cut this all off," she said out loud.

"Don't do that." Hunter rolled over on the blanket to watch her swim toward the pond's edge and pull herself out of the water.

"Do you have any suggestions for what I can do to this hair besides more of the usual?"

"Quit your whining. Let me braid it for you."

"You? Braid hair?" Sinclair dried herself with a towel, paying particular attention to her woolly hair.

"Don't look so shocked. I'm good for more than a few spectacular rounds in the sack, you know."

Sinclair choked on her laughter. "No, I didn't know."

"So what do you say?" Hunter sat up and stretched. "Can I braid your hair for a kiss and another fun outing?"

Sinclair thought about it. "I guess. But if it looks bad the bet is off."

"You insult me, city girl."

Sinclair threw the wet towel at her. "Do we do it now or later on when you're less . . . horizontally inclined?"

"Now is fine, smart-ass."

Sinclair retrieved her comb from her bag and sat in front of Hunter on the blanket. She leaned into the other woman as the hands in her hair gently began to comb through the thick strands of hair.

"You have beautiful hair," Hunter said in a low voice. "You shouldn't cut it."

"Well, it's not like yours. I have to actually battle with it every morning before it does anything remotely resembling what I want it to."

"Maybe you're just not being gentle enough." Her hands slid through her scalp, massaging as she combed. Sinclair murmured her agreement as she sank back into the gentle touch.

"Hmm. You're entirely too good at that."

"There's no such thing as too good. As long as the ladies are satisfied, I consider it a job well done."

"You must have plenty of satisfied customers on the island."

"Not as many as I'd like." Was that wistfulness she heard in Hunter's voice or something else? "When I moved back to the island a few years ago, I was the new dyke meat for a lot of straight aka bi-curious women here. Even the tourist women I ran into wanted a piece of me. But I soon realized that being the tropical flavor of the moment was even less satisfying than being alone."

"Was that before or after you hooked up with Della?"

The hands in her hair stilled. "So you know about that too, huh?"

"Of course, it's not like you two keep it a secret."

Hunter released an exaggerated sigh. "This island is way too small. Used to be I could seduce a naive virgin and no one would ever know. Now it's broadcast in all the papers from here to Manchester."

"That's the price you pay for being so wanted."

"By you?"

"Maybe."

Her low chuckle vibrated against Sinclair's back.

"That was before Della and I became lovers. She was an escape for me, a reprieve. We had a nice year together."

"I'm assuming from what you just told me that you didn't come fully formed from the wilds of this place. Lydia talks about your notorious days in England, but I've never heard you mention them."

"There's not much to say." Hunter shrugged. "My parents took me from here to England when I was fifteen. After they died I came back. End of story."

"Really? There was no great love in England that you were escaping, no dyke determined to end your days of bachelor-hood?"

"Oh, that's your story, Sin, not mine. Love for the island pulled me back here."

"It must be nice to have such pure motives for coming home."

"It is." She heard the smile in Hunter's voice.

Sinclair sighed and leaned back into the cradle of warm flesh behind her. The faint scent of the other woman floated to her on the breeze. Hunter's hands drifted through her hair, already tightening bits of the kinky mass into the promised braids.

"She's not worth all this, you know." Her hand touched the back of Sinclair's neck briefly before returning to the hair. "If she was worth half your sighs she would have been here with you apologizing on her knees for hurting you."

"Oh, I know she's not going to apologize. I doubt that she even sees anything wrong with what she did."

Hunter was quiet above her, patiently twisting Sinclair's hair, and lending the solid warmth of her body to the other woman as comfort. "You'll feel whole again. This pain is only temporary."

Sinclair could only nod. It was true. Already the Regina-induced pain was fading to a mild sting. With a start of surprise, she realized that it was her pride that was hurt more, not her heart. She pushed the thought of her ex-lover away and decided to change the subject.

"Della took me to see my mother's grave yesterday."

After a moment's hesitation, Hunter went with it. "Why?"

"I don't know. I was hoping you might give me some insight into that."

She felt Hunter shrug behind her. "Unfortunately, I have little insight into the motives behind a lot of Della's actions."

"I thought you two were close."

"Lydia's been giving up more information again, I see." Hunter snorted in annoyance. "Della and I are good friends. She may just be my best friend on the island, but there are still a lot of things I don't know about her. And it's not because she's secretive; she'll probably tell me if I ask. But I allow her whatever privacy she needs."

Sinclair felt the subtle slap on the wrist. One good friend protecting another. "I'm not discussing her personal business all over the island, although it does seem that my mother was part of that business." She scratched at a dried patch of skin on her knee. "At the cemetery it felt strange being with her. I miss my mother, and I was content to leave her private business in the past. But it keeps confronting me here. First when I found out that my father cheated on her with Lydia's mother and who knows how many other women, and then I found out that she cheated on him, too, with Della and who knows how many other women." She made a sound that could have been interpreted as a laugh. "But I suppose I shouldn't worry. It's all in the past, right?"

"Della sometimes lives in the past. A lot of us indulge her. But you're right, you don't have to be a part of that. I'm sorry she made you feel uncomfortable."

"You have nothing to be sorry for, Hunter. I don't think any of us do."

Hunter breathed softly above her, and said nothing.

An hour later when Hunter finished, her hair was wreathed in tiny braids that brushed her shoulders and back. Sinclair stared down at her reflection in the water, impressed. "You're very good."

"I told you, no woman has ever left my care unsatisfied." She grinned at Sinclair before standing up to stretch. "In case you missed it, that means if you ever have any complaints, keep them to yourself." She threw Sinclair a teasing glance before diving into the water.

At her father's gate much later that afternoon, Hunter shut the door to her Jeep and walked Sinclair to the door.

"Thank you for a lovely time," she said. "I enjoyed you."

Irresistible laughter bubbled up in Sinclair's throat. "And I enjoyed you. We should do it again soon."

"I'm free tomorrow after six o'clock."

"Very funny."

"I'm not joking." Hunter stepped closer. "I could lock all my windows if that's what you want. No one will hear you scream my name." Her breath tickled Sinclair's mouth, made Sinclair part her lips and moisten them. "Kiss me."

Sinclair brushed her lips across Hunter's. The taste was so good, yet so subtle that she had to lean in for another. Her fingers slid into the thick wet hair to pull Hunter closer. The soft mouth opened under hers, inviting her in with a flicker of tongue, a squeeze at her waist. Sinclair accepted the invitation, moving into the dark woman with a slide of tongue and wet lips. Her legs fell open and she pushed, gently, against Hunter's hips. The other woman pulled back, breathing deeply.

"Only because we're right in front of your father's house," she rasped.

Sinclair nodded and bit her tongue to prevent herself from begging Hunter to come in.

"I have to go now." Hunter stepped back. "My right hand and I have an appointment to keep."

Sinclair watched her hop into her truck and take off down the road as if she did have an urgent appointment elsewhere.

"Sinclair, is that you?" Nikki came to the front door as Sinclair was unlocking it. Something she saw in her stepdaughter's face made her smile. "Did you have a good time?"

"Yes." Her face heated and she looked away. "I did."

Nikki closed and locked the door behind Sinclair. "You sound surprised."

"Yes, I thought—" Sinclair stopped herself from saying something about having to fight Hunter off. She remembered in time who she was talking to. "I just didn't think I would."

"But you still went."

Sinclair laughed. "Yes."

"Stranger things have happened, I guess." Nikki's smile was teasing.

"True enough." Sinclair looked around, noticing for the first time how quiet the house was. "Where are the boys?"

"At a movie. Some kung fu thing." Nikki shrugged.

"Ah. Boys indeed." She could see where Nikki had made herself comfortable on the sofa with a book turned face-down and a bookmark sticking out from between its pages. Nearby on the coffee table sat a platter of sweet biscuits and a glass of amber colored liqueur.

"I'll let you get back to your quiet evening, then." She started to walk through the living room.

"No. Stay." Nikki made room for her on the couch.

Sinclair came back and sat down, tucking her bag in the corner between the wall and the coffee table.

"So," Sinclair said to break the silence. "What are you doing this evening?" The inanity of the question made her want to roll her eyes.

Nikki giggled. "You can do better than that, right?"

"At another time, maybe. Hunter has my mind doing all kinds of crazy cartwheels today." Too late, she realized what she just hinted at.

"She is a challenge, isn't she?" Nikki looked at Sinclair as if inviting her to share a secret. "Lydia thought she could handle her, but she can't."

Well, in for a penny, in for a pound. "It's not about can't. She just won't."

"I doubt that."

Nikki sounded fairly certain of what she was talking about. It made Sinclair wonder. "What do you know about Hunter?"

"Not much. But I can see that *you* want to know her better."

Sinclair felt a blush climb hot and fiery up her throat. She coughed on air and turned away from her stepmother's teasing smile. The phone rang and saved her from responding. Nikki stood up and disappeared into the kitchen to answer it. Moments later she was back with the cordless phone in hand.

"It's for you."

"Hey, it's Hunter." The woman's voice caressed her ear through the phone.

"I know. Is everything all right?"

"Yes, fine. Why shouldn't everything be OK?"

"You're calling me when I just saw you less than half an hour ago."

"So you don't want me to call you, is that it?"

"No, that's not it. Quit putting words in my mouth." Too late she heard the teasing note in Hunter's voice. "What do you want?"

"You. For dinner tomorrow evening. Is that possible?"

"Um." Sinclair swallowed past the lump in her throat. "I don't see why not."

"Good. I'll be by to get you at four thirty."

"OK. See you then." Sinclair ended the call, avoiding Nikki's eyes. "Yes, I do want to know more about her," she finally said, feeling her face heat up again.

Nikki's smile was full of mischief. "No crime in that."

A question took hold of Sinclair's tongue. "Not that I'm trying to find conflict where there is none, but why are you so OK with this?"

"Why shouldn't I be? I know people think that everybody in the Caribbean wants to stone gay people and blame their visit to foreign countries for 'turning them gay,' but I had a lot of good girlfriends growing up who still play the games we used to play as children. They're still my schoolmates. I'm not going to stop being their friend just because they don't like what I like in the bedroom."

That was the longest sentence Sinclair had ever heard the younger woman speak. She smiled, feeling a sudden rush of warmth for her stepmother. "Thank you."

Sinclair and Nikki shared the glass of Grand Marnier and

conversation until nightfall. When Victor and Xavier came home, Nikki excused herself to tend to her boys and Sinclair went out into the dew-dusted night to be alone with her camera and her thoughts.

When Hunter knocked on the door the next evening wearing a powder blue dress shirt and black slacks that fell in an elegant wave of cloth over shiny black loafers, Sinclair was relieved. She didn't want to be the only one to dress up. Hunter gave her apple-green silk dress a long appreciative glance before greeting Victor Daniels.

"Hello, Mr. Daniels."

When the doorbell had rung he had put down his paper to answer it but Sinclair beat him to it, dashing out of her room in the gauzy, slim-fitting dress. Now he looked from one woman to the other with curiosity. Beside him, Nikki smiled at Hunter.

"Good to see you again," she said.

Hunter nodded and gave her one of her lazy smiles.

"I'll be back later on," Sinclair said.

"We'll probably be in bed when you get back." Nikki was careful not to smile as she said that.

"That's OK. I have my key."

"Be careful then," Victor said with a slow nod. "Drive carefully out there."

"Yes, do," Sinclair said to Hunter as they closed the door behind them.

"Of course." Hunter opened the passenger door of her Jeep for Sinclair. "I wouldn't want to end our date before it begins."

Sinclair rolled her eyes. Hunter did drive slowly this time, entertaining Sinclair with details of her eventful day at the university until they pulled up at the beachfront restaurant. Coconut trees swayed in the front driveway with a sound like quiet laughter, welcoming them into the faux-thatch-roofed building.

The thickly muscled host in a yellow tie led them through the meagerly peopled restaurant out to the large back deck only a few feet from the water. Out here, only three of the dozen or so tables were occupied. Hunter pointed to the table farthest from the others that was tucked in a corner by the railing.

"We'll take that one."

The host pulled out their chairs and laid two menus on the table. "Your server will be right with you." He disappeared back into the restaurant.

"This is gorgeous." The beach stretched beyond them for a few yards before falling into the hypnotic quiet of the sea. Tonight the moon was barely a sliver in the inky sky.

"I'm glad you like it. My cousin, Clifton, is the owner and he's pretty proud of the place."

"It doesn't seem very crowded though."

"It's only five o'clock. He gets most of his business from the late dinner crowd and the brunch set on the weekends."

"How come we didn't have reservations for later, then?"

"It should be pretty obvious to you, you're not a stupid woman."

"Humor me anyway."

Hunter winked. "I wanted you all to myself, of course."

The waitress approached before she could say anything else. "Good evening, ladies." The woman was tall and voluptuously built with large high breasts, easily the size of Sinclair's head each, and full womanly hips held tight by her red dress. She gracefully placed two glasses of water in front of the two women. "Welcome to Celestial."

"Hey, Hyacinth."

The woman looked at Hunter for the first time. "Hey, girl. How are you doing?"

"Good, good. Can't complain, you know."

"Oh, yes. I understand." Her eyes slid over Sinclair. "This your new girl?"

Sinclair hid her smile.

"I'm trying, but you know how slippery some women are."

"Slippery, huh? Interesting turn of phrase, my dear."

Hunter chortled. "Behave, Hyacinth."

"Why? Life is too short." She winked at Sinclair. "Can I get you anything to drink?"

"The house port, please," said Hunter.

"Hmm, seduction wine." Hyacinth grinned and turned to Sinclair. "And you, my dear?"

"Gilbey's and tonic for me, please."

"Coming right up." She did a sassy turn on her high heels and left them alone.

"Sorry about that." Hunter gave the other woman a look of chagrin. "I should have known better than to bring you here."

"It's all right so far. The waitress is fun." Sinclair glanced down at her menu. "Do you bring girls here all the time?"

"No. Not all the time. Della came here with me once. Usually I'm here alone with my laptop." Hunter gestured to the restaurant. "Sometimes it's just nice to be among other gay people."

Sinclair looked around in surprise, noticing for the first time the refined flamboyance of a few of the male customers and the rainbow-colored Christmas lights threaded along the railing of the deck. "This is a gay restaurant?"

"Not exclusively. But a lot of the clientele and staff are. So is the owner."

"Your cousin?"

"My cousin."

"Here you go, my dear." Hyacinth twisted open the bottle of wine and put it and two glasses on the table. I'll be right back with the gin and tonic."

Hunter had just finished pouring wine into her glass when the waitress came back with Sinclair's drink. "Your Gilbey's gin and tonic." She presented it with a theatrical flourish. "Do you know what you'd like for dinner?"

"I know what I'd like, but I'm not sure if—" began Hunter.

"I'm ready, too," Sinclair said. "Can I have the steamed parrot fish with rice and peas?"

"You can have anything you want, sugar."

She arched an elegantly plucked eyebrow at Hunter. The other woman grinned as she gathered up the two menus and handed them to Hyacinth. "Chicken roti for me with a side of corn. On the cob and roasted."

"Yes, ma'am."

After Hyacinth left, Hunter lifted her glass in a toast. "To a pleasant evening."

Sinclair echoed the toast. "And thank you for bringing me here. The view and company alone so far have been well worth it."

"Anytime you want me to repeat the experience just let me know."

They shared a smile and drank deeply from their glasses. The light caught the gleam of burgundy the wine left on Hunter's mouth. Sinclair tasted the gin on her own lips wishing suddenly for a taste of port, preferably from the pair of lips across from hers.

"Don't you think it would be wrong if we got involved?" she asked suddenly.

Hunter put her glass down. "In what sense?"

"Morally, of course."

"Why? I'm not involved with anybody and, as far as I know, neither are you."

"And Lydia?"

"What about her? I never fucked her so there won't be any mixture of sisterly body fluids on my toys or in my mouth."

Sinclair's thighs clenched at the vivid imagery but she pressed on. "What about your emotional attachment?"

"Damn near nonexistent at this point." Hunter sipped her wine. "As far as I'm concerned, what she and I had has nothing to do with us. She's the past. You and I are right now."

"Easy for you to say."

Hunter smiled. "It is. You can say it with me if you want."

Sinclair nudged her foot under the table. "Will you please be serious?"

"You want me to be serious? Really? Then how about this? Your tits look amazing in that dress, the perfect size for my mouth." She lifted the wineglass by the rim, dangling it by her fingertips. "I want to lap you up like you were my last meal on earth. I want to fuck you with my tongue and my fingers until you come so hard and so much that your pussy juice drips into my palms. And after I tie you to the bed and make you ready for my dick I'll be able to lick my hand off and taste you all over again."

Sinclair released her breath in a slow, shuddering sigh. But Hunter wasn't done yet. She leaned back in her chair and unzipped her pants. Her lips parted and her eyes fluttered closed briefly before she pulled a slick finger from beneath the tablecloth.

"See how wet I am for you?" She leaned close, tilting her wet finger toward Sinclair, who could smell the briny damp of her, pungent and tempting. Her own body clutched at emptiness, wanting to feel that finger, Hunter's tongue, anything, inside. She bent quickly, a snakelike motion of her head and licked the other woman's finger, sliding her tongue between it and its neighbors to clean it of all its flavor, sucking the long digit deep into her mouth. At first Hunter drew back, surprised. Then she leaned closer, lips parted, breath coming heavily. Sinclair grasped her wrist and pulled her closer, her mouth sucking steadily on the finger, her tongue stroking. Hunter groaned.

"I see you started dinner a little early."

They both jumped back guiltily at Hyacinth's voice. Hunter dropped her hand in her lap and Sinclair blushed painfully and looked down at the table. They made room for the large steaming platters of food the waitress set down before them.

"Enjoy," she said and left them to their meal.

"Fuck!" Hunter breathed when they were alone again.

Yes, please. Sinclair took a steadying breath. "The food looks good." She picked up her fork and held it poised over the fish.

Across the table, Hunter looked flustered. She drank deeply from her water, finishing half the glass in one greedy gulp. When that didn't do what it was supposed to, she drank the whole glass then took a healthy sip of her wine.

"I think you won that round," she said at last.

"I'm just trying to keep up with you." Sinclair forked a bit of the flaky, golden simmered fish into her mouth. It was perfectly flavored with pale curls of onions, bits of pimiento, and tiny tomatoes, wilted and draped across it like bits of confetti. Still her mouth watered for another taste of Hunter. Preferably direct from the source.

"Trust me when I say that you do keep up." With her fork, Hunter dug into the soft flour wrapping of her roti, exposing the curried chicken, potatoes, and spices inside. Sinclair noticed that she used her left hand with no difficulty. Her right hand was still in her lap. *Ambidextrous?*

"Do you have any after-dinner plans for us?" she asked.

"As of a few minutes ago, yes. But I'm not sure that you'd agree to them."

"If those plans involve any sort of exchange in body fluids, then you're right."

"Tease."

"You started it."

Hunter laughed softly. "I did, didn't I?"

Sinclair hummed her agreement around a bite of rice and fish.

"Then give me a chance to finish it. I promise that I'll make it worth every second."

I'm sure you would. Sinclair shook her head. "Perhaps some other time."

Between the two of them they managed to finish off the

bottle of wine and two very large plates of food, pushing aside the sexual tension to satisfy their more immediate oral craving. Still, when Sinclair fed bites of her fish to Hunter she couldn't help but notice the other woman's moist pink tongue as she parted her lips to accept each morsel of food.

"Thank you for dinner, it was wonderful," Sinclair said after Hunter put down money for the bill. They stood and walked out of the restaurant together.

Hyacinth spotted them as they were leaving. "Come back to see us again soon, Hunter darling." She brushed Hunter's shoulder with manicured fingers as she passed to tend to another table of customers. "And behave yourself now."

"She knows you well, huh?"

"Sadly, yes." Hunter laughed. "It makes it hard to keep a secret in this town."

"I'm sure you have some that the fawning majority haven't figured out yet."

"Maybe." Hunter took Sinclair's hand. "Walk down to the water with me."

"A walk on the beach?" Sinclair looked at her. "Are you kidding me?"

"Come on, don't be a spoilsport. It's corny but fun. And I promise not to push you down in the sand and have my way with you."

"Then what's the point of going then?"

"Ah, I'm rubbing off on you." Hunter pulled her away from the parking lot and toward the water. "Come on."

They walked in silence toward the water, hand in hand. Sinclair had tried to pull her hand from Hunter's before but after several seconds of futile struggle she gave up. Besides, the other woman's hand in hers felt good, solid and warm.

"Tell me," Sinclair said. "What's England like?"

Hunter looked at her as if surprised she would ask that question. "It was a place to live. Nothing special. At least not to me."

"Specifics, please. Pretend you liked it a little. Give me the highlights."

"I take it you've always wanted to go but never did?"

"You take it correctly," Sinclair mocked her proper tone. "You are such a stick up the ass sometimes."

"Me?" Even in the dark, she could tell that Hunter was rolling her eyes. "You're the last person who needs to call anybody uptight."

"Shut up and get on with the story."

"Well, let's see. It's rainy and wet. Where I lived it doesn't really snow so much as ice over. And if you're unprepared you can spend a horrendous hour or two slipping and sliding home, holding on to iron fences or, failing that, crawling on your hands and knees over the pavement." She laughed at Sinclair's expression. "That was in south London. They often didn't bother de-icing my street. In nineteen ninety six, I moved to Manchester, just in time for the IRA bomb that blew away most of Exchange Square. Though that wasn't necessarily a bad thing since the place looks much better now that they've rebuilt, refurbished, and invited the homos in to redecorate."

"Are you saying that you didn't have a single good experience in England?"

"I didn't say that. I definitely enjoyed my life there. Don't get me wrong." Hunter's eyebrow rose. "There's just nothing that I find aesthetically appealing about the country."

"Fine. You'll just have to take me there so I can see for myself."

"Will you, as the Americans say, put out?"

"Is that all you think about?" Sinclair asked.

"When I'm with you that's definitely in the top five."

"Pig." Sinclair laughed, not knowing whether to be flattered or insulted.

"I get called so many names, all for lust of a beautiful woman."

Still laughing, Sinclair pulled away from her, the Gilbey's

and wine beginning to truly sing in her veins. Foam tipped waves splashed up her legs and knees, cleaving the dress to her skin. "I get the feeling that lust is not an uncommon thing for you to feel. The woman is irrelevant. Your pussy doesn't care who it throbs for."

The moonlight floated silver on the water and over Hunter's face. The scientist knelt to take off her loafers and socks then rolled her pants up. She tossed her shoes and socks a safe distance up on the dry sand.

"At this moment it throbs for thee." Hunter ran into the waves, splashing Sinclair's thighs with the salty water. She tugged on Sinclair's dress, using it to pull her close. "Isn't that enough? Can't it be enough for now? Come home with me." She bit Sinclair's bottom lip, then sucked it into her mouth. "I'll be gentle if you want." Her voice was rough.

Sinclair melted against Hunter, slid her arms around her neck, and returned the wine-flavored kiss. Sinclair stopped thinking. Her body, however, chanted yes with its aroused nipples and wet mouth, the hands grabbing Hunter's ass through her slacks, and the soft panting noises it made. But she wanted to be sure, not overwhelmed like she had been with Regina. Sinclair didn't want to be a victim of her hormones again. She pulled away.

"I can't."

Reluctantly, Hunter let her go. Later, as they pulled up to the gate of the Daniels' house, she touched Sinclair's thigh. "I'm not going to give any false promises. I'm not going to lie to you. My honesty is what I can offer that's better than what you had before. Think about that."

Sinclair climbed out of the Jeep, unlocked the front door and walked inside, all without once looking back. It was going to be a long night.

Chapter 16

Hunter didn't call. Sinclair prowled around the house with her camera, taking photo after photo of the backyard, of Nikki's garden, even of the unsympathetic telephone. People called, but no one she wanted to talk to. Yesterday, she thought that she had good reasons for not giving in to her feelings for Hunter, but today she couldn't think of what those reasons were. When Nikki and Xavier came home in the late afternoon with both their faces smeared by chocolate ice cream, Sinclair was still standing in the yard staring listlessly at the garden.

"What are you doing?"

Sinclair waved her camera at them. "Taking some pictures."

"Is the yard that depressing?"

"What? Oh, no." Sinclair shook her head. "I was just thinking." She dredged up a smile for Xavier. "I don't suppose you brought me any ice cream, huh?"

"We didn't think you'd be home." Nikki's smile teased her. "Leave the flowers alone and come in and help us make dinner. You're just making them sad by hovering over them like that."

Sinclair wrinkled her nose at her stepmother but followed her into the house anyway. "What are we cooking?"

"I don't know. Let's look in the cupboard and see what's here."

Xavier went off to wash his hands and face while the two women headed into the kitchen. Nikki washed her face at the kitchen sink and used a paper towel to pat it dry.

"How was dinner last night?" she asked.

"The food was very good."

Nikki peeked at Sinclair around the door of an open cupboard. "Was Hunter?"

Sinclair felt her face grow hot but didn't rise to the bait. "Not especially, but she was pleasant company nevertheless."

"Should I make enough for her this evening?"

"I don't think so. She has a lot of work to do at home."

"Excuses, excuses." Nikki pouted. "I don't think she likes us anymore."

"You know they say that too much thinking isn't good for you." Sinclair grinned then picked up her camera from the dining table. "Let me go put up my camera then you can just order me around the kitchen. Tell me what you need me to do and I'll do it."

"Is that what you told Hunter today?" Nikki called out behind her as she walked down the hall to her room.

"Funny. Very funny."

By the time Victor came home two hours later dinner was already done. His plate lay warming in the oven and his daughter, wife, and son sat on the living room floor playing checkers and eating their dessert. He eyed the gigantic slice of rum cake sitting, half eaten, between Nikki and Sinclair.

"Did you leave any for me?" he asked and kissed his wife on the forehead.

"Nope." She tilted her mouth up for a real kiss. "But there's plenty of food for you in the kitchen."

When he left for the kitchen Nikki turned to Sinclair. "He doesn't like rum cake. Says it's too fruity."

Sinclair laughed. "He probably doesn't want to contaminate his rum with the cake."

"That's very possible," Nikki agreed, wrinkling her nose with amusement.

"King me, Clair! King me!" Xavier waved his triumphant red checker in the air at Sinclair.

His sister stuck her tongue out at him. "Fine, but I don't have to like it."

Sinclair went to bed early. At least early for her. After Nikki and her father abandoned her for their own bed, she left Xavier asleep on the pullout sofa and turned off the television.

In her room, she closed the door and undressed before slipping under the thin sheet. Hunter still hadn't called. Sinclair sighed and stared out the window, preparing herself for a restless night.

A noise at the window woke her up. Sinclair's eyes snapped open in time to see a dark shape climb over the windowsill and into the bedroom.

"What are you doing here?" She sat up, watching Hunter slip into the bed next to her.

"I've been thinking about you." Hunter shrugged off her shirt. "I can't get any work done. I needed to see you."

Her pants and underwear quickly followed, falling away to the foot of the bed. Shadows of her nakedness appeared to Sinclair, the smooth line of breast and rib, a bare throat, the shape of lips settling close.

"I was going to wait until you made the first move, until you knew that you were ready. But, you know what? You leave in two weeks. And at the rate that you're going, neither of us will get laid this year." She pressed Sinclair into the bed, her body taut with the excitement of her words. Sinclair gasped. "I know you worry that they'll hear you." Hunter pulled something from one of her discarded pockets. A bit of silk. "So I brought something for you." Her breath fluttered against Sinclair's mouth, warm and teasing. "If you don't want it, if you say no, then I'll put it away." Her hips pressed into Sinclair's. "I'll leave."

Over the throbbing of her pulse and the need singing through her body, Sinclair heard the threat and panicked. "No." She grabbed Hunter's arm. "Stay."

The first kiss was an explosion of want, of previously compressed desire expanded suddenly, catching Sinclair in a wave so powerful that it stole her breath. She clawed the thin sheet from between their bodies, anxious to feel all of Hunter, not just her provocative heat through the cotton. Soft, mewling noises left Sinclair's throat. It seemed like she'd waited so long for this. She couldn't understand why she'd denied herself this satisfaction of desire, this vicious pain.

Her mouth opened to devour and to claim the dark woman. Hunter's thigh fell between hers, pressing against the dampness that had flooded her the instant she'd seen her face at the window. The thigh flexed and she shuddered. Hunter's mouth burned her body, her mouth, her throat, the tight peaks of her breasts. She gasped and moved against the heaviness above her, sliding her palms down the sleek, muscular back and restless hips. The silk brushed her mouth.

"Should I tie you up now?" There was raw laughter in the other woman's voice, a promise that Sinclair wouldn't be able to stay quiet tonight.

They whispered softly to each other, their words a mere brush of breath against flesh, a movement of lips.

"Is that the only way you can think of to control me?"

"Control isn't the word tonight, sweetheart. I want to fuck you. Believe it or not I was pretty content without sex until you came along. But when I saw this ass—" she grabbed Sinclair's behind and lifted it hard against her thigh. Through Sinclair's breathless moan, she continued, "I knew I didn't want to be celibate anymore."

Sinclair widened her legs against the thrust of Hunter's

thigh, gasping her passion into her lover's sage-scented hair. Her body swam with sensation, a liquid rush that bathed her in heat, tingled her clit, made her breasts ache. A fine mist of sweat appeared on her skin.

"Then . . . stop talking about it and do it."

"I don't want to break you on your first go-round."

Another trembling gasp broke through Sinclair's laughter. "You don't know what . . . I can . . . handle."

"We're about to find out, aren't we?"

Hunter covered Sinclair's mouth with her own, swallowing the soft, panting gasps as her thigh pumped against her lover's dripping pussy. Sinclair's belly clenched at the frantic stimulation. "Inside. Come inside."

"Not yet, baby. Not yet." Hunter's fingers plucked at her nipples, squeezing the hard points in rhythm with her thigh's movements until Sinclair grasped at her back, digging her fingers into the damp skin. Her back arched and she shuddered in Hunter's embrace, falling from the dizzying peak of orgasm with her mouth held firmly by her lover's.

As Sinclair's body quieted she noticed Hunter's hawklike stare, the brown eyes fierce on her wet mouth.

"You want something from me?" Sinclair asked.

"I wonder whatever gave you that idea."

"I don't know." Sinclair slid a hand between them to cup Hunter's pussy. Her fingers were immediately wet. She remembered what the woman tasted like, the mingled flavors of mango and salted honey. "Maybe this?"

Hunter groaned and pressed herself into Sinclair's hand. Again.

"Put those lips right here," Sinclair ordered, tapping an index finger against her own mouth.

"I thought you'd never ask." Hunter slid up Sinclair's body to crouch over her face.

"Well, technically, I didn't." Though she was ready to beg if Hunter had refused her. The sight of her woman's flesh, with its inner maze of pink and damp, made her wet her lips.

"If you're not going to put your mouth to good use, then I suggest you shut—" Hunter swallowed the rest of her words at the first touch of Sinclair's mouth.

The first taste of her was like a mouthful of clean, ocean air. Sinclair dove down for more. Deeper inside, Hunter was more substantial, like the flesh of the mango she'd eaten yesterday, wet and ripe. Juice dripped down her chin. Sinclair's tongue slid faster over the slick flesh as dark thighs widened and Hunter's hand cupped the back of her head.

"Slow down," she gasped. "I don't think that I can—" Sinclair swirled her tongue through the moist folds and held on, grabbing the clenched ass cheeks as Hunter's flesh began to pulsate against her mouth. The dark woman gasped again and tightened her fingers in Sinclair's hair, pushing her into the contracting flesh as she growled low in her throat.

"Damn." Hunter's thighs released their vice hold from around Sinclair's ears as she fell gently backward. Her hair flooded over Sinclair's belly and thighs. "That wasn't exactly my sexiest moment, huh?"

"Actually, that's the nicest compliment anyone's ever paid me."

"Sweet of you to say."

"It's OK." Sinclair rubbed her cheek against Hunter's thigh and smiled at the delicate shudders that vibrated the muscles under her skin. "You'll make it up to me."

"I will, I swear." She stretched voluptuously against Sinclair, wriggling her hips and back in delight. "That felt so damn good, though." She sighed and relieved the other woman of her weight, sliding over to lie beside her on the bed.

Sinclair's body tingled in the aftermath of pleasing Hunter. She felt swollen again, wet and ready. "I hope you're not tired." Her long fingers traced Hunter's face in the semidarkness, touching the soft cheeks and the curved lips that opened for her.

"Hm, not at all. I was just thinking the same thing about you."

"What do you have in mind?"

"I can show you better than I can tell."

"I'm all yours."

"Promises, promises." Hunter chuckled softly in the dark. "Sit here."

With Sinclair sitting on the edge of the bed, Hunter tied the silk cloth around her mouth, then knelt between her spread thighs. She leaned closer until her nose brushed the untidy curls at the top of the other woman's thighs. She drew in another breath, and kissed her. The touch of Hunter's lips was soft, a light brush against the sensitive hairs. The second kiss touched Sinclair lower, made her breath catch and hold. When Hunter lifted her head, her mouth came away wet.

"I thought the first cum would make me less hungry for you"—she licked her lips clean—"but it didn't." Hunter spread her thighs wide and slid even closer, draping one long leg over her shoulder and down her back. When her mouth touched Sinclair again her whole body jumped to attention.

Hunter's tongue stroked Sinclair with a firm, delicious pressure that sent her body into a sensual shock. Goose bumps peppered her skin, her breath shallowed, then grew loud and ragged under the silk scarf. Hunter held Sinclair apart and used her tongue to extract every ounce of sensation from her. Sinclair's legs spread wider. Hunter's head moved like a snake between her thighs, undulating with each movement of her tongue. Sinclair was warmer, then burning. Heat sprung from between her thighs to engulf and enfold her, making her legs burn and spread as wide as they could for Hunter. Slim hands hovered over the dark head, wanting to touch her rough silk hair, to spread it over her thighs, but pleasure rose up and caught her in the throat. Sinclair curled her hands in the sheets and clenched her teeth against the mewling gasps that still tumbled free.

Sinclair's breasts felt heavy and tender. She wanted Hunter's hands on them, to feel the dark woman against the swollen flesh of her nipples.

With a soft moan from beneath the silk, she grabbed Hunter's hands and put them on her breasts, panting softly as she hurled through the flames with Hunter's tongue and lips moving over her aching pussy with deep, indelicate slurps.

The springs of the mattress squeaked and groaned as her hips surged toward Hunter's mouth, begging for more. She felt sweet, overflowing with sticky cotton candy mess as her lover feasted, ate her up until she wanted to cry out, to scream, but she didn't. The silk was thin. Trapped in her own silence, Sinclair could hear the noises that Hunter made, the slurp and lick and release, that kiss and suck of lips, the soft, soft float of tongue across her clit that made her feel like fine velvet that was about to get wet.

Her hips moved mindlessly, bucking against the hungry mouth pushing her to a place that was like pain, but much, much sweeter. Her whole body was hot and sweating and focused on that one spot that Hunter devoted herself to so well. The dark woman was like a kitten with a bowl of milk, lapping her up, licking her cream-slicked thighs then back again to her throbbing pussy where she needed it most. Her body was raw and tight with sensation. It wanted. It wanted so much.

Sinclair pushed against Hunter's mouth and grabbed her hair. With a low groan, Hunter pulled Sinclair hard against her face, tumbling pillows and sheets to the floor. Sinclair dropped back against the bed, gasping. Hunter's tongue plunged inside her and the bed began to shake. She fell over the edge screaming behind the silk.

Hunter left before dawn just as the rest of the house was beginning to stir. "Call me later," she whispered to a limp Sinclair as she disappeared out the window and into the soft gray light.

The exhausted woman could only nod before rolling over and falling back deeply asleep. At some point Nikki knocked on the door asking Sinclair if she wanted to go to work with her. Sinclair could only utter a sleepy moan. Nikki must have taken it for a no, because she made a funny noise of her own and left Sinclair alone until much later in the day.

Sinclair woke up feeling tender and bruised. With a low groan she reached over to touch the source of that ache, and when her clutching hand encountered only rumpled bedsheets, she grimaced in disappointment and sat up. *Why stay in bed then?* She stumbled to the bathroom to begin her day.

"Did you have company last night?" Nikki asked Sinclair as the two of them sat on the verandah sharing an early evening drink. Xavier sat nearby, puzzling over his homework.

"Why do you ask?"

"I thought I heard noises coming from your room last night."

Sinclair adjusted the air in her throat. "Hunter came over for a bit."

"Ah, I see."

She probably did see, and all too clearly. Sinclair felt her face heat up, but she strove for nonchalance.

"Are we going to have her over for dinner tonight, then?"

"You're obsessing about this a bit much, aren't you?" Sinclair finally looked up from her examination of her fingers. "Did she come over when she was seeing Lydia?"

"Not really. But then Lydia doesn't live here. Last month she went with us to Dunn's River Falls, though. Even Della was there."

Sinclair winced at the thought of how Della and Lydia must have gotten along. "I can invite her over and see what she says."

"Tell her to come on the weekend so I'll have enough time to cook up something nice." Nikki's eyes twinkled.

"I'll be sure to pass on the information."

The sound of a car stopping at the front gate made them both look up. It was Lydia's Cadillac. They watched Lydia get out of the car and walk up the gravel-lined footpath. The line of flesh between her tight black jeans and blouse played peekaboo as she stepped closer.

"'Evening," she called out.

"Hey, there," the two women chorused.

Xavier grinned up from his pile of books. "Hey, Lydi."

"You two look cozy." She looked at the two women as if a conspiracy was afoot.

"Is there a reason we shouldn't?" Sinclair asked.

"Not really, it's just that it usually takes Nikki at least a year to warm up to people." She sat down on the top step and leaned back against the small stone column. "I might have gotten her to talk to me in more than two word sentences after six months. It's been less than three weeks and you two are acting like best friends."

"I like Sinclair's company." Nikki smiled at the American. "And it's not like I have a whole bunch of time to get to know her."

Sinclair shrugged and drank deeply from her glass of carrot juice. Lydia looked like she was in the mood for a confrontation. But Sinclair wasn't. That would come soon enough when she had to tell her about Hunter.

"Hm." Lydia made a vague noise of agreement then glanced up at Sinclair as if trying to figure something out.

"You want some juice?" Nikki offered from her chair.

"Sure, thank you. But no ice though."

When Nikki left for the kitchen Lydia turned to Sinclair. "I haven't seen you in a while, big sister. Did I scare you off with that craziness at Phyllis and Nance's?"

"Nope. I don't scare very easily. You just haven't come to get me. Remember, I'm not exactly mobile while I'm here."

"I'm surprised that you haven't rented a car."

Sinclair shook her head. "I don't drive."

Lydia laughed. "There you have it then, a really good excuse why I haven't seen you these past few days." She looked up as Nikki came back with her glass of carrot juice. "Thanks,

Nik." She took an obligatory sip, then set the glass beside her on the tile. "So what have you been up to then?"

From the corner of her eye, Sinclair saw Nikki perk up. "Taking photos of the island, mostly. Going with Nikki to work in the mornings then hanging out with Hunter until it's time for her to go home."

"When does the fun happen?" She turned to Nikki. "No offense, Nik."

Nikki rolled her eyes. "As far as Lydia is concerned if someone's not dancing 'til the wee hours of the morning or meeting scores of eligible people then there is no good time."

"Damn right." Lydia lightly tapped Nikki's foot. "Speaking of as you put it, meeting scores of eligible people, can I kidnap you lovely ladies and gentleman"—she tugged at Xavier's naked foot—"and take you to the reggae show in Queenstown?"

The little boy squeaked, "Yes!" then looked at his mother. "Can we?"

Nikki didn't waste any time thinking about it. "Sure. Victor can fend for himself when he gets home tonight."

The fairground was packed. Its crowd, consisting of a fairly mixed group of younger and older people, seemed friendly; unlike the last time Lydia and Sinclair had been out together. Kids ran through the grassy area, chasing and calling out to each other in loud excited voices.

"We don't have to stay that long," Lydia said, linking hands with Xavier and Nikki. Sinclair tried to walk a little behind the three of them, but Nikki grabbed her hand.

"Stay close, daughter." Her eyes danced with laughter.

Sinclair squeezed her hand and smiled. "I'm all grown up, you know."

"Yeah, but you're a grown woman who could easily get lost in this mob."

Sinclair wrinkled her nose at Nikki but kept up anyway. At six in the evening the sun was still high and brilliant in the

Friday sky. Vendors, with their carts overflowing with every variety of juices and desserts, lined the avenue leading to the stage. Xavier dragged his group of women toward the carts, eyeing the flaky pies and cakes with more than casual interest.

"I think he's more excited about the food than about the people onstage," Lydia said as they pulled him away from yet another stand.

"If we walked faster then he wouldn't be able to see all these goodies," Sinclair said, although she was getting tempted herself.

They sped up but had to stop when Xavier saw a group of his school friends. The couple chaperoning them looked harried, turning around every few seconds to make sure that all five of the children weren't getting into any trouble. Xavier jumped in the midst of his friends and started chattering away like a little magpie.

"My name is Alton," the man introduced himself to Nikki over the children's heads. "Father to those two, uncle to the rest." His companion hovered nearby, looking worried. "That's Kathleen over there."

"I'm Nikki. All three of these are my children."

Lydia laughed at his expression. "Stepchildren, she means. At least us two. That one over there is Sinclair. I'm Lydia."

"Good to meet you," Alton said with a smile. "I was just about to say that you don't look your age, Nikki."

"She looks every day of her twenty-two years, so don't you dare try to tell her otherwise." Lydia slipped her arm around her stepmother's waist, chortling.

"Alton, help me out here, please." Kathleen's desperate voice interrupted their lovefest.

"Excuse me." Alton went to help gather the fleeing children.

"Come on, Xavie. You can visit with your friends later." Nikki took his hand and waved at Alton and his brood, then they were off again.

"They were nice people," Nikki said.

"Yeah, that Alton guy kept staring at your breasts the whole time."

"Shh!" Nikki shushed Lydia, pointing to her son.

"Sorry to burst your parental bubble, but he already knows what breasts are."

"He does not!" She looked at Sinclair for support, but her stepdaughter merely shrugged and walked ahead.

Lydia grinned and gave her brother a hundred-dollar bill to buy the ice-cream cake he was so obviously ogling. They all waited while he got his cake and the change before forging their way through the crowd to get to the main stage.

Two hours later, with darkness coming swiftly on the heels of the falling sun, they piled into the convertible and headed for home.

"That was the best!" Xavier hopped up and down in the backseat, straining against his seatbelt. "Spragga jumped so high and sing so fast!"

"That's what he got paid to do." Lydia guided the car through traffic, smiling.

"We had a really good time, Lydia," Nikki said, resting her fingers lightly on her son's neck. "Thanks for coming by to get us."

"No problem."

Lydia seemed to have needed the distraction of their company as much as Xavier had needed this outing. She looked a little tired.

"Everything been all right with you, Lydia?"

"Good. Everything is good." She looked back at Nikki in the rearview mirror as if still trying to convince her.

At home they put Xavier and Nikki to bed, poured two glasses of something stronger than carrot juice and sat on the verandah. Sinclair was the first to speak.

"So is everything really OK, Lydia?"

"Not really. But you know people are always saying that, if you say that something is, then it will be."

"Right." Sinclair was unconvinced. "So what's wrong?"

"You know that Hunter and I broke up last week, right?"

Sinclair stiffened. Had it only been a week? "I didn't know for sure, but I suspected when Papa made such a big deal about you not bringing her to the beach cookout."

"Did you?" Lydia sipped her Grand Marnier. "I guess I wasn't being as subtle as I thought."

"What happened?"

"The details aren't that important. We hadn't really been talking for a few days, then I tracked her down at the party to get some things out in the air. I let it slip about why I couldn't let her touch me and she broke it off." She sighed. "I thought I'd be relieved, but I'm not."

"Do you want her back?"

"No. It's not even that. She's the best looking woman on this island. The most eligible dyke bachelor so to speak, but I—" she sighed. "I *do* want her back."

"Does she know that?"

"No, not yet. But I'm going to let her know this week."

"Don't you think you're being a little flighty?"

"What do you mean? It's a woman's prerogative to change her mind, isn't it?"

"Not when it means jerking somebody around emotionally." Would Hunter jump at the chance to have Lydia back if she was willing to put out?

They both looked up as the door opened and Nikki came out of the house rubbing her eyes. She had the telephone in her hand. "It's for you, Sinclair."

"Thanks. Excuse me, Lydia."

She took the phone and walked into the house behind Nikki. The younger woman slid her a quick look but said nothing before disappearing into her bedroom door.

"Hello?"

"You didn't call."

Sinclair leaned back against the kitchen wall, smiling stupidly. "Is that why you tracked me down?"

"I was going to come over, but I thought two nights in a row might be a little bit much."

"A bit much for what?" Sinclair's voice was breathless, low. She forgot about Lydia waiting for her on the verandah.

"Not that. Definitely not that. I just didn't want to turn your father's house into my personal playroom."

"Logic. Sometimes it sucks." She took a trembling breath. "I want to see you. In the daylight. I know you have work to do, though."

"That's what all-nighters are for."

"I thought we already had one of those."

"Very funny, Ms. Sinclair. Tomorrow. I can pick you up tomorrow. We can spend the day together, go sightseeing or something."

Sightseeing? "That sounds fine."

"Don't sound so excited. I'll make it worth your while."

"I'm sure you will." She heard a noise from outside. "By the way, Lydia is here."

"She's not invited on our field trip."

"She—oh, never mind. I guess she'll talk to you about it herself. I'm not going to get in the middle of things." *Though it might be a little late for that.*

"What are you talking about?"

"Don't worry your pretty little head about it. I'll see you tomorrow."

Hunter made a rude noise. "Fine. Tomorrow."

She hung up the phone and went back out to Lydia.

"Hmm, you certainly look sparkly and new," her sister said, raising her glass. "Must have been quite a phone call."

"It was." Sinclair picked up her glass and took a sip. "So what are you up to for the rest of the night?"

After a smirking look she shrugged. "I hadn't really thought about it beyond the visit here. I've been seeing a woman in the valley on and off, so I might go see her tonight. She's always good for a bit of fun."

"So you want Hunter and this girl, too? What's that about?"

"Don't be so judgmental, Sinclair. This woman was giving me what I couldn't get from Hunter. It was never emotional between us."

"And that makes it all right?"

"It does, believe me. I'm sure Hunter is getting her kitty stroked by someone else. She isn't moping around waiting for me. Della's probably never stopped getting her regular dose of Hunter in the two years since she's been here."

"That's not fair. Just because you've been cheating on the relationship doesn't mean that Hunter had been too."

"Why do you care so much anyway? You don't know Hunter well enough to know that she wouldn't cheat on me. According to the dyke news around here, when Hunter and Della were together they were all over each other. Della was always letting everybody know how she was getting her sex, how often, and how good it was. If all that was true, how could she give that up?"

Sinclair resisted the urge to roll her eyes. "I don't know. Like you said, you've known these people longer than I have so your guess is much better than mine." She stood, draining the rest of her drink. "I'm going to turn in for the night."

"Isn't it a little early for you?"

Sinclair's evil twin spoke up. "Usually, but I didn't get much sleep last night."

After Lydia left, Sinclair stayed on the verandah a little longer, absorbing the night's quiet and the faint twinges of unease she felt about her sister and Hunter. She blinked at the moon wondering if this was what they called dyke drama?

Sinclair rode the early morning bus that Nikki normally rode to work. This time she was alone, sitting up front near the driver so she wouldn't pass her stop. Her fellow passengers were silent, swaying in an early morning stupor with the bus's movements, staring straight ahead or out the open windows at the passing landscape.

"Here you go, miss." The driver stopped the bus and pointed down the road. "Take that road to the left and it will take you straight to Rincon Street."

"Thanks." She got off the bus and stepped away from the road to wait for it to pass on its way higher up the hill. This was a stop below where Nikki usually got off and, according to the driver, should get her to Hunter's street faster. Ten minutes later, she knocked at Hunter's door. It was six thirty in the morning.

"Don't you look all touristy," Hunter said when she opened the door.

Sinclair grinned and twirled on the doorstep, giving her a glimpse of her loose floral sundress and the matching wide-brimmed hat she wore tilted low over one eye.

"I came early on the off chance that you were here and awake. I hope you don't mind."

"Not even a little bit." Hunter tugged her into the house and kissed her quickly on the mouth, lending Sinclair the faint flavor of mint tea from her tongue. "Come in."

Hunter waved her into the hallway and into the immaculate living room. "I'm doing some work in the study. Give me ten minutes to wrap up and I'll be right back."

"Take your time." Sinclair dropped her hat and bag on the coffee table. When Hunter came back almost a half an hour later, she was propped up on the sofa with her shoes off, reading a history book about the Nanny and the Maroons.

"Did I mention how great you look?" Hunter asked, dropping to her knees beside the sofa.

"No, not yet." Sinclair marked her page with the attached red ribbon and set the book aside.

"Well, let me just say," she kissed Sinclair's knee, "that you look," then the other, "fabulous." Hunter's mouth pressed briefly against the top of her thighs. "Do you feel like breakfast?"

"Like *being* breakfast?" Sinclair's thighs parted slightly at the thought. "Or having breakfast with you?"

"Either. Both." Hunter put her arms around Sinclair's hips and drew her to the edge of the couch. "You pick, food or fucking." Hunter nibbled on her pouty lower lip.

"What do you think?" She slid her legs around Hunter's waist. "Feed me." Laughter bubbled easily to her lips.

"Slut." Hunter tasted her mouth again. "Come into the kitchen and help me."

Between the two of them they managed to put together a more than decent meal. Meaning that Sinclair provided distracting pinches and kisses to Hunter's butt, back, and neck while the besieged woman made scrambled eggs, seasoned potatoes, and hominy corn porridge flavored with coconut milk, nutmeg, and vanilla.

"You are so useful," Sinclair said later as they sat at the kitchen table sharing their breakfast. "Talented hands for every room in the house. I like that."

"I hope you can show me just how much. Later on." Hunter blew her a kiss over a spoonful of porridge.

After breakfast the dark woman showered and dressed, then they left the house to go on the promised sightseeing trip.

"This is going to be fun," Hunter insisted as they drove up the hill toward Fairfax Castle. The national landmark was a place referred to in all the guidebooks as exotic and mysterious, and one of the most beautiful lookout spots on the island.

"Some Englishman apparently built the place in the image of his ancestral home, complete with stone walls, servants quarters, and a little upstairs prison for his certifiable wife." At Sinclair's startled expression, Hunter laughed. "I'm not even joking. It says so right there in the guidebook. Look." She pointed to the folded brochure in Sinclair's hands. "And the best part is that they have tours of the place every two hours."

"I didn't figure you for a history buff, Miss High-Tech."

"Oh, I am. And so much more." She chuckled and guided the Jeep farther up the mountain.

Hunter was right. The view *was* breathtaking. From the top of Mount Rosanna to sea level the marker said it was 1,219 meters. Sinclair did a quick mental calculation. That was about 4,000 feet. Below them sat a sprawling vista of jungle plants, exotic houses built into the mountainside, and far, far out, the sea. They stood at the entrance to the castle, giggling like teenagers at the booth where a tiny man with tired eyes took their money and gave them flimsy paper tickets in return. He wore a drooping version of some sort of British uniform, dark blue with red stripes down the sides of the trousers that disappeared into knee-high black boots. Hunter dragged her away to follow the crowd walking away from them up the stone path to tour the tumble-down structure.

The place really was gorgeous, with long arches of marble marking each doorway, and thick green vines that slid up through all this impervious rock. It was a fairy-tale house, one that had more in the way of beauty than practicality. The beauty came from nature, the elements that had over time slipped in uninvited to make the marble and stone warmer, more approachable and photographable.

The tour guide, who introduced herself as Mavis, reminded Sinclair of one of her old teachers with her thick, flyaway hair pulled back into a bun and the dark-rimmed glasses shoved high on her nose.

"She's kinda sexy, isn't she?" Hunter whispered behind her.

"Stop it, she reminds me of the teacher I had in basic school."

The dark woman snickered. "You wanted to lick all over her, didn't you?"

"Shh! She's saying important things."

"This was built in the late seventeen hundreds when Lord

Braithwaite realized that he would never be able to leave Jamaica for good." The woman's proper English and curvy behind really did make her very appealing. "Come with me upstairs—" Mavis's voice faded away under the sound of treading feet as she and the crowd of sightseers disappeared up the stone staircase.

"Doesn't that ass just make you want to follow it anywhere?" Hunter palmed Sinclair's ass from behind then stepped close briefly to press her breasts against her back.

"You are not nice," Sinclair murmured, rushing to catch up with the group. But it was too late, she didn't hear a thing the woman said. All her awareness was focused on Hunter, on her warmth behind her, the teasing hands that touched and fondled when no one was looking. They drifted higher into the stone castle until they stood in the madwoman's bedroom. Time and a cannon blast had opened up most of the room to the mountain air. Off the main room was a smaller anteroom with only two and a half of its walls remaining, one with barred windows looking down at the shifting waves of jungle greenery and the sea beyond it. In a back room that was only the size of a walk-in closet, there was more open space. The sky above radiated a brilliant blue.

"Down there," Hunter pointed to a speck of white in the distance, "is where I was born. In my Aunt Eunice's house. I came too soon so they had to make some adjustments."

"And you've been shaking things up ever since then, right?"

"How did you know?" Hunter chuckled and turned back to Mavis.

The tour guide pointed out the woman's mad scribblings that neither time nor war had diminished, scribblings that were etched deep into thick walls that would have made it impossible for anyone to hear her screams or her angry recriminations against the husband who had brought her here away from her genteel society in England. Mavis's matter-of-fact recounting of the woman's madness sent a collective shudder through the group of tourists. They could well imagine being isolated from their comforts, forced to tolerate primitive conditions.

"Does that make you shudder too, Ms. American?" Hunter asked.

"Not especially."

"Then what would?"

The question trickled down Sinclair's spine and settled firmly in the cradle of her hips.

"All right, ladies and gentlemen." Mavis paused at the top of the stairs. "Our next destination is the former slave quarters, a place that the mistress, as well as the master of this house, visited at regular intervals."

The group trooped down the stairs after her. Hunter grabbed Sinclair's hand when she started to follow.

"There's something she forgot to show you," she said.

Sinclair smiled. "What's that?"

"This." Hunter pulled her into the circle of her arms and kissed her.

"But I've already seen that."

"Really? How about this?" She pressed her hips against Sinclair's and the slighter woman pushed back, sighing in the rising heat from Hunter's body. Then she felt the extra thickness, a hard length where the woman's softness should have been. Sinclair hissed. "Well? Do you want it?"

Oh. "Yes."

Hunter kissed her again then pulled her away from the stairs, toward the small back room with its barred windows and glimpse of paradise. Sinclair's body was wet with anticipation.

"They won't come up here, don't worry."

Sinclair wasn't worried. It didn't matter if the whole group of tourists came back, as long as Hunter fulfilled the promise in her trousers.

"Hold on to the bars," the dark woman instructed. "Please." Her breath tickled the back of Sinclair's neck.

Sinclair shuddered at the sound of Hunter's zipper. She bit her lip. Fireflies danced through her stomach, slipping down between her thighs as Hunter's long fingers moved her dress out of the way.

"I only want you to feel good," her lover whispered behind her. "Do you understand?"

"Yes. God, yes."

Cool mountain air washed over Sinclair's naked ass and between her parted thighs. Hunter touched her wetness, the drip of want that already coated her thighs. She sighed her delight into Sinclair's neck and palmed a soft breast through the dress. Then slid the dildo deeply, firmly into her. Sinclair gasped and arched her back to take more of the fullness.

"Thank you," she breathed.

Their breaths shivered together and a deep shudder traveled through their bodies as Hunter began to move. Sinclair was a mass of tingling, hyperstimulated nerves, slick and hot as Hunter slipped into her shallows and depths, creating exquisite friction. She moved against Sinclair's tightening ass, and breathed against her neck while Sinclair stood, legs braced apart, fingers clenched around the bars of the window. Her sweat-slick palms amplified the metallic smell of the bars, searing it forever in her sense memory. Sweat and sex and iron and Hunter.

Sinclair's body was prickling, aching, and wet. Hunter whispered her name and she breathed quickly, begging her not to stop. She didn't. Her hips moved faster, rushing to meet hers with a slap of flesh that made her gasp and push back into her.

Though buried in sensation, Sinclair thought she heard footsteps. Her body tensed and, despite her earlier bravado, fear of being caught ricocheted through her body. She tried to push Hunter away, but the other woman held her, trapped between the wall and her body. Her hips moved jackhammer fast against Sinclair. She felt Hunter groan against her back, then the dark woman overflowed like a river bursting free of its dam and washed her clean.

Hunter's fingers loosened from Sinclair's thighs and she slowly withdrew. Limp and still trembling, Sinclair could only brush her dress down and blink, panting, at the landscape beyond the bars. When she could walk again, she turned around. Hunter had already gotten herself together and was staring at the walls as if absorbed in the dead madwoman's fevered writing.

"Are you ready?" she asked.

"Whenever you are." Hunter dipped her head to kiss Sinclair's throat then stepped back to allow her lover to walk ahead of her. "I'm starving. Let's go find something to satisfy my other hunger, hm?"

They went to lunch, back to Celestial. This time Hyacinth wasn't there, but Hunter's cousin was. He looked up from the cash register, slim and dark with glowing gold eyes and Hunter's saturnine mouth.

"Hey, Cliff."

"Hunter! Hey, baby." They shared a long hug. "You look good. And it looks like you're running with a better class of company too." He winked at Sinclair.

The restaurant was crowded, both inside and out, but Cliff found them a table on the patio.

"You going to the family barbeque next week?" he asked.

"I think so. I haven't seen a lot of those guys in weeks."

"Good. So if I don't get the chance to come back out I'll see you there then."

"Later, cuz."

He turned to kiss Sinclair's hand. "I hope to see you again, fair Sinclair." Cliff disappeared back into the busy restaurant.

"The people in your family are unusually attractive," Sinclair said.

"What does that mean?" Hunter looked up from her menu. "You think we sold our collective soul to the devil for these looks?"

Sinclair laughed. "The thought hadn't occurred to me, but now that you mention it, I do smell the stink of brimstone on you."

"Is that what you call it?" Hunter leaned closer. "I could have sworn it was Sinclair's cum."

"Stop it." She blushed and slapped at her lover's knee.

The waitress arrived at their table. "Can I get you ladies anything to drink today?"

"Some manners for her." Sinclair pointed to her unrepentant lunch companion who gave her a lazy smile for her trouble.

"I'm a waitress, miss, not a miracle worker." The woman grinned at Hunter. She obviously knew her well.

"What's going on, Dee?"

"Hey, bad woman." She smiled at Hunter, flirtatious and familiar. "You see Cliff yet?"

"I was just telling him how nice and crowded the place looks."

"Yeah, and most of them are good tippers too."

"I'll remember that."

Dee slipped back inside the restaurant after taking their order for drinks.

"She wants you," Sinclair giggled.

"Already had me. I'm sure she's over it by now."

Sinclair hid her surprise at that bit of information. "I bet she's not."

"Unfortunately not everyone is as enthusiastic and delighted about my attentions as you." Hunter grinned. "Then again, maybe it's not so unfortunate. I could only handle this kind of chemistry only once per lifetime."

When the waitress reappeared Sinclair looked at her more carefully, noting her high, generous ass as she leaned over the table with their drinks, the full bosom, and the coltish wildness of her movements. Dee was young. Younger than Lydia, but she was definitely all woman.

"Are you trying to make Dee nervous or something?" Hunter asked.

"No. Why?"

"You look like you're evaluating her as a prospect for an afternoon of hot sex."

"Oh, please. I was just trying to see what your type of woman is."

Hunter snorted with laughter. "That should be fairly obvious to you by now."

"Yes, it is. You're an ass woman."

"That's true. Any other key observations?"

"Nothing remarkable, but I'll let you know."

"Do that." Hunter sipped her water. "What about you, Miss Cool and Collected. What kind of woman do you like? What's your type?"

"I'm not sure if I have a type. You're only the second woman I've been with."

Hunter leaned back in surprise. "What about the first one, then? The bitch from the city?"

"Regina is . . ." Sinclair's voice trailed off as she tried to recall images of Regina that she could tie descriptions to. "She's thin. With a take-charge kind of attitude."

Hunter rolled her eyes. "Does she wear pants or dresses?"

"Both," Sinclair grinned. "But mostly skirts."

"And she came after you?"

"Yes."

Hunter leaned across the table and lowered her voice. "That cool exterior of yours is very seductive. It's a wonder that some intrepid dyke hadn't tried to climb onto your face before then."

Sinclair snorted.

"That sound, however, was not seductive."

Sinclair blew a raspberry at her lover then, noticing Dee's return, leaned back in her chair so that the waitress had enough space to maneuver their food onto the table. Sinclair blew Hunter a kiss over the waitress's ass.

That evening Sinclair beat everyone home and surprised them all with dinner. Steamed fish, stewed chicken, butter-simmered corn, and an iced pitcher of Grace's Calypso Punch fresh from the can.

"Did you make all this?" Nikki asked after her first mouthful.

"Of course not. It's restaurant takeout."

Victor laughed. "Even I knew better than to ask that question, Nik." He reached for his glass of punch. "Good job, daughter. No matter how the food got here, thank you. I don't think anybody in this house wanted to cook tonight."

"I did," Xavier said from his chair, raising his hand high as if he was still in class.

"I stand corrected," Victor said.

"What's the occasion?" Nikki's smile was pure mischief.

Sinclair ignored it. "None at all. I just thought how nice it would be for someone besides the two . . . uh, three of you cooked for once. And since I wasn't about to set anything on fire, then a restaurant meal seemed the perfect thing."

"You're a brilliant and perceptive woman," Victor said, raising his glass.

"So I've been told."

After dinner, Victor and Xavier stayed in the kitchen to wash the dishes, then do homework while Nikki and Sinclair went for a walk around the neighborhood.

"You look happy," Nikki said as soon as they left the house.

"I am. It's a little scary."

"Since when is happiness a scary thing?"

"Since I know it's going to end when I leave here. And, even more important, because I've found it with my sister's ex-girlfriend."

"Agh!" Nikki made a dismissive motion. "No one cheated on anybody so it should all be fine. As for the long-distance thing, I know people who've made it work."

"But I'm not that naive. I know that there are plenty of women on the island. A lot of them much more appealing than I am, and very willing to satisfy Hunter's desires. I would never want her to deny herself because of me. That was something that Lydia did and despite our similar looks we're definitely not the same woman."

"No one ever said you were the same person. Calm down." They walked in silence. "What if Hunter wanted to make a long-distance thing work?"

"She wouldn't. Trust me." Sinclair stopped. "Listen, can we talk about something else for a while? This whole subject of my sex life is a little boring right now."

"Fine, fine." Silence. "So when are you going to tell Lydia about you and Hunter?"

Chapter 17

Sinclair looked up from her book as she heard rhythmic footsteps against the Breckenridges' expensive Spanish tile floor.

She smiled as Hunter stepped through the door. "Hey, gorgeous."

Her lover was breathtaking in her university clothes—belted black slacks and a white button-down shirt neatly tucked and pressed. A thick onyx circlet trapped her hair at her nape, preventing it from falling into her face. Sinclair put her book facedown on the window seat next to her when Hunter drew closer. She practically glowed.

"Want to go for a ride with me?" Hunter's mouth brushed hers before lightly nuzzling her throat.

"Should I dress up, too?" Sinclair grinned, intrigued by her exuberance.

"Nope. You are perfect. Just bring your camera."

She looked down at her pale green sundress and shrugged. "OK. Let me just let Nikki know that I'm leaving."

"I already told her when she let me in." Hunter nibbled on her collarbone. "She knows you'll be safe with me."

They left the Breckenridges' and walked back to Hunter's house with the dark woman frolicking like a puppy in front of, then beside her. She tugged at Sinclair's loose dress, flattening it against her belly and breasts.

"I love your tits," Hunter said, pulling closer. "They're so . . ." Her eyes touched them while Sinclair blushed and stood tongue-tied, not knowing what to say. She had never seen her like this.

At Sinclair's look of confusion Hunter backed away, smiling. "I love your coolness," she said. "I love it when you melt and show me your soft spots. I love how you make me want to be less cynical, more like the kid I was when I left this place."

This time when she came closer, Sinclair grabbed her hand. "You make me happy." She spoke the words against Hunter's mouth, feeling secure in saying them for the first time.

Hunter laughed and ran ahead of Sinclair. At her gate, she lifted the latch and motioned ahead of her. "I'm taking you out on a little road trip," she said. "Isn't that what you call it in America?"

Sinclair ignored her and walked ahead to open the garage door. After Hunter pulled the Jeep out, she brought the door back down and climbed into the passenger seat.

They drove away from the house, up a steep hill with a path that seemed barely big enough to fit the Jeep.

"What's gotten into you today?" Sinclair brushed Hunter's leg through the fine crease of her pants. "Not that I mind or anything."

"You better not." Her eyes were full of infectious mischief, winking in the afternoon sun as she carefully navigated the Jeep up the mountainside. "I think I got the happy bug from all the kids I ran into on campus today," she said. "And I was thinking of you." The smile on her face let Sinclair know exactly what kind of thoughts those were. Her hand brushed Sinclair's knee, then moved back to the gearshift.

They drove through dirt and forest, through narrow passes that allowed the branches of trees to dip inside the open windows of the Jeep and tickle their hair.

"When I was planning to come back to the island I read a lot about it," Hunter said. "Its history, its present, its landscape. Everything. My first few weeks back I was in the mountains almost every day when I wasn't working, determined to find out as much as I could that wasn't in most guidebooks." The Jeep roared as it struggled over a large root in their path. "It was on one of those wanderings that I found this place." She gestured to the forest around them.

The sun was a different quality up here, brighter with the contrast of shadowy trees enfolding it. Everything it covered—leaves, vines, tree trunks, moss—seemed to welcome it, stretching luxuriantly under its golden touch. The air felt cooler here, rarified.

They stopped at the foot of one of the largest trees Sinclair had ever seen. It was easily as big as Hunter's house with gigantic branches that stretched out and up, shining bright in the sun. Green and brown vines hung down from these branches, some brushing the forest floor. Sinclair blinked as a flurry of varicolored butterflies tumbled through the air close enough for her to see the fine powder on their wings.

"Beautiful, aren't they?" Hunter tucked the Jeep's keys in her pants pocket then turned to the other woman. "I wonder if you realize how much you've fucked me up?" Hunter didn't wait for her to respond. "With you I feel like a damn virgin again, all sweaty palms and wet pussy. You make me think of fucking and making love all the time." She touched Sinclair's face. "Or about just being with you. I want you to think about that when it's time for you to go back." Her lips covered Sinclair's.

Sinclair pushed into the kiss, amazed by her words and by the heat flaring quickly between them.

"Come on," Hunter rasped, pulling away. "Before I change my mind."

"What if *I* changed your mind?" Sinclair pushed her fingers into Hunter's shirt, parting buttons to find warm skin.

The dark woman gasped then chuckled against Sinclair's mouth. "Whatever you want, baby."

Their tongues slid hot and electric against each other, tasting moistness and heat and want. Sinclair climbed over the gearshift to straddle Hunter's lap and pull her shirt from the slacks.

"Whatever you planned, we can do later." She feasted on the softness of Hunter's mouth, the hard slide of teeth, and on the breath that Hunter gasped for her. The dark woman's hands danced up the backs of Sinclair's thighs under the dress and abruptly pulled down her panties. They ripped. She palmed Sinclair's ass, squeezing the soft flesh and pulling her close. Sinclair pushed Hunter's shirt and bra aside, blindly seeking her breasts, those mounds of soft flesh that seemed so different from the rest of her. She nipped them with her teeth, raking the hardened nipples as Hunter groaned, squeezing Sinclair against her. Hunter's fingers distracted her, thrust into her, abruptly, deeply.

"Baby . . ."

"Drop—drop the seat back," Hunter gasped into Sinclair's hair. When she pulled the lever they almost flew in the backseat. Hunter's fingers slid from Sinclair's heat.

"No! No . . ."

"Shh. I'm coming for you, baby. Just . . . yeah, open your legs like that." She filled her again, slipping more of her fingers inside as Sinclair nibbled and suckled her and undid her pants. Hunter didn't have any panties on. Sinclair almost sobbed with relief at finding her slick and ready. Hunter's legs widened even as her fingers fucked Sinclair, moving inside her with an insistent rhythm that made Sinclair long to feel the heat of Hunter on her own fingers.

"Not inside," Hunter whispered as Sinclair's hands slid against her soft flesh and teasing the delicate petals apart. Sinclair brushed her clit, then moved away. The indirect stimulation pulled a moan from Hunter and thrust her hips hard against Sinclair. Her brain was going up in smoke with each stroke of Hunter's fingers. She bent double in Hunter's lap, feasting on her breasts as her lover brought her closer to the edge. The wicked fingers went even deeper and Sinclair fell, crying out. Her body spasmed, shuddered, then tried to move away when Hunter stroked its hypersensitive clit.

"Stop!" Sinclair pushed her hands away and Hunter gasped into her hair, whispering her apology in a litany of moans as her hand clutched the back of Sinclair's neck tighter and tighter. Sinclair touched her clit again, lightly stroking her, then harder as she took a dark nipple deep into her mouth. Hunter jerked hard against her.

"Oh, fuck!" Her fingers dug into Sinclair's neck. "Fuck!" Her body trembled and wept, shuddered and quaked. Sinclair held on.

"I swear," Hunter said when she could speak coherently again. "I didn't bring you up here just for this."

"You had better not. You know you can have me any-where." Sinclair kissed her softly and licked at the slightly swollen mouth.

"If only that were true."

"Trust me. It is."

She looked at Sinclair with a slow grin. "I'll remember that."

Sinclair slowly pulled away until she was sitting back in the passenger seat. "So what was the real reason you brought me into the woods?"

"Ah, so now you want to see."

"Of course, since my immediate needs have been satis-fied." She pulled off her ripped panties and tossed them in the backseat. "For now."

Hunter put her clothes back to rights and jumped out of the Jeep before grabbing a blanket and throwing it over her shoulder. "Come on then."

They stepped through the curtain of vines then stood still as it settled closed behind them. Sinclair gaped.

"*This* is the reason I brought you up here."

It was a sanctuary, a hidden garden of exotic blooms, or-chids, lilies, hibiscus, all sporting colors that Sinclair had no idea existed in nature. Butterflies of every hue and size flitted from flower to flower, delighting in the chaos of color and scent. The sun lay over the glade like a blanket, warm and golden.

"There's a hot spring on the other side of the gardens. We can soak in it later on if you like."

"I would definitely like."

They found a clear spot and spread the blanket out, being careful not to crush any of the carelessly flittering butterflies in the process. Hunter sighed as she lay down with her head in Sinclair's lap.

"This place is so peaceful, so perfect." Her eyes drifted closed. "It's almost like I can feel the rest of the universe when I'm in here."

"It *is* lovely. I'm surprised that other people haven't found out about it."

"I'm a little surprised too. Or maybe they know about it but just make sure that when they come they leave the place just as they found it. That's fine with me too."

Sinclair rubbed her lover's stomach through the shirt, pleased that Hunter had chosen to share this moment and place with her. Happiness warmed her, nearly burning away the awareness that she would soon be leaving for America.

"Aw, isn't this sweet."

Sinclair jumped at the unexpected intrusion. Hunter froze in her lap then turned, slowly, in the direction of the voice. It belonged to one of two men, who stood much too close to them in the clearing. One held a machete in his hand. Sinclair's pulse started a panicked riot in her body.

"You gals look really good together. Especially back there in the Jeep." He rubbed his chest and stared hard at the two women.

Hunter slowly stood up, watching them walk closer. "Hey, there," she said. "Can we help you boys?" Her voice was vicious with scorn.

"Yeah, you can help us," the one with pale eyes and the

bare chest said. "You can give us another show like the one you did in the truck."

"Or," his friend laughed breathlessly, "you could just keep on doing what you were just doing. We'll take care of the rest." The front of his trousers bulged.

Fear prickled over Sinclair's skin. *This was not happening. Not again.*

"I'm afraid we can't do that," Hunter said.

"Well, foreign woman. We're not going to give you a choice."

In a blur of motion the men flew at them. The one with the machete went for Hunter. He hurled his body at her with the long blade held behind him. His eyes widened when Hunter's foot flew up and slammed into his belly. She danced out of the blade's way. Then Sinclair had her own problem to deal with and couldn't watch anymore. The other man abruptly materialized in front of her and slapped her hard across the face. She tripped on the edge of the blanket and fell on her backside. The man lunged at her. Galvanized by fear, Sinclair scrambled backward, reaching desperately for a weapon to hold him off with. With a sob of relief her hand closed on something. Her camera. She swung it by its strap, hitting him full in the face. Stunned, he staggered back and fell in the grass. Blood rushed up, splashed across his skin and the grass. She came up after him, slamming the heavy Nikon in his face over and over even after he brought his hands up to protect himself against her assault. Then, he stopped moving.

Sinclair stumbled back from his battered and slack face. Her harsh breath was loud in the clearing. *Where was Hunter?* She looked around at the sudden glint of steel in the sun.

"Hunter!"

The dark woman held the machete in her hand, the blade descending in an arc toward the prone man's chest. Her foot pressed hard against his throat.

"What?!" she snarled.

"Don't."

"Don't what? Do you know what they were going to do to us, Sinclair?" She held the weapon above his bleeding chest, arms trembling with the effort of not striking. "They were going to fuck us to death." She released a harsh breath. "You know, they find dead bodies in the bush every day. Two more, especially the bodies of two rapists wouldn't make that much difference."

"No, baby. No. Don't defile this place any more."

"Defile? Don't talk about defilement to me—"

"Let's leave them. Let's go before they wake up." She didn't ask Hunter this time; she pulled her lover's arm, forcing her to drop the machete in the grass. "Come."

Hunter turned once to look at the two men sprawled in the afternoon sun, their faces and bodies bloody. She spat in the grass then turned and walked back to the Jeep.

Sinclair gathered the pieces of her camera and its film and dropped them in the unused picnic basket before picking it and the blanket up and following her lover. With each step she slowly became aware of her body's aches. Her jaw was beginning to sting from where the boy had slapped her. An unpleasant sense of déjà vu made her stumble as she tried to get into the truck. Hunter was silent during the drive down the mountain, her mouth hard and set. At a crossroad, she turned to Sinclair.

"Do you want me to take you home?"

"Home with you, yes. We need to go to your place and get you cleaned up."

Blood ran sluggishly from a gash along Hunter's cheekbone. The knuckles of both hands were raw and bleeding. She drove on without another word. At the house, they parked the Jeep and walked inside together. Once in the safety of her blue haven, Hunter collapsed. Her stony façade crumbled and she leaned against the wall, trembling.

Cooing words of comfort, Sinclair led her to the bedroom where she gently undressed her lover and tended to her wounds. Hunter curled up on top of the sheets.

"You know, Sinclair," she said. "I love this place. I really do. But when things like this happen . . ." her voice roughened and she stopped. Sinclair slipped her arms around the dark woman and held her close. She quietly shook, her body vibrating like a plucked string in Sinclair's embrace.

"The island is beautiful," Sinclair said. "But it's also poor. A lot of desperate people live here, and desperate people do desperate and awful things. You have to love Jamaica still, with all her faults. You just have to."

"I do. But it hurts." Her voice broke. "Sometimes it hurts too damn much."

"I know. I'm sorry." Sinclair rocked her trembling body, feeling tears begin to run down her face. "I'm sorry. I know."

They slept. Their emotional exhaustion laid them out on the bed and pulled their eyes closed to the bright sun just outside the large windows. At some point Hunter woke, undressed Sinclair, then fell back asleep. The sun was gone when Sinclair opened her eyes again.

The dark woman lay propped up on one elbow, watching her. "Hey."

"Hey, yourself." Sinclair yawned and carefully stretched her bruised body. "How are you feeling?"

"Better."

"Good. I was getting worried for a minute there."

"So was I."

Sinclair touched Hunter's face, traced its smooth lines, even the bandaged cheek, before moving to the slash of a nose and the curved mouth. Her lover closed her eyes.

"You are an amazing person," Sinclair said. "And I am glad to know you, to be close to you."

Hunter kissed her wandering fingers before pulling them away from her face. "I should be saying those words to you." She sighed again. "I've been here for two years, and in that time I've heard of so many horrors, so much brutality happening on the island. A time or two I even encountered some of that craziness myself, and I was terrified. But none of that came close to what I felt today when those men came after us." Her fingers stirred around Sinclair's. "Thank you for being there with me. Thank you for being here with me now."

"Where else would I be?" They both looked surprised at the words that came out of Sinclair's mouth. Yet neither woman rushed to put them away. That evening Sinclair called her father to let him know that she wouldn't be home until tomorrow. After an unguarded heartbeat of silence, he told her to be careful and wished her a good night.

When morning came Sinclair was the one who woke first. She left her sleeping lover, who looked vulnerable and unexpectedly sweet with her face tucked into the pillow, to make an attempt at breakfast. The kitchen was meticulous and intimidating but she managed to make decent scrambled eggs with cheese and toast. She brought the food to the bedroom where Hunter was still peacefully sleeping, and put the tray on the bedside table.

Sinclair woke her with kisses, lingering over the warm skin of her face before trailing down to her neck, the skin between her breasts, then her stomach. Hunter stirred beneath the soft touches but did not open her eyes. Sinclair paused at the juncture of her thighs when a familiar scent reached her nose.

She laughed. "Open your eyes, you faker."

Instead Hunter with her eyes still closed, widened her thighs and gently nudged Sinclair's head down. "I thought you were going to continue this to its logical conclusion."

Sinclair batted her hand away and moved back up the bed. "I was trying to wake you up with breakfast not an invitation to sex."

"Hmm, but you can do both." She opened her eyes. "That's the beauty of a woman like you."

Sinclair lightly pinched her arm. "Wretch."

Hunter flinched away then groaned as she sat up. "Careful of my battle wounds, temptress."

"Oh, shit. Sorry about that." Sinclair sat back against the headboard. "I forgot."

"If only I could forget, too, and pretend that none of this ever happened."

"At least we left them alive and you don't have to live with the regret of killing them."

Hunter growled. "I wouldn't have called that regret."

Sinclair's troubled gaze flickered over the other woman then away. "Have some breakfast. I don't cook very often so it's a rare treat. Eat up."

"Don't try to change my mood, woman."

"I'm not trying to change your mood." Sinclair retrieved the tray and sat it between them on the bed. "Have some breakfast, dammit."

"Some merciful angel you are," Hunter said, reaching for the food. "This is good," she murmured after a few mouthfuls.

"Glad you like it."

Sinclair stole a piece of toast and watched as Hunter devoured the meal, sitting cross-legged on top of the white covers. She was gorgeous in her nakedness; even the sadness in her eyes and the pale bandage on her cheek added to her beauty.

"I think you should rest," Sinclair said. "Take it easy until tomorrow when you feel a little better."

Hunter shook her head. "I doubt that I'll feel any better tomorrow, so I might as well try to make a dent in the work piling up on my desktop today."

Which meant that she wanted Sinclair gone. "That makes sense, I suppose. But don't overdo it." She stood up and went back into the kitchen on the pretense of getting more orange juice. Her face stung with the slap of rejection. At least now she knew the quicker way to catch the bus back to her father's house. Sinclair brought Hunter back another glass of orange juice and stayed only long enough to change the dark woman's bandage and wipe her wounds down again with witch hazel.

"I'll talk with you later on," she said from the doorway of the bedroom. "I'll let myself out."

All the way back to her father's house, she was angry at Hunter for letting her go without a word of protest. Then she chided herself for being passive-aggressive and too weak to tell Hunter what she wanted from her. *Which was . . . what exactly?*

At home that night she let Nikki know what happened, told her about Hunter's reaction and her own sudden possessiveness.

Nikki sat close to Sinclair on the sofa. "You said all that happened with Hunter and what she was feeling, but what about you?" Her voice was low. "Do you feel the same way she does?"

Sinclair shook her head. "I don't know." She had been so caught up in taking care of Hunter, in trying to give her lover what she needed that her own fear had been erased from the equation. She shivered, remembering the intent on those men's faces, the jutting penis and feral look of the one who had raised his hand to her and forced her to break the camera.

"I left my camera in Hunter's Jeep," she said inanely.

"You can get it from her tomorrow." Nikki touched her hand. "It's OK to be afraid, you know."

Sinclair shook her head. "I know. And I was. I was so afraid for her, so afraid of not being able to see you or Papa again." She took a cleansing breath. "I'm just glad we got out of there alive and without getting raped."

"So am I." Nikki squeezed her hand and they sat, silently, in the dark.

"Do you think she'll want to see me tomorrow?"

"She'd be stupid not to."

When Sinclair walked up to Hunter's house the next morning, she heard laughter. She hesitated a moment before knocking. Hunter came to the door looking relaxed and calm, much better than the day before, in her loose drawstring pants and a white T-shirt. The bandage on her cheek was fresh.

"Hey, come in." She kissed Sinclair briefly on the mouth. "This is a day for visitors. Della is here with me in the backyard."

"Oh, that's the sound that I heard."

"We must have been pretty loud for you to hear us at the gate."

You said it, not me.

"Hello, Sinclair," Della greeted her as she stepped out into the backyard. "Would you like something to drink?" She gestured to the folding table set up with a pitcher of something red swimming with ice cubes and, next to it, a tall carafe of water.

"No, I'm all right. Thank you, though."

"Have a seat, Sin." Hunter pointed her to the stone bench where she must have been sitting beside Della. She sank into the grass at the older woman's feet.

"Hunter was just telling me about what happened in the hills," Della said.

Sinclair sat down. "It was pretty awful."

"I tell you this country is going to hell in a handbasket and it's us Jamaicans who're taking it there."

"We're not all to blame, Della." Hunter squinted up at her ex-lover in the sun.

Sinclair took her sunglasses out of her bag and passed them to Hunter. Without pausing her conversation the dark woman smiled her thanks and slipped them on. "There are bad elements everywhere, back in Manchester and London and certainly in the U.S. I'm trying not to be bitter about this whole experience."

"You're a sweet, naive thing." Della said, brushing her hand through Hunter's hair. "That's why the rest of us have to look out for you. Isn't that right, Sinclair?"

"I'll do what I can, although so far she's done an excellent job of taking care of herself."

"A mere illusion." She poured a glass of water and gave it to Hunter. "Drink up before you fall over in the heat."

"I'm not a delicate flower, Della." Hunter took the water anyway and drank deeply before passing it back. With a low sigh, she lay back in the grass and crossed her ankles. "See what I've been putting up with all morning?" She directed a look of long suffering at Sinclair. "Della is convinced that I'm going to fall apart any minute now just because those boys roughed us up."

Despite Hunter's bravado, Sinclair noticed that the incident in the garden had left a faint shadow in her eyes, a shadow that she knew would linger for some time. Although the boys hadn't touched Hunter, at least not in a sexual way, she still felt violated.

Della rolled her eyes. "When she called this morning to tell me what happened, I couldn't just stay at the shop languishing in the air-conditioning while she was here probably suffering from post-traumatic stress or some such. I left my niece to watch the shop before I came down."

"I didn't know that you had a shop," Sinclair said, turning an interested look on the older woman so Della would give Hunter a little breathing room.

"I sell my pottery and sculpture out of the back of my house. A lot of the rich white tourists buy them so I can keep myself in women and food."

"She is minimizing what she does," Hunter said. "Della is actually quite successful around the island. She even has made a name for herself here. People keep wanting to whisk her off to New York or London to do a show and sell even more than she does here, but she's not interested."

"How wonderful," Sinclair leaned slightly toward Della. "Maybe one day I can see your workshop?"

"Come up anytime. If I'm not there then my niece, Sofia, should be."

"Great. I'll drop by sometime this week."

Della nodded and handed Hunter another glass, this time it was filled with whatever juice was in the pitcher. The dark woman shook her head and pointed to the water.

Watching them it would be easy to think that they were still lovers. That lingering stare of Della's and the solicitude she showed to Hunter in nauseating abundance said that she still cared deeply for the dark woman. Her attentions sent little prickles of annoyance racing along Sinclair's nerves. She didn't deceive herself by pretending that she wasn't jealous. Meanwhile Hunter acted . . . like herself. Sinclair smiled then stood up.

"I'm going to head out and leave you two to chat," she said. "I just stopped by to make sure that you were all right." She knelt down to kiss the dark woman in farewell. Hunter sat up and grabbed her arm.

"What's going on with these sudden exits? Have I become that unbearable so soon?"

"Don't be ridiculous. You have company and I know you two want to catch up."

"Della is not company. We can 'catch up' with you here." She pulled Sinclair closer until she was almost in her lap. "Stay." Their lips were inches apart. Hunter shoved the sunglasses to the top of her head to reveal her pain-flecked eyes. "Please."

"OK. I'll stay." Sinclair stood up and reclaimed her seat on the bench.

"Well, this is interesting." Della said, looking at the two women. "How long has this been going on and why didn't I know about it?"

Sinclair looked down with too-warm cheeks. The dark woman shaded her eyes again and lay back down in the grass. "A few days."

"But you're leaving. Right?"

Did Della want to make sure of that fact? "Yes, I am. But I'm going to stay for a few more weeks than I had initially planned." The decision made itself the moment those words left her mouth. She'd wanted to prolong her time with her family and her new lover. Since she hadn't taken a vacation in three years, it should be more than possible. She just had to call Shelly and have her make sure.

"Are you now?" Della looked down at Hunter. "That dangerous charm of yours strikes again."

The dark glasses shielded Hunter's eyes from view, but her mouth was smiling. "As long as the charm works on the ones I want then I'm not complaining. Are you, Sin?"

Sinclair grinned. "Not at all."

Della left them an hour later, to get back to the shop, she said. Hunter walked her out while Sinclair lingered in the backyard, taking sips from Hunter's abandoned cup of water and replaying the afternoon's conversations in her mind. She stretched out on the bench and put her feet up. Della didn't seem at all jealous that she and Hunter were together. Rather toward the end of her visit she had smiled oddly at Sinclair and said something about wishing that Sinclair could stay because Hunter needed some stability in her life. Stability? The older woman might as well have called her boring.

"What are you smiling about?" Hunter let the back door swing closed behind her as she walked back to Sinclair.

"Stability. Excitement."

"Don't let Della get to you. Ever since we stopped being lovers she's been playing mummy and trying to find a suitable girl for me to marry."

Is that what she was doing? "Wasn't Lydia suitable?"

"Apparently not." She moved Sinclair's feet out of the way and sank down on the bench beside her, draping the long legs across her lap. "Have dinner with me tonight." Hunter watched Sinclair with a soft smile curving her mouth. "I want to give you a sweet reward for taking care of me yesterday."

"Sweet, huh?" Her insides just officially turned into mush for this woman.

"Definitely." Hunter's fingers played over the fine bones of Sinclair's feet, tracing the veins just under her skin.

"With such promises, how can I refuse?"

At Hunter's insistence, they ate dinner in the backyard, spread out on a blanket with the food laid out between them. Watching Hunter cook the meal and being unable to taste it had built a steady fire under Sinclair's hunger. By the time the dark woman had set the plates out, she was starving.

"Where do I start?" she asked as Hunter presented the meal.

"With this."

Hunter took a thick, scarlet-colored fruit from a pile of three others in a white bowl and broke it in half. A honeycomb of bright red seeds lay in the pale membranes.

"Pomegranate." Hunter took a piece in her hand and used a finger to detach a sprinkling of seeds. "You can eat the seeds if you want to. For fiber." She put them near Sinclair's mouth. "Open."

The flesh-covered seeds were sweet, exploding between her tongue and palate with only the slightest pressure. Sinclair tried to suck off the juicy bits and spit the hard seeds into her hand, but it was messy and she wasn't keeping enough fruit in her mouth.

"Try eating the seeds. You might find that more satisfying."

She did. They ate until all that remained of the pomegranate was a shell that lay open like a crushed flower on the white juice-stained dish.

"Are you ready for the rest of the meal?"

Hunter fed Sinclair a steaming plate of run-down, its slow-simmered flavor of coconut milk enhanced by pink curls of shrimp and the delicious burn of scotch bonnet peppers. She poured the richly scented stew over boiled green bananas, ripe plantains, and firm, round dumplings. At the first bite, Sinclair released a breath of pure astonishment.

"This is even better than my grandmother's." She threw Hunter a look of mock anger. "You've made me blaspheme." She took another bite. "But this tastes so good."

"And all I have to do is cook to have you make those noises? I think you're about to turn me into a chef."

Sinclair laughed and raised her fork to Hunter before returning to the serious business of eating.

"I really, really like the way you cook," she said after the second helping. Her mouth was still full, this time with the starchy sweet combination of dumplings and boiled plantains. She chewed with her fingers covering her mouth. No need to express her thanks by spraying Hunter with food. Besides, it was too good to waste.

"Well, I like the way you eat," Hunter returned with a smile, her fork poised over a modest-sized plate.

Sinclair winked. "Save that kind of talk for later, missy. One oral indulgence at a time is all my poor little heart can take."

"Really? I took you for a multitasker."

"Not where you're concerned."

"In that case, I might have to take back your all-access pass."

"I'd like to see you try." Sinclair let go another orgasmic moan. "If you cooked this well for Della no wonder she doesn't want to let you go."

"She was the one who let me go, not the other way around."

"That's surprising."

"Why?"

"She just seems a little . . . possessive of you, like she hasn't completely let your past relationship go."

"That is definitely not the case. She put me aside like a child, like she'd given me as much of her time as she could before setting me free, so to speak."

"Were you angry?"

"For a while, yes." She shrugged and sipped her water. "Then I wasn't."

Sinclair nodded, content with that explanation. They ate the rest of their meal in companionable silence, each swept up in the eddies of their own thoughts.

When the meal was over Sinclair stood up to help Hunter with the dishes. In the kitchen, she ran hot water over the small pile already in the sink. Thankfully, Hunter was the kind of chef who washed as she cooked. The kitchen was nearly spotless, with only their dishes left behind to clean.

"Go ahead and make us some tea while I take care of these," Sinclair said, glancing over her shoulder at the other woman.

After she finished the dishes, she escaped to the backyard to lie on the blanket that had been cleared of all remnants of their dinner. Sinclair looked up at the sky. Daylight was just beginning to fade. Other stars were still pale shadows hidden by the brightness of the sun, but that brilliant star was preparing to make its exit. She released her breath in a long sigh of appreciation. The sound mingled with those of the swaying leaves and the wind ruffling the grass near her. The back door creaked open.

"You are not going to fall asleep on me," Hunter murmured near her ear. "I have other plans for you." She set the tray of tea in the grass beside the blanket.

Sinclair opened her eyes, smiling. "I wouldn't dream of ending our day so soon."

"Good. Have some tea with me."

The brew was simple yet fragrant, a mixture of fresh orange leaves and honey. Sinclair took a few sips before leaning into the shelter of Hunter's arms, replete.

"You are a wonderful cook. A beautiful, ravishing woman," Sinclair murmured, well on her way toward a nap. "And sweet. Like a pomegranate."

Hunter chuckled and gathered her closer. When Sinclair opened her eyes again, the sky was wreathed in stars.

"You're awake then?" Hunter asked, nipping gently on

her ear. At Sinclair's sleepy smile, she grinned. "Good. Let's move this party indoors then, shall we?"

Hunter locked the night out and left the blanket and tea cups in the kitchen to be dealt with later. She took Sinclair's hand and walked toward the bedroom. Once in the room Sinclair excused herself to go to the bathroom. When she came back Hunter was turning down the sheets on the bed. A trio of candles glowed from the windowsill.

"Very nice."

She came up behind Hunter and dragged the T-shirt from her body, taking time to touch the warm skin with its shifting muscles and irresistible womanliness. Sinclair was careful not to aggravate her bruises.

"I finished the painting," Hunter murmured.

Sinclair's hands paused their exploration. "Really? When can I see it?"

"When you turn around."

The painting hung suspended on the wall between the two large bedroom windows, a study of greens, copper, and reds. The woman in the painting—because this untamed creature couldn't really be Sinclair—lay on a bed of ferns with her head tossed back and her hair spread in a cottony cloud over upraised arms. The top two buttons of her white blouse were undone, giving a teasing glimpse of her breasts. The long legs, accentuated in tight blue jeans, were strewn in a pose of postcoital relaxation. Only her cheek, the graceful slope of her neck, and the corner of a moist-lipped Mona Lisa smile could be seen. The rest of her face was lost to her coyly turned-away head. It could have been a photograph, the image was so real.

"You like?" Hunter asked.

"Very much." Sinclair looked at the large painting again. Was that how Hunter saw her? "I'm never going to see that painting again, am I?" she asked.

"Of course you will. Whenever you come into my bedroom, it'll be hanging right there." Hunter kissed the back of her neck and anchored her hands on Sinclair's hips. "Now, where were we?"

Sinclair chuckled and turned around. "Right here, love."

Her fingers loosened the drawstring pants and pulled them down Hunter's legs. The dark woman was wearing panties, of a soft, white Victorian lace, the kind that sat low on Hunter's hips to show off the flat expanse of belly and the inviting slope that led to her pussy. Sinclair took a peek at the back. The lace lay high across Hunter's ass like butterfly wings, leaving the sleek bottom half of her cheeks bare. Sinclair wet her lips.

"Were you expecting to get lucky today, Miss Willoughby?"

A shrug sent delightful ripples across her cleavage. "It didn't hurt to be prepared."

Hunter's eyes challenged Sinclair to continue her exploration, to hook her fingers in the waistband of the panties and fling them to some corner of the room. But she wasn't ready to get rid of the gorgeous wrapping quite yet. Instead, Sinclair's hands touched dark hips and pulled them close to her nose. With a low trembling sigh she inhaled the smell of Hunter, the delicate musk of her that was like the earth after rain.

"May I?"

"Please do." Hunter's voice was rough.

Sinclair laid her cheek against the pale lace, feeling the heat with her face, indulging herself in the powerful, primal scent of her lover. Patient, Hunter breathed slowly above her even though her body obviously begged for satisfaction.

"You can take them off if you want."

Sinclair smiled. "Thank you." She caressed the dark skin through the white lace, excited by the increased pungency of the other woman's scent.

Hunter groaned. "Do you just get off on torturing me?"

"Is that a rhetorical question?" Sinclair laughed softly.

"Very funny." Hunter pulled her to her feet and with spare

quick movements undressed her. "Come, let me show you something."

"I remember hearing that line before."

"Then you know this won't hurt." She pressed Sinclair down into the bed. "Not even the tiniest bit."

Hunter kissed Sinclair. She was gentle, her exploration curious rather than passionate. But Sinclair invited her to do more, opening her mouth under Hunter's and sliding her fingers into the other woman's hair. Her legs captured Hunter's, curling around her like twin snakes so she wouldn't take the pleasure away, so she would keep pouring heat and wetness into her body until Sinclair forgot everything. The smooth curves of her lace-clad ass undulated under Sinclair's hands.

"Hunter . . ." Her voice trembled with need.

Hunter's body truly came alive then, rising up over Sinclair like a dark tide. She pressed her thigh between Sinclair's and shoved her hands above her head. She moaned and pushed into her, desperate to have Hunter's body against her sensitive nipples.

"I loved feeling your pussy on my face," Hunter whispered. "You taste like ackee and saltfish. I could eat you all night." She licked her throat and followed the arched line to her breasts. Sinclair could feel her hovering, could feel her breath, waiting. Hunter's mouth covered her nipple. She sighed, drowning in the liquid delight. Hunter sucked her nipples into the warm wet of her mouth, sucking, milking until Sinclair gasped and writhed against the bed. She took Sinclair's breasts into her hands, pressing one into her mouth then the other. Sinclair trembled under her.

"What do you want?" Hunter bit her nipples and stained them again with her tongue.

"I want your fingers, your mouth, anything." Sinclair thrust her hips against Hunter, beyond pride, begging.

Her hands slid between Sinclair's legs, searching for the ache. "Here?"

"Yes."

The fullness was a surprise. It was only one finger, but it felt so good. Sinclair's body arched off the bed, stung by the sweet pressure Hunter finally offered. "More."

With the second finger she would have promised Hunter anything. Sinclair's hands clawed her back, sinking into the solid muscles that moved as Hunter nipped at her sensitized nipples and fucked her with agonizing slowness. Hunter lifted her head, sending her hair dancing over Sinclair's heated skin.

"You've ruined me for other women." Her fingers moved steadily inside her. "I hope you know that." She bit a blood-flushed nipple.

The pain sparked a higher flame inside Sinclair. She panted and arched into Hunter, sliding on the long fingers until she was crying from the sensation, her hips rocking against Hunter's palms, moving to the tempo she set. "I—oh!" The stroke of her fingers stole Sinclair's breath, until she was whimpering with need, her belly tight and trembling. The bed shook as she exploded in Hunter's hand, shaking and arching her breasts against her lover's mouth.

Hunter released her slowly, licking her breasts in lazy, circular strokes and holding her body still as shudders of satisfaction rippled through it.

"Not fair," Sinclair gasped. "This was supposed to be my show."

"You weren't fighting me off." She kissed Sinclair's chin then buried her face in the damp neck. "But don't worry. You'll get your turn soon."

Hunter lay back on the bed and her body relaxed into the rumpled sheets, soothed by Sinclair's wandering hands and soft, warming kisses. She hummed her approval when Sinclair touched her skin, still clothed in its Victorian lace panties that made it look like dark silk. The contrast of white lace against bitter chocolate skin made Sinclair's body heat again. *So beautiful.* Hunter waited patiently while her lover lay quietly against her thighs.

Her hand touched Sinclair's hair. "Teasing at this stage of the game isn't very nice."

"No. That's not it." A weak laugh trickled from Sinclair's lips. "Give me a second."

The dark woman quieted. Sinclair kissed the smooth line of Hunter's stomach and watched, amazed, as the muscles rippled under her touch. Her body was wet again. Had it ever been dry in Hunter's presence?

She pushed the lace out of her way to better feel the heating flesh and the rough spring of hair under the tiny panties. Her scent was hypnotic. She touched her nose to Hunter's flesh again. The dark woman squirmed under her, but didn't resist when she tugged at the white lace. The panties peeled away with a sigh, revealing their moist treasure. Above Sinclair, she hissed.

"Can I see?"

Sinclair looked up and saw her nod. Hunter widened her legs. The dark curls were wet, glistening around a deep pink snail that thrust its head out even further as she watched. Her tongue tingled.

There it was again, that faint taste of mangoes and wildness. She grasped the tight ass cheeks and pulled Hunter closer, diving into the banquet before her. Salted honey flooded over her nose, down her chin and neck, still she ate, licking and sucking until Hunter's thighs tightened around her ears and all she could hear was the hammering of her own heart and the thirsty sound of her mouth. Fingers grasped her head, pulling her deeper into the feast, encouraging the hungry movement of her tongue and the frantic snaking search of her mouth between slick thighs. The fingers tightened on her head, the thighs trembled, hips shuddered, and the soft flesh streamed wetness as it undulated under her tongue. Hunter's fingers loosened and fell away.

"Damn." Hunter's thighs relaxed against the bed. "I have to say . . . that was really worth the wait."

"I should hope so." Sinclair kissed her lover's thigh and moved up to snuggle under her chin.

Hunter shuddered again and tightened her embrace. "You are . . ." Her voice drifted away in a sigh. ". . . incredible."

"Hey, Nikki." Sinclair rolled over in the bed and adjusted the phone at her ear. "I don't think I'll be home tonight. Is that OK?"

She heard her stepmother laugh. "It should be fine. Just don't forget to tell Hunter that she's invited to dinner one night soon."

Sinclair cursed Nikki for making her blush again. Instead of bothering to deny who she was with she sighed. "I'll tell her. See you tomorrow morning."

"Trouble?" Hunter took the phone and put it back in its cradle.

"No. But Nikki does want you to come over for dinner with me before I leave."

"Ah. To check me out as your suitor instead of Lydia's. Interesting developments." She trailed a hand between Sinclair's breasts down to the soft curve of her belly.

"Not really. I think Nikki really likes you and wishes you'd come around more often."

"Don't try to bullshit a bullshitter, baby." She kissed Sinclair lightly on her nose, moving her hand farther south. "It's fine. I'll come to dinner with you one day to satisfy Nikki's curiosity. To be honest, she and I have yet to have a real conversation so that could be interesting."

"What?" Sinclair had stopped listening the moment agile fingers dipped between her thighs. Her breathing deepened.

"Never mind," Hunter's voice deepened. "We can talk about all that later on."

That next evening they went out together to a barbeque in Mandeville Hills.

"It's informal, I promise," Hunter said before they left. "And no more surprises."

"Please and thank you. I don't think my heart can stand any more of your surprises."

"I don't know, you seemed to hold your own pretty well." Hunter pulled on a white tank top and smoothed it over her belly. Her smile was just a tad too self-satisfied.

"Brat." Sinclair put on a stripe of postshower deodorant, then checked herself for hickies. Her neck was faintly bruised, but there was nothing to be done about it. She buttoned her shirt. Hunter had lent her some clothes, a pair of jeans and a long-sleeved shirt that somehow looked more feminine on her than they ever did on her dark lover. "The least you could have done was let me go home and change into something of my own."

"Why? I like how you look in my clothes." Hunter chuckled. "It marks you as mine."

Sinclair politely showed her the middle finger.

"Later. We have somewhere to be right now."

At the barbeque, they walked out of a sprawling British colonial style house to a backyard full of Hunter look-alikes. Women, boys, old men, little girls, all various versions of Hunter, possessed of some feature she wore all too well; the dark skin, the fleshy mouth, even the look of cynicism that Sinclair thought was cultivated. Now she had proof that it was genetic.

"No surprises, huh?"

"What? This is a barbeque."

"With your family."

"So what? They don't act like deranged wildebeests or gnaw on each other in front of company."

"I'm not amused."

"Yes, you are." Hunter grinned. "Come on. Let's go say hello."

She marched Sinclair straight over to a slim, pale-skinned woman who stood over a bowl of punch looking at it like it was the worst disaster since disco. Her expression changed once she saw Hunter. She hugged the dark woman as if she hadn't seen her in months.

"Good to see you, prodigal Hunter. We haven't seen you over here in a while."

"Well, you know, work for the university keeps me busy."

"I know you work at home so don't try that on me, young lady."

Hunter had the grace to look slightly embarrassed. "I'm not here five minutes and you're already making me feel bad."

"Well, if you came around more often—" the older woman made a dismissive noise. "Let's not get into this old argument in front of your guest." She turned toward Sinclair, extending her hand. "Since my niece is too rude to introduce us, my name is Eunice Keller."

"Uh, sorry. Aunt Eunice, this is Sinclair."

Sinclair put on her most polite smile. "Good to meet you."

"Are you the new girlfriend?"

She blinked at the unexpected question. "I'm just here for another few weeks."

"That's not what I asked you."

"Aunt Eunice, stop." Hunter tucked Sinclair behind her and gave her aunt a stern look. "She's here to have a good time, not to be badgered by you."

"Darling, we all want to know. We're concerned about your happiness." Eunice brushed Hunter's cheek with the back of her fingers.

"I know, but ease off. Please. If you treat all the girls I bring over this way then you'll never see me safely married off."

"What girls? You never—"

"We'll talk more later. I have to say hi to everyone else.

Bye." Hunter pulled Sinclair away, but not before she saw Eunice's look of amused speculation.

"Is this going to be an obstacle course?"

"Not really. She was the most important person for you to meet. Everyone else will come over to us in their own good time." She released a sigh of relief. "Now it's time for food!"

More family members did come up to them as the afternoon wore on. Most were merely curious, looking at Sinclair with a speculative gleam in their collective eyes, though few were as direct as Eunice had been. After an hour of subtle interrogation, Sinclair had enough and escaped into the house for a drink.

At the bar in the sunroom, she ordered a Gilbey's and tonic and sat back to take in the view through the wide French doors. A familiar curve of ass caught her eye and Sinclair wolf-whistled in appreciation. Then she looked closer. No, that was not Hunter. Sinclair quickly turned around on the bar stool, hoping that the woman hadn't heard the high, piercing noise. She waited a few minutes before turning to look at the woman again.

The Hunter look-alike was very attractive. Tight brown leather pants hugged her slim hips and a white tank top showed off small, well-shaped breasts and a flat belly. She saw Sinclair looking at her and winked. Hunter suddenly appeared from somewhere in the house and sat next to her at the bar.

"That's my cousin, Ebony."

The woman looked exactly like Hunter only her hair was long and wavy, trailing down to her hips in a silky cloud.

"You see anything you like over there?"

"She is very attractive." Sinclair had a moment of déjà vu. Would Hunter ask her cousin to join them tonight in her bed?

"Well, that's too bad because you're taken."

She hid her sigh of relief. "I am? By whom?"

"Well, if it's not obvious then I guess I'm going to have to show you."

Sinclair was suddenly afraid. She backed away as much as she could on the bar stool. "No, it's OK, I believe you."

Hunter laughed and brushed her lips against the vulnerable spot just beneath Sinclair's ear. She shivered.

"See, it wasn't that bad, was it?"

Yes, it was. Apparently Hunter had already discovered one of her more sensitive erogenous zones. Sinclair put the glass to her mouth.

"What is this that I'm getting into with you?" she asked.

The other woman shrugged. "This is us having fun for as long as you're here. Don't feel pressured because I brought you here and you've met my family. This doesn't quite mean the same thing here as it does in America."

"Fair enough." Sinclair leaned toward her dark lover and lightly nipped her ear. "Does this mean we can come here and use their hot tub whenever we want?"

"How did you find out about the tub?"

"Unlike some women, who shall go nameless"—She patted Hunter's thigh. —"the people around here are a mighty informative bunch. They already outlined all the perks of being your girlfriend. One of them being twenty-four-hour access to the hot tub to do whatever I want with or without said perceived girlfriend."

"Really? What are the other perks?"

"If I told you then I'd have to kill you," Sinclair deadpanned.

"Do little deaths count? If so, we can get started on that right now. My old room is free and it has a nice fat lock on it." Hunter wiggled her eyebrows.

"You are incorrigible."

"As my perceived girlfriend, it's a good thing for you to know. It'll make everything go that much smoother." She kissed Sinclair quickly on the mouth. "Now come on, let's go dance. They're finally starting to play some good music."

* * *

A long time later Sinclair pled exhaustion and left Hunter on the dance floor shaking her ass to the fast-paced calypso music. She asked the woman behind the bar for some fresh carrot juice, but she looked at Sinclair as if she didn't know what the Americanized woman was talking about. With a glass of water in hand, Sinclair left the bar in search of more intelligent life.

"Where are you going, Sinclair?" Eunice called out to her from her lawn chair. She sat ringside with some half-dozen other members of the family who'd gotten tuckered out by the heat, dancing, or the children. "Come sit. Have some rum punch with us."

"No thank you for the drink, but I will sit with you."

They made room for her on a padded lawn chair next to Eunice. Sinclair was beginning to sense some sort of conspiracy.

"Everybody here knows Sinclair, right?"

Several people nodded. Sinclair remembered meeting them but couldn't be sure of all their names, all except for Ebony. "For those who don't know, this is Hunter's new girl."

"I am not her new girl." Sinclair scowled at Eunice who gave her a look that was all innocence. "We're just keeping each other company while I'm on the island."

Ebony laughed. "You say that, but I bet if one of us tried to push up on you Hunter would take us out."

"Damn right." A thin man with pale gold eyes grinned. Sinclair remembered that his name was Cliff. He owned the restaurant on the beach.

"So you're Hunter's girl," Ebony stated, laying back in her chair. "Subject dismissed."

Eunice nodded. Sinclair was glad to fade into the background once again as they began talking about something else. She quietly sipped her water and watched Hunter's family.

"Conchita sent some money from America the other day,"

Eunice was saying, "not much money, just two hundred-dollar bills."

"Didn't she marry that American dentist last year?" Tima, an Indian-looking cousin with her hair cut stylishly short, asked. Her amber eyes glowed in the afternoon sun.

Eunice waved her hand for silence. "Yes, she can afford to send much more than that, but that's not why I'm telling the story."

People in the group laughed or sucked their teeth, whichever their inclination.

"She sent it to Bailey's house and you know Bailey sent little Michael to the bank with money to cash."

"No, don't tell me," Cliff groaned.

"Yes, man. The thieving woman at the bank told the boy that the American money was no good and sent the boy home without any money."

"What?!" Winsome gasped. She was the quiet one who looked like Billie Holliday at the peak of her career, complete with a white flower in her pressed hair.

"My God, this is worse than those crooks at the post office who open all the mail from foreigners, steal whatever money that happens to be in there, then toss the letters in the rubbish bin not expecting to get caught."

"Poor Michael," Tima said, shaking her head.

"Is he stupid or something?"

Ebony threw her head back and laughed. "Leave my cousin alone. He's still at the age when he thinks that all grown-ups tell the truth."

"Hopefully after this he realizes that is just not so."

"You talking about what happened to little Michael?" Hunter leaned over Sinclair, looking sweaty but still energetic in the tank top that clung to her torso. "Ease up, Sin. Let me sit behind you."

"You're all sweaty and wet."

Hunter abruptly drew off her tank top and used it to dry

her neck, stomach and arms before tossing it behind the chair. "Better?"

"Much."

Wearing a black sports bra, Hunter slid into the lawn chair behind Sinclair. She leaned back into her lover with an inaudible sigh, ignoring the pairs of curious eyes on them.

"Yes, Bailey's boy," Eunice said, smiling at her niece. "Remember the fiasco with the bank?"

"Yes, man," Hunter replied. "I went down there to raise hell, but of course nobody knows who was on duty then or what happened to the two hundred dollars."

"Thieving crooks."

Cliff lifted his glass to Tima's comment. "Amen."

"The country is poor, man." Ebony said. "What else are poor people supposed to do?"

"Not steal from their countryman, for one thing," Winsome muttered.

"Don't be so damn idealistic. People just trying to put food on the table."

"If somebody works in a bank, chances are they don't have to worry about the children in the house dying of starvation." Tima raised a well-plucked eyebrow in Ebony's direction. "What that woman in the bank did was wrong. That wasn't any sort of Robin Hood gesture. Bailey and those kids need the money a hell of a lot more than they do."

"Why don't you go down there and give it to them then?"

"Uh-oh," Hunter whispered at her back. "This is about to get ugly."

Eunice finished her glass of rum punch and held it out for a refill. "Calm down, Ebony. Let's not make this personal."

The long-haired woman was about to say something else, but Hunter kicked her bare foot and slid her a warning glance.

"Well at least somebody didn't kill Michael for that little bit of money," Tima said with a delicate shudder.

"Not that they wouldn't have done it if they knew what he was carrying down the street."

"Well, the neighborhood kids know that he has people abroad, so that wouldn't have been such a big leap." Eunice sipped her rum punch. "A lot of folks around the island get killed every day over money or some other stupid thing. If it wasn't for security in all those big houses on the hill, a lot of those white people would be dead in their two-car drive-ways."

"What about Jamaicans who leave for years then come back to settle on the island? Is their situation the same as those so-called expatriates?" Cliff asked.

"You mean people like me?" Hunter asked with a sardonic twist to her mouth.

"Not exactly like," Felix shook his head. "I mean just the other day, a woman from Portmore, who was in England for some twenty years, came back to settle in the house she was born in. Some local boys broke into the house, broke her neck, and took all her money plus all the nice things she brought back from foreign lands for her family."

Hunter shifted against Sinclair's back. "I remember that story from *The Gleaner*. The two girls she had here said that she had a lot of ideas about turning the country around, that she wanted to give something back to the place where she was born."

Sinclair absently stroked the condensation on her glass. *So even straight people had to worry about violence on the island.* Like most visitors, Sinclair had initially imagined Jamaica as a place of gently swaying hammocks and turquoise seawater overflowing with fish. Peaceful. Even though they knew the realities of living on the island, Nikki and her father managed to be happy here. And she knew that Lydia wouldn't leave even if someone gave her approved immigration papers tonight.

"Does that make you worry about your safety?" Sinclair asked Hunter. "Your accent isn't strictly Jamaican anymore.

Someone on the street might hear you talk and think that you have a lot of money."

"That's the chance I take. I'm not going to up and leave here for what some people think I have. Everybody around here knows that I don't have much."

"Still, it's a lot more than most Jamaicans have. A Jeep in the garage, a fancy computer, a nice house with a yard you don't have to farm to make your living." Ebony nodded. "That's a lot."

"I worked hard for what I have. I'm not going to let some irrational fear of my own people make me hide or even leave this island."

"I'm not saying be fearful. Just be cautious." Eunice forcefully tapped her glass.

"Living here, I haven't been any less cautious than when I was in the middle of London or even Miami. You know that, Ebony." Hunter reached down to lightly touch her cousin's hand. "Besides, unlike you, I work for money. I don't just stand around and wait for people to hand me their cash."

At Sinclair's questioning look, Hunter shook her head. "My cousin is a con woman. Runs a game like no other on the island."

"And that's bloody hard work, thank you very much."

"Here we go again," everyone within earshot chorused.

Hunter laughed as her cousin defended her own work ethic. Tima stood up saying something about looking for a toilet to vomit in. Cliff just rolled his eyes before taking his leave as well. He didn't give an excuse. Eunice lay back in her chair and pretended to dose under her sunglasses. After Ebony ran out of steam, Hunter nudged her cousin's foot.

"I don't know why you try the same shit whenever we get together. Nobody is going to approve of your lifestyle, you little criminal. Just be thankful that Tima or somebody else hasn't turned you in by now."

"That's because Tima is a good cop, not like a lot of these

bastards running about in their fake British uniforms harassing and killing with impunity." Ebony shrugged. "But enough shop talk." She turned to Sinclair. "Where did my egghead cousin meet someone as gorgeous as you and do you have a sister?"

Chapter 18

"Welcome home, stranger," Nikki glanced up from the television as Sinclair walked into the house. She made a show of looking at her watch then at the late afternoon sun burning outside the window.

Sinclair rolled her eyes and smiled. "Yes, I know that I said I'd be back in the morning." She dropped a quick kiss on her stepmother's forehead and kept walking. "I'll be right back." In the kitchen, she sat down at the table and dialed her work number.

"Volk Publishing. Bliss Sinclair's office."

"Good afternoon, Shelly."

"Hey, boss. I didn't expect to hear from you so soon."

Sinclair smiled at the sound of Shelly's voice. "Surprise."

"So what's going on? Are you calling to make sure that I'm hard at work and not tippling your good whiskey in the executive washroom?"

"Not at all, my little underpaid poet. Tipple away if that's your fancy." Sinclair chuckled. "I want you to tell Jonas that I'm staying an extra two weeks and to take that time out of my vacation bank."

Shelly laughed. "Are you serious?"

"Yes. There shouldn't be a problem. Make up some dire reason for my extended stay if you have to, but let them know I'll be back in three weeks."

"You are not kidding. Wow. First we can't get you to take a vacation and now you don't want to come back." Shelly laughed again. "What's her name?"

Sinclair hung up on her, still smiling. The house was quiet except for the babble of the television. No Xavier. No Victor. She stuck her head in the living room. "Is Papa in?"

"No, he took Xavier down to see his auntie, then went to the bar with friends."

Sinclair sat next to her stepmother and dropped her bag beside the couch. "Good."

"You don't want him to know about you and Hunter?"

"I think he already knows. I just don't want to face him right now. I feel a little guilty for not telling him outright."

"If he's paying attention, he'll see that you're not trying to trick him. Then things should be fine."

"Is it that simple?"

"Of course." Nikki grinned. "So when is Hunter coming over for dinner?"

"Christ, I was hoping you'd forget about that."

"Are you joking? Especially after you extended your trip just to be near her?"

"How did you know about that?"

"I have ears, silly. So when is she coming?"

Sinclair rolled her eyes at Nikki's persistence. "This Friday."

"Great. I need to start planning now. Do you know what she absolutely doesn't eat?"

"As far as I can tell, she eats anything."

"Even better."

They shared a smile. Nikki was bubbling over with curiosity, but she kept her mouth shut, only glanced at Sinclair with her lower lip caught between her teeth, and her eyes wide with mute inquiry. Sinclair was under no obligation to acknowledge the unspoken question. But she did.

"Things went well."

"Good."

"She wasn't upset with me, she just needed a little time alone and with her friends."

"You mean Della."

Sinclair nodded and was surprised when Nikki rolled her eyes. "What?"

"I love that woman, but sometimes she is worse than Xavie."

Sinclair chuckled. "Let me guess. She can't decide whether to keep the old toy or throw it away?"

Nikki giggled. "I'd never thought of Hunter as a toy before but that description will work."

"Hunter thinks she's being motherly."

"She is. Then she remembers what it was like to have Hunter in her bed and Della starts wanting her again."

"I saw her over there yesterday, actually."

"And?"

"And nothing. She wished us luck, talked about random things then left to go back to her shop. Despite her past relationship with my mother I still like her."

"Past relationship?"

Oops. "Nothing. Don't worry about it." Sinclair got up to leave. "Is there anything to eat around here?"

Nikki dragged her back down on the sofa. "She and Beverly used to do what you and Hunter do?"

Sinclair cursed her own big mouth and sighed. "Probably some variation of it, yes."

Nikki's eyes went wide. "Are you serious?"

"Not at all, I do this comedy routine just for you." Sinclair stood up again. "If you insist on talking about this let's at least go to the kitchen so I can find some food."

"I can't believe this!" Nikki followed Sinclair and sat at the table while her stepdaughter searched the fridge for edibles. "She never told me."

"Are you best friends or something? Is there any reason that she should have told you?"

"I'm a regular customer. She and I talk all the time."

"Obviously not about some things." She found the ingredients for a corned beef sandwich and set about making one. "In the lesbian community it's apparently common knowledge."

Nikki leaned back in her chair. "You think that's why she didn't tell me? Because I'm not one of you?"

That surprised a laugh out of Sinclair. "Or it might have something to do with the fact that you're Beverly's husband's new wife."

"Oh."

"Is that all Nikki said?" Hunter looked up from her contemplation of the road under her feet.

"Pretty much. And, by the way, dinner for Friday is fine. She did ask me what you liked to eat though."

"Besides you?"

"Stop." Sinclair blushed. "I didn't tell her that."

The two women walked up the hill toward Victor and Nikki's house where Hunter had left the Jeep. Sinclair had already finished the ice-cream cone that they'd left the house to get and was eyeing the scant remains of the one Hunter was working on.

"Just tell her that I'll eat just about anything as long as it's well-seasoned," Hunter said.

"I already did."

"What about your father?"

"What about him?" Sinclair watched her lover suck the last of the ice cream from the cone, then pop the last bite in her mouth.

Hunter slid her a lazy look as she chewed. "Does he know that she's invited me over?"

"I would assume so, although I haven't talked to him myself about that, or about us."

Hunter stopped walking. "You're not hiding this, are you?"

"Hardly." Sinclair kept walking. "Oh, come on, the house is only around the corner. Don't make me stop now." The other woman caught up with her. "He knows where I spend most of my nights and days. He and I have just never talked about it." She tossed Hunter a grin. "If you're so anxious to be out and proud then come Friday dressed in your lesbian best."

"Very funny."

Sinclair chuckled. "I thought it was."

Hunter lightly pinched her waist. "Then you better run, funny girl, 'cause I'm coming to get you."

Sinclair screamed and took off running toward her father's house. She flew up the badly paved street, almost breaking her ankle in a pothole, but kept going, dashed through the gate, under the crape myrtle trees sprinkling their lavender-colored blossoms in the late morning air, and up the gravel walkway. Hunter caught her when she stopped to unlock the door, fumbling at the keyhole with fingers that shook from her uncontrollable giggles. Hunter pinned her against the door, pressing her belly against Sinclair's back.

"Do you know what funny girls get?"

Sinclair laughed and finally slid the key in. "No, but can I please find out soon?"

The lock turned but she didn't open the door. It felt so good to have her lover's body against her, to feel her warm length and be surrounded by her smoky sage and sandalwood scent.

"Let's take this inside, then. I don't want to give a show to the people passing by."

Sinclair stumbled over the threshold and pulled Hunter after her. She locked the door behind them, shoved the keys in her jeans pocket and jumped on Hunter. The other woman gasped her surprise, but quickly slid her palms under Sinclair's ass as Sinclair wrapped her legs around her waist and kissed her, slanting her mouth hungrily across the receptive lips.

"Bedroom," Sinclair muttered. Her breasts ached beneath the abrasive cotton of the T-shirt. They needed the softness of the other woman's skin, her mouth.

Hunter stumbled through the beaded curtains that separated the sitting room from the narrow hallway leading to the bedrooms. The beads knocked together, discordant and loud. Some caught in Hunter's hair, but she impatiently pulled away, turning right into Sinclair's temporary bedroom and slammed the door behind them. The buttons on Hunter's shirt separated from their holes under Sinclair's quick fingers. Her hands found the hard-softness of the dark woman's nipples and she sighed. They fell backward on the bed with Hunter pinned under Sinclair's body and ravening hands, gasping under the greedy mouth and at the fingers that pinched and stroked her nipples. She tugged at Sinclair's zipper. They didn't hear the door open, but the high squeak of surprise and quickly drawn breath warned Sinclair.

"I can't believe this!"

They jumped apart, guiltily. Or at least Sinclair did, rolling off the supine Hunter to sit on the bed. The dark woman slowly pulled the edges of her shirt together and stood.

"Hullo, Lydia. What an unexpected surprise."

Sinclair felt herself flush wine red. Her face prickled with embarrassment.

"What the fuck is this, Sinclair?" Lydia glared at her sister before turning to the other woman. "Hunter?"

Her ex-girlfriend shrugged and began to button her shirt. "This is definitely not the best way for you to have found out."

"What do you mean the best way? This shouldn't even be happening." Lydia took in Sinclair's flushed face and the hard points of her nipples visible through her T-shirt. Then she turned around and walked out.

Sinclair stood up to follow but Hunter stood in her way.

"That probably wouldn't be the best idea," she said.

"Then what—" Sinclair sank back to the bed. "I don't know."

Outside, they heard a car start up and drive away.

"Give her a little time." Hunter's mouth twisted into a grimace. "Sorry about all this."

"It's not your fault. I should have told her before now."

"Well, you know hindsight and all that." Hunter sat down beside Sinclair. "Are you all right?"

"Not really." Sinclair sighed. "I'm going to talk to her later."

"Tomorrow."

"Tomorrow," she agreed, collapsing backward on the bed. "That was fucked."

"Do you want me to go?"

"Yes. No. Shit, I don't know." She turned to look at Hunter. "I feel awful."

"Not unexpected. Tell you what, I'll go, you relax and try not to think too hard about this mess."

"So you're just going to leave me?"

A tiny smile curved Hunter's mouth. "I'll keep you company if you want me to."

"Yes. Distract me."

Hunter looked at her trembling lower lip and the frustrated tears that lurked at the corner of her eyes. "Come on," she said. "Put on your bath suit. We'll go for a swim and wear you out so you won't have to think about this so much."

"That sounds better than the initial abandonment idea."

"Drama queen."

Hunter packed Sinclair up with sandwiches and drinks into the Jeep and took her to the beach.

"I'm miserable. This outing isn't working."

"Well, you look gorgeous and edible," Hunter said, nibbling playfully on her ear.

She didn't look so bad herself in the pale blue bikini she'd pulled from the backseat of her Jeep. It was a tiny thing made up of string and three pieces of scrap that showed off her lean body with its sweet swell of breasts and casually worn muscles. It almost made Sinclair forget about Lydia's untimely interruption. Almost. Then Hunter pulled her into the cold water and her mind became completely focused on other things.

* * *

The next day, she showed up at her sister's house. The Cadillac sat in the driveway and the savory smells of a curry dinner floated outside, teasing her nose. Sinclair rang the doorbell. She thought she heard someone approach the door, but when it remained closed she knocked again.

"Lydia, open up. I know you're in there."

Still no answer. Sinclair ignored the pinch of annoyance she felt and instead lay down in the hammock draped across her sister's elegant, colonial-style verandah. This was a peaceful middle-class neighborhood. The Blue Mountains soared just behind the house, the only trace of untamed nature in the manicured surroundings. When Sinclair had first met her sister she was surprised that Lydia lived here, but now she could see how the other woman fit into this carefully cultivated setting. Sinclair glanced at her watch.

"This is stupid, Lydia." She got up and knocked on the door again. "You have to talk to me." Her fist pounded the door in a loud, continuous staccato rhythm that jerked shockwaves of pain into her wrist and hand. The door flew open, startling Sinclair.

"I don't have to do shit." Her sister stood in the doorway in shorts and a T-shirt with a food-splattered spatula in one hand.

"Are you throwing a tantrum?"

"Why don't you just go back to Papa's house and leave me the hell alone?"

"Because we need to talk about this."

"I don't think that's necessary. You're fucking Hunter. End of story."

"That's not the end of it." Sinclair's voice rose. "Stop acting like a child."

"Oh, for fuck's sake." Lydia looked down her driveway to the empty street. "Come in. I don't want my neighbors watching the dykes brawl on my front lawn."

"Thanks. I think." Sinclair stepped inside the house.

Lydia slammed the door behind them and walked through the living room to the kitchen. "I can't believe you came to my house," she muttered.

"What else was I supposed to do when you wouldn't answer the phone?"

"Take a hint and not try to contact me at all." Lydia dropped the spatula in the sink and turned down the flame on the stove. "So you're here. Now talk."

Sinclair released a tense breath. "I'm sorry about what happened yesterday. That's not how I wanted you to find out."

"Like I said, there shouldn't have been anything for me to find out. After I confided in you, told you how I felt, you still went to her." Lydia narrowed her eyes. "Is that how they do things in America?"

Not again. "Stop using America as an excuse for every fucking thing that's wrong with us, with this family! I fucked her because I wanted to. My Americaness does *not* factor into this. You didn't want her, and I did. It's as simple as that."

"What about family loyalty?"

"When was it ever disloyal to have a little friendship with your sister's unwanted ex?"

"Friendship?" Lydia gave a short bark of laughter. "That's a good one." She paced away from Sinclair. "If it was all so blameless then why did you keep it from me?"

Sinclair opened her mouth but nothing came out. The two women looked at each other.

"I should rip your lying tongue out," Lydia said.

"Now just wait a damn minute. I don't go for any of this fighting over a sex partner bullshit."

"Then why did you touch her? You knew it would have to come to this."

"No, I didn't," Sinclair said. "If I knew you'd threaten to cut out my fucking tongue and act like a psycho over a woman you didn't want, then I wouldn't have touched her."

They both realized that she was lying at the same time.

Lydia's look was poisonous. Sinclair shook her head, laughing ruefully. "OK, I take it back." She released a steadying breath. "Do you really hate her that much?" Her question was soft, barely above a whisper.

"I don't hate Hunter. I love her."

"Is this how you show your love?"

"Yes," Lydia hissed. "She deserves better than a cheap imitation of what she can never have."

Sinclair jerked back in shock. It wasn't like she hadn't thought the same thing herself, but hearing her sister say the words made it hurt worse. "You had your chance, Lydia. You had Hunter and because she'd been with someone you didn't like, you threw her away like an old toy. She's worth more than that. And I show her."

"I bet you do." They glared at each other across the narrow space.

"Don't worry. It's not like I'm going to marry her and take her back to the States with me."

Lydia gasped as if the idea had never occurred to her. That someone could physically take Hunter away.

"Don't flatter yourself into thinking that that's going to happen," she said. "You're nothing more than a piece of ass, a way to scratch the itch that I didn't."

"Don't be crass, Lydia. It doesn't suit you."

"What the fuck would you know about what suits me?"

"OK." Sinclair backed up. "I see that this isn't getting us anywhere. I'm going to leave now."

"Good riddance. I don't know why you came here in the first place." She turned back to the stove. "You know your way out."

Sinclair walked out and didn't look back.

Chapter 19

On the night of the dinner party, Sinclair helped Nikki cook. She didn't know half of what her stepmother was making, having been put to work chopping, pureeing, and being the general kitchen slave. Nikki knew how her discussion with Lydia had gone two days before and had spent that time trying to distract her since Hunter was off somewhere earning her computer scientist's salary.

Victor was quiet that evening, sitting behind his newspaper or overseeing Xavier's homework. Before Hunter was due to arrive he went to water the plants in the yard.

"Is Papa OK?" Sinclair looked up from setting the dinner table. They had expanded the table to its full width and unearthed one of the two extra chairs that went with it.

"He's fine," Nikki said as she wiped down the kitchen counter with a wet rag. "I think he talked to Lydia, though. She might have told him that she was mad at you but not why. It's not like she ever let him know that she and Hunter were girlfriend and girlfriend."

"True. But he acknowledged them as a couple. Remember how he asked about Hunter at the cookout?"

Nikki slid a fresh jug of carrot juice in the fridge. "You worry too much. Everything will be fine."

Hunter came at seven on the dot, dressed in her best jeans and a button-down linen shirt. She brought wine for the grown-ups and ginger biscuits for Xavier. Sinclair greeted her at the door.

"Hey. Right on time."

"I didn't dare be late today." She kissed Sinclair lightly on the mouth. "How is everything going?"

"Good, I think. Lydia may have talked to Papa and bad-mouthed me but I'm not entirely sure."

"Nothing to be done about that. We're here to eat and be social and be happy."

Sinclair led her into the living room, holding her hand and the bottle of wine. Xavier looked up from his toys as the women walked in.

"Hunter!"

"Hey, big boy. What are you doing?"

"Waiting for dinner. Mama says we can't eat until you come."

"I'm here." Hunter grinned.

Xavier smiled back and hopped up from his mess of toys scattered in front of the television. "Food!" He raced into the kitchen ahead of the women.

"I think somebody is hungry," Hunter said.

Victor walked into the kitchen at the same time that they did. The already small room suddenly felt very tiny.

"Hunter." He inclined his head toward the dinner guest. "How are you?"

"Fine, Mr. Daniels. No complaints."

"Good, good." He washed his hands under the kitchen tap and sat down at the table. "Sit beside me, Xavier."

Everyone sat at the table and said grace over what Sinclair finally identified as stew peas and rice with sweet corn fritters and a bit of steamed cabbage on the side for health. Xavier wasn't the only one pleased at what Nikki turned out. They attacked their food at once, immediately making low sounds of appreciation and praises to the cook.

"Fabulous, as usual, Nikki," Sinclair said, lifting a forkful of stew and rice.

"As usual? I was hoping for out of this world since Hunter was our guest tonight."

Hunter smiled at the smaller woman. "Trust me when I say this is a stellar meal, Nikki. I haven't had it this good in a long, long time."

"Thank you." Nikki swept a pleased glance around the table, her cheeks blooming with subtle color.

Not to be outdone, Xavier raised his empty fork in the air. "This is the best stew peas ever."

"Thanks, sweetheart." She lightly touched the back of his neck.

Victor picked up a corn fritter. "So, Hunter. Nikki tells me that you and Lydia are no longer . . . friends."

Sinclair almost choked on her carrot juice. She turned to Hunter as her lover slowly put down her fork.

"That's not necessarily true," she said. "Lydia and I are still friends. Or at least we were until a few days ago. We just don't have the same relationship that we used to."

"The kind of relationship you used to have with Lydia, that's what you now have with Sinclair?"

"No. Sinclair and I have something better."

Victor nodded and bit into his fritter. "Is Lydia OK with that?"

"I don't think so, but she and I ended our involvement before Sinclair and I got together so there shouldn't be any hard feelings on her part."

Victor glanced at Sinclair then back again at Hunter. "You're very honest. I like that."

Nikki cleared her throat. "How is Della doing these days, Hunter? I haven't seen her in forever."

"She's doing all right. Things have been real busy at the shop ever since you told the Breckenridges about her work. She can't make those goddess pots fast enough."

"That's good, then. But I still miss her."

"Why don't you run by the shop and see her one of these days? I'm sure she would be glad to see you."

"I just might do that."

"Good."

Nikki kept sneaking peaks at Hunter as if reevaluating a former opinion, watching how she ate and responded to the not-so-subtle inquiries Victor threw her way. Despite the succulent flavor of Nikki's meal, Sinclair was too nervous to eat. She picked at her plate, tasting the tender bits of pork-infused red beans and the thick red-tinged sauce that perfectly complemented the white rice. It wasn't like she was going to marry the woman. Still her appetite remained sparse and her hands were cold with nerves.

"My dinner not good enough for you, Sinclair?" Nikki teased. Sinclair glared at her stepmother. Nikki knew damn well why she couldn't eat.

"Stop teasing, Nikki. You know that the food is good. I'm just not really hungry right now."

Four pairs of eyes looked at her as if she'd just flown over the moon in her underwear. Her father patted her hand and smiled.

Sinclair kept quiet. After the main meal they moved to the living room for dessert. Xavier quickly went through half the bag of cookies that Hunter brought him. It wasn't long before Nikki put him to bed, tucking him into her and Victor's bedroom until later on when she could move him. Victor brought out the cards and they sat down around the coffee table to play gin. Hunter was an aggressive player, unforgiving of Sinclair's inexperience and Nikki's niceness. She and Victor played in deadly earnest until, unexpectedly, Sinclair's father stood up to get drinks for the women—bottles of Guinness for himself, Sinclair, and Hunter, and carrot juice for Nikki. He and Hunter boasted loudly about who was the better player, slapping down cards amid laughter and chortles of amusement from the other women. They didn't talk again of serious matters, of Lydia or the relationship, or the fact that Sinclair was leaving in less than three weeks.

Later in the night, Hunter and Nikki teamed up against

the other two in bid whist, becoming a true team of trash talkers while Victor and Sinclair beat them soundly at every game, laughing quietly to themselves even as their lovers grew louder in their defeat.

At three in the morning, they reluctantly packed up the cards and Hunter gathered her things to go. Sinclair walked her out to the night-blanketed verandah and, away from the curious eyes of her parents, gently kissed her. "Thank you."

"You're making me work hard for this, aren't you?" Hunter growled into Sinclair's throat.

"You didn't have to come tonight."

"Like hell I didn't."

Sinclair laughed. "Will I see you tomorrow?"

"Why wouldn't you?"

"Smart-ass."

"Better that than a dumb-ass." Hunter nuzzled her throat again. "Come to the house after dinner. Spend the night with me."

"Maybe."

Hunter laughed and pulled away. "Tomorrow." She walked backward down the short steps leading from the verandah to the gravel footpath.

Sinclair blew her a kiss and watched her walk out to her Jeep. She didn't go back inside until long after Hunter had driven away.

Chapter 20

"I want to go horseback riding."

"Then go." Nikki turned to look at Sinclair. "There should be a few places on the beach that have horse tours."

The two women lay stretched out under an oversized beach umbrella while Xavier sat on the beach, building a fortress out of sand for his toy soldiers. It was the weekend again, and Sinclair was finally able to lure Nikki away from Victor to go to the beach with her. This time, they took a taxi at Sinclair's expense so they wouldn't have to wrestle with the umbrella on the motorcycle.

"I don't want to do the tourist thing, though," Sinclair said.

"Maybe Hunter can help you out. She knows a lot of rich people on the island. She might be able to find you a private tour or something."

"Hunter!" They looked up at Xavier's shout. The boy abandoned his fort to greet the woman and pull her over to see the results of his labor. She took something out of her backpack and gave it to him. Xavier looked puzzled, then after a few words with him, he nodded and put his gift, another toy soldier, with the others who were lined up to go into the fort.

"You know I think the reason he likes her so much is because she always brings him gifts."

Nikki smiled. "There's nothing wrong with that."

Sinclair rolled her eyes.

"Hey, ladies." Hunter left the fort to join them.

"Speak of the devil and she shall appear."

"Should I take offense?" Hunter sat in the sand beside them and gave Sinclair's butt a playful pat.

"It's not like we're telling you something you don't already know," Sinclair grinned. "Nikki was just saying you might know about a private horseback riding tour. I haven't been on a horse since my grandma took me to Montana when I was eighteen."

"I can't guarantee you any experience you have here is going to be like Montana when you were a teenager."

"Hmm, I could think of at least one." She exchanged a heavy lidded gaze with Hunter, swept her eyes over the other woman's taut body in its cutoff shorts and thin T-shirt. The exhilaration of her first ride had been coupled with a healthy dose of fear and breathlessness. Not unlike the time Hunter had taken her at the castle, her body hard and sweaty as it pounded against Sinclair's from behind.

Hunter coughed. "My apologies, you would certainly know better than I."

"So what about the horseback riding?"

"I have some friends who own horses." She lay back in the sand and watched Xavier chase little seabirds away from his fort. "I'll call them this evening."

"So what brings you out of your dungeon on such a gorgeous day," Sinclair asked. Over the past few days, Hunter had been working feverishly on a project that left her little daylight time to spend with her lover.

"You, of course." Hunter flashed her a smile. "I brought you something."

Beside them, Nikki suddenly stood up and went to join her son in the sand.

"Really?" Sinclair sat up. "What is it?"

Hunter opened her backpack and pulled out something heavy wrapped in cheesecloth. "Here."

It was a camera. One very much like the one that Sinclair had broken in the mountains, only it was older, an antique where hers had merely been old.

"Oh my God!" Sinclair took the camera, marveling at its metal and leather housing that gleamed in the sun.

"This one is metal, so in case you decide to beat someone's face in with it, it'll survive the attack, and the guy at the shop said that it works just fine with the 35 millimeter film you were using before. It's from 1972 or something. All I knew was that yours was old so I looked online then ran down a guy in Kingston that happened to have this." Hunter took a quick breath as if to stop herself from talking. "Is this close enough to what you had?"

"Are you kidding?" Sinclair let out a squeak and grabbed Hunter in a fierce hug. "This is wonderful. Thank you. I can't believe you did this for me."

"Why wouldn't I?" Hunter's palms were hot against Sinclair's back and neck. "You mean a lot to me. This is nothing."

"It's hardly nothing, you crazy woman." Sinclair kissed her mouth. "This is very unexpected. Thank you."

"Good. I'm glad you like it. The film from the broken camera is in the plastic bag too. I think you can save some of the photos." Hunter reluctantly pulled back from their hug. "I have to go. Work."

Sinclair groaned in disappointment. "Really?"

"Yes. But I'll be done with this project by Tuesday." She brushed her fingers over Sinclair's cheek. "Come to my house on Wednesday morning by seven. I can arrange for us to go riding then. OK?"

"OK." Sinclair grinned, clutching her new old camera as she watched Hunter wave at Nikki and Xavier then walk away toward her Jeep. After she drove away, Nikki came back to sit next to her stepdaughter.

"Nice," she said, pointing at the camera.

"Yes, it is. So is Hunter."

"She gave Xavie a new toy." Nikki dimpled. "A girl soldier."

They both laughed.

"At first, he didn't even know what to do with her. He had no idea they made girl soldiers."

"But I'm sure Hunter set him straight." Sinclair looked down at the camera. "God, it's going to be so hard to leave."

"That's two weeks away. Don't think about it now, just enjoy the time you do have."

A bittersweet smile tugged at Sinclair's mouth. "You're right." She touched the younger woman's arm. Nikki made a low noise and hugged her tight.

It just happened that Hunter *did* know some rich people with horses, friends she'd known in England years ago. The Rai-Spencers were an attractive, charming couple. Madeline was an English barrister who had enough of London's rain and noise and decided to move back to the country where her parents were born. Her wife, Radha, was a dancer who had been forced into early retirement by a knee injury and who now wrote bestselling novels for British lesbians. The women looked vaguely familiar to Sinclair, but she couldn't quite place where she'd seen them before.

"Good to see you again, Hunter." Madeline hugged her friend. "Twice in one week. Rare but most welcome."

Radha took her turn in Hunter's arms. "Yes, we know it's not quite a social call, but we love seeing you anyway." She turned to Sinclair. "And this is the woman you told us about?"

"Yes. This is Bliss Sinclair. Sinclair, these are my very good friends."

When Madeline turned to Sinclair, she remembered where she'd seen them before. At the party three weeks ago. They were the same beautiful couple she hadn't been able to take her eyes off of.

"It's good to finally meet someone who she's dating."

Madeline pulled Sinclair into a tight embrace. Her skin held the tang of indoors, air conditioner, and expensive soap. "You have no idea the pains she goes through to keep her love life secret from us."

"Don't exaggerate, Maddy."

"Ha! She doesn't at all exaggerate." Radha kissed Sinclair warmly on the cheek. "A pleasure."

Madeline looped her arm though Sinclair's. "Come and have a drink of something cold before you run out to play with the horses."

The women plied them with fruits and drinks before showing Sinclair around the large two-story Spanish-style house. It was a gorgeous space, cool with ceiling fans spinning lazily in every room and walls the color of Jamaican fruits.

"Hunter is familiar with everything in the stables," Radha said with an impish smile. She flipped her long braid over her shoulder as she spoke. "The horses know her. Just have a good time and come in to see us when you get back."

In the stables, Sinclair watched Hunter with the animals. She *did* know what she was doing, greeting each horse by name and fishing a carrot from the bulging pockets of her cargo shorts for them. She was gentle and teasing and the horses responded well to her. The smell of horse, manure, and leather marinating in the heat made Sinclair eager to leave the confines of the neatly kept four-horse stable, but as Hunter soothed the animals with her soft voice and sure hands, Sinclair, too, became soothed and was content to simply watch.

"Radha and Madeline are very nice women," Sinclair said.

"They are. I knew Madeline when I lived in London. She'd been unhappy there for as long as I could remember. Only when she and Radha met did she want to do anything about her unhappiness." Hunter looked up at her with an odd smile. "They're good for each other."

"Were you and Madeline lovers?"

"No. But we thought about it. After Radha came on the scene there was no chance, of course. Love at first sight and all that."

Sinclair's eyes followed the sleek lines of Hunter's body. "That's beautiful."

"Yes. It is."

Hunter disappeared into a stall to saddle a quiet brown horse. The plaque on the door named her Dahlia. She led the horse out and handed the reins to Sinclair.

"Just hold her gently. She won't bite or anything. I'm going to saddle up Glimmer and walk them both out."

When she was finished, she quietly took the reins back from Sinclair and led the horses into the paddock just beyond the barn door.

"Do you remember much from your teenage riding lesson?" Hunter asked, her mouth a curving tease.

"Only to sit my ass down, hold on to the reins, and follow the horse in front of me."

Hunter chuckled. "That won't help you in this case, I'm afraid."

She showed her how to mount on the left side using the mounting block, how to turn the horse, and how to prevent Dahlia from galloping away if she saw something tempting ahead. The height from atop the shifting horse was disconcerting and took some getting used to. Sinclair held the reins tightly then remembering Hunter's advice, relaxed her grip.

"That's good. Now stay loose in the saddle. Allow her movements to guide you." Hunter gracefully mounted her horse without the aid of the mounting block. "Watch me." She and Glimmer walked around the paddock. The movement of Hunter's hips atop the pale horse was hypnotic. It wasn't long before Sinclair forgot why she was supposed to be watching her lover in the first place. She simply stared, admiring the lean and graceful body that swayed in the saddle.

"You watching?"

"Absolutely." Sinclair smiled lazily at her.

Hunter walked Glimmer back to Dahlia's side. "Really?"

"I swear." Sinclair had only enough courage atop Dahlia to reach out for her lover and slip her fingers through the ends of Hunter's thick hair. "But I can watch you even closer if you'd like."

Hunter chuckled and leaned in to complete the motion Sinclair began, meeting her lips and accepting their moist warmth. The horses snorted at each other then shifted, pulling them apart.

"I guess this means that they're eager to get started," Hunter murmured with a smile.

"Me, too." But Sinclair was talking about something else entirely.

They took the scenic route from the Rai-Spencers' densely green backyard with its acres of grass and fruit trees and color dappled flowers blazing under the sun. Once they stepped through the iron gate and crested the rise of the hill, miles of gold-washed mountain land spread out like a tapestry before them.

"I don't remember much of this growing up, but my mother used to talk about seeing the island by horseback all the time." Hunter and Glimmer moved at Sinclair's side. "She hated the island, but once she was away it was all she ever talked about. How could I have loved England when she served up visions of this," she waved her hand at the vista below them, "to me everyday?"

They rode steadily down the mountain, ducking their heads to pass beneath low hanging tamarind trees thick with vines. Hunter pointed out hidden oases of wildflowers growing in the green forest—the scarlet ginger and bright orange bougainvillea and white jasmine and red hibiscus. Their colors were dazzling.

At midday they stopped to eat the sandwiches and water Hunter brought along in her backpack, leaving the horses to graze a short distance away on the abundant grass.

"Thank you for doing this for me," Sinclair said, leaning back against a thick shade tree. "It's been a perfect day."

Hunter bit into her sandwich. "My pleasure."

Sinclair expected some smart-ass comment from her, but was surprised by Hunter's look of quiet satisfaction and nothing else.

Even with stops to get food and water for the horses and to take photos of nearly everything between the Rai-Spencer house and their destination, they made it down to the beach well before dinnertime. The sun hung teasingly near the horizon, still full and white in the sky, while under it the Caribbean Sea sparkled a luminous turquoise. Glimmer and Dahlia quickly trotted down the well-worn path from the mountain to the water's edge, eager for a change in terrain. The horses splashed in the water, kicking up white sand and seawater on the women's bare legs and arms. They tossed their necks over the water, whinnying.

"They probably want to play in some water they can drink," Sinclair said, laughing as another splash caught her.

"Me, too." Hunter slid Sinclair a laughing look. "Food now, I think."

She and Glimmer led the way to a nearby seaside restaurant. The women tied the horses to a hitching post near a gigantic trough of water and walked in to have a proper dinner.

"Fun times, good company, *and* food." Sinclair lightly bumped Hunter's hip with her own as they walked into the restaurant. "You are, hands down, the best guide out there."

"Of course I am. Wait until you see what I have to show you when we get back."

"If it involves more of your wet skin then I'm all for it," Sinclair said.

They sat out on the deck so they could keep an eye on the horses while they ate. As Sinclair looked around the restaurant indulging in a bit of people watching, a familiar face caught her eye.

"Lydia is here."

"Really?" Hunter didn't look up from her menu. "What are you in the mood for?"

"Something tasty. When was the last time you talked with her?"

"The day she almost caught us naked at your father's house." Hunter looked up and saw something over Sinclair's shoulder that made her grimace. "Damn, I hate dyke drama." She put her menu down and stretched her lips in a bad imitation of a smile as her ex-girlfriend drew close. "Hullo, Lydia."

"Hey, kids."

Lydia was not sober. She sat down at the table with her customary grace, but Sinclair could smell the alcohol on her.

"How are you, Lydia?" she asked.

"I'm not really dealing well with my sister's betrayal. Other than that, I'm fine."

Hunter made a rude noise. "Get over yourself, baby. This is not about you."

Sinclair stared at Hunter in surprise. Her lover looked annoyed and not in the mood to hide it.

"How can you say that when she took you away from me." Her voice rose. "I wanted you back."

Sinclair looked down at the table. This was either going to get really ugly, or it already was.

"I'm not a toy to be—" Hunter stopped and stood up. "Tell you what, Lydia. Come with me for a second. Let's talk somewhere private." She didn't look at Sinclair.

The younger woman threw her sister a narrow-eyed look as she stood up and followed Hunter. People turned to stare at them and, after the two women disappeared from view, watched Sinclair to see what would happen next. Sinclair bowed her head over her menu, annoyed and embarrassed.

"Hello, lovely."

Sinclair looked up to see Hunter's cousin standing near the table. "Ebony, right?"

"At your service, beautiful lady. I'm pleased that you remember my name." She sat down in Hunter's chair. "So why is a pretty girl like you sitting here looking so sad? My egghead cousin put you off already?" She leaned back and propped her feet up on an empty chair. The silver ring in her right nipple winked at Sinclair through the tight shirt.

Despite her annoyance, Sinclair chuckled. "No, she hasn't done a thing to 'put me off.' I'm just having a bit of a family raucous at the moment."

"You mean with Lydia?"

"How do you know about that?"

"She and I came here together." At Sinclair's raised eyebrow, she grinned. "She's trying out some new things these days." Ebony picked up the menu. "So I guess they're off somewhere talking, then?"

Sinclair nodded.

"Lord knows how long that's going to take and I'm already hungry." The waitress chose that moment to walk over to their table. "Perfect."

After they ordered, the two women sat back to watch each other. Ebony's mouth tilted in a crooked smile. To Sinclair, it seemed pained.

"I hope you don't feel bad about being a substitute for Hunter," she felt compelled to say.

Ebony chuckled. "Not at all. I know that girl doesn't want me. She doesn't want my cousin either. We're both subs. That's life. At least I'm getting to enjoy the perks of that arrangement."

"You're both substitutes? What do you mean?"

"For Della. The girl never really got over her. Especially since Del left her for Hunter." Ebony shrugged. "I don't get that. A woman dumps me, I move on. Not try to fuck the girl she left me for just to prove something."

Things suddenly became a little clearer. "But why is she still stalking Hunter if it's Della she wants?"

"Don't ask me to explain the minds of crazies, my lovely." She looked up when the waitress came back with their food, the large tray almost overflowing with the lobster dinner, its various side dishes, and Sinclair's rather modest crab cakes and seasoned rice. "Ah! I've been looking forward to this all day."

The two of them were well on their way through their meal when Hunter reappeared, minus Lydia. She sat down and greeted her cousin with a nod. "Sorry about that."

"No problem, Hunt. We made the best of it despite being abandoned by our dates." Ebony scraped the last bit of lobster from the collection of shells on her plate and forked it into her mouth. "Where is Lydia anyway?"

"I left her in the parking lot. She might come back in here, but she might not."

"Then I guess I better go find her." Ebony finished her glass of wine and wiped her lips with the napkin before standing up. "Good to see you again, Sinclair." She looked at her cousin. "If you want to keep this one you should start acting better." She bared her teeth at Hunter. "Later."

Sinclair nibbled on her rice. Hunter slowly turned to face her, her mouth twisted into a less than humorous expression. "I really am sorry about that. But her childishness was really getting on my nerves."

"And that's all, huh?"

"What more could there be?" Hunter brushed her thumb across Sinclair's bottom lip. "You had some ... sauce on you." She licked the speck of white off her thumb. "Is it too late for me to get something to eat?"

"Maybe. How late do you want to keep the horses out?"

"Good point. I'll just grab something to go." She raised her hand for the waitress.

They rode back into the mountains with the sun chasing them all the way. Hunter's teasing slowly melted away whatever misgivings Sinclair had about the long talk she'd had with Lydia. She even offered to share her chicken sandwich, laughing when the slight woman ate most of it, saying that it was Hunter's fault that she had been too keyed up at the restaurant to eat.

"I didn't know that Della and Lydia used to be together," Sinclair said as they trotted up the mountain.

"Me either until fairly recently." Hunter slid her an ironic look. "Small world, isn't it?"

Sinclair nodded. "Ebony was just telling me about that whole mess. Are you OK with it?"

"Yes. I have to be. When Lydia and I talked at the party a few weeks ago, I found out that this thing . . . was never really about me. Lydia still loves Della. And with all that going on she could never make love with me, much less love me. You know?" Hunter stared straight ahead as her body moved like a graceful metronome in the saddle. "That's why it made me so angry today that she was attacking you for *stealing* me, someone who she never really wanted." She shook her head. "Women."

Sinclair's eyes caressed the other woman's profile. "You're the one that I want," she whispered. "No other."

Ahead of them, the mountains were beginning to catch fire. The gold of full sun gave way to the stunning brilliance of sunset, steeped in shades of amber and orange and red. Beside her, Hunter, too, was draped in fire, her darkness haloed and magnified and magnificent as she rode quietly at Sinclair's side with her mouth curved in a faint smile.

"What are you smiling about?"

"Why do you ask? Can't I just be happy?" The smile remained, taking the sting out of the words.

"I suppose." Sinclair rolled her eyes, but felt a smile tug at her own lips.

"Want to go a little faster?"

"What?"

"It's easy. And the horses are restless. We'd be doing them a favor." She grinned. "Trust me." And she took off galloping up the gentle slope. Because Dahlia knew who was boss, the brown mare followed, forcing Sinclair to hold on for dear life.

Hunter bent forward on Glimmer's back and the horse's mane, tail, and the dark woman's hair streamed out like a black and silver banner. Laughter poured out behind her. The hooves pounded across the mountainside, flying through the grass and dirt toward the woods leading them back to the stables. Glimmer began to slow down, so did Dahlia until the horses were at a canter, their chests heaving with their recent effort. Hunter's chest, too, was heaving, and the look of her made Sinclair's body flush hot.

"Sexy, sexy, Miss Willoughby." Sinclair playfully licked her lips.

"Baby, you say the most flattering things . . ."

They shared a heated look then rode quickly the rest of the way home.

The next day Sinclair was so sore from riding that she could barely make it out of bed. Hunter knew, and showed up at her father's door not long after everyone had gone with a jar of something sweet-smelling to rub her down with.

"Just cut off everything below the waist so I can feel better," Sinclair groaned when she opened the door to let Hunter in.

Her lover, of course, looked disgustingly fit and pain-free in beige chinos and a white button-down shirt. "That's more pain in the long run for us all," she said. "Come on. Get back in bed."

"That's the best thing I've heard anyone say to me all day."

"It's barely nine o'clock."

"And I've already experienced three hours of constant pain. Come fix me."

She lay back on the bed and took off her robe so that Hunter could work on her.

"You know that's not really necessary, right?" she said,

gesturing to Sinclair's nakedness. "Not that I'm complaining."

"Then shut up and touch me."

Hunter rubbed Sinclair's legs and thighs until she was jelly, until the pain receded to the back of her mind and she was falling back asleep. Dimly she heard her lover say something about being teased without the promise of satisfaction. Sinclair yawned from the pillow of her arms and rolled over to her back.

"If you want it so bad then take it," she murmured then moaned softly when Hunter took her up on the invitation, stroking her throat and breasts with her tongue. That woke her right up.

Chapter 21

The sun splashed like fine gold around Sinclair. Rain from last night had come and gone, rinsing the island clean and leaving behind the crisp scent of newness. Sinclair lay on her blanket in the sand. Coconut trees rustled nearby in the breeze, their subtle music almost drowned out by the shrieking children running along the beach, playing tag with each other and with the waves galloping up on the sand. A few people lay on towels or sat in beach chairs a few feet away. Their presence was welcome; their conversation a soothing counterpoint to the clamor in Sinclair's head.

In a week she would leave, pack up her American clothes, and go back to where she came from. The thought hurt. She would miss her family. Their cooking, their laughter, the feeling of belonging. And she would miss Hunter. Sinclair rolled over and pillowed her suddenly wet face in her arms.

"Is there room on this blanket for one more?"

Lydia stood next to Sinclair looking down at her through amber-tinted sunglasses. Surprised, she wiped at her eyes and sat up.

"Sure." She curled her legs under her and moved aside so Lydia could sit down. Her sister faced her in silence, sliding her sunglasses to the top of her head.

"I wasn't sure where you'd be today."

"Papa and Nikki usually know where I am."

"Yeah. Nikki told me where to find you."

"So now that you have . . ." Sinclair looked at her in expectation.

Her sister actually blushed and fidgeted. A sigh escaped her. "I came to apologize."

"Why? I thought you were pretty clear about what you were feeling last time we talked."

"I was clear, but I was also being stupid. I'm sorry about what happened at the restaurant and I'm sorry about what I said when you came to see me. I don't own Hunter. I never did."

Sinclair nodded. "OK. If you don't mind me asking, what brought on this change?"

"I thought Hunter would have told you what happened."

"Whatever went on was between the two of you. I was just . . . unhappy that you chose to confront the situation in such a public place and on a day when I was feeling really good."

Lydia winced and looked away. "I'm sorry. The liquor I had before I got there was working on me and I didn't show the best judgment when I raised my voice at you in front of all those people. My conversation with Hunter made me realize that." She looked fully at Sinclair. "It also made me realize that I had no right to be angry because the two of you found happiness with each other while I . . ." Lydia shrugged. "Anyway, I messed up."

"You said some awful things to me. It's hard to forget that."

"I meant them at the time, believe me." Her mouth twisted with bitter humor. "But I was wrong. My motives were wrong."

"Apology accepted." Sinclair drew her knees up and rested her chin on them. "Thank you for coming to find me."

Lydia stayed with Sinclair for a little while longer, chatting about nothing in particular then later promising to get together for a drink before Sinclair left for America. Then the younger woman drove away, leaving Sinclair to bask in the slow burn of the sun.

Chapter 22

"Hey, Papa. You're home early."

"Do you have plans for the house that I don't know about? Should I find an excuse to leave or something?" His eyes danced.

Sinclair shook her head. "Not funny."

"I thought it was." He looked over her shoulder. "What are you cooking?"

"Boiled sweet potatoes, cassava, and dumpling. The ackee is already done."

"It looks good. What restaurant did you get it from?"

"Believe it or not, I cooked it—with a little help from Hunter."

"That girl can cook?"

Sinclair grinned. "Can she ever."

"Hm, you find out all kinds of things every day." He peeked in the ackee pot and sniffed with appreciation. "Nikki and Xavier are visiting some relations in Stony Hill. They won't be back until late."

"Then it's just going to be you and me. That's fine."

"As long as you don't mind your old man's company."

"As long as you don't give me a reason to mind his company." Sinclair smiled cheekily at her father.

They sat down at the kitchen table with freshly made carrot juice and two plates piled high with food.

"For a skinny girl you sure can eat."

"I'm not that skinny."

"True. Not as skinny as when you first got here. You gained a little weight since last month."

He was right. Sinclair remembered standing in front of the mirror at Hunter's house staring at what she had suddenly realized was a new body. Her ribs, concave stomach, and hip bones that had stood out like bayonets were all now covered by healthy new layers of flesh.

"Thanks. I feel really good. Thank you for allowing me to stay with you for my trip."

"I'm glad that I have the home to share. When I saw you in that airport looking so much like your mother it made me feel close to her again. It's been a happiness having you here. I know Nikki feels the same way, although for different reasons."

Moisture tickled the corners of Sinclair's eyes. That was the last thing she'd expected her father to say, especially after the disturbance caused by her affair with Hunter.

"So you're not angry about Hunter and me?"

"No. I'm not thrilled about it, especially since Lydia ended up being hurt, but I'm not angry. Nikki and I have been talking about this and she helped me realize that we all need companionship, whether it's for a lifetime or for a week, we crave it. It doesn't matter that you find it with a woman. At least it doesn't matter to me. I've never been in a position to tell another grown person what to do with their life, I'm not going to have illusions that I am now."

"You know you're pretty enlightened for an old man stuck in the backwoods of Jamaica." Sinclair teased him with her smile.

"I should hope so." He pierced a slice of cassava with his fork.

After dinner, they moved to the verandah with a bottle of white rum and sat on the steps to share it. The night was fragrant and still. Moonlight turned everything to silver, includ-

ing the fat clouds hovering low in the sky. Crickets and fireflies serenaded Victor and Sinclair with their night music as
father and daughter talked and breathed in the sweet, dew-
lathered scent from the crape myrtle trees at the gate.

"I know you've had a good visit so far, but with less than
a week to go, is there anything you'd like to do?"

Sinclair leaned back against the column and thought about
it. Everything had been so perfect—well, except for a few unpleasant moments here and there. "I'd love for us all to do
something together before I leave. The family, Hunter, maybe
even Della."

"I'm sure we could arrange that."

"Good."

Chapter 23

The day of Sinclair's get-together dawned bright and sunny. She woke up with butterflies in her belly after she turned over and noticed that Hunter was gone. During the night, her lover had simply held her, breathing with her until the first trickles of light began to leak across the horizon. Sinclair had felt her pull away but instantly fell back into sleep even before the window slid open to let her out. Now, finally awake, she hated the cold spot next to her, and wished that Hunter had stayed.

She left the bed for a shower, staying under the lukewarm spray until her skin pruned and the water turned cold. Nikki knocked on the bathroom door and came in, still in her night clothes, to talk. She stayed in the bathroom when Sinclair left to get dressed. Xavier was excited, chattering about the coming backyard cookout to anyone who would listen. He tugged Sinclair's skirt as soon as she stepped out of the bedroom, asking if Hunter was coming. When she told him yes, he bounded off, even happier, to get something that he'd made in school for his friend.

Her father asked if she was OK. She reassured him, but could not reassure herself as she wandered through the day in a daze, appetite set on ravenous, but being unable to focus on anything except the floating feeling inside her. It wasn't pleasant.

When the time came for the party, she showered and changed again, was prepared to be social and gregarious and charming, because this was the last time she'd see all these people in the same place again. Della came first, floating up the walk in something light and gauzy that made her look like a mother sex goddess. She greeted Sinclair with lavish kisses and extravagant compliments on her appearance and on how much Sinclair's visit had meant to her.

Hunter and Xavier walked into the backyard together, giggling at some shared joke. Lydia came in behind them. Sinclair embraced her sister, touched her hair and face for what she felt might be the last time, then greeted her lover with a fierce hug. Hunter felt her tremble and held on tight, whispering Sinclair's name. This wouldn't be the last time for them, she reassured her.

With the fire lit and blazing high, everyone gathered around laughing and eating. They pulled Sinclair into a circle of warmth and love. Her father talked to her quietly by the fire as they watched Nikki and Xavier play, darting through the trees like moths with the firelight flickering over them. Soon Della joined their play, then Hunter. Victor laughed, saying that he didn't know that he'd invited big children to the cookout, but it was a joy to see them play. Sinclair wanted to join them, but she couldn't. Her spirit was too heavy. Lydia and Della circled each other like wary piranhas, but managed not to shed any blood. Hunter rewarded them with frequent shouts of her laughter and teasing conversation that drew everyone in and made them forget about their differences for a while.

People were slow to leave. They ate and played long after the fire dimmed, moving to the verandah to finish whatever games they had gotten started. Sinclair drank her carrot juice, rolled its milky sweetness over her tongue, and watched them. When it was time to go, she said long good-byes. She held on to Della's hand, to Lydia's, and to Hunter's for as long as they let her before they slid beyond the myrtle trees and out the gate.

After her family retired for the evening, she lingered in each room, touching everything with her eyes and fingertips, stretching out the moment before she, too, had to rest. Then, it was three in the morning. Then four. Then five. Her body got tired. She climbed into the bed, turned to the cold spot where she wished Hunter's body was then, finally, drifted into a light sleep.

Chapter 24

And then there were just two days left. Sinclair sat at the Breckenridges' kitchen island on a bar stool, watching Nikki cook the evening meal.

"For old people, they have a lot of parties up here," Nikki said. "At least once a month. That's when I have to get at least two other people to help me with the cooking."

"Do they ever invite you?"

Nikki looked horrified. "No. Why should they?"

A knock sounded on the back door. "Who could that be? Nobody makes deliveries this late."

"Afternoon, ladies," Hunter called out. Despite her cheerful greeting she looked tense.

"What are you doing here?"

"Coming to see you." She leaned on the kitchen island next to Sinclair. Up close her body was tension itself, coiled and waiting for something.

Sinclair touched her arm. "Is anything wrong?"

"Not really, but I'd love for you to come home with me now."

Sinclair and Nikki exchanged a look. "OK. Let me just get my bag. I'll meet you outside."

At the Jeep, Sinclair looked at Hunter's tense face again. "Are you sure that you're all right?" she asked.

"I'm not. But I will be." Her hand curled around Sinclair's.

"You have at least two days before you have to go. You can spend the last day with your family. Today is mine. Yes?"

When Sinclair nodded, Hunter drove them down the hill to her house. Once there, she pulled Sinclair into her bedroom. "I love you." She kissed her. "No. Don't say anything."

Her tongue stroked Sinclair to life, pressing her body's need into hers until Sinclair clung as viciously as Hunter did to her. She dragged the straps of the tank top down Sinclair's arms, baring her breasts. Heat slid under Sinclair's skin as Hunter's mouth claimed her nipples. She pushed Sinclair against the wall.

"Will you stay?"

Sinclair's body panted and wept yes but it couldn't speak. Hunter's fingers moved inside her, loving, fucking, shoving her against the wall and all Sinclair could do was say Hunter's name as she took what she wanted, what Sinclair wanted her to take. Her name tumbled from Sinclair's mouth when her body started to shake, thighs trembling, fingers twisting in the snaking hair, sweat weeping behind her knees and under her breasts, down her back, rubbing into the skin over her taut muscles. Hunter followed her as she slid down the wall, still pumping her fingers as Sinclair shuddered and came and screamed her dark goddess's name.

But Hunter wasn't finished. She peeled Sinclair off the floor and took her to bed, covering Sinclair's body with hers, washing her with her sweat, her cum, her tongue. Hunter plunged deep for more milk from her lover's body, squeezing until Sinclair thought that she had nothing left. She was a supernova, rawness and pain pushed aside for the rapture that Hunter's hands brought.

The dark woman pushed into her and Sinclair pushed back, thighs straining apart so Hunter could take more of her.

"I need you to stay."

Limp. Sinclair was limp when Hunter tied her arms to the headboard, spread her legs wide and tied them down too. Her teeth nipped Sinclair's ankles and toes, and the flesh of her legs and thighs. "But if you want to leave me, I'll let go. I won't make a scene." But she lied. Sinclair was helpless to the press of Hunter's tongue and fingers inside her, pulling the trembling out until she flexed taut as a bow.

Sweat bathed her skin, stinging her eyes, salting her lips and tongue. She wanted to beg, for what, she wasn't quite sure. But the words kept escaping her, slipping away in the tides of sensation that buffeted her body.

Hunter's teeth closed on her clit and her slim fingers slid even deeper into Sinclair's pussy. The whimper caught them both by surprise. Tingles scuttled under her hair, traveling down her neck and shoulders, into her hips. The cum shattered her, shrieking through her like pain. Sinclair sobbed. She fell back to earth, dimly aware of the throbbing ache of her entire body and her tireless lover licking the sweat from it. Her eyes closed. An after-shudder rippled through her as she tried to push Hunter away. But her hand sagged back to the bed and she fell heavily asleep.

"There's nothing for you in America." Sinclair lay trapped in an exhausted slumber when she heard Hunter's voice from far away, she felt the steam of her seducer's breath on her neck. Like a fish diving into water, Hunter slid into her and Sinclair rose up from sleep. Her belly pressed against Sinclair's back, dark hips cupped her ass, a new part of her, hard and firm, buried inside her. Sinclair clawed at the sheets and arched her back. Hunter's name left her throat in a long, ragged moan.

She was wet. An ocean, swallowing her, moving beneath her, with her. "Hunter . . ."

"Stay, Sinclair."

Hunter slid deeper inside, taking her body to a place of fire and ice. The wave of heat left Sinclair gasping, the cold clenched her and she sobbed Hunter's name again.

"Stay." Her hand spread under Sinclair's belly, lifting her up to her knees, until her face was against the pussy-smelling sheets, her fingers curled into the soft cotton under her.

Hunter folded herself over Sinclair's body and pushed into her. When she touched Sinclair's clit, the flesh beneath hers shuddered.

"Tell me you'll stay," she groaned into the back of Sinclair's neck. "I'll do anything you want."

"I—I can't—oh, sh—oh!" Sinclair's world fell to pieces.

When her body quieted, after the shivers of sensation had bled away, leaving her limp and sated, she opened her eyes to see Hunter propped up on her elbow watching her.

"I've waited a long time for you," Hunter said. "Some days I look at you and feel that you're the reason I left England. It wasn't to find some idealized dream of an island that I knew less than nothing about. It wasn't even to reconnect with my family. It was to meet and love you." Hunter traced a pattern in the drying sweat on Sinclair's belly. "Don't say anything. I just wanted to tell you that before you left."

Sinclair couldn't speak. Tears leaked from her eyes and ran down into her hair. No one except her Gran had ever made her feel this special, this essential to happiness. She needed Hunter, too, more than even she could understand. Her bones ached for the dark woman. And she was terrified. Sinclair had trusted Regina and even started to love her. That betrayal had been as painful as it was unexpected. What she felt for Regina then was like a pebble compared to this avalanche of emotion roiling through her. Sinclair knew that she would break if Hunter abandoned her. And because that made no sense, she cried.

Hunter brought her breakfast in bed. "I'm sorry about last night. I wasn't quite thinking." She saw the look on Sinclair's face. "Not about the sex, I loved fucking you. I loved the way you called my name." A rueful smile shaped her mouth. "I *am* sorry about asking you to stay. That was out of line. I won't do it again."

She fed Sinclair sliced mangoes from her hand, and eggs and toast and cherries. "After your shower I'll take you back home."

Sinclair didn't know quite what to say. Her body was exhausted. She hadn't gotten more than two hours of sleep and her thoughts were sluggish. Yet she was alert enough to realize that today was her last day on the island and she needed to spend it with her family. "All right. Let me . . . let me get started." Sinclair stood up. "Come. Shower with me."

They undressed and climbed into the tub together, shrouded in silence and the heavy sadness of Sinclair's leaving. The shower spit and hissed as Hunter turned it on. She soaped her washrag and bathed Sinclair's body, taking every opportunity to show how much she would miss her. Only after the lukewarm water sluiced the suds from Sinclair's body did Hunter speak.

"You already know how I feel about you," she said. "If it's that real for you, too, then come back to me. If it's not, then don't fuck with me. Don't call or promise to write, and please don't send me any of those insipid 'wish you were here' postcards."

Beneath the rain from the shower's nozzle, Sinclair promised, kissed her lover, blessed Hunter's skin with her hands, and promised.

Chapter 25

"Look at the sky juice man." Xavier piped up from the backseat of the Honda. "Can I have some sky juice?"

"Not now, baby. We have to get to the airport." Nikki rubbed the back of her son's neck.

Sinclair's mouth suddenly felt dry, longing for a taste of the syrupy bag juice with its crushed ice. Banana was her favorite flavor. Sinclair remembered, as a child, curling her tongue around the cool plastic straw as she sucked for as long as she could without taking a breath.

"That sure would feel good in this heat though," Sinclair murmured, meeting Xavier's eyes in the rearview mirror. The boy grinned. "The plane isn't supposed to take off for another three hours. We should have enough time."

Her father pulled the car over before the last word left her mouth. Xavier started hopping up and down in the backseat, while Nikki just looked pleased. They parked the car on the shoulder of the perfectly paved road, the sort of road that was rare up where they lived, and locked it.

"'Afternoon." Victor greeted the old man with the gray-flecked beard and oversized hat sitting on top of his thick, knee-length dreadlocks.

"'Afternoon, brethren. What can I get for you today?"

"Four bags of sky juice." He looked at his family. "Pick your flavors."

Back in the car, they all sucked quietly on their straws, while Sinclair told the story of the first time she had sky juice. Her father chimed in, too, because he had been there to buy it. He bought the second one, too, after she dropped the first one on the ground and started crying as if she'd just lost her best friend. Nikki laughed until she snorted and juice sprayed out of her nose, hitting her giggling son in the face.

"It wasn't quite that funny, people," Sinclair muttered.

"Right." Victor laughed softly as he maneuvered the car toward their destination with one hand.

Still, Sinclair smiled at the memory. Her mother had been just as dismayed, especially since the bright yellow juice had hit the ground and splashed up on her new slacks. But Beverly had laughed, too, swinging the crying Sinclair up in her arms and held the new juice bag while her daughter suckled happily from the straw. Sinclair remembered the feeling of being carried by her mother, remembered the smell of jasmine and oil sheen in Beverly's hair.

"I'm going to miss you," Sinclair said.

"Does that mean you won't make it another twenty years before you come to visit us again?"

Sinclair shook her head and swallowed her mouthful of light banana syrup mixed with fresh water and grated ice. "I won't let it be that long before I taste Nikki's cooking again."

"In the meantime, you better eat something. You can't come back to this country looking like a refugee."

"Trust me, I won't let that happen again either."

At the airport, there were strained good-byes. Xavier started to cry and a sniffling Nikki tried to comfort him with the promise of more sweets on the way home. Victor shrugged and pulled his daughter into a crushing hug. "Get there safe."

"And call us when you land," Nikki said juggling her son in her arms to hug Sinclair one last time.

Sinclair felt tears of her own well up. "I will."

A red-hatted porter trotted over to help her with her two large suitcases. "What airline, miss?" When she told him, he slung the bags on his trolley. "This way."

Sinclair turned to hug Nikki and Xavier again, then waved at them as she trailed behind the porter. A frantic half hour later she was checked in and waiting at the boarding gate with the hundreds of other passengers who would share the same plane with her. Sinclair checked her purse to make sure that all her paperwork was in order before taking out a book to read. But she couldn't focus. Her eyes ricocheted off the printed page to watch what was going on around her.

Everywhere she looked people seemed excited about getting to the city. Some faces sagged with the world weariness of the well traveled, others held the dreamy afterglow of a blissful honeymoon, while others seemed simply anxious for the plane to come and take them back home. Sinclair quietly acknowledged that she was none of these. Just as quietly, questions began to form. Why? Why was she going back to the city? Were any of the excuses she'd given herself really valid? Her oversized apartment? Her vapid job at Volk? All the friends she'd made while living in the city? Right. And what was she leaving behind?

Sinclair remembered the first time Regina touched her and the waves of sensation she felt. It was like diving underwater, those first few moments of disorientation, of wonder. She felt those things just by looking at Hunter. A couple walked into her line of vision, a slim young man and his more voluptuously built woman. He looked at her intently as she spoke. It wasn't until they passed that Sinclair noticed he held her hand in his and that his thumb moved lightly over her knuckles. The woman carried her own bag.

Sinclair watched them then felt an inexplicable sense of loss when they disappeared around the corner. *He loves her,* she thought. A moment later she reopened the novel her father had given her from his collection. Something British, he'd said, but she might like it anyway. The words in the first paragraph swam before her eyes. *He loves her.* Sinclair looked up, surprise settling on her face. She stood and grabbed her carry-on bag and her purse. Before she knew it she was dashing through the airport, her loose hair bouncing around her head. The blast of warm air when she stepped outside the airport doors made her pause. What was she doing? Sinclair saw the line of taxis waiting, and her fingers spasmed around the strap of her purse.

"Where are you heading?"

She turned automatically to answer, but her breath caught in her throat. "Um . . . back."

"Can I give you a ride?" Hunter's smile was pure sin. Her unfastened hair stirred in the balmy afternoon breeze, brushing the shoulders of the man-tailored shirt she wore unbuttoned over a white tank top and black jeans. She looked freshly scrubbed, as if she was going courting.

A smile slowly shaped Sinclair's mouth. "Yes. Yes you can." She followed Hunter to the Jeep and threw her bag in the back before climbing into the passenger seat. They sat staring at the line of cars ahead, feeling the soft caress of the afternoon breeze. Hunter fiddled with her keys but made no motion to start the truck.

"So," Sinclair said softly. "What are you doing here?"

Hunter looked startled, as if she'd been prepared to wait in the silence forever. "I wanted to tell you something that I forgot to the other day." She cleared her throat. "You matter to me. It's not about the sex or the other things we do together. All those things are good—shit, they're fantastic." Hunter shifted in her seat but didn't look away. "I want you to understand that I care for you. Deeply. You're the first. If you say that I have to move to your big city so that we can be together then I'd do it. For you I'd do it. No bullshit."

"I thought you weren't going to bring this up again?" Sinclair teased, allowing her smile to slowly show itself.

"I lied. Sorry. Am I being a total asshole here?" She seemed to notice Sinclair's smile for the first time. "This is good?"

Sinclair looked into the smiling face of her lover, knowing her cheeks were creased just as deeply with the signs of her happiness. "I love you," she said.

"This is good." Hunter laughed softly. "I guess we can sort out the rest of it later?" She nodded, answering her own question. She started the Jeep and began to slip back into the slow-moving stream of traffic. Her hand drifted to Sinclair's thigh. Their fingers linked.

Sinclair leaned back into her seat, feeling the wind's teasing fingers through her hair. On the horizon she could see light sprinkles of rain, but beyond that the sun waited. She took in a deep breath, feeling for the first time in her life, satisfied.

"This is good."